Leisure Studies in a Global Era

Series Editors:
Karl Spracklen, Professor of Leisure Studies, Leeds Metropolitan University, UK
Karen Fox, Professor of Leisure Studies, University of Alberta, Canada

In this book series, we defend leisure as a meaningful, theoretical, framing concept; and critical studies of leisure as a worthwhile intellectual and ped-agogical activity. This is what makes this book series distinctive: we want to enhance the discipline of leisure studies and open it up to a richer range of ideas; and, conversely, we want sociology, cultural geographies and other social sciences and humanities to open up to engaging with critical and rigorous arguments from leisure studies. Getting beyond concerns about the grand project of leisure, we will use the series to demonstrate that leisure theory is central to understanding wider debates about identity, postmodernity and globalization in contemporary societies across the world. The series combines the search for local, qualitatively rich accounts of everyday leisure with the international reach of debates in politics, leisure and social and cultural theory. In doing this, we will show that critical studies of leisure can and should continue to play a central role in understanding society. The scope will be global, striving to be truly international and truly diverse in the range of authors and topics.

Titles include:

Brett Lashua, Karl Spracklen and Stephen Wagg (*editors*)
SOUNDS AND THE CITY
Popular Music, Place and Globalization

Oliver Smith
CONTEMPORARY ADULTHOOD AND THE NIGHT-TIME
ECONOMY

Karl Spracklen
WHITENESS AND LEISURE

Karl Spracklen
DIGITAL LEISURE, THE INTERNET AND POPULAR CULTURE
Communities and Identities in a Digital Age

Soile Veijola, Jennie Germann Molz, Olli Pyyhtinen, Emily Hockert and Alexander Grit
DISRUPTIVE TOURISM AND ITS UNTIDY GUESTS
Alternative Ontologies for Future Hospitalities

Udo Merkel (*editor*)
IDENTITY DISCOURSES AND COMMUNITIES IN INTERNATIONAL EVENTS,
FESTIVALS AND SPECTACLES

Brenda Gardenour Walter, Gabby Riches, Dave Snell and Bryan Bardine (*editors*)
HEAVY METAL STUDIES AND POPULAR CULTURE

Leisure Studies in a Global Era
Series Standing Order ISBN 978–1–137–310323–6 hardback
978–1–137–31033–0 paperback
(*outside North America only*)

You can receive future titles in this series as they are published by placing a
standing order. Please contact your bookseller or, in case of difficulty, write to
us at the address below with your name and address, the title of the series and
the ISBN quoted above.

Customer Services Department, Macmillan Distribution Ltd, Houndmills,
Basingstoke, Hampshire RG21 6XS, England

Heavy Metal Studies and Popular Culture

Edited by

Brenda Gardenour Walter
Saint Louis College of Pharmacy, USA

Gabby Riches
Leeds Metropolitan University, UK

Dave Snell
Waikato Institute of Technology, New Zealand

Bryan Bardine
University of Dayton, USA

First published 2016 by
PALGRAVE MACMILLAN

Palgrave Macmillan in the UK is an imprint of Macmillan Publishers Limited, registered in England, company number 785998, of Houndmills, Basingstoke, Hampshire RG21 6XS.

Palgrave Macmillan in the US is a division of St Martin's Press LLC, 175 Fifth Avenue, New York, NY 10010.

Palgrave Macmillan is the global academic imprint of the above companies and has companies and representatives throughout the world.

Palgrave® and Macmillan® are registered trademarks in the United States, the United Kingdom, Europe and other countries.

ISBN 978–1–137–45667–0

This book is printed on paper suitable for recycling and made from fully managed and sustained forest sources. Logging, pulping and manufacturing processes are expected to conform to the environmental regulations of the country of origin.

A catalogue record for this book is available from the British Library.

Library of Congress Cataloging-in-Publication Data
Heavy metal studies and popular culture / [edited by] Brenda Gardenour
    Walter, Gabby Riches, Dave Snell, Bryan Bardine.
       pages   cm
    Includes index.
    ISBN 978–1–137–45667–0 (hardback)
    1. Heavy metal (Music)—Social aspects.   2. Heavy metal (Music)—
    History and criticism.   3. Popular culture.   I. Gardenour Walter,
    Brenda S., 1971–   II. Riches, Gabby, 1985–   III. Snell, Dave.
    IV. Bardine, Bryan Anthony, 1968–
    ML3918.R63H45 2015
    781.66—dc23   2015028740

Contents

Tables

Preface

The academic study of heavy metal as a genre of music continues to grow. Arguably beginning with the seminal works of Gaines (1991), Weinstein ([1991]2000) and Walser (1993), the body of knowledge concerning this previously maligned form of music continues to expand exponentially (Spracklen et al., 2011). Prior to 2007, excluding the three previously mentioned works, academic accounts of heavy metal were mostly contained within edited volumes concerning subcultural research. At conferences, presentations on the topic were included within symposia wherever the best fit was thought to be by organizers, resulting in their inclusion (regardless of actual content) alongside topics including culture, media, or in relation to anti-social themes such as alcoholism and deviancy. But during the early 2000s a burgeoning body of scholarship focusing on metal began to materialize, most of which came from doctoral students and early career researchers. Metal music scholars have maintained that the increased scholarly attention dedicated to the musical genre developed alongside a dramatic shift in journalistic and popular culture representations of metal music and its culture, a connection that is significant to metal music studies' development (Spracklen et al., 2011). In many ways this edited collection emphasizes metal's relationship with other forms of popular culture and the value these connections offer in expanding 'what we can understand *about* metal and what we can learn *from* metal' (Hill & Spracklen, 2010, p. vii). As metal music and its culture continue to entice intellectual curiosity, these growing dialogues illustrate metal's potential as being an important medium for understanding, sharing and transformation.

Due to the diversity of metal music and the scholars that study it, attempts to categorize the research or find a scholarly home have been difficult for scholars within the field of metal music studies. Weinstein (2011) highlights that research on metal music has never been a linear trajectory which advances from a singular discipline or methodological approach; rather, it has been and continues to be a highly multidisciplinary project. As noted by Riches and Spracklen (2014), research on heavy metal 'has become a growing part of the subject fields of musicology, sociology, women's studies, leisure studies, and cultural studies' (p. 149). The field not only includes these cultural aspects, but also extends to the natural sciences through journals that cater to the full spectrum of the discipline: publications such as *Metal Music Studies*. With the advent of a peer-reviewed journal and numerous international conferences devoted to the musical genre, it can be argued that metal music has finally found its scholarly home. However, there are concerns that metal studies, as a disciplinary field, could potentially become insulated, where particular theoretical and methodological tendencies become commonplace and legitimations of metal and its culture are privileged (Kahn-Harris, 2011). Weinstein (2011) argues that if the benefit of having a coherently defined field of 'metal studies' is that it 'provides a rubric for bringing together diverse research proceeding from different disciplines, theoretical perspectives and methodologies, then it follows that it is a mistake to attempt to define that field precisely, either in terms of content or the forms through which to study that content' (p. 243). The contributors in this edited collection seek to probe and challenge metal's ideological, definitional and gendered boundaries, thus offering readers a critical and nuanced perspective on its history and relationship to popular culture that goes beyond the music itself. The varied approaches to understanding metal music *differently*, as a musical genre and complex cultural practice, are recognized and exemplified by all of the chapters in this edited collection.

The importance of researching beyond metal's musical boundaries was particularly evident at the *Heavy Metal and Popular Culture Conference* held at Bowling Green State University in Ohio from the 4th to the 7th of April 2013. While being held in America, this conference attracted attendees from the United Kingdom, Finland, Germany, Puerto Rico and New Zealand (among others). Symposia on heavy metal addressed issues relating to its production, reception and consumption. Sessions included (among many others) topics such as 'Rethinking Heavy Metal,' 'Women & Gender in Heavy Metal,' 'Global Dimensions,' and 'Comics, Sci-Fi and Superheroes: Metal Meets Fiction.' Attendees and presenters included academics who were fans of the music, but also those who were not. Such diversity of approaches, subject areas and backgrounds highlights the depth of the discipline. This conference represented the vibrant present and promising future of metal studies. This edited collection comes from the proceedings of that conference.

The keynote speakers at the conference were Laina Dawes (writer of *What Are You Doing Here?*) and Dr. Keith Kahn-Harris. For those unfamiliar with Keith's work, he is a London-based sociologist and writer and the author of *Extreme Metal: Music and Culture on the Edge*. Published in 2007, this was the first book-length study of extreme metal and could potentially have been one of the contributing factors that led to the academic spotlight being cast upon heavy metal music in the first scholarly conference devoted entirely to the subject in Salzburg in 2008 (Shepard, 2008). Keith's keynote at the conference entitled 'Metal after Metal Studies: What Comes Next?' regarding the future of metal studies, and in some cases metal music more generally, prompted numerous discussions. In particular, he posed four key themes – Metal as Resilience, Metal as Memory, Metal as Critique and Metal Beyond Metal. These themes were put forward as potential challenges for both metal studies and heavy metal as a genre. Keith challenged attendees to consider the ways in which metal is or is not fulfilling these elements.

The chapters contained in this volume represent academics in the field of metal studies taking up Keith's challenge and beginning a conversation on where metal music has come from and where it may go – academically, musically and socially. They are presented here within the categories as first suggested by Keith in his keynote. Our hope is that they will encourage further debate and subsequent scholarship regarding metal's past, present and future, in particular how metal music can be used in critiquing a range of phenomena but also how it can be self-reflexive as a way of being critical of its own processes and how it can further develop and grow moving forward.

We would like to thank Dr. Keith Kahn-Harris for his input in the writing of this publication's Introduction and also for his cooperation in this endeavor from conception to production.

We would also like to thank all the contributors for accepting our invitation to engage in these discussions and for their hard work in putting together their individual chapters.

Works Cited

Gaines, D. (1991) *Teenage Wasteland: Suburbia's Dead End Kids* (Chicago: University of Chicago Press).

Hill, R. & Spracklen, K. (2010) 'Introduction,' *Heavy Fundametalisms: Music, Metal and Politics*, eds. R. Hill & K. Spracklen (Oxford: Inter-Disciplinary Press), pp. vii–x.

Kahn-Harris, K. (2011) 'Metal Studies: Intellectual Fragmentation or Organic Intellectualism?' *Journal for Cultural Research*, 15(3), pp. 251–253.

Riches, G. & Spracklen, K. (2014) 'Raising the Horns: Heavy Metal Communities and Community Heavy Metal Music,' *International Journal of Community Music*, 7(2), pp. 149–151.

Shepard, J. (2008) 'World's First Heavy Metal Conference Hits Salzburg,' *Guardian*, 29 October. Retrieved: http://www.guardian.co.uk/education/2008/oct/29/research-music.

Spracklen, K., Brown, A. R., & Kahn-Harris, K. (2011) 'Metal Studies? Cultural Research in the Heavy Metal Scene,' *Journal for Cultural Research*, 3(15), pp. 209–212.

Walser, R. (1993) *Running with the Devil: Power, Gender, and Madness in Heavy Metal Music* (Hanover: University Press of New England).

Weinstein, D. ([1991]2000) *Heavy Metal: The Music and Its Culture* (New York: Da Capo).

Weinstein, D. (2011) 'How Is Metal Studies Possible?' *Journal for Cultural Research*, 15(3), pp. 243–245.

Contributors

Gerd Bayer is a tenured faculty member (Akademischer Oberrat & Privatdozent) in the English department at the University of Erlangen, having held teaching or visiting positions at Canadian, American, French and Estonian universities. The author of a book on nature in John Fowles's writing (2004) and the (co)editor of seven books, including *Heavy Metal Music in Britain* (2009), he has also written articles on postmodern and postcolonial literature, early modern fiction, Holocaust studies and mockumentary film. He is completing a monograph on paratextual poetics in the Restoration novel.

Andy R. Brown is a sociologist who works in a media department at Bath Spa University, UK. His teaching/research interests include popular music, music journalism, global music industries, media and youth consumption, with a specific focus on heavy metal music culture(s). He has published widely on metal and subculture; the metal magazine; gender, class and metal; metal and moral panics; and metal and cultural legitimation.

Osvaldo González-Sepúlveda is a PhD student in Clinical Psychology at the Ponce School of Medicine & Health Sciences, Puerto Rico. He has directed various movie projects, including *No me visites* (Do not visit me) (2011), which was presented at the XXXIII Movie Festival in La Habana, Cuba. He directed the documentary 'The Distorted Island: Heavy Metal and Community in Puerto Rico.'

Keith Kahn-Harris is a London-based sociologist. He is the author of *Extreme Metal: Music and Culture on the Edge* (2007) and has written many articles on contemporary metal culture.

Brad Klypchak is Assistant Professor of Liberal Studies at Texas A&M University-Commerce. A popular culture scholar, he holds a PhD in American culture studies from Bowling Green State University. While he has taught and done research in film, theatre, sport, performance and mass media studies, his particular emphasis has been on heavy metal music. His book, *Performed Identity: Heavy Metal Musicians 1984–1991*, reflects this interest. Among other publications, he has contributed chapters to a number of edited collections including *Heavy Metal: Controversies and Countercultures, Global Glam and Popular Music* and *Rammstein on Fire.*

Jenna Kummer is an MA student in Sociology at the University of Lethbridge in Alberta, Canada. She is finishing her thesis on glam metal's style and significance, which compares the subculture's structural homology in the 1980s to its present-day revival in television. Her research interests include popular music and discourse, identity, style and gender representations.

Sigrid Mendoza holds an MA degree in social community psychology and is a PhD student from the same program at the University of Puerto Rico. She has presented her work on heavy metal studies at the *Heavy Metal and Popular Culture Conference* and at the *Annual Convention of the Puerto Rican Psychological Association.* Her research interests include gender dynamics and feminism, heavy metal studies, ethnography, social construction of sexuality and neo-tribal community theory.

Colin A. McKinnon is an independent scholar with a background in biological science and a passion for metal, which led him to participate in and serve on the steering committee for two of the *Heavy Fundametalisms: Music, Metal and Politics* conferences. He is also a member of the board of the International Society for Metal Music Studies. His passion for metal, however, is slightly predated by his passion for comics. As both a comics geek and metalhead, he is fascinated by the correlations between the two subcultures. He lives and works in Switzerland.

Jamie E. Patterson is a master's student in Folklore at the University of North Carolina Chapel Hill completing her thesis, an ethnography with female-identified death metal fans in Raleigh, North Carolina. Her research examines gender, race, class and identity in folk life-narrative construction among fans in the American South. Her other research interests include music and rural landscapes, ritual studies and trauma narrative research, particularly in Kenya and the southern US. A long-time extreme metal fan and musician, she teaches cultural anthropology at Western Carolina University.

Eliut Rivera-Segarra is a clinical psychologist at the Ponce Health Sciences University in Puerto Rico. His research interests include stigma theory, serious mental illnesses and heavy metal studies. His work on heavy metal studies has appeared in the *Journal of Community Music, Metal Music Studies, Journal of Community Psychology* and a chapter in the book *Hardcore, Punk and Other Junk*. He has also presented this work at the *Convention of the Puerto Rican Psychological Association,* the *EMP Pop Conference, the International Conference on Heavy Metal and Popular Culture* and the *Grimposium*.

Niall W. R. Scott is Senior Lecturer in Ethics at the University of Central Lancashire and Chair of the International Society for Metal Music Studies. He is editor of *Helvete, a Journal of Black Metal Theory*, co-editor of *Metal Music Studies* and has published widely and spoken internationally on heavy metal, philosophy and politics.

Anthony J. Thibodeau serves as an instructor in the Department of Anthropology. Northern Arizona University, Flagstaff, Arizona. After several decades managing Native American art and material culture in museum collections in Santa Fe, New Mexico, he graduated with a master's degree in popular culture in 2014 from Bowling Green State University, Ohio. His general research interests include contemporary Native art, ethnomusicology and the intersection of traditional and popular music.

Nelson Varas-Díaz is a social psychologist and professor at the University of Puerto Rico. His work on social stigma and communal identities has appeared in the *Interamerican Journal of Psychology, Journal of Community Psychology and Music, Metal Music Studies, Qualitative Health Research, American Journal of Community Psychology, AIDS Education & Prevention, Qualitative Report* and *Global Public Health*. His research has focused on the social stigmatization of disease (i.e. HIV/AIDS, addiction), marginalized groups (i.e. transgendered individuals) and cultural practices (i.e. metal music, religion). He is the principal investigator for the first systematic study of heavy metal music in the Caribbean.

Introduction: The Next Steps in the Evolution of Metal Studies

Keith Kahn-Harris
Birkbeck College, London

This edited collection originates from the _Heavy Metal and Popular Culture_ conference that was held at Bowling Green State University in April 2013. Although not the first scholarly metal conference, it was at that stage the biggest. The conference also saw the formal announcement of the establishment of the International Society for Metal Music Studies (ISMMS) and its journal, _Metal Music Studies_. While the development of what had previously been a disparate, loosely linked network of metal scholars into a coherent discipline called 'metal studies' had been noted previously (Spracklen et al., 2011), the Bowling Green conference saw metal studies take on a concrete institutional form.

Metal studies is still very much in the process of formation, but its growth is undeniable. Indeed, metal studies has reached the stage where it is reflecting on its own history (Hickam, 2014). The online ISMMS metal studies bibliography is growing all the time. The very fact that a journal is sustainable is noteworthy in and of itself.[1] While a perusal of the journal and the online bibliography demonstrates that a wide range of metal-related topics are receiving attention, there are still areas where metal studies has made less of an impact. As I have argued elsewhere (Kahn-Harris, 2011), the musicology of metal remains underdeveloped and metal studies scholars are sometimes not sufficiently informed about the wider popular music studies literature. Nonetheless, there is every reason to think that metal studies is well on the way to establishing a profound understanding of metal as a musical, social and cultural form. All this is to be welcomed, but it's vital to ask an important and difficult question: What is the _aim_ of metal studies?

At one level, the answer to this question is obvious. The aim of metal studies is to engage with metal in a scholarly fashion. This project needs no justification. Any socio-cultural phenomenon can and should be

1

studied as part of the general scholarly effort to understand the world. If ancient Greek vases or the class structure in Sri Lanka are worthy topics for study, then so is metal.

Yet there can also be a greater purpose for metal studies than simply the worthy accretion of scholarship. The position of metal studies in relation to metal itself offers the opportunity for *engaged* scholarship. Most metal studies scholars are also engaged with metal as fans and metal scene members – but critically so. They are part of the phenomenon which they are describing. This is not unique to metal – to give a couple of examples, punk and hip-hop scholars are often similarly engaged – but it is sufficiently rare in popular music studies as to be worthy of note.[2] Metal studies scholars can be and often are Gramscian 'organic intellectuals' (Kahn-Harris, 2011), critically engaged in the politics of metal scenes themselves. Even if, as Michelle Phillipov's (2012) work implies, such a politically oriented engagement in metal scenes may – ironically – lead to critics underplaying or ignoring those aspects of metal that cannot be politically reclaimed, there is no doubting the personal investment in metal that motivates many metal studies scholars.

While it would be wrong to state that metal scenes are always receptive to scholarly ideas,[3] there are abundant examples of instances where 'practitioners' engage seriously with metal studies scholars and vice versa. For example: Nelson Varas-Díaz and colleagues[4] have worked closely with members of the Puerto Rican metal scene to document its history; the Bowling Green conference featured metal scene members without a scholarly background as panelists and participants; the 2011 *Heavy Metal and Place* conference in Birmingham, UK, was closely connected to the 'Home of Metal' project that has celebrated and documented the role of Birmingham and the Black Country in metal history.[5] More broadly, metal has long been a highly literate culture, with books and mythological canons drawn on extensively in metal lyrics and symbolism. The black metal scene is probably the site where the collision between literary culture and metal is most intense. The various 'black metal theory' symposia and publications (for example, Masciandaro, 2010) have mined a rich seam of playful philosophical discourse that is less analytical so much as it is an outgrowth of black metal culture itself.

In my own experience, while my own book on metal derived from my PhD research and uses predominantly scholarly language, it has certainly been read and reviewed outside of the academy.[6] Further, I have often been interviewed for metal magazines and fanzines.[7] In my ethnographic work on metal, I received little resistance – and a great deal of interest – from metal scene members to the idea of scholarly engagement with metal culture. Indeed, the gap between academia and metal often seemed surprisingly narrow: when I wrote for *Terrorizer* magazine in the late 1990s and early 2000s, both the editor and I, together with a significant portion of the writers, were working on master's degrees and doctorates (although I was the only one studying metal itself). More recently, I made the decision to publish my keynote lecture at the Bowling Green conference as a series of posts on the webzine *Souciant*[8] as it had a track record of publishing work that crossed the boundaries between scholarship, criticism, journalism and music scenes themselves.

There are, of course, potential dangers in this relationship. If metal studies scholarship is too oriented toward metal itself, then it can lose contact with wider trends and issues in popular culture. Clearly, metal is not entirely *sui generis* and metal studies scholars have to work to remind themselves of this. In this respect, as Niall Scott's chapter in this collection points out, metal and metal studies need to be positioned within a wider relationship to popular culture.

In thinking through the aims of metal studies then, we therefore have to take into account the possibilities and responsibilities that derive from the field's sometimes close relationship with metal scenes themselves. Metal studies is, potentially at least, in a position to make an impact on metal itself. The question is, to what end?

Four aims for metal studies

I would like to highlight four aims for metal studies. These aims address the question: *how should we build on the possibilities that metal studies scholarship sometimes has and could have in the future for influencing metal practice?* My assumption is that the role of metal studies within metal is to *raise issues that are difficult to raise within the metal scene itself.*

What ties these aims together is *the promotion of reflexivity.* As I have argued elsewhere (Kahn-Harris, 2006), metal scenes have developed an odd kind of reflexivity. While scene members demonstrate a considerable sophistication in reflexively managing the complex work of scene-making, it is a reflexivity that is sharply limited. Indeed, it is often turned against itself in the strange phenomenon of 'reflexive anti-reflexivity' in which scene members demonstrate considerable sophistication in appearing incredibly unsophisticated (Kahn-Harris, 2006, pp. 144–152). The end result is that in metal scenes certain questions, issues and challenges are ruled largely out of bounds.

So the four aims that I will outline here are all based on nurturing the more thorough kinds of reflexivity that metal often lacks. The promotion of a more thoroughgoing metal reflexivity may actually be necessary if metal is to survive. Metal's limited reflexivity may have served it well in the past, but as I will argue it has arguably left it ill-equipped to face the challenges that it faces now and in the future.

Nurturing resilience

The first aim of metal studies should be to nurture metal's *resilience*. By resilience I do not mean that metal should remain unchanged into the indefinite future. Rather, the aim is to nurture the reflexive tools necessary for metal to confront both the 'external' challenges it faces, and its own internal politics.

Metal studies scholars can boost metal's resilience through helping the scene protect itself against external assault. It is sad that metal studies never existed in the heyday of attacks on metal in the US in the 1980s and early 1990s. A larger body of engaged metal scholars – as opposed to the small group of pioneers that were around at the time[9] – could have helped in countering the often absurd arguments that were leveled against metal. It should certainly be a priority for metal scholars to act when metallers and metal scenes become the target of unjustified assaults and prejudice. When it appears that metal is going to be cited as a factor in a court case, metal scholars should be proactive in offering themselves, either individually or collectively, as expert witnesses. When metal is cited as a 'problem' by governments, official bodies or politicians, metal scholars should be there to push back. When metal is censored and its fans persecuted by undemocratic and fundamentalist regimes, metal scholars should alert the world, as Mark Levine did in his 2010 Freemuse report on the censorship of heavy metal in the Middle East, North Africa, Southeast Asia and China.[10]

Nurturing resilience is about more than simply defending metal against attack. Metal scenes can be threatened by much more than simply outside malicious forces. Metal is part of a fast-changing world in which no institution or cultural practice can ever be guaranteed to endure. Metal's complex institutional and aesthetic archipelago was built up in times that were different to the present and while they have proved resilient so far, that does not mean that they will continue to be so indefinitely. Metal scene members may be exceptionally adept in maintaining and navigating metal's scenic infrastructure, but they do not always have the breadth of vision to understand the wider context within which they act. Indeed, deep involvement in metal can, in those instances when it is based on a reduction of involvement in the non-metal world, actually endanger scenic reflexivity through maintaining the illusion that life can be lived through metal alone. Here again, metal scholars, through placing metal in the context of wider social change, can make a real contribution.

Nurturing memory

The second aim for metal studies should be to nurture metal's *memory*. That is not to say that metal is not conscious of its history. Deep knowledge of metal's manifold artists and sub-genres is highly prized in metal and so is loyalty to metal artists over time. But metal's memory has its blind spots. Canons are always based on exclusion and on the smoothing out of historical complexity. Metal will be in a better place to face the challenges of the future if it is more open about the complexities of its past. Part of what metal studies can do is to raise challenging examples and remember that which some would prefer to forget. One example is the exclusion of black artists and black music from metal's collective memory, in which a figure as pivotal as Jimi Hendrix can be totally marginalized (Wells, 1997).

Nurturing critique

My third aim for metal studies is to nurture critique. This is one area where metal studies has already made a distinctive contribution. Metal studies scholars have tried to highlight areas where metal can be prejudiced, discriminatory and even abusive. Crucially, this has been done in a spirit of generosity that does not condemn metal in its entirety, but has tried to find ways to make the metal scene more responsive to the needs of minorities within the scene. While it is hard to pin down the exact contribution that metal studies has made here, what we can say is that, at the very least, it is no longer so unusual to find unabashed critiques of sexism and racism from metal scene members themselves and that metal studies may have played a role in bolstering this welcome trend. The critic Laina Dawes is one example. As a writer, she has ensured that the position of black women in metal has received greater prominence (Dawes, 2012). Having presented a keynote lecture at the Bowling Green conference, she has become associated with metal studies while still being an important voice within the scene itself.

Metal studies can be a place where hard questions and difficult issues can be raised with a measure of restraint and nuance. It can be a place from which supportive critiques are disseminated to change metal itself.

Looking to the future

Reflexivity is about 'knowing how to go on,' to face the future through an unflinching look at the past and the present. What will metal be like in 10, 20, 50 and 100 years' time? Will there be such a thing as metal in 500 years' time? And does it matter anyway?

It is this future orientation that is most absent in the metal scene. In fact, it is part of a more general absence in both lay and scholarly reflection on popular music. Serious reflection on popular music tends to be confined to understanding the past and the present. Attempts to speculate on the future are largely confined to understanding the short to medium term impact of changes in music technology and the music business. There has been little attempt to predict the longer-term aesthetic, social and cultural shifts that will mark popular music in the future.

In some ways, this ignoring of the future is ironic, given that post-war popular music has been at the forefront of dramatic social changes. Indeed, as Jacques Attali (1985) has influentially argued, music provides both a harbinger and a stimulus to the shifts in socio-cultural tectonic plates. It is hard to imagine the manifold changes that occurred in the West in the 1960s apart from the dramatic changes in the place and the nature of popular music that both catalyzed them and signaled their coming. Some popular musicians have been actively interested in the future as a theme in their work; the pre-eminent example of this is Kraftwerk, and in metal we can think of the obsession with nuclear war and apocalyptic destruction that marked thrash metal in the late 1980s.

Yet post-war popular musicians have rarely made a conscious, reflexive attempt to grapple with the long-term future of music itself. Even if artists have often sought to push forward the possibilities of music through exploiting new technology, it is much rarer to find artists speculating on what the place of music will be in 50, 100, 1,000 years' time. 'Futuristic' music of the Kraftwerk-kind is tinged with a sense of self-parody, a consciousness that nothing dates faster than visions of the future. Futuristic music rarely tries to imagine new possibilities for how music might be embedded institutionally within society.

Critics and scholars play an essential role in tracking changes in popular music, but they rarely 'lead' musical innovation – they do not create or specify the sounds of music. Developments in popular music are led by musicians and those who run scenic institutions. Critics and scholars, in highlighting some artists and not others, may affect the trajectory that scenes and musical developments take, but no one either predicted in advance the groundbreaking innovations that the Beatles, Slayer or Kraftwerk made. This blindness to the future has actually served post-war popular music very well. The shock and surprise that new developments like punk or black metal have caused is part of their power and pleasure. But there is increasing reason to think that popular music's future-blindness is not serving it well in the present. We have, I would argue, entered a period of fundamental crisis in the condition of popular music – and metal is no exception.

It is this final aim that I addressed most directly in my keynote address at the Bowling Green conference. My presentation, which was subsequently published in a series of blog posts[11] and will be reworked into a book in due course, argued that metal was facing a 'crisis of abundance.'[12] In an age in which even the most obscure metal texts are instantly accessible, metal is losing its distinctiveness and metal scenes are losing their definition. Any sense of historical movement is undermined as nothing is ever rendered obsolete. Against this background, metal scenes have responded piecemeal or not at all – and it is this lack of reaction that constitutes a crisis. The fundamental building blocks of metal culture are under threat yet metal all-too-frequently responds, if it responds at all, by clinging ever more desperately to these building blocks. For this reason, metal needs to think about the future and look ahead to what I have called 'metal beyond metal.' What might metal look like if it abandoned many, most or all of its most cherished elements? How could 'metalness' be reworked into the future in ways that transcend the crisis of abundance?

* * *

The contributions to this collection can be viewed through the lens of these four aims. Doing so can bring together separate pieces of scholarship into a framework that drives metal studies forward and further embeds its reflexivity into the reflexivity of metal itself. Further, examining the contributions to the collection in the light of my own attempt to think about metal's future can help bring out the ways in which the metal scholarship presented in this book may offer implicit and explicit versions of what the future of both metal and metal studies can and should be.

As mentioned before, the papers presented here stem from the Bowling Green conference and the discussions that emerged from it. Almost all of the contributors presented at the conference. Some of the contributors do engage with my own contribution to the conference, which is not to say that my arguments are universally accepted. But a concern for metal's future certainly does permeate this collection, whether or not this future is viewed through the 'metal beyond metal' lens.

A concern for metal's future inevitably brings up questions of normativity – what we think metal *should* be. This can be difficult within scholarly traditions that focus on the descriptive rather than the prescriptive. Niall Scott's chapter in this collection grasps this nettle firmly. He argues:

> I am not particularly interested in what *is* the case, rather in what *ought* to be the case, in other words I am interested in pursuing what heavy metal can do not just at a practical level, but at a normative level.

Moreover, Scott also sees metal studies as having an important part to play in developing this normativity, working in cooperation with artists and journalists. For Scott, metal should be a source of 'resistance' – a concept that is related to, but not reducible to 'resilience' as I have discussed it. Drawing widely on cultural theory and on metal research, he eschews simplistic ways of thinking about power, resistance and popular culture. Rather, metal's relationship to power is complicated, since 'on the whole metal culture does not represent an oppressed group,' although 'it does suffer oppression in certain geographical locations and within the metal scene there are pockets of oppression.' While metal is not always resistant, it is important to point out those spaces where resistance is stronger than elsewhere. Scott points to examples across the globe, in contexts as apparently disparate as Israel/Palestine and Flint, Michigan, 'where metal music is dynamically engaged in many forms of resistance to power structures and ideologies.'

The form of metal resistance that Scott sees most potential in is resistance to 'popular culture.' Although metal discourse has long been predicated on disparagement forms of popular culture, Scott points out that metal is itself a form of popular culture in that it 'emerges from the popular.' This embeddedness represents metal's greatest potential and its greatest challenge. It requires, in Scott's deliciously paradoxical phrase, that metal be 'resistant to itself': 'a self-reflexive resistance, dealing with edifices of power and domination that the subculture has built up over time.'

Scott's chapter does not shirk this challenge. In both pointing to areas of problematic power relations within metal, and highlighting challenges to them within metal itself, Scott treats metal as a living tradition that is constantly emerging – with everything left to play for. The possibility of a form of popular culture that would be based on its own critique and that would promote its own 'unmanageability' is a tantalizing one.

Viewed from Niall Scott's perspective, Gerd Bayer's chapter illuminates some of the complexities and possibilities of metal resistance. Bayer examines the documentary films *Anvil: The Story of Anvil*, *Metallica: Some Kind of Monster* and *Heavy Metal auf dem Lande*. He argues that these films 'appropriate generic qualities drawn from sentimental genres' in ways that subvert conventional hyper-masculine images of metal. As Bayer shows, the documentaries reveal male metalheads to be emotionally fragile, embedded within family and community and far from the image that they often represent. Drawing a comparison with the film *Priscilla Queen of the Desert*, which similarly familiarizes gay subculture, Bayer suggests that:

> What the three films discussed in this essay demonstrate, I would like to argue, is that heavy metal culture is trying to step out of a closet…a public perception of heavy metal that places and defines it as a masculinist, violent, anti-intellectual, and anti-emotional domain within popular culture…it communicates to a larger, maybe even non-fan audience that heavy metal is nothing to be frightened of.

Demonstrating that metal is 'nothing to be frightened of' may seem to be a strategy that is anything but resistant. Yet at the same time it clearly subverts hegemonic representations/understandings of masculinity in both metal and the wider society. What Bayer's chapter shows, then, is that developing a more complex picture of what metal is and could be – in documentary films or, indeed, in metal studies – can simultaneously threaten metal and suggest new directions for its future development. The line between the two is perilously thin.

The same is true with regard to analyses of metal's history and memory. The chapters by Brad Klypchak, Andy Brown and Nelson Varas-Díaz all demonstrate the ways in which scholarly work on metal's past and its relationship to the past can overturn old certainties and offer new possibilities for the future.

Brad Klypchak's work on 'panicmetalmemories,' which he defines as 'the postmodern blurring of metal's past and present into an unsettled and re-reflexive cycle of self-reference,' problematizes any simplistic understanding of metal history. Rather, he identifies 'experiential and nostalgic blends of memory thereby blurring versions of "the known" into constructed hybrids of truth, non-truth, and selective inclusion and/or omission.' Within what I have termed the 'age of abundance,' metal continually refracts 'panicmemories informed by the past yet regenerated and re-inscribed simultaneously through its ever-accessible presence.' As Klypchak shows, one of the ways in which this process plays out is through ongoing controversies over the 'authenticity' of long-established metal bands when they change members. Recent 'reversionings' of bands such as Guns N' Roses, Queensrÿche and KISS lead to debates over what the authentic nature of a band is; debates that are caught up in practices of nostalgia and selective remembering. Klypchak extends his argument to the personal: as he argues, metal studies scholars such as himself are confronted by the often glaring contrast between their own selective and nostalgic metal memories and a scholarly commitment to subject them to scrutiny.

Andy Brown's exploration of the history of the heavy metal ballad also deals with the discomfort that an unflinching look at metal history can provoke. He argues that the ballad 'has been removed from contemporary accounts of heavy metal history.' The metal ballad, whose heyday was the 1980s, is too often seen as a 'commercial aberration' from metal's triumphant history. As Brown argues, if we accept this judgment, we close off important questions regarding the history and development of metal. Further, the often gendered assumptions about what 'authentic' metal consists of are ripe for deconstruction. The 'continuum' between hard rock and metal is subject to controversies over how to draw the line between genres, controversies that involve issues of gender and commercialism. As with Klypchak, Brown's contribution to metal studies is to provoke a productive discomfort over the question of what metal is and should be.

Nelson Varas-Díaz and colleagues discuss a different kind of absence from the history of metal. In their discussion of the Puerto Rican metal scene, they argue that 'the story of Heavy Metal in Puerto Rico has been systematically overlooked in light of archaic conceptualizations of what is culturally appropriate music.' Assumptions of what is 'culturally appropriate' can be common to both metal and non-metal understandings of what Puerto Rican music is and should be. While the Puerto Rican scene is clearly peripheral (but not insignificant) to the global metal scene, the authors rightly argue that 'a truly encompassing historical account of metal music, now part of a globalized world, needs to include the experiences and stories of those living outside the epicenters of metal production and consumption.' The project that Varas-Díaz and colleagues undertook, to write the unwritten history of Puerto Rican metal, is groundbreaking both in the close connections it forged between scholars and metalheads and in the richness of the information it yielded on how metal scenes form and develop over time.

From its inception, one of the major preoccupations of metal studies has been gender. Deena Weinstein and Robert Walser, in their pioneering works on metal, pioneered the nuanced approach to gender that characterizes much of metal studies work in this area – engaging with sexism and the marginalization of women in metal, while at the same time highlighting the often surprising opportunities that metal affords for non-sexist forms of engagement. Jamie Patterson and Jenna Kummer, in their contributions to this collection, continue this tradition. Patterson's fine-grained ethnographic discussion on her involvement with a group of female metal fans in North Carolina highlights the complexities of gendered metal identities. The women she studied are both the objects of sexism in metal, yet they play with their metal and feminine identities in complex and reflexive ways. In particular, their relationship to pop musicians, such as Britney Spears and Lady Gaga, both subverts and affirms simplistic forms of boundary-making between metal and mainstream music. As Patterson concludes: 'the rigid categories between authenticity and superficiality, resistance and conformity, mainstream pop and extreme metal, that I had internalized as sources of power are ... fluid, nuanced, and complex.' Kummer's chapter, which also draws on research with female metal fans, also demonstrates the simultaneous prevalence of both sexism and female empowerment in metal. Her respondents are fully aware of sexist practices in metal, yet they refuse to accept their marginality as a given. Instead, as Kummer concludes, they 'illustrated tremendous hopefulness and independence with regard to resistance by way of how they were found to reappropriate their femininity and redefine what it means to be feminine in the heavy metal subculture.'

The final two chapters in the collection point toward new possibilities in the future development of metal. Anthony Thibodeau's discussion of 'Cascadian black metal' shows how a small group of artists based in the Pacific Northwest both drew on and transformed the conventions of black metal, opening up new horizons in the process. Drawing on 'anarcho-primitivism' and embedded in the specificities of the local environment, bands such as Wolves in the Throne Room have rethought black metal in radical and avant-garde ways. Discussing Wolves in the Throne Room's 2014 album *Celestite*, Thibodeau argues that it constitutes an example of what I have called 'metal beyond metal,' 'in which metal is not defined as identifiable aesthetics, or even by affiliation in an existing metal genre or scene, but through specific kinds of social values, as hard as these may be to pin down.' He demonstrates that however much the album may depart from black metal's musical conventions as usually understood, it nonetheless remains part of the genre and its scene in other ways.

Colin McKinnon's discussion of comics and metal points out the similarities between the two forms, and the similarities include the fans of both forms and the frequent disparagement and persecution that both arts have attracted. But the parallels go beyond this; both comics and metal are often infused with mythology and transgression. While McKinnon shows that there have been crossovers between comics and metal, he argues that they could go much further. In particular:

> The strengthening connections between the two art forms may be one way in which comics could help metal negotiate through its crisis of abundance, specifically for creators and fans of metal to use this different medium to cast fresh light on their reflexivity around metal, allowing perceptions to be challenged in a different way.

Again, metal can reach beyond metal through exploring other forms and resources that both honor metal's past and transcend it.

* * *

In reading through the engrossing chapters in this collection I was struck – as I was at the Bowling Green conference itself – by the growing 'maturity' of metal studies. This is not just a matter of the growth of the field that I discussed earlier in this chapter; the field has matured in the sense that today's metal studies publications can now build on a considerable amount of previous work. With much of the groundwork now laid in broad studies such as my own, metal studies scholars do not have to establish and detail the principal aspects of metal in order to make a contribution. Rather, it is now possible to produce increasingly specialized studies of aspects of metal (as in the Varas-Díaz and McKinnon chapters, for example) that elucidate more general questions. There are dangers here as well. I have previously argued that the 'fragmentation' of metal studies into a host of disparate studies would weaken the potential of the field.[13] For that reason, metal studies needs to remain highly conscious of itself as a field if its potential is not to dissipate. My own suggestions of the aims of metal studies (and also Niall Scott's in this volume) provide a possible path for ensuring the future potency of the field.

Another sign of the maturity of metal studies that struck me in reading this book is the possibility it affords for the production of 'revisionist' accounts that challenge widespread assumptions that are prevalent in metal (as in Andy Brown's chapter) or in metal studies. In reading Jamie Patterson's chapter, I was reminded of her original paper at the Bowling Green conference, which was part of an all-female panel on metal and gender. The participants implicitly and explicitly challenged the emphasis on sexism in metal in earlier studies such as my own, arguing that they did not give sufficient attention to the agency of women in metal. This struck me, both at the time and now, as an important moment: when one's own work is challenged, it is a sign that the field is moving on, which is exactly as it should be.

This collection, then, exudes intellectual excitement that has accompanied metal studies' development, before, during and after the Bowling Green conference. The following chapters respect and honor metal, but they are not afraid to critique it, to look honestly at the past and to envisage a different future. Both metal and metal studies have much to say and much to offer. What comes next is bound to be, at the very least, fascinating.

Notes

1. Retrieved from: http://www.ucmo.edu/metalstudies/metal_studies_home .html
2. I am grateful to members of the email list of the International Association for the Study of Popular Music (IASPM) for sharing their experiences of non-academic involvement in popular music studies. Note also that in the early 1980s, the IASPM had a substantial non-academic element which was rapidly lost. As popular music scholar, Simon Frith argued in 2012: 'I think one thing IASPM failed to do was to really keep connections with other ways in which Popular Music was being studied, worked on, analysed outside the academy . . . it seems to have lost connection with that world.' In 'Simon Frith and Politics: An Interview.' http://livemusicexchange.org/blog/simon-frith-and-politics-an-interview/.
3. For a thoughtful discussion of these issues, see O'Boyle, T. (2013). *Semesters in the Abyss: Metal's Town and Gown Lock Horns* in The Quietus. Retrieved from: http://thequietus.com/articles/12385-heavy-metal-academics.
4. See later in this volume and also Varas-Díaz, N., Rivera-Segarra, E., Medina, C. L. R., Mendoza, S., & González-Sepúlveda, O. (2014). Predictors of Communal Formation in a Small Heavy Metal Scene: Puerto Rico as a Case Study. *Metal Music Studies*, 1(1), 87–103.

5. http://homeofmetal.com/.
6. A number of reviews and articles on my book are collated on my website here: http://www.kahn-harris.org/books/extreme-metal-music-and-culture-on-the-edge/.
7. A number of interviews with me are collated on my website here: http://www.kahn-harris.org/media-appearances/.
8. Collated on my website here: http://www.kahn-harris.org/metal-beyond-metal/.
9. Most importantly, Donna Gaines, Robert Walser and Deena Weinstein: Gaines, D. (1990). *Teenage Wasteland: Suburbia's Dead End Kids*. New York: Harper Collins; Walser, R. (1993). *Running with the Devil: Power, Gender and Madness in Heavy Metal Music*. Hanover: Wesleyan University Press; Weinstein, D. (2000). *Heavy Metal: The Music and Its Culture* (Volume 2). New York: Da Capo Press. Jeffrey Arnett is sometimes cited as part of this generation of scholars, but his view of metal culture essentially accepts that metal is somehow problematic in and of itself: Arnett, J. J. (1995). *Metalheads: Heavy Metal Music and Adolescent Alienation*. Boulder, CO: Westview Press.
10. Headbanging Against Repressive Regimes – Censorship of Heavy Metal in the Middle East, North Africa, Southeast Asia and China. Retrieved from: http://freemuse.net/archives/1540
11. Collated at http://www.kahn-harris.org/metal-beyond-metal/.
12. While this concept is my own, my work in this area was heavily informed by the work of Simon Reynolds (2011) *Retromania: Pop Culture's Addiction to Its Own Past*. London: Faber and Faber.
13. Kahn-Harris, K. (2011). Metal Studies: Intellectual Fragmentation or Organic Intellectualism. *Journal for Cultural Research*, 15(3), 251–254.

Bibliography

Arnett, J. J. (1995) *Metalheads: Heavy Metal Music and Adolescent Alienation* (Boulder, CO: Westview Press).

Attali, J. (1985) *Noise: The Political Economy of Music* (Manchester, NA: Manchester University Press).

Dawes, L. (2012) *What Are You Doing Here? A Black Woman's Life and Liberation in Heavy Metal* (New York, NY: Bazillion Points).

Gaines, D. (1990) *Teenage Wasteland: Suburbia's Dead End Kids* (New York, NY: Harper Collins).

Hickam, B. (2014) 'Amalgamated Anecdotes: Perspectives on the History of Metal Music and Culture Studies,' *Metal Music Studies*, 1(1), pp. 5–23.

Kahn-Harris, K. (2006) *Extreme Metal: Music and Culture on the Edge* (Oxford: Berg).

Kahn-Harris, K. (2011) 'Metal Studies: Intellectual Fragmentation or Organic Intellectualism,' *Journal for Cultural Research*, 15(3), 251–254.

Masciandaro, N. (ed.). (2010) *Hideous Gnosis: Black Metal Theory Symposium 1* (CreateSpace Independent Publishing Platform).

O'Boyle, T. (2013) 'Semesters in the Abyss: Metal's Town and Gown Lock Horns,' The Quietus. Retrieved from: http://thequietus.com/articles/12385-heavy-metal-academics.

Phillipov, M. (2012) *Death Metal and Music Criticism: Analysis at the Limits* (New York, NY: Lexington Books).

Reynolds, S. (2011) *Retromania: Pop Culture's Addiction to Its Own Past* (London: Faber and Faber).

Spracklen, K., Brown, A., & Kahn-Harris, K. (eds.). (2011) Special Issue: 'Metal Studies? Cultural Research in the Heavy Metal Scene,' *Journal for Cultural Research*, 15(3), pp. 209–353.

Varas-Díaz, N., Rivera-Segarra, E., Medina, C. L. R., Mendoza, S., & González-Sepúlveda, O. (2014) 'Predictors of Communal Formation in a Small Heavy Metal Scene: Puerto Rico as a Case Study,' *Metal Music Studies*, 1(1), pp. 87–103.

Walser, R. (1993) *Running with the Devil: Power, Gender and Madness in Heavy Metal Music* (Middletown, CT: Wesleyan University Press).

Weinstein, D. (2000) *Heavy Metal: The Music and Its Culture* (Vol. 2) (New York, NY: Da Capo Press).

Wells, J. (1997) 'Blackness 'Scuzed: Jimi Hendrix (In)Visible Legacy in Heavy Metal,' *Race Consciousness: African-American Studies for the New Century*, ed. J. A. Tucker (New York, NY: New York University Press), pp. 50–63.

Part I
Resilience

1
Heavy Metal as Resistance

Niall Scott
University of Central Lancashire

In this chapter I aim to show that heavy metal music and its culture is in a good position to develop as a form of popular culture capable of offering political and moral resistance. In considering heavy metal as a form of resistance, we have to first delineate what it is standing in resistance to, or what it has the possibility to resist. These questions arise as challenges in the work of Theodor Adorno but are refined when considering Stuart Hall's views on popular culture. I wish to argue that heavy metal has much promise politically speaking in its resistance in the political sphere, its resistance to certain features of popular culture, which it is also simultaneously embedded in as a form of popular culture, and also the possibility of resistance to itself. In doing so I will draw on Stuart Hall's definition of popular culture, which is firmly embedded in a socialist political framework, treating popular culture as a site where resistance to hegemonies and power hierarchies of dominant cultural ideology is played out. I will draw on a range of examples to illustrate this point, but also recognize the complexity of heavy metal's situation in a market-driven popular culture context.

To start with, then, it is worth reminding ourselves of another cultural theorist, whose interaction with popular music culture in a different era presents us with a continuing challenge. Theodor Adorno's criticism of jazz in the 1930s and 1940s (Adorno, 1989) may offer important questions regarding the state of heavy metal today, with an eye on what the metal genre and subculture has to offer. However, we can treat heavy metal with perhaps more optimism than Adorno had for the evolution of jazz. Adorno's view of jazz is one of initial hope for a genuine shift in musical style and evolution, which for him was eventually saturated with disappointment and failure. He holds: 'The aim of Jazz is the mechanical reproduction of a regressive moment...' (Adorno,

1989, p. 207). Instead of seeing jazz develop musically into avant-garde directions, he thought it moved ever closer to the processes of standardization and pseudo-individualization of the popular music industry (Strinati, 2001, p. 65). Adorno paired this with a scathing criticism of popular music and those who consume it. Although supporting an elitist separation of popular culture and high culture, Adorno's view does provide heavy metal with some probing questions. He thought that popular music generated standardization in its structure that was in direct opposition to the ideals of individuality in liberal society (Strinati, 2001, p. 66), but the music also had a superficial effect of novelty in each separate musical product, giving rise to an illusion of individuality in each piece. Heavy metal needs to find a way of avoiding becoming infected with sameness, avoiding standardization, as Adorno would say, in order to retain its resistant and transgressive qualities. One can easily criticize Adorno's elitist taste and misguided expectations regarding jazz music, yet still take much of value from his work. Adorno's work provides an ever-present warning concerning the damage that can be done to creativity and art's political edge in succumbing to the domination of market forces, reproduction and repetition. In this piece, I will explore the possibility that heavy metal oscillates between the opportunity to be not just a space for musical innovation but also holds promise in maintaining a critical and resistant stance as a form of popular culture.

Heavy metal as resistance in the sphere of politics

To identify the spheres of resistance in a political sense in the subculture of heavy metal is not an impossible task, but the diversity of positions expressed in the metal movement do make it impossible to draw any general conclusions. One would be tempted to immediately pose the question, resistant to what, politically speaking? It is certainly the case that in all corners of popular music we see the articulation and driving forward of political perspectives that are subversive and challenge power structures and dominant ideologies, for example the oppressive features of capitalism. This is brought to the fore strongly when one considers the attempts to censor musical expression by government and regulatory bodies. John Street (2003) makes the claim that 'music has long been a site of resistance. From the folk songs of rural England to the work songs of slaves, from antiwar protest songs to illegal raves, music has given voice to resistance and opposition' (p. 120). The imputation of resistance to popular music, Street claims, is also a familiar theme in liberal society, where he asserts that the consumption of popular music is linked to 'acts of defiance or "rituals of resistance" [*sic*]'(p. 121). The field of cultural studies has shown, he claims, that popular music culture is a space where 'acts of resistance could be articulated' and 'forge counter-hegemonic accounts' of the world of popular music fans in subcultures (Street, 2003, p. 121). Research in cultural studies as well as political science, specifically in the case of black music and the civil rights movement, Street (2003) writes, have 'revealed the extent to which political interests and movements were intimately linked to the development of musical form but also how the music developed and shaped the politics' (p. 122). Hjelm et al. (2011) in *Heavy Metal as Controversy and Counterculture* point out the way in which heavy metal retains an antagonistic stance in a range of social contexts by being transgressive.

Heavy metal culture keeps its position of political resistance by maintaining a momentum of controversy wherever it rears its head. The direction of this resistance is broad, ranging from extreme left wing to the extreme right wing areas of the political spectrum. Contrast for example the left wing leanings of many grindcore bands, such as Napalm Death, Extreme Noise Terror, Carcass and Terrorizer to the other side of the spectrum where we find National Socialist Black Metal (NSBM) such as Absurd, Burzum or Graveland and American hatecore, as described in Sharon Hochhauser's 2011 essay, *The Marketing of Anglo-Identity in the North American Hatecore Metal Industry*. Heavy metal expresses views that are liberal and conservative, politically active, inactive and apolitical. Indeed it is metal's position as apolitical that seems in many contexts to be given the strongest voice. Scott Wilson (2011) links the apolitical in metal to its sound, referring to metal also a form of *amusic* and that this is at the heart of its creative force and its rebellious form. I have argued elsewhere that the apolitical aspect of heavy metal culture actually presents its strongest political threat to mass and popular culture in what I have termed 'Heavy Metal's great refusal' (Scott, 2011, p. 238), adopting Herbert Marcuse's phrase from *One Dimensional Man* (Marcuse, 1991, p. 63). Marcuse adopts this phrase to describe art's capacity for 'the rationality of negation' (p. 63). Here I have argued that metal is politically apolitical, in that it promotes the apolitical as a value and is capable in this vein to 'protest against that which is' (p. 63). However, as I shall repeat below, in metal the music tends to take precedence over and above any other discussion.

Heavy metal faces a continuous challenge, met by some and ignored by others, of using its posturing as an antagonist and rebellious resistant movement for social, moral and political change. Some readers may immediately disagree and reject any argument that wishes to place a normative requirement on metal; after all that's not what the music and scene is about. This ignores many positions taken up by artists, scholars, journalists and fans in the scene, as will be seen clearly in Machine Head's Rob Flynn's stance against racism detailed below. That the success of turning heavy metal's transgressive stance into definitive social change or at least its capacity to be effective beyond its own front door has been particularly questioned by Keith Kahn-Harris's early (2004) work on black metal. He concludes that although it has failed to generate a racist practice, which is a good thing, it fails in turning its 'transgressive aesthetics and underground structures toward a thoroughgoing critique of large scale structures of domination' (Kahn-Harris, 2004, p. 109). This point will be further relevant when considering the third area of resistance – metal being resistant to itself.

The diversity in metal as mentioned above makes it difficult to near impossible to identify a single area of resistance. Where resistance is articulated as a defining feature of popular culture, this generally concerns opposition to hegemonic and dominant power structures. On the whole, metal culture does not represent an oppressed group, yet it does suffer oppression in certain geographical locations and within the metal scene there are pockets of oppression. The latter needs to be resolved from within metal culture itself; the former concerns metal as a popular culture form that is combatting power, oppression and discrimination imposed upon it from outside. Problematic issues within the metal scene such as racism and sexism can and are being dealt with through public rebuke by fans and musicians taking a vocal stand against such problems. Rob Flynn who will be mentioned again shortly, for example, took a stand against racism expressed at some of his gigs in an open letter disseminated in the metal media. He had been criticized for supporting the posting of flyers in San Francisco proclaiming 'Black Lives Matter' in response to the deaths of black men at the hands of the police in several places across the USA, including Ferguson, Missouri. He asserted:

> Apparently metal musicians aren't supposed to have opinions on the issues of the day. We're just supposed to 'rock and party bro.' And while we still do that with the best of 'em, all of my favourite bands had some kind of moral consciousness.' He continues pleading: 'Where are the god damn protest songs? Where are the 'War, What Is It Good For's'? Where are the 'Fight The Power's'? Where are the white metal bands protesting about Ferguson and Staten Island? Why don't metal bands stand for anything anymore?
>
> (Pasbani, 2015)

But where metal succeeds in resisting oppression in all contexts it sends a message to popular culture at large. It has the capacity to be a beacon demonstrating Hall's view of popular culture, which will be expanded on in detail in the next section, as a site were the 'struggle against the powerful is engaged' and is an example of an 'arena of consent and resistance' (Hall, 2009, p. 518).

Examples of this struggle come from very different places in the globe. I will discuss examples from the United States, Israel/Palestine and Malaysia/Singapore, although there are many more. The first is from Flint, Michigan cited by Al Jazeera news as one of the most dangerous places to live in the USA because of the combination of poverty and violence (Gliha, 2013). It is a small post-industrial city that has seen huge declines in its social stability and wealth as its population contracts. It is also a scene for heavy metal resistance. The hardcore band King 810 have taken their predicament of growing up in Flint and expressed the suffering and violence with critical creativity, both echoing a countercultural sentiment and challenging what heavy metal can achieve in poetic recognition of their struggle.[1] They voice a desire to stay in Flint, rather than relocating to another city, due to the success of their debut album *Memoirs of a Murder* (Lawson, 2014). Dom Lawson describes their release as a work of art in a world where the metal scene is dogged by vacuity. In an interview with King 810 in Flint on this very topic, Lawson quotes the band's lead singer David Gunn:

A lot of people who live through this shit just let it eat 'em' David nods. 'A lot of people I know and have known, people that are gone, it definitely affects 'em in a different way, and they end up dead. This life is just a hamster wheel, and you're just in it and you do it until you die. When you have a purpose and you understand that there is something beyond yourself that's happening, there's a fork in the road where you choose what's important. (p. 56)

Such a choice encompasses a critically resistant stance to domination and the bands lived experience vocalized in the song War Outside:

I hear all these critics talk but I listen to none/Cuz none of them have ever been where music comes from/And none of them have ever stepped foot inside a slum/And none of them have ever wrapped their hands around a gun/And squeezed till its empty and it locks up and it's done/And feel the man on the other sides last breath leap out his lungs/I've been doing this here since I was young/ So next time you speak about me just cut out your fucking tongue.

(Gunn, 2014)

The impact of how the market damages identity is explored in the song 'State of Nature':

Remember when a man was a man not a product or a title or a brand/Now everything's changing these people aren't real and we have no heroes/They're pink in the middle/They don't say what they mean they don't do what they say they won't stand here and die for it.

(Gunn, 2014)

Moving to a different kind of violence entirely, the Israeli band Orphaned Land set an example of resistance to war and injustice in their homeland. Orphaned Land's collaboration with the Palestinian band Khalas (meaning 'enough!') and their very vocal stand against political violence in the Middle East and the plight of children and innocent victims of the war in Syria is at the heart of the 2013 album, All Is One. When Orphaned Land were awarded a Golden Gods at the Metal Hammer ceremonies in June of the year it was released, singer Khobi Fhari, insisted on sharing the award with Khalas's singer, Abed Hathut, in a public show of unity (Metal Gaia, 2014).

From a different corner of resistance, Liew and Fu (2006) have documented moral panics and social disdain targeted at the metal scene in Malaysia and Singapore. The metal music culture is treated as 'subverting the conservative socio-political ethos in both Malaysia and Singapore' (p. 103). Consistent resistance to power structures is perpetuated in the stability of a youth culture that stimulates fear and anxiety in the establishment, especially of the decadence of encroaching Western values (ibid.). They chart a history of fears of political subversion generated by metal music that go back to the 1970s and 1980s, as well as the perceived hippie culture and long hair worn by men and those that mirror the moral panics surrounding metal music in the USA and UK. In more recent times they notice a difference in attitudes toward metal music between Singapore and Malaysia, where the resurgence of Islamic conservatism in Malaysia, most particularly concerning black metal led to a police clamp down on the youth culture involved in the extreme music scene, expressing itself through heavy metal, whilst in Singapore a greater degree of tolerance started showing itself, due in part, Liew and Fu report, to the sheer physical volume of imported music sales going up. The authors speak of youths in 2001 finding themselves as targets of social surveillance both by the state law enforcement agencies as well as religious authorities. '... police raids were conducted on shopping centres and schools with an estimated 700 youths detained or questioned for alleged criminal activity relating to religious desecration, devil worship, drug use and promiscuous behaviour'(p. 116). A more recent example of heavy metal's agitative stance and resistance to state power can be seen in Iran, where in 2013 it was reported that 200 fans were arrested at a Dawn of Rage concert in Tehran, despite the event being sanctioned by the Ministry of Culture and Islamic Guidance (Freemuse, August 2013).

Although the context and background to these examples are radically different, one cannot compare Tehran, Malaysia, Singapore, Israel/Palestine and Flint Michigan, there are countless more examples across the globe where metal music is dynamically engaged in many forms of resistance to power structures and ideologies, sometimes at a high cost to the musician and fan.

Heavy metal as resistant to popular culture

Heavy metal has the capacity to be resistant in the sphere of popular culture. Stuart Hall in his 1981 essay, Notes on Deconstructing the Popular,' identifies three possible ways of defining popular culture coming from a socialist political perspective. The first, which he is critical of, concerns those things that are popular simply because large numbers of people participate in them and what the masses consume. Hall rejects this as, although it presents a fact of consumer behavior, it also treats the masses as uncritical, passive 'cultural dopes' (p. 512). The alternative popular culture in this first definition concerns popular culture embodying the authentic things that working classes are involved in, do, and have done. This is dismissed by Hall as well, as it is too all encompassing and provides no critical weight. In this he furthermore rejects popular culture defined as a heroic authentic alternative working class that is not 'taken in by the commercial substitutes' (p. 512).

Hall's second definition concerns treating popular culture as 'those things that "the people" do or have done' (p. 513) and is thus descriptive. The trouble with this is that it can encompass anything that 'the people' happen to do. More importantly though he rejects this definition because it fails to draw out the very distinction that matters in popular culture – its existence as wholly other than dominant culture or elite culture. It thus fails to address structural differences and processes that usefully distinguish the popular from other categories.

It is a third definition that he views as most relevant and one that I think is of value in heavy metal's capacity for resistance. This definition is one in which popular culture is positioned as a flexible, changing dialogical arena where trends and ideas shift (pp. 514–515). In other words, today's news is tomorrow's fish and chip wrapper. It maintains the descriptive features of popular culture but sees them as in an antagonistic relationship to the dominant culture at any given time. The key opposition Hall maintains is between popular culture and the power bloc it opposes. This can be envisaged as being present within a subculture as well as in popular culture in general, and opposition to power blocs arguably outside popular culture. Popular culture thus exemplifies itself in movements of resistance and conformity. Hall speaks of this in terms of shifting dominant and subordinate formations.

Heavy metal, in its complexity and diversity, is a culture that has its own power blocs and resistances to them. For example heavy metal has seen shifts in the increased participation of women, challenging the masculine power blocs that existed as characteristic of metal's identity in the past, as explored in Sonia Vasan's 2011 work on women in death metal, Rosemary Overell's 2014 study of the grindcore scenes in Australia and Japan and Gabby Riches forthcoming work on grindcore noting its increasing female fan base. Another example which can be found throughout popular music is the embracing of crowdfunding initiatives, building a relationship directly between the artist and fan base, initially undermining the traditional status of the record company and promoter. This is still an explorative space not without its problems; it may not be as utopian as it seems (Beaumont–Thomas, 2014). Nonetheless it is an area where dominant and subordinate forces are involved in a process of redefining their field, indeed challenging and rethinking market hegemonies in the music industry. Yet another example could be grunge music's overhaul of the commercial heavy metal of the 1980s. More such examples will be discussed below. If we are to accept Hall's view of popular culture, the call then for metal is to be ever prepared to maintain its position as resistance, as opposition to dominant power blocs external to metal but also those that exist within metal. Resistance is secured, Martinez (1997) points out, where 'subcultures transform their parent culture creating a highly variable repertoire of responses to hegemony' (p. 270). Thus heavy metal is in a position to be part, if not at the forefront, of a struggle which Hall argues, explicit in his socialist aims, is a site where the 'struggle for and against the powerful is engaged' (Hall, 2009 [1981], p. 518). The processes and changing dynamics in this understanding of popular culture admit that popular culture arises in a certain context. In the case of music, that context includes market forces and the music industry, not just a romanticized ideal, a pure relationship between the fan and the artist.

The difficulty in this is that heavy metal is part of popular culture and in a sense it has two or more parent cultures; one could cite blues music and classical music for example, but also pop music in general. Treating metal music and its culture as a part of popular culture admits the status of metal as a form of popular culture in the sense that it emerges from the popular. This is in line with Stuart Hall's third definition of popular culture as a music form that emerges under certain material and social conditions, where Hall defines the popular in terms of an antagonism, relationship with, and in an influential tension to, the dominant culture. It includes a relationship of change where things are not fixed.

In the same manner, heavy metal can be seen as moving through periods of transgression, which in time can become rather mundane or lose their efficacy in a contemporary context, being relegated to historical narrative. The shock generated by the activities of one generation can lose their effect in the next generation. The perceived threat to the Christian Conservative Right from 'satanic heavy metal' is not as threatening now as it was in the 1970s and 1980s. For example, Klypchak points out that Alice Cooper, Black Sabbath and KISS, all of whom were targets of scorn and moral panic, have 'become ubiquitous in mainstream popular culture' (Klypchak, 2013, p. 36). The significance of moral panics with regard to heavy metal may have receded in some places but, as Hjelm, Kahn Harris and Levine maintain, because of metal's global reach they now surface in different cultural contexts, such 'as in the contemporary campaigns against metalheads in Islamic countries' (Hjelm et al., 2011, p. 5)

However, a greater challenge for metal to rise to is to develop a capacity to resist popular culture as a form of popular culture itself. This of course stirs up normative questions (what metal ought to do), rather than descriptive ones. I am not particularly interested in what *is* the case, rather in what *ought* to be the case, in other words I am interested in pursuing what heavy metal can do not just at a practical level, but at a normative level. As seen from the examples above and in the following section, heavy metal can promote values in opposition to dominant power structures and damaging hegemonies such as oppression, restricting freedoms of expression, racism and sexism and thus also address political issues raised in the previous section. Can metal have a normative force where it *ought* to pursue an opportunity to resist popular culture? Does it have the capacity to continue to express cultural struggle as it certainly did in its working-class/blue-collar origins? I think that it can and does. I have argued elsewhere (Scott, 2013) that the political aspect of heavy metal culture actually presents its strongest political threat to mass and popular culture. However, the unreflective position will think that heavy metal is simply yet another popular culture expression that conforms to the demands of the market. Complementary to this, one may think that heavy metal most clearly exemplifies Herbert Marcuse's insight of the damage that the market does to any possibility of moral or political value poking its head above the parapet of consumer power. Marcuse (1991) writes: 'In the realm of culture, the new totalitarianism manifests itself precisely in a harmonizing pluralism where the most contradictory works and truths peacefully coexist in indifference' (p. 61). The damning effect of this point is that even when any politically resistant stance is expressed, it will always be subsumed under the power of market forces and commodification. But when considered with Stuart Hall's view on popular culture as a dynamic and contested space, we have cause for optimism concerning heavy metal's capacity to maintain its transgressive resistant stance. Hall quotes Gramsci: 'What matters is the criticism to which such an ideological complex is subjected. [...] The old collective will dissolves [*sic*] into its contradictory elements since the subordinate ones develop socially.' Then he holds that: 'Popular culture and tradition is a battlefield' (Hall, 2009, p. 516). Part of being able to accept some of the messages articulated by voices of performers in metal culture has to do with knowing the individual who articulates, knowing whether something is expressed with integrity or for the sake of image production. Rob Flynn of Machine Head delivered an impassioned speech at the 2012 Bloodstock festival, highlighting their success, thanking their fans despite never having been on the radio or MTV. Flynn continues to speak up in favor of the power of music over and against monotonous, electronic syncopated background music (https://www.youtube.com/watch?v=hpakWSgQ_AI).

Behind this point of view lies the general criticism of inauthenticity against the damaging effects on creativity mass/pop music culture brought about by unskilled use of computer programming technology in musical composition, as well as an attack on the contemporary wave of talent shows delivering instant success, such as the X Factor, demeaning the process of musical growth, sometimes through hardship, but definitely requiring life experience and time. This criticism needs to be tempered though with the recognition of the role of technology in metal music, both in its production and composition challenging the narrow idea of authenticity as purity. Mark Mynett et al. have explored the production of heaviness in studio mixing of modern heavy metal, questioning a superficial understanding of the meaning of authenticity in metal (Mynett et al., 2010). Instead, though, I think these utterances on authenticity are awkward expressions of a different point. That is, there is an intuitive difference between music generated from a lived experience and music manufactured as superficial affective entertainment. Such a view is further expressed regarding the Japanese pop metal phenomenon of Babymetal, criticized for being a manufactured product and not reflecting the 'lived' nature of metal music (Hudson, 2014). The expression of the 'lived' nature of metal has strong resonances with heavy metal's and rock music's hard work and touring ethic – contrast Babymetal's constructed product with King 810 and the differences are all too clear.

Heavy metal as resistance to itself: Self-reflective resistance

Heavy metal's resistance to popular culture exposes areas where it can be resistant to itself, a self-reflexive resistance, dealing with edifices of power and domination that the subculture has built up over time. This recognizes the possibility that metal descends and ascends; it has its own bourgeoisie that shifts and changes depending on the conditions under which the particular form of metal emerges. This can range from a sonic response to an image response, for example the drone reaction to speed and thrash involves a slowing down of the music through the removal of virtuosic guitar solos and fast drumming. The Los Angeles thrash metal scene emerged as a response to glam and hair metal, not just a change in sound, but a change in image away from makeup and hairspray back to denim, dirt and leather. Metal has seen the move from 'prog' complexity to blues simplicity and back. Things that used to stand as resistance may no longer be so; the working class heritage of the fandom/following of metal arguably is no longer relevant, but of course that depends on what kinds of struggles/resistance metal represents. Above, we saw clear examples of areas of resistance that still persist and represent the normative question: what ought metal to stand for? In addition to metal being worth listening to simply for its own sake, this question has its place where metal (as well as other music and art forms) has the opportunity to communicate messages of political resistance, for example injustices, inequality and oppression. In this vein, Hall argues for the popular as exhibiting 'the people against the power bloc' – but he adds an important reminder: those blocs can exist internal to the things that that people adhere to. The power-bloc management, commodification and so on can be part of the identity of metal itself.

Heavy metal has the capacity to be resistant to excesses of corporate greed. When Ghost and Gojira played a UK tour in 2013, tickets were being sold at five pounds, with sponsorship from Jägermeister (Hicks, 2013). Gojira is a metal band that openly promotes environmentalist thought in their lyrics and in interviews (Anderson, 2009). So collaboration with a promoter whose main concern is to sell its product and thus sponsors a tour, reducing ticket prices to boost consumption of its product, seems to be ideologically opposed to Gojira's political credentials. One may look at this as downright contradictory, or else see it a useful collaboration allowing a band to reach out to more of its fans and even a new audience. In a remark made to me by a friend in the industry it was pointed out that as a marketing ploy this may be seen as cynical and then he followed with the somewhat rhetorical question 'but who loses?' At a more considered level one can point out worker exploitation, fans being lured in with cheap tickets, who then spend their hard-earned cash on merchandise, drink and so on; Jägermeister's brand certainly wins no matter what. Yet another industry contact explained that the Jägermeister tour promoter genuinely wanted to give fans the opportunity to see bands that they might not normally see or could not afford to see. One can question whether this is a genuine example of resistance or the opportunity presented by Jägermeister sponsorship. I think it is a problem open for debate; on the one hand it gives an example of how corporate interest can work better in the music's interest and goals and provide a platform for a band such as Gojira to turn more people on to their message. On the other hand, it is nothing other than a clever marketing strategy. To tease out where power (bloc) and exploitation lie can be a difficult task especially where mutual benefits and exchanges are experienced by those engaged in an event or the scene in general. This mutual collaboration can for example be illustrative of Marcuse's claim above of the peaceful manifestation of a contradictory indifferent harmonizing pluralism where the corporate market values and interests of the sponsor and promoter (Jägermeister) share a space with a band (Gojira) who are expressly opposed to such values.

When one looks at heavy metal culture, one is easily confronted with a scene that is intelligently reflective, despite Keith Kahn-Harris' identification of intentional unreflexivity in some areas and individuals involved in metal. Even this is entertained as a knowing position; it is a dynamic music culture, confronted with opportunities for development. This is of course not unique to metal, but can be found in other forms of popular music culture. Scholarship that looks critically at heavy metal's more problematic issues, such as sexism, racism and conservative insularity mirror arguments and challenges that emerge from within heavy metal's core. Amit Sharma's interview with Opeth's frontman Michael Arkerfeldt delivered a similar claim, where Arkerfeldt insisted that: 'metal should be rebellious, even within its own genre' (Sharma, 2014, p. 39). This claim is not just about exploring different avenues in musical experimentation and composition, but also heavy metal's reflection on its own state of affairs and definitions. For heavy metal, music is the primary object of interest in its culture; it is both the essence and expression of its culture (Scott, 2014). Where metal shows an internal resistance to itself, this may well be good for its own creative musical evolution, but it can also be criticized for being too self-obsessed when metal has the opportunity to resist oppressing power structures. In this respect, the metal community certainly has its work cut out, as I would insist that it is in turn resistant to normative pressure, be it political or moral. But musical creativity and expression is very much part of that articulating voice of resistance. Scholarship and journalism certain have a role to play here in foregrounding that resistance, and examples such as Laina Dawes' (2012) excellent work combatting racism and sexism in the scene in her *What Are You Doing Here? A Black Woman's Life and Liberation in Heavy Metal* thunders a serious demand that the metal world wake up to moral and political problems within its ranks. She points out in her chapter 'The lingering stench of racism in metal' (p. 133) that she was drawn to certain grindcore bands precisely because of the social commentary provided in their work. However, she also draws attention to the resistance to normative change in the metal community where one of her interview subjects, Jason Netherton, bassist of Misery Index claims that fans prioritize the music over lyrical content: 'When artists promote social and political messages, the responses are mixed, to say the least' (Dawes, 2012, p. 148). Fans like the music, the energy and the anger, and definitely the lyrics come second if not last for a lot of people, notes Netherton. 'It's unfortunate, but I don't think that people would appreciate more socially conscious lyrics or lyrics that are critical of racism or homophobia. I tend to find that the more blatant you are with your message, the reaction or response you get will get is more critical' (Dawes, 2012, p. 149). Fortunately, there are bands that provide a counter to this; Napalm Death, already mentioned, is probably one of the most well-known bands to do so. Not only does Napalm actively promote an antifascist and anti-racist stance as well as green political views, they can also be found indulging in reflective criticism within the scene regarding the image and symbolism represented in the performance space. An example to illustrate this comes from my own experience seeing Napalm Death at Hammerfest in Wales in March 2014. In a sarcastic well-humored dig, the singer Barney Greenway about to be enveloped in CO_2 said from the stage: 'Can you turn the smoke off? We don't need any smoke on stage you know, we're not that kind of band. We're not Cradle of Filth, you know? We want everyone to see us. Thanks.' This statement alluded for me not only for the band members to want to be visible and transparent to their audience, but I took it as a statement about the visibility of their political presence – they want to be heard, and visual transparency contributes to being heard, being listened to. Their music is not about entertainment although it may be entertaining; it concerns Napalm Death's primary aim of communicating a worldview, one that ought to be paid attention to by anyone attending their gig. Although Scott Wilson reiterates the point made by Netherton above that 'In metal images and words are always subordinate to sound' (Wilson, 2011, p. 205). Napalm Death in their quip use a point concerning their image to focus attention on their lack of image – there are no gimmicks on stage, just the band and what they stand for. Another clear area where metal is engaged in an internal resistance is in the contested arena of gender politics. Sonia Vasan's 2011 critical analysis and research of women's practices, participation and tolerance of misogynistic, sexist and androcentric culture in the Texan death metal scene indicated that much needs to be done to challenge the power structures that either exclude women or make it a difficult space for women to participate in. The extensive research by Rosie Overell (2014) on brutality and belonging in the Australian and Japanese Grindcore scenes also sheds light on misogynistic and sexist views and practices that have no place in the contemporary metal scene. The research being generated on gender politics in heavy metal is a growing and exciting field where soon more critical work will be published. Heavy metal scholarship is not simply a movement of academics that express their allegiance to metal by writing about it, but it is involved in the production of knowledge. In this sense, it is delineating, in cooperation with artists, and journalists a genuinely different way of thinking about (popular) cultural resistance by outlining new forms of knowledge and discourse; defining terms and also setting out structures in normative directions.

Conclusion

Heavy metal is trapped between being a form of popular culture as resistance and a movement that has the capacity to resist popular culture. Where heavy metal culture expresses an imperative task to resist popular culture, it exposes itself too easily to failure in this task. At the UK Bloodstock festival in 2012, Rob Flynn's speech promotes the creativity and diversity in heavy metal music as well as a defense of its authenticity and rejection of simulation, reproduction and monotony. Heavy metal, both its music and culture, are in a position to resist the popular where the popular in music is an infantilized submission to sameness. Heavy metal can satirize the worn out and the ruined state of popular music, yet often falls prey to the very values and sounds of some forms of popular music it rejects in its commodification, institutionalization and standardization. This is a key problem for heavy metal as a potential form of resistance, notwithstanding the plight of metal musicians and fans as consumers in certain parts of the globe where it is sometimes dangerous to be a metal head. Heavy metal in affluent, liberal 'Western' music culture does not stand or represent an oppressed group per se, in the way that oppositional cultures often do. Yet heavy metal culture has at its disposal tools to perform subversive resistance in its use of language, image and capacity to lampoon and mock commodified popular music culture and at the same time not promote a notion of a dominant legitimated culture as opposed to a popular culture. Instead it has the capacity to expose the repression of an intellectual critique of popular culture whilst at the same time make popular culture unmanageable for those who consume it in the manner of standardization and pseudindividualization that Adorno was so critical of.

Note

1. It has been pointed out though that a different narrative concerning King 810 has been reported. Retrieved from: http://www.metalsucks.net/2014/08/07/king-810-may-actually-flint-michigan/. However, as a close acquaintance to the journalist Dom Lawson I have no reason to doubt the veracity of his report in its context.

Bibliography

Adorno. T. (1989) 'Perennial Fashion-Jazz,' *Critical Theory, A Reader*, eds. E. Bronner & D. MacKay Lellner (London: Routledge), pp. 199–209.

Anderson, E. (2009) 'French Metal Band Spreads Eco-Friendly Message'. Retrieved 30 August 2014 from: http://www.dailyiowan.com/2009/10/08/Arts/13446. html.

Beaumont-Thomas, D. (2014) 'Can Fan Campaigns Reinvent the Music Industry?' Retrieved 01 February 2015 from: http://www.theguardian.com/music/2014/ jun/17/can-fan-campaigns-reinvent-the-music-industry-kickstarter-crowd funding.

Dawes, L. (2012) *What Are You Doing Here? A Black Woman's Life and Liberation in Heavy Metal* (New York, NY: Bazillion Points).

Freemuse. (2013) 'Iran: Over 200 Rock Fans Arrested at Heavy Metal Concert.' Retrieved 1 September 2015 from: http://freemuse.org/archives/6641.

Gliha, L. J. (2013) 'Growing Up in America's Most Dangerous City.' Retrieved 29 August 2014 from: http://america.aljazeera.com/watch/shows/america -tonight/america-tonight-blog/2013/10/24/growing-up-in-americasmost dangerouscityflint.html.

Hall, S. (2009) 'Notes on Deconstructing the Popular,' *Cultural Theory and Popular Culture A Reader*, ed. J. Storey (Harlow: Pearson Longman Books), pp. 508–518.

Hicks, A. (2013) 'Ghost/Gojira/the Defiled, *Metalmouth*, Live Reviews.' Retrieved from: http://metalmouth.net/2013/04/index-50/.

Hjelm, T., Kahn-Harris, K., & Levine, M. (2011) 'Heavy Metal as Controversy and Counterculture,' *Popular Music History*, 6(12), pp. 5–18.

Hobart, M. (2005) *Top 10 Most Ridiculous Black Metal Pics of All Time*. Retrieved 30 August 2014 from: http://www.ruthlessreviews.com/1124/top-10-most-ridiculous-black-metal-pics-of-all-time-2/.

Hochhauser, S. (2011) 'The Marketing of Anglo-Identity in the North American Hatecore Metal Industry,' *Metal Rules the Globe*, eds. J. Wallach, H. M. Berger, & P. D. Greene (Durham, NC: Duke University Press), pp. 161–179.

Hudson, A. (2014) *Did Babymetal Invent Cute Metal and What is It?* Retrieved 25 October 2015 from: http://www.bbc.co.uk/newsbeat/28217125.

Kahn-Harris, K. (2004) 'The Failure of Youth Culture: Reflexivity, Music and Politics in the Black Metal Scene,' *European Journal of Cultural Studies*, 7(1), pp. 95–111.

Klypchak, B. (2013) 'How You Gonna See Me Now': Recontextualizing Metal Artists and Moral Panics,' *Heavy Metal Controversies and Countercultures*, eds. T. Hjelm, K. Kahn-Harris, & M. Levine (Bristol: Equinox), pp. 36–49.

Larin, H. (2011) 'Triumph of the Maggots? Valorisation of Metal in the Rock Press,' *Popular Music History*, 6(1–2), pp. 52–67.

Lawson, D. (2014) 'King 810: Welcome to Hell,' *Metal Hammer*, 260, pp. 53–59.

Liew, K. K. & Fu, K. (2006) 'Conjuring the Tropical Spectres: Heavy Metal, Cultural Politics in Singapore and Malaysia,' *Inter Asia Cultural Studies*, 7(1), pp. 99–112.

Marcuse, H. (1991) *One Dimensional Man* (London: Routledge).

Martinez, T. (1997) 'Culture as Oppositional Culture,' *Sociological Perspectives*, 40(2), pp. 265–286.

Metal Gaia. (2014) 'Orphaned Land Frontman Speaks Out About Middle Eastern Violence'. Retrieved 25 October 2015 from: http://metal-gaia.com/2014/08/13/ orphaned-land-frontman-speaks-out-about-middle-eastern-violence/.

Mynett, M., Wakefield, J. P., & Till, R. (2010) 'Intelligent Equalisation Principles and Techniques for Minimising Masking when Mixing the Extreme Modern

Metal Genre,' *Heavy Fundametalisms: Music Metal and Politics*, eds. R. Hill & K. Spracklen (Oxford: Inter-Disciplinary Press), pp. 141–146.

Overell, R. (2014) *Affective Intensities in Extreme Music Scenes* (Basingstoke: Palgrave Macmillan).

Pasbani, R. (2015) 'Machine Head's Rob Flynn Comments on Selma, Racism and Phil Labontes Recent Comments,' *Metal Injection*, January 22. Retrieved 01 February 2015 from: http://www.metalinjection.net/latest-news/ machine-heads-robb-flynn-comments-on-selma-racism-and-phil-labontes-recent-comments.

Riches, G. (2015) 'Use Your Mind?: Embodiments of Protest and Grotesque Realism in British Grindcore,' *Global Metal Music and Culture: Current Directions in Metal Studies*, eds. A. R. Brown, K. Spracklen, K. Kahn-Harris, & N. Scott (London: Routledge).

Scott, N. (2011) 'The Deafening Threat of the Apolitical,' *Popular Music History*, 6(1–2), pp. 224–239.

Scott, N. (2013) 'The Deafening Sound of the Apolitical,' *Heavy Metal: Controversies and Countercultures*, eds. T. Hjelm, K. Kahn-Harris, & M. Levine (Sheffield: Equinox Press), pp. 228–243.

Scott, N. (2014) 'Seasons in the Abyss: Heavy Metal as Liturgy,' *Diskus*, 16(1), pp. 12–29.

Sharma, A. (2014) 'Angel of Retribution,' *Metal Hammer*, 260, pp. 36–45.

Street, J. (2003) ' "Fight the Power": The Politics of Music and the Music of Politics,' *Government and Opposition, and International Journal of Comparative Politics*, 38(1), pp. 113–130.

Strinati, D. (2001) *An Introduction to Theories of Popular Culture* (London: Routledge).

Unknown Author. Retrieved 28 August 2014 from: http://freemuse.org/archives/ 6641.

Vasan, S. (2011) 'The Price of Rebellion: Gender Boundaries in the Death Metal Scene,' *Journal for Cultural Research*, 15(3), pp. 333–349.

Wilson, S. (2011) 'From Forests Unknown: "Eurometal" and the Political/Audio Unconscious,' *Reflections in the Metal Void*, ed. N. Scott (Oxford: Interdisciplinary Press), pp. 149–161.

2

Sentimentality and the Heavy Metal Documentary

Gerd Bayer
University of Erlangen

The traditional conception of metal as an art form dominated by violence, noise and youthful immaturity is forcefully disrupted by recent heavy metal documentaries. Various films present a new narrative that draws on generic conventions that were hitherto not associated with metal. In a range of films, the focus on personal, biographical, and relationship issues emphasizes emotional and human qualities. In doing so, these documentaries add a new facet to the way heavy metal culture is viewed and perceived by a larger audience, thereby unsettling and putting into play the closeted existence of metal culture. Sentimentality in metal films not only invites outsiders to reconsider their views about the values and practices within metal culture, but also supports those within the metal scene who resist sexist and machismo tendencies that spill over from hegemonic cultural spheres into this subcultural element. By looking at three recent documentary films, Sacha Gervasi's *Anvil: The Story of Anvil* (2008), Joe Berlinger and Bruce Sinofsky's *Metallica: Some Kind of Monster* (2004) and Andreas Geiger's *Heavy Metal auf dem Lande* ('Heavy Metal in the Countryside,' 2006), this chapter discusses how these films appropriate generic qualities drawn from sentimental genres, which can look back on a literary and painterly history of various centuries, for the portrayal of metal music and the social environment from which it grows.

Each of these films follows a different but related trajectory. Gervasi's portrayal of Anvil's two master-minds circles around their friendship and the unlikely story of their eventual return to musical success. Though ostensibly about the making of a new Metallica album, *Some Kind of Monster* turns into a very tense portrayal of the band members' psychic and emotional state of mind. Geiger's film is framed as a kind of *Bildungsroman*, where the hero, Markus Staiger, overcomes various obstacles to turn his brain-child, the record label Nuclear Blast, into a successful venture. All three cinematic documents present heavy metal in a rather unusual way in that they allow their male protagonists to demonstrate their emotionality and fragility in a manner that appears to contradict widely held perceptions about heavy metal. While feelings like anger, rage, lust and desire are frequently evoked in connection with this musical genre, the films' tenderness and what I discuss in the following as their sentimentality introduce a different quality, one that questions the perceived understanding of its gendered identity. In disrupting supposedly stable forms of metal masculinities, the three films discussed here confirm claims by scholars who resist 'a unitary masculinity' and instead propose an approach to types of masculinities that allows for the kinds of 'internal contradiction' (Connell & Messerschmidt, 2005, p. 852) that, in the context of heavy metal, sees hypermasculinity accompanied by more sentimental and emotional forms of masculinity.

The way male figures are presented in recent metal documentaries shows masculinity to be more complex and fluid than one would normally admit for the supposedly masculinist genre of heavy metal. It is only appropriate, one could add, that such re-adjustments play out within a cinematic context, where filmic conventions allow 'characters' to present themselves in a particular light, even within a documentary. Such performances frequently highlight the very fault lines that exist in a particular sphere. When Judith Butler asks 'Is drag the imitation of gender, or does it dramatize the signifying gestures through which gender itself is established?' (1990, p. xxxi), her suggestion can be applied to the masculinities that perform themselves in the films discussed here. In choosing the sentimental masculinities that dominate these three documentaries, the filmmakers might be said to have subverted, or even dramatized, the inherently inaccurate portrayal of conventionalized metal masculinities.

From masculinist metal to the sentime(n)tal

The manner in which heavy metal employs gendered performances, imagery and discourses related to sexual dynamics has been a staple feature of the scholarship devoted to this musical genre. Robert Walser, whose 1993 monograph on metal bears the subtitle 'power, gender, and madness in heavy metal music,' begins his comments on gender by noting that 'heavy metal often stages fantasies of masculine virtuosity and control' (1993, p. 108) and goes on to claim that the musical genre as a whole 'is, inevitably, a discourse shaped by patriarchy' (1993, p. 109). Walser concentrates mainly on the early phase of heavy metal, a time when concepts like metrosexuality (Pompper, 2010; and see Shugart, 2008) and the socio-cultural discussion of what Susan Faludi, in the subtitle of her 1999 book, *Stiffed*, has described as 'the betrayal of the American man,' were still overshadowed by a wide-spread consensus according to which men were almost exclusively committed to the kind of 'hegemonic masculinity' outlined by R. W. Connell (1995). By now, Walser's focus on what he describes as metal's reaction to 'the "threat" of women' (1993, p. 110) feels slightly dated.[1] The dominant imagery within heavy metal culture has moved beyond the blatant sexism as found in its early music videos;[2] or at the very least it seems less exceptional when compared to the collective pornographication of popular music (see Levande, 2007), almost regardless of the genre.

While gender discussions continue in many professional and academic contexts, there are some indications for changing attitudes that see the two sexes engage in a less confrontational manner. And while, on the surface, some metal genres still seem committed to gendered stereotypes of masculinity and femininity, as for instance described by Rosemary Overell's discussion of brutality and song lyrics within an Australian grindcore scene, the move toward sentimentality in metal documentaries attests to developments in metal culture that challenge the clichés about gender and metal. Even the disembodied and de-intellectualized growls of grindcore can be seen as a turn toward affect, and thereby constitute a challenge to the general 'male aversion to articulation of feelings' (Overell, 2011, p. 208).

Scholarship like this addresses the fact that the historical changes in gendered identities in the early twenty-first century have also arrived in heavy metal. In her influential 2000 monograph on heavy metal, Deena Weinstein had still described metal's attitude toward gender as based on 'antifemale posturing of heavy metal stars' and their 'misogyny' (2000, p. 67), noting also that 'the macho image of the metal artist' (68) subjects even female metal musicians to the one-dimensional role of 'sexual objects' (68). In a more recent essay, however, Weinstein revises her earlier claims and now concludes that in metal 'women are of no concern,' meaning by this that within metal culture 'no invidious elevation of one gender over the other' exists (2009, p. 18). She suggests that when male metal musicians cultivate masculinities they are moving in spheres outside of gender differences, trying instead to 'affirm an imaginary of power' and to create a sense of 'forceful individuality' (Weinstein, 2009, p. 28).[3]

Similarly, Nedim Hassan offers a re-evaluation of the 1988 film *The Decline of Western Civilization Part II: The Metal Years* in which he analyzes the Los Angeles metal scene as less sexist and misogynist than conventionally agreed. Hassan's discussion of this early metal documentary shows that, even then, the male-centered objectification of women in the metal scene was frequently and insistently undermined, suggesting for instance that many of the aspiring metal musicians 'are almost entirely dependent upon women for finances, a place to stay, or booze and drugs,' thus handing to women in the metal scene 'power and agency' (Hassan, 2010, p. 257). Some male band members also openly prostituted themselves, both in hetero- and homosexual ways, further eroding the sense that metal is built on the objectification of women. While conventional patriarchal structures co-existed with such reversals of sexual roles, *The Metal Years* nevertheless testifies to a certain instability at the heart of metal's gender identity, allowing Hassan to describe parts of this film as constituting 'a series of vulnerable, often contradictory, self-presentations' (2010, p. 261). Sentimentality, it seems, has been part and parcel of metal documentaries for quite some time.

If vulnerability is read as referring to mental states (rather than alluding to physical conflict), then it already indicates that emotional qualities are being addressed that were hitherto assumed to be absent from this genre. This opens the door for the sentimental in metal. In approaching the question of how implementing generic traits from sentimentality reshapes the public perception of heavy metal, let me draw on a canonical work about how men relate to other men, Eve Sedgwick's *Between Men: English Literature and Male Homosocial Desire*. In her book, Sedgwick asks whether it makes sense to differentiate between homosexual and homosocial male relationships, in other words, between male-male contact that is driven by homoerotic activity or by what is often described as male bonding, producing the kind of old-boys' networks that mostly center on the principle of prolonging patriarchal structures. What Sedgwick describes as the 'continuum between homosocial and homosexual' (1985, p. 2), I would like to disrupt further through the literary tradition of the sentimental, which allows for male-male relationships that center on themes like friendship and reliance without relating to themes of sexuality or gender politics.

Sentimental literature became popular in the eighteenth century and is closely related to a female readership as well as to a de-sexualization of romantic love and to other morally un-suspect emotions. While clearly committed to patriarchal gender relationships, as for instance visible in the marriage themes that structure Jane Austen's novels, sentimental themes nevertheless aim to bypass the sexual, focusing instead on humanist notions of proper moral conduct.[4] The concept of the sentimental was first made popular by Laurence Sterne's 1768 *Sentimental Journey*, and it became widely known in philosophical circles through G. E. Lessing's translation as '*empfindsam*' (see Jäger, 1969). While the word went a little out of fashion following the scandalous publication of Goethe's *Werther* in 1774, with Schiller's distinction between naïve and sentimental art (1795/1796) further turning the tide, sentimentality has its firm place in the literary canon as a movement that subscribed to the idea that moral judgment frequently takes its origin in the emotional capacity. As Enlightenment and Romanticism fought out their battle over what Austen aptly portrayed as the conflict between sense and sensibility, sentimentality was frequently coded as female and in opposition to male rationality. By evoking the sentimental, then, heavy metal films set out to show that even heavy metal allows men to be in touch with their anima and with those features like sentiment that, according to C. G. Jung,[5] are needed to create a healthy and stable mental mindset.

What the tradition of the sentimental thus allows me to do in my discussion of heavy metal documentaries is to move beyond the supposed continuum between homosexual and homosocial and instead concentrate on emotionality, with the sentimental opening up a conceptual space in heavy metal studies for all aspects of emotion-based human relationships. By studying sentimental tropes, this essay continues the arguments made by Weinstein and others about the non-confrontational gender politics within heavy metal culture.

A story of brotherly love: *Anvil*

One cinematic place where such sentimentality is given ample room is *Anvil*, the film named after the band it celebrates. While frequently taking inspiration from *Spinal Tap*, with the famous 'Hello, Cleveland' invariably intoned while the band walks through confusing backstage corridors, this rockumentary nevertheless mostly adopts a serious tone, bordering if anything on the tragicomic. After all, the film reminds its viewers that in the metal industry, like in life at large, justice does not necessarily prevail, and it is accordingly not always the most deserving bands that garner all the fame and fortune. This sense of failed justice already hints at the literary affinities that underwrite this documentary since it is precisely the notion of poetic justice that the film *Anvil* undermines. Taken from classical tragedy, poetic justice refers to the kind of dramatic development that sees a play's villain eventually punished for his (or sometimes, her) evil deeds. With the audience's sense of justice thus flattered, creating the famous moment of catharsis that embodies the release of pent-up feelings and frustration, tragic plays neverthe-less act as a reminder that actual justice, outside the aesthetic realm, does not necessarily follow such a principled progression, with the play-ground bully frequently escaping unpunished. The rise and fall of Anvil provides a good example of the frequent unfairness of life in general, of the fact that theatrical tragedy, in the sense that it serves up a deserved punishment, does not easily translate into the extra-literary. In its aban-donment of classical tragic conventions, the film thus draws on the tragicomic, which is built on 'the desired progression from calamity ("tragedy") to a felicitous resolution ("comedy")' (Schmidt, 2013, p. 16). Like the early seventeenth-century appropriation of tragicomedy, the tendency in some recent metal documentaries to blend generic traits serves as a reminder that the conventional approach to metal as a cul-tural phenomenon is seen as in need of correction. The film *Anvil* offers a case in point in that it presents the story of one (more or less) major metal band through rather unexpected tropes and images.

In the mid-1980s, when new albums by Metallica, Megadeth and Anthrax raised the bar for fast-playing and aggressive metal, formerly promising and even musically progressive bands increasingly sounded dated: 'Power metal bands like Anvil, still dressing in red leather bondage outfits and playing guitar solos with phallus-shaped vibra-tors, felt the chance for mass popularity slipping through their fingers' (Christe, 2003, p. 136). The film *Anvil* provides quotes from numerous famous metal musicians, all of whom seem to agree that the impor-tance that Anvil had for the formation of various metal genres is not well reflected by their commercial status or overall success in the music industry.[6] Nobody seems to be able to explain their later fall from grace, with Lars Ulrich speculating that 'something didn't translate all the way up to the next level' (3:30). The band's failure to capitalize on their extensive cultural capital, on their extensive investment in what Keith Kahn-Harris discusses as 'mundane' or 'subcultural capital' (2011, pp. 210–215), as well as their inability to transcend the inner circles of the metal scene,[7] all stand as a stark reminder that heavy metal, while being a musical art-form in its own right, does nevertheless exist within the real world. Too frequently seen as a playground of fantasies and as a sphere of culture detached from reality, metal is thus returned to the social reality of the various band members who try to build their lives around the music and its culture. This worldliness of metal also stresses the humanity of its agents and thereby opens pathways, for the films' viewers, of affect and empathy.

The literary affinities in *Anvil*'s generic sub-structure are strengthened further by its commitment to sentimental tropes and scenes. The focus on sentimentality is supported by the film's overall sense of serenity, which prevents its audience from approaching the film exclusively from the kind of comic angle that the intertextual references to works like *Spinal Tap* suggest. The pervasive sense of emotional attachments – not just to an artistic ideal, but to specific individuals – in fact marks this documentary. The film is less a documentary that celebrates the music or cultural importance of one particular band, but instead an almost tender portrayal of the band's two major players: guitarist/vocalist Steve 'Lips' Kudlow and drummer Robb Reiner. Both protagonists are shown through the prism of their long-standing personal friendship, and their frequent bickering and subsequent declarations of love turn their relationship into a showcase of sentimental feelings that are not often on display in works dealing with heavy metal music. Their sentimental relationship also attests to the fact that metal culture is not built on a desire to 'assert masculinity by co-opting femininity' (Walser, 1993, p. 134), but instead frequently envisions alternative forms of masculine identities.

Sentimentality and emotional encounters structure numerous scenes in *Anvil*. As the film accompanies Lips, Robb and the other band members on their ill-fated tour through the backwaters of the European club scene, Lips's comments concentrate on his commitment to the idea of his band. However, while heavy metal music provides the soundtrack to this journey, the rhetorical realm is determined not by the kind of musicological self-fashioning that dwells exclusively on the perceived purity or authenticity of a particular metal sub-genre, but instead by the frequent insistence on the band's emotional commitment to their fan base. One of the most frequent words to describe this relationship is love: for performing on stage, for being with the other band members, for investing time to get the band ahead and, more generally, for being a musician. It is this overwhelmingly emotional attachment to the project of heavy metal that stands out and that also provides some of the high points of the film. Such a focus on sentimentality in metal documentaries is really rare, and this becomes obvious when the film is compared, for instance, to directors Greg Olliver and Wes Orshoski's *Lemmy* (2012), a biopic devoted to Motörhead's mastermind. In this film, Lemmy at one point is asked what in his memorabilia-filled apartment he treasures most and, rather nonplussed, points to his son, sitting next to him on the couch. While Lemmy's soft core is also addressed elsewhere on the DVD (tellingly, hidden amongst the bonus material), his overall persona relies substantially on a rather martial aura of seasoned metal-veteran, with this emotional outbreak seeming rather out of character. The *Anvil* film, by contrast, elevates such sentimental moments to become a central leitmotif.

Right from its beginning, *Anvil* indeed confronts its viewers with images that go against the conventions of metal documentaries. The opening scenes, before the title frame, introduce the band and its central role in the early days of global metal through historical live footage and through testimony given by major metal figures like Lars Ulrich, Lemmy, Scott Ian, Tom Araya and Slash. The film proper then begins with a scene shot from within a moving car. The atmosphere during this winter morning is marked by the extreme brightness of a rather typical Toronto day, with few clouds in a deep blue sky. The suburban open park-scape complements the bucolic quality of this opening, with the dark silhouettes of various trees providing a clear contrast to the snowy plains. The sunny morning functions as a metaphorical setting that speaks about the optimism that comes with a new day and thus introduces an important emotional quality into the film, namely the almost insurmountable belief in a better future that drives the band's two main members. The film in this scene accompanies Lips on his way to work, showing him soon after as he collects the various orders of frozen food items he will deliver on his morning run for a company that provides catering to schools. Working in the cold interior of a giant freezer room, Lips wears a ski-hat (replaced in a later scene, shot in the same location, by a hairnet) that provides a stark contrast to his 'normal' long-haired metal persona. In fact, reversing his status as a metal musician and thus something of a social misfit, he seems to be content to fit in with his fellow drivers, saying 'I am one of those ten drivers,' only to add that his real fulfilment still derives from his membership in a band: 'Anvil gives me happiness. [...] It gives me the joy, the pleasure that you need to get through life.' Somehow he seems to combine a stoic acceptance of the present with an unflinching belief in a brighter future, offering as his philosophy of life the statement: 'It can only get better' (5:30).

A similar strategy of alienation is used for introducing drummer Robb, whom viewers encounter as he works with a powerful pneumatic drill, sporting safety goggles and a breathing mask. He quickly explains that what seems like moonlighting in construction work in reality forms part of his routine in dealing with emotional balance: 'It's part of my psycho-active therapy session – and my doctor says I'm doing well' (7:01). He gladly admits that he would much prefer to be on tour and on stage.[8] Lips quickly supports this sentiment, saying there is nothing he likes more than performing for his fans. For him, the greatest thing is 'Being in the same room with people that love you' (7:40). A little later, as the band is about to embark on a new tour, they note that this is all about 'the fans and the people who love the band' (16:10). It is truly remarkable with which frequency the band members describe their professional identity as heavy metal musicians through language that is highly emotional. The film widely excludes statements about the music's aggression, the band's loudness or the authenticity of their musicianship. It instead relies on a language of emotions, inviting its viewers to become emotionally invested in the wellbeing of the film's protagonists.[9] While there is still plenty of metal in the film, through concert footage that relies on various time-tested visual and acoustic tropes, *Anvil* presents both Lips and Robb as two otherwise average guys who are exceptionally devoted to each other and to their job, which happens to be playing heavy metal.

However, their mutual devotion and friendship is variously tested as they go on tour. While they appear to enjoy playing even in very sleazy locations, some of which lack a proper stage, forcing the band to perform standing amongst the audience members, they eventually encounter tensions when their personal relationship suffers under the strain of touring. The film's first major crisis occurs when Lips and Robb are fighting over whether it makes sense to continue the tour, a scene that anticipates their subsequent altercation while recording their new album in England. In the later scene, the verbal abuse is accompanied by shoving and pushing, ultimately leading to Robb walking away from the studio and Lips saying into the camera about the drummer that 'he's fired, I mean, what can I say' (55:00). When they make up soon after, the tearful scene has Lips express his devotion to Robb, stating 'you're my fucking brother, man,' and suggesting that he should be able to say anything to Robb, 'Because I love you, that's why' (57:10). The band, then, is built less on a shared idea about what metal should sound like, even though that remains important as well, but relies substantially on the emotional ties and mutual trust between its two core members. Or rather, the film concentrates on such sentimental tropes over and beyond presenting the band as built around shared musical taste. While the actual dynamics amongst the band members might indeed be different, the film's focus on emotional aspects betrays a clear preference for re-adjusting common perceptions about metal.

The musical couple at the center of *Anvil* even shows various matrimonial tendencies, and their utter devotion to each other is acknowledged (albeit sometimes grumpily) by their spouses and relatives. Given the legacy of Tipper Gore's Parents Music Resource Center (PMRC) attack on bands like Anvil – and the film includes a historical document showing Lips being grilled in a talk show over the band's very explicit lyrics – it comes as something of a surprise that what constitutes the heart of Anvil turns out to be good old family values. Even before the band goes into their studio retreat that reveals the soft underbelly of its metal veterans, Lips is filmed during a very emotional meeting with his older sister, without whose financial support the band would have been unable to afford the trip to England. With a rather tearful eye she explains 'He's my dear brother, and I've always loved him,' causing him to respond, into the camera, 'My big sister, man; cool' (48:00). Love is in the air, it seems, yet it consists less of the explicit sexuality conventionally assigned to metal culture but instead of a tender and asexual devotion to somebody else, like a close friend or sibling, which is best described as sentimental. In a study on Canadian mosh-pits, Gabby Riches comes to a similar conclusion when she notes that the 'heavy metal lifestyle is sensual, affective and emotive' (2014, p. 101). The closing scenes in *Anvil* reinforce these sentiments. They celebrate not only the band's successful concert in Japan, but also show two buddies hugging each other, walking through a glitzy Japanese city center and celebrating their friendship during a quiet moment at a beautifully landscaped shrine, where their long-haired metal appearance may remind viewers of fierce samurais, whose chivalric devotion to pure principles well echoes the sentimental ethos represented in the film *Anvil*.

Bonding to be a band: *Some Kind of Monster*

Sentimentality also sounds odd when used in discussing Metallica, by any measure one of the major metal acts and thus an icon of toughness. The film *Some Kind of Monster* begins at a moment in time when the band struggles, in the aftermath of its split with bass player Jason Newsted, to record the songs that would turn into their eighth album, *St. Anger* (2003). The film in fact opens with the album completed and selected journalists being invited to listen to some songs before the album was released. The actual film then goes back in time and begins with an exterior shot of the – somewhat un-metallic – Ritz-Carlton Hotel in San Francisco and the band's meeting with Phil Towe, introduced through subtitles as 'Therapist/Performance Enhancement

Coach' (3:50). Towe's work with the band during the recording sessions served as a catalyst for the breaking out of substantial emotional tensions, but it also contributed to their resolution. What the film portrays is less the making of a new metal album but the relationship between Metallica's band members,[10] most importantly between singer/guitarist James Hetfield and drummer Lars Ulrich, who are shown as being engaged in a rather brutal battle over the leadership role in Metallica after the band's interior balance was lost with the departure of Newsted. One can assume that both Newsted and guitarist Kirk Hammett had previously managed to smooth over these conflicts. In his review of the film, the late Roger Ebert (2004) aptly described Hammett's role within the band as that of 'the child in a dysfunctional marriage who has learned how to stay below the radar.' With savvy and professional producer Bob Rock completing the group during the recordings, the film thus has a wide range of emotional qualities from which to build its dramatic developments.

Similar to *Anvil*, the central dynamic in *Some Kind of Monster* circles around the partnership of two musicians, with the Metallica film revealing that this particular couple is far less harmonious than their Canadian counterparts. The film also suggests that being in a band may be a highly abusive experience, demanding both emotional and artistic compromises that feel painful to some of those directly involved. A comment by Hammett about his new hobby of surfing is highly telling in this regard. He notices that 'There is a certain individualism also about surfing that I like; I mean, when it's your moment, man, that's your moment, and yours alone; and no-one can help you' (11:10). His words attest both to the need to create distance from your professional environment, maybe in particular when that consists of a metal band, and to the fact that being in a band requires that you rely on the help and support offered by the other band members. This turns out to be a disabling experience as it confronts individuals with their own insufficiencies. *Some Kind of Monster* painfully reminds its viewers that bands consist of individuals, and that the supposed uniformity of artistic creation to which a recorded song attests frequently is the result of fierce battles and contesting opinions. As there is no established formula about what makes a good (metal) song, musicians have to rely on whatever musical talent they have when composing, arranging and performing.

Tellingly, some of the most direct conflicts between Ulrich and Hetfield are triggered by disagreements over what is needed in a particular song, with both trying to verbalize their disagreement in such a way that their statements are not seen as too critical of their band members'

contributions to the song. In the end, though, they are both too insecure and vulnerable to accept somebody else's opinion, and the scene
accordingly ends with door-slamming and anger. This battle shows that
what appear to be conflicts over musical style, playing technique, or
compositional decisions, are substantially affected by the interpersonal
dynamics in the band. The situation in the recording studio becomes a
proxy war over ownership and group leadership, thereby acknowledging
the all-too-human factor in metal music.

The real monster in the film, accordingly, turns out to be the interior workings of a band. Like the unfortunate creature in Mary Shelley's
1818 novel about Frankenstein, to which the musicians briefly allude,
the band consists of poorly matched individual parts that fail to con-
geal fully into the body of a band. While Niall Scott has described the
film's monstrosity as pointing to 'radical evil in human nature' (2007,
p. 205), the interpersonal dynamics portrayed in the film do not necessarily point to such negativity. Instead, what *Some Kind of Monster*
showcases is the banality of rock-stardom: it insists that, in the end,
what determines the way a band functions (or otherwise) is its members' ability to collaborate and embrace each other's idiosyncrasies. It is a
matter of emotional involvement, of work/life balance and of the acceptance of responsibilities for one's own deeds and for the wellbeing of
one's dependents. Hetfield's prolonged stay in a rehab facility, which
interrupts the recording sessions and, at least for a while, puts the very
survival of the band in doubt, aims to address his alcoholism, but it also
sets new personal limits to the way he relates to his monstrous band,
which post-rehab he describes as a 'beast' (52:55).

While the film clearly presents more than one band member as lacking in interpersonal skills and emotional integrity, the importance lent
to these ideas and concepts in a metal documentary creates space for an
affective engagement on the side of the viewers, thus inviting the kinds
of responses that Charles Altieri, in *The Particulars of Rupture* (2003), has
presented as an alternative to rational or cognitive attitudes toward art.
As the therapy sessions start, Ulrich emphasizes that throughout the
recording sessions, everybody in the band will be 'completely equal'
(11:20); which sounds rather hollow when compared to his general
tendency to control the band's direction and image. In flashbacks that
discuss the recording of an earlier album, the 1990 sessions for *Black
Album*, Bob Rock emphasizes that, in the past, Metallica's band members were excessively territorial, with each band member's individual
contribution being non-negotiable by the other musicians. To counter
these secessionist tendencies, Metallica created a 'Mission Statement,'

assumedly under the guidance of their coach. One part of that statement refers directly to the way the band members interrelate with each
other like family members:

> Throughout our individual and collective journeys…sometimes thru
> pain & conflict…we have discovered the true meaning of FAMILY.
> It is both our mission and our destiny to manifest this ideal. (14:20)

As the statement is read out by Towe, Hammett offers supportive expla-
nations, but the scene also catches Hetfield taking a rather cynical or
skeptical view. As viewers come to understand later, Hetfield not only
has problems accepting his own role and responsibilities as a parent –
something that is related to his own childhood – he also feels that not all
of his band members will be able to live up to the spirit of this Mission
Statement. The film immediately cuts to a scene in the recording studio
where Hetfield is sitting on the couch with a toddler on his lap as he is
singing into a microphone, with Ulrich playing with another child in
the foreground. The idyllic quality of this cozy closeness soon crumbles,
stressing the lack of authenticity in the band's emotional make-up.

Coaching confronts Hetfield with various demons, eventually leading
to his long absence for treatment. At the recording sessions after his
return, tensions with Ulrich again flare up, with both musicians apparently relating to each other through a love-hate spiral of abuse and
dependence. The tensions reach a climax in a scene where the whole
band is sitting around a table as Ulrich voices his discontent, culminating in him yelling, at the top of his voice, the word 'fuck' right in
Hetfield's face. They both are clearly engaged in a fierce struggle over
issues of respect and control, and both cannot quite come to give voice
to positive feelings about their musical partner. Love and devotion are
frequently mentioned, and the emotional toll of collaborating in this
musical partnership becomes clearly visible. The machismo that marks
some of the band's habitual stage posturing is fully undermined by the
fragility of ego and self-imagery, and the battle between Ulrich and
Hetfield only slowly turns into the kind of positive energy that can be
channeled into the writing of music. As the band is about to go on tour
with their new material, Ulrich specifically refers to the 'positive energy'
that went into the highly aggressive music on their new album (2:08:55).

As *St. Anger*, the title of the album, eventually shows, there is something positive to be learned from anger. The message somehow sanctifies
negative emotions, but only as long as they are appropriated for positive
outcomes. This process, in the case of *Some Kind of Monster*, is aided by

the fact that the band can rally around their mutual dislike of certain management decisions, as when they are being asked to do a radio promotion for a credit company. In reaching for a certain level of integrity that they all obviously share, they find common ground on which to build a future for the band. What holds them together in the end, at least within the confines of this documentary, is not their shared commitment to a particular musical vision but rather a rekindled emotional bonding, a reattachment to the sentimental core at the heart of their friendship.

Another aspect that appears to contribute to this development is the band's past: both the dismissal of Dave Mustaine in 1983 for alcoholism-related attitude problems and the death of Cliff Burton in 1986 are evoked in the film as reminders of the fragility of any band and even of the precariousness of life, which Judith Butler around the same time described as 'the experiences of vulnerability and loss' (2004, p. xii), following the 9/11 attacks on New York. This re-turn to sentimentality, accompanied as it is by a re-evaluation of postmodernity's discussion of simulacra, surfaces also in other areas of male culture. In her study on masculinity and rock climbing, Victoria Robinson notes that in this cultural context, too, 'male climbers are now more capable of publicly and legitimately showing emotion' (2008, p. 103). The toughness of rock climbing parallels the conventionalized ethos of metal bands in that both spheres require from its (male) group members a specific type of masculinity. Out of a confrontation with the precariousness of lives, for instance through the permanent threat of a climber falling off from great altitudes, a more sentimental attitude arises. As Metallica's band members reflect about the consequences of alcoholism or mental health problems, they finally come to treasure what they have in the band, and to accept that this also involves accepting other people's needs and shortcomings. In the end, then, the film celebrates a certain interpersonal attitude that is highly sentimental.

The small town family man: *Heavy Metal auf dem Lande*

While Metallica as a band has almost global name-recognition, the label Nuclear Blast is a slightly better-kept secret with which few outside the (extreme) metal scene will be familiar. *Heavy Metal auf dem Lande* formally departs from the average metal (or rock) documentary in that it does not focus on a single band and only indirectly on a particular genre but, like Dave Grohl's *Sound City* (2013) about a legendary recording studio, instead concentrates on the underlying institutions within the business and the people who make it happen. Andreas Geiger's made-for-TV movie was occasioned by the filmmaker's return to his small home town in the Swabian hills of Southern Germany, an area known for both its entrepreneurial spirit and its conservative values. What struck him in the otherwise rather unremarkable Donzdorf, a 10,000-people community 50 km east of Stuttgart, was the sheer size of the Nuclear Blast warehouse and offices in the town's small industrial park. Started in 1987 by Markus Staiger, the label began with hardcore punk bands but has over time metamorphosed into one of the world's most influential labels for various extreme metal genres, its catalog including albums by such important bands as Dimmu Borgir, HammerFall, Machine Head, Blind Guardian, Sepultura, Agnostic Front and Nightwish, the latter even topping some countries' album charts.

Drawing on the tension between the highly successful company and its rural environment, the film focuses on heavy metal as a family experience, as something that plays out, affects and is affected by the manner in which its protagonists relate to their human environment. For instance, it presents various situations where metal is listened to and appreciated across generational boundaries; or where it has at least become accepted as being a normal aspect of popular culture. The film returns a number of times to a family where the two grown sons (probably aged 16–20) still live at home but cultivate their metal identities, including long drum practices, without any major tensions with their parents, who apparently have accepted that no particular threat for their children emerges from this particular musical taste. While the mother even seems to be able to recognize individual bands, she also voices her dislike of the graphic nature of some album covers, a theme that is prevalent throughout the film.

To counter these graphic excesses, the film also presents Staiger as going through some sort of identity crisis, where he questions his CEO-level commitment to his company, the excessive work routine that has prevented him from finding the kind of work–life balance that contemporary human resource rhetoric proclaims as necessary for healthy and productive work routines. The viewers accordingly follow Staiger to a horse-riding class – where the energetic manager cannot repress his impatience with the animal's rather sedate pace – and repeatedly see him going through yoga sessions with an instructor who tries to reconnect the man to his body. The extreme corporeality of heavy metal, so frequently transcended into grotesque and superhuman figures in the visual language of its music videos and band characters, is here returned to the rather mundane matter of breathing patterns and stretch exercises. The banality of normal everyday culture, also evoked in the film through shots of members of the local community harvesting apples or hanging their laundry on a clothesline, becomes intimately linked to heavy metal. The various people committed to this musical culture are presented as rather average, and if they deviate from social norms then this occurs frequently through exceptional talent or positive values. One local fan is accordingly quoted as saying '*tolerante Menschen tun einfach harte Musik hören und ein bisschen verwahrlost rumrennen*' (36:00; 'tolerant people just listen to hard music and run around a little unkempt'). There appears to be a modicum of resistance and individuality attached to the metal community, but by and large the self-image is one of belonging to a group that is, if anything, exceptional in its levels of commitment, and revolutionary only when it comes to disobeying calcified remnants of conservative social practices.

At the same time, though, the film even suggests that Nuclear Blast, and its sometimes extreme metal bands, fits in oddly with the conservative lifestyle of a small rural town, where people attend church, sing in the local choir and mostly go about the kinds of jobs that follow in their grandparents' footsteps. What both realms share is a dogged persistence to prevail, a stoic ability to continue through hardship. The sale of extreme music and of the (at times) macabre fan paraphernalia that makes up much of the daily business of Nuclear Blast nevertheless form a stark contrast to the more folkloristic soundtrack that accompanies rural life outside the metal community. Accordingly, one of the strangest scenes in the film consists of a pre-listening media event held at a local restaurant. While the regular guests meet over a beer, various international journalists sit in a backroom to get a first impression of a new release. There seems to be a certain level of resignation amongst the local regulars about the sonic quality of the music blasted at such events, but also an unspoken (and highly Swabian) respect for the business success that the music label has had in the past.

The film in fact extensively attests to Staiger's business acumen: not only does he frequently refer to the commercial success of his company, taking the film crew around his town in his flashy German sports car and gazing at his golden-record filled wall of fame, he also apparently managed to convince the film's director to place extensive footage of band videos by artists like Nightwish in the documentary. Supporting the normalizing effect that the sentimental focus on family and emotionality creates, this insistence on the corporate success story further justifies his professional choices. Having pulled metal in from the fringe through its sentimental focus, *Heavy Metal auf dem Lande* takes one further step and suggests that metal in fact can claim a leadership role, at least when it comes to its commercial side. And commercial success offers the ultimate justification, at least in the mindset of Staiger's social environment.

The film also spends time with other local characters, for instance the son of a local knitwear factory owner who uses the machines in his parents' company, which normally churns out what amongst more mature customers might count as stylish cardigans, to produce unique fan-items that celebrate his favorite bands. For him, individuality runs supreme, and he accordingly notes that one of his major fears consists of going to a concert in a band t-shirt also worn by somebody else. Through the highly conservative medium of knit-wear garments, this metal character celebrates what Weinstein has described as the genre's commitment to 'forceful individuality' (2009, p. 28). However, his devotion to a renegade sense of individuality is somewhat belied by the fact that he also poses, shyly but proudly, in front of his bourgeois mansion, the kind of ostentatious rural single-family home which attests to a successful Swabian biography.

Upsetting gender perceptions in metal

What the three films discussed in this essay demonstrate, I would like to argue, is that heavy metal culture is trying to step out of a closet. Not, for various reasons, the closet of heteronormative desire, of gay pride – or, a little more current, of same-sex marriage legislature – but a container all the same: a public perception of heavy metal that places and defines it as a masculinist, violent, anti-intellectual and anti-emotional domain within popular culture. *Anvil*, *Some Kind of Monster* and *Heavy Metal auf dem Lande* go to lengths in presenting heavy metal musicians, fans and managers as the kind of emotionally complex human beings that the general public's clichés have never allowed them to be. This focus on the emotions, what I have tried in this essay to describe through the literary tradition of sentimentality, thus predominantly serves a rhetorical purpose: it communicates to a larger, maybe even non-fan audience that heavy metal is nothing to be frightened of.

And it is with this move, away from negative semantic associations and toward positively labeled characteristics, that I would like to turn to a final example; an example, admittedly, that few will expect in the context of heavy metal studies but one that nevertheless allows me to show that the kind of strategy I have outlined above has in fact already found currency with other filmmakers before finding its way into metal documentaries. A film that follows a similar trajectory is the wonderful *The Adventures of Priscilla, Queen of the Desert* (1994), an Australian movie about crossdressing, disco-loving drag acts directed by Stephan Elliott.[11] Like the metal documentaries discussed earlier, *Priscilla* sets out to realign the public perception of a fringe group within society, one conventionally assigned marginal existence at best. *Priscilla* avoids portraying sexual contact (if one ignores the campy banter) and thus desexualizes gay and transgendered identities. The US-remake of *Priscilla*, the rather lame *To Wong Foo* (1995), went one step further and alienated many in the gay community by removing almost all sexual content from the film, allowing Patrick Swayze to say in an interview that the film 'had to be about heart' (cited in Evans, 2009, p. 44). Indeed, the later film relies on 'the asexual nature of the drag queens' (Evans, 2009, p. 45), replacing the sexual with the kind of sentimentality described in the present essay as a substantial element in recent metal documentaries. While clearly the more provocative and explicit film, *Priscilla* also avoids too direct presentation of gay sexuality, with its most scandalous scene centered on the explosive genital prowess of a female stripper. It instead concentrates on the characters' emotional and social attachments to other people, on their deep friendships and commitment to parenthood, for example. In doing so, the film redefines the discourse about homo- and transsexuality and, through its immersive activation of emotional features, somehow normalizes a group of people who are all too frequently de-humanized.

The sentimentality in *Priscilla* and in the three heavy metal documentaries analyzed earlier thus serves to de-marginalize sub-cultural groups and to engage in what Lauren Berlant, in *Female Complaint*, describes as 'fantasies of emplacement, exchange, and transcendence' (2008, p. 11). Such a desire for acceptance and inclusion, itself a reaction to the negative clichés harbored in the non-fan community, now increasingly surfaces within the metal community as well. What the films discussed in this essay hope to effect is a social echo that allows them to re-claim their legitimate membership in the political and cultural sphere. By drawing on sentimental tropes, the films activate the generic traits that replace sexuality with emotional attachment, and desire with friendship. By thus investing heavy metal figures with characteristics which society views in a positive manner, these documentaries contribute to a redefinition of what it means to be part of the metal community – less for those inside the community, many of whom have always known about the dominant ethics within their cultural sphere,[12] but to those outside who were too confused by the music's intensity and the sometimes rather excessive visual markers to accept metal culture for what it has always been. The sentimentality in all three films deconstructs these supposedly stable identities, doing so by emphasizing the range of masculinities that exists within metal. Butler's definition of gender identity as 'the stylized repetition of acts through time' (1988, p. 520) is based on an understanding of gender as potentially instable. The sentimental male metal characters discussed in this essay also offer 'a different sort of repeating, in the breaking or subversive repetition of that style' (Butler, 1988, p. 520), and by doing so they not only make a crucial contribution to our understanding of the various ways in which metal and masculinity interact, they also link up, as my discussion of *Priscilla* shows, with how non-mainstream social groups are presented cinematically, suggesting that popular culture continues to leave room for subversive engagements with mainstream society and its oftentimes intolerant values.

Notes

1. Walser (1993, pp. 120–124) cautiously discusses a change of tone in the way metal engages with gender, but he does so through examples (like Bon Jovi) that are not fully convincing since they go along with a generic re-invention of metal's outer limits.
2. See Kaplan, whose discussion of hair metal videos addresses these issues.
3. In a further essay, Weinstein discusses metal's hybrid gender identities under the heading 'Playing with gender in the key of metal' (Weinstein, forthcoming).
4. The sentimental allows for a focus on emotionality and even tenderness that entirely avoids the sexual; it thus continues, albeit through a non-political outlet, the medieval tradition of courtly love. By allowing strong emotional responses that are untainted by all matters of (sexual) desire and, more generally speaking, physicality, sentimental works were almost ideal outlets for a puritanical engagement with matters of love that was acceptable to nineteenth-century readers.
5. For a first introduction to Jung's work, see Young-Eisendrath and Dawson's collection of essays (2008).
6. The music industry is not always supportive of metal, often requiring bands to develop their own strategies for survival (see Bayer, 2000); or to adapt to commercial expectations (see Earl, 2009).
7. For a survey of how notions related to scene can be applied in metal scholarship, see Phillipov (2012, pp. 12–15).
8. The film here alludes to mental illness in a rather indirect way, evoking memories of Elizabeth Wurtzel's 1994 memoir *Prozac Nation*; the extreme music community knows about this topic also through the song '*Prozac People*,' from English post-punkers Killing Joke's 1996 album, *Democracy*.

9. On how emotions, empathy and affect relate to how people respond to stories, see Suzanne Keen (2007).
10. See also the chapter on the film in Irwin (2007).
11. Walser's comments on the androgynous nature of some glam metal bands, while acknowledging homophobia (1993, p. 130), do not explain these acts as challenges to conventional masculinity (or clichés about heavy metal) but instead suggest that bands like Poison wanted 'to claim the powers of spectacularity for themselves' (p. 129), that is to say, they draw on the gendered gaze as it consumes popular culture. Ian Christe's assessment, that glam metal was merely a materialization of 'insecure young males' (2003, p. 156), sounds closer to home.
12. The British newspaper the *Guardian* ran a series of reports during the spring of 2014 about sexual harassment as part of student culture and behavior at various clubs. Some entries in the substantial comments section on the newspaper website mentioned that the aggressive attitude found in mainstream club culture seems to be largely absent in the metal scene, where a more respectful code of conduct largely prevents abusive excesses; see Young-Powell.

Bibliography

Altieri, C. (2003) *The Particulars of Rupture: An Aesthetics of the Affects* (Ithaca, NY: Cornell University Press).
Anvil: The Story of Anvil (2008) Directed by Sacha Gervasi (Canada: Metal on Metal).
Bayer, G. (2000) 'The Band J.B.O. and Exploding the Serious Side of Pop Culture,' *Journal of Popular Culture*, 34(3), pp. 109–128.
Berlant, L. (2008) *Female Complaint: The Unfinished Business of Sentimentality in American Culture* (Durham, NC: Duke University Press).
Butler, J. (1988) 'Performative Acts and Gender Constitution: An Essay in Phenomenology and Feminist Theory,' *Theatre Journal*, 40(4), pp. 519–531.
Butler, J. (1990) [2007] *Gender Trouble* (New York, NY: Routledge).
Butler, J. (2004) *Precarious Life: The Powers of Mourning and Violence* (London: Verso).
Christe, I. (2003) *Sound of the Beast: The Complete Headbanging History of Heavy Metal* (New York, NY: HarperCollins).
Connell, R. W. (1995) *Masculinities* (Berkeley, CA: University of California Press).
Connell, R. W. & Messerschmidt, J. W. (2005) 'Hegemonic Masculinity: Rethinking the Concept,' *Gender & Society*, 19, pp. 829–859.
The Decline of Western Civilization Part II: The Metal Years (1988) Directed by Penelope Spheeris (USA: Columbia Pictures).
Earl, B. (2009) 'Metal Goes "Pop": The Explosion of Heavy Metal into the Mainstream,' *Heavy Metal Music in Britain*, ed. G. Bayer (Farnham, VA: Ashgate), pp. 33–51.
Ebert, R., 2004. 'Review of *Metallica: Some Kind of Monster*.' Retrieved 30 January 2015 from: http://www.rogerebert.com/reviews/metallica-some-kind-of-monster-2004.

Evans, A. (2009) 'How Homo Can Hollywood Be? Remaking Queer Authenticity from *To Wong Foo* to *Brokeback Mountain*,' *Journal of Film and Video*, 61(4), pp. 41–54.

Faludi, S. (1999) *Stiffed: The Betrayal of the American Man* (New York: Morrow).

Hassan, N. (2010) ' "Girls, Girls, Girls"?: The Los Angeles Metal Scene and the Politics of Gender,' *Decline of Western Civilization Part II: The Metal Years. Popular Music History*, 5(3), pp. 243–263.

Heavy Metal auf dem Lande (2006) Directed by Andreas Geiger (Germany: Arte).

Heavy Metal Parking Lot (1986) Directed by John Heyn and Jeff Krulik (USA: Factory 515).

Irwin, W. (2007) *Metallica and Philosophy: A Crash Course in Brain Surgery* (Malden, MA: Blackwell).

Jäger, G. (1969) *Empfindsamkeit und Roman: Wortgeschichte, Theorie und Kritik im 18. und frühen 19. Jahrhundert* (Stuttgart: Kohlhammer).

Kahn-Harris, K (2011) ' "You Are from Israel and That Is Enough to Hate You Forever": Racism, Globalization, and Play within the Global Extreme Metal Scene,' *Metal Rules the Globe: Heavy Metal Music Around the World*, eds. J. Wallach, H. M. Berger, & P. D. Greene (Durham, NC: Duke University Press), pp. 200–223.

Kaplan, E. A. (1987) *Rocking Around the Clock: Music Television, Postmodernism, and Consumer Culture* (New York, NY: Methuen).

Keen, S. (2007) *Empathy and the Novel* (Oxford: Oxford University Press).

Konow, D. (2002) *Bang Your Head: The Rise and Fall of Heavy Metal* (New York, NY: Three Rivers).

Lemmy (2012) Directed by Greg Olliver and Wes Orshoski (USA: Damage Case).

Levande, M. (2007) 'Women, Pop Music, and Pornography,' *Meridians: Feminism, Race, Transnationalism*, 8(1), pp. 293–321.

Metallica: Some Kind of Monster (2004) Directed by Joe Berlinger and Bruce Sinofsky (USA: Radical Media).

Overell, R. (2011) ' "I Hate Girls and Emo[tion]s": Negotiating Masculinity in Grindcore Music,' *Popular Music History*, 6(1/2), pp. 198–223.

Phillipov, M. (2012) *Death Metal and Music Criticism: Analysis at the Limits* (Lanham, MD: Lexington).

Pompper, D. (2010) 'Masculinities, the Metrosexual, and Media Images: Across Dimensions of Age and Ethnicity,' *Sex Roles*, 16, pp. 682–696.

Riches, G. (2014) 'Brothers of Metal! Heavy Metal Masculinities, Moshpit Practices and Homosociality,' *Debating Modern Masculinities: Change, Continuity, Crisis?* ed. G. Riches (Basingstoke: Palgrave), pp. 88–105.

Robinson, V. (2008) *Everyday Masculinities and Extreme Sport: Male Identity and Rock Climbing* (London: Bloomsbury).

Savage, J. (1991) *England's Dreaming: Sex Pistols and Punk Rock* (London: Faber and Faber).

Schmidt, G. A. (2013) *Renaissance Hybrids: Culture and Genre in Early Modern England* (Farnham, VA: Ashgate).

Scott, N. (2007) 'God Hates Us All: Kant, Radical Evil and the Diabolical Monstrous Human in Heavy Metal,' *Monsters and the Monstrous: Myths and Metaphors of Enduring Evil*, ed. N. Scott (Amsterdam: Rodopi), pp. 201–212.

Sedgwick, E. K. (1985) *Between Men: English Literature and Male Homosocial Desire* (New York: Columbia University Press).

Shugart, H. (2008) 'Managing Masculinities: The Metrosexual Moment,' *Communication and Critical/Cultural Studies* 5(3), pp. 280–300.

Sullivan, N. (2013) 'The Good Guys: McCarthy's *The Road* as Post-9/11 Male Sentimental Novel,' *Genre*, 46(1), pp. 79–101.

The Adventures of Priscilla, Queen of the Desert (1994) Directed by Stephan Elliott (Australia: PolyGram).

To Wong Foo, Thanks for Everything, Julie Newmar (1995) Directed by Beeban Kidron (USA: Universal Pictures).

Waksman, S. (2011) 'Arenas of the Imagination: Global Tours and the Heavy Metal Concert in the 1970s,' *Metal Rules the Globe: Heavy Metal Music Around the World*, eds. J. Wallach, H. M. Berger, & P. D. Greene (Durham, NC: Duke University Press), pp. 227–246.

Walser, R. (1993) *Running with the Devil: Power, Gender, and Madness in Heavy Metal Music* (Hanover: University Press of New England).

Weinstein, D. (2000) *Heavy Metal: The Music and Its Culture*, Revised Edition (New York, NY: Da Capo).

Weinstein, D. (2009) 'The Empowering Masculinity of British Heavy Metal,' *Heavy Metal Music in Britain*, ed. G. Bayer (Farnham: Ashgate), pp. 17–31.

Wurtzel, E. (1994) *Prozac Nation: Young and Depressed in America* (Boston: Houghton Mifflin).

Young-Eisendrath, P. & Dawson, T. (eds.). (2008) *The Cambridge Companion to Jung* (Cambridge: Cambridge University Press).

Young-Powell, A. (2014) 'Stalked and Beaten Up: Student Stories of Sexual Violence in Clubs,' *The Guardian*, 24 March. Retrieved 30 January 2015 from: www.theguardian.com/education/2014/mar/24/stalked-and-beaten-student-stories-sexual-violence-clubs?

Part II
Memory

3
The Ballad of Heavy Metal: Re-thinking Artistic and Commercial Strategies in the Mainstreaming of Metal and Hard Rock

Andy R. Brown
Bath Spa University

The aim of this chapter is to put the ballad back into the history of heavy metal. This is a controversial issue for a number of reasons, not least because to all intents and purposes the ballad, understood as a slow or mid-tempo song with strong melody, chorus and harmony, has been removed from contemporary accounts of metal's history or that history has been redefined to exclude bands and songs that fit this description. As for example, Gary Sharpe-Young's *Metal: The Definitive Guide* (2007), which states, 'this book is about Metal with a capital M. Ask AC/DC, Aerosmith, KISS, Bon Jovi, or Def Leppard if they are metal – you'll get a resounding "No"!' (p. 9)[1]

Yet, Lena and Peterson (2008), in their exhaustive survey of US music genres crucially reserve the term 'heavy metal' for the metal/hard rock and glam styles (including the bands named above), whose major period of success in the Billboard Top 100, was in the 1984–1991 period; a period, as a Billboard report put it, when 'metal owned the land [and] everyone else was just paying rent' (Laurin, 2013, p. 57). Or as *Rolling Stone* declared, 'last fall [1988] a steady stream of moody ballads by Bon Jovi, Def Leppard and Guns N' Roses topped the pop charts delivering as many Number One Hits in four months as the entire hard-rock and metal fields had in the preceding two decades' (Ressner, quoted in Metzer, 2012, p. 448).

Sharpe-Young (2007) reserves the term 'heavy metal' for the classic bands Black Sabbath, Budgie, Judas Priest, Motörhead, Ozzy Osbourne and the Scorpions. The problem with this selection is that, like the 1970s and early 1980s bands they share a history with, they have penned a number of ballads[2] – indeed, Judas Priest probably more so than any other metal band. But also in the case of Ozzy Osbourne and the Scorpions, such ballads, 'Goodbye to Romance' (1980), 'So Tired' (1983), 'Mama, I'm Coming Home' (1991), 'No One Like You' (1982), 'Still Loving You' (1985) and 'Wind of Change' (1991), form part of the commercial domination of the charts by metal and hard rock bands, in the 1984–1991 period, even as they preceded it. This suggests that there is a greater continuity in the relationship between classic hard rock/metal music and the perceived formulaic, commercially driven glam metal or 'big hair' bands, than many metal academics and fans are prepared to acknowledge.

Even Metzer's (2012) recent study of the power ballad is initially troubled by the notion of the 'heavy metal power ballad' in that such songs 'may seem to be an aberration, so far apart are heavy metal and ballads' (p. 488). Yet, not only do such songs exist, they 'made it all the way up the pop charts' (ibid.). Indeed, the 'power ballad' phrase gained currency in the mid-to-late 1980s largely in reference to songs by rock and heavy metal bands, glam metal bands in particular, that successfully combined the conventions of the romantic ballad with a hard rock and metal sound. Songs, such as Whitesnake's 'Is This Love' (1987), Aerosmith's 'Angel' (1988), Skid Row's 'I Remember You' (1988), Poison's 'Every Rose Has Its Thorn' (1988), Warrant's 'Heaven' (1989) and Bon Jovi's 'I'll Be There For You' (1989), continue to signify that decade as well as comprising a central part of the repertoire of 'power-ballad playlists.'

Caught in the crossfire: Counting the cost of commercial success

Rejecting the period of metal's history identified with the power ballad, specifically its association with outrageously androgynous glam metal bands and melodic hard rock,[3] as some sort of musical and commercial *aberration*, actually closes off a number of areas of inquiry that are important in understanding that wider history. One of these is the question of what role the ballad played in hard rock and heavy metal repertoires prior to the 1984–1991 period and why this changed? This in turn raises the issue of artistic and commercial strategies and how these shift and change depending on the stability of relations between bands, industry and audiences. There is no doubt that the penning and strategic release of 'power-ballads' was a crossover strategy employed by a number of hard rock and heavy metal bands in the 1984–1991 period. Crossing-over is inherently risky. If it works you gain access to a larger audience but this could be at the expense of your core audience or fan-base. It often means making musical and artistic compromises and the key issue here is how these are symbolically communicated to your core fans. In the case of the power ballad, negotiating the perils of the pop/metal boundary is crucial in terms of how success, if it occurs, is represented. As Moore (2001) argues, while '[o]bjectively speaking [...] the commercial/authentic polarity is illusory, since all mass-mediated music is subject to commercial imperatives [...] what matters to listeners is whether such a concern appears to be accepted, resisted, or negotiated with, by those to whom they are listening, and how' (p. 199).

Throughout the history of heavy metal music such border-crossings have been understood not just in terms of a *discourse* but also a *demographics* of gender. For example, as Robert Walser (1993) argues, not only did heavy metal become the 'dominant genre of American music' in the 1980s it did so, in the case of the success of bands like Bon Jovi, by fusing the 'intensity and heaviness of metal with the romantic sincerity of pop' (pp. 11, 13). But this 'fusion' was achieved through collaboration with an external songwriter (Desmond Child)[4] and by emphasizing the 'I,' first-person, or female-address of songs, particularly in ballads. How such songs were viewed, particularly by metal's core male audience, depended on how the ballad sat in relation to the other material put out by the band, particularly the balance of rockers or higher-tempo songs in the overall repertoire. It also depended on how bands positioned themselves in press coverage and in MTV videos promoting such songs. Symbolically, this positioning was not a defense of 'going pop' but of securing the integrity of heterosexual masculinity, to the extent that the ballad was identified with love, loss and the 'feminine,' bands would engage in sexual braggadocio and casual misogyny. For example, the video for Poison's 'Every Rose Has Its Thorn' (1988), inter-cuts footage of the band bonding in sweat-soaked performance and backstage, with footage of the singer alone with his acoustic guitar and girlfriend. This girlfriend figure, irrespective of whether the song is about romantic love or loss, is always sexually objectified, reclining on the singer's unmade-bed or dancing in their apartment. Or in the case of the actress and model Tawny Kitaen, in videos by Ratt and Whitesnake, dancing in and half-out of the singer's car or performing a seductive dance on top of it.[5]

Whereas in the past hard rock and heavy metal bands gained exposure through live performance and working their way up the bill in touring circuits, there was a significant shift in this period toward crafting songs in the studio that could gain crossover appeal, when released as singles. Prior to this the ballad occupied a minor but significant role within the hard rock and metal album, usually one or two songs, occurring at a strategic point in the track-order; most often to be followed by an all-out rocker. By contrast, the power ballad was often a stand-alone song released prior to the album. Indeed it seemed to be a commercial strategy of some bands to have at least one power ballad per album aimed at the pop charts. Success gained there would then be reflected in increased album sales. The reason for this was that while hard rock and metal bands would expect to get airplay on album-oriented-rock (AOR) stations, a power ballad might gain exposure on contemporary-hit-radio (CHR) and thereafter Top 40 airplay, effectively allowing hard rock and metal bands to crossover to a mainstream audience. For example, the success of Poison's 'Every Rose Has Its Thorn' pushed the sales of their album *Open Up and Say....Ahh!* (1988) from three to four million units. Or as one AOR promotion executive put it:

> Now let's talk massive – you cannot make it massive without CHR. Sure, Guns n' Roses cracked a million units through word-of-mouth, some rock radio airplay and MTV. But with 'Sweet Child O' Mine' going to Number One, they went up to 3.5 million, then went over 6 million with the Top Ten follow-up, 'Welcome to the Jungle.' If you get one hit under your belt, it's a gone gator.
>
> (quoted in Ressner, 1989, p. 22)

Sernoe's (2005) analysis of pre- (1981–1990) and post- (1992–2001) *SoundScan*[6] Billboard Top 100 chart data shows that the hard rock and metal genre never had fewer than six albums in the top 100 (1998), while having a record of 24 in a single year (1988) (p. 650). This chart success remained constant 'with metal/hard rock albums placing among the year-end top ten in 15 of the 21 years studied (no other genre has produced a year-end top ten album more often)' (ibid).

Clearly the late 1980s were the best years for this genre. The No. 1 album of 1987, Bon Jovi's *Slippery When Wet*, was one of the 17 metal/hard rock albums among the top 100 that year. Metal/hard rock albums accounted for 1,245 points and 24 of the year's top 100 albums in 1988, including three of the top 10 (Def Leppard's *Hysteria*, No. 3;

Guns N' Roses' *Appetite for Destruction*, No. 6; and Aerosmith's *Permanent Vacation*, No. 10) (ibid., pp. 651–652).

Although record companies in this period brought in experienced producers (and sometimes writers) to guide the songwriting and development of hard rock and metal bands, single releases would alternate between ballads and rockers. This sequencing was believed to be crucial to retaining a core male audience, where romantic ballads appealed more to female fans, crossing-over from the pop charts. For example, 'the release order of singles from [Bon Jovi's] *Slippery When Wet* was carefully balanced between romantic and tougher songs' (Walser, 1993, p. 124); Skid Row released the tough, socially conscious ballad '18 and Life' (January 1990) before the romantic, 'I Remember You' (March 1990); Poison's 'Fallen Angel' (July 1988) was followed by the number one hit, 'Every Rose Has Its Thorn' (October 1988). Or as Joe Elliot, of Def Leppard, put it, 'Rule one, don't lose your hardcore fans or you can end up with a 95 per cent female audience, who you know aren't going to be there next year unless you release another hit single' (quoted in Dickson, 1995, p. 139). So, although 'the pop-metal power ballad played a crucial role in the success of bands like Skid Row and Poison,' as Pillsbury argues, it did so 'by appearing to set aside for a moment the bravado and hedonism of the rest of those bands' music' (2006, p. 54).

Before the dawn: Exploring the history of the ballad in hard rock and metal

Frith and McRobbie (1990) in their scathing critique of the musical field of the 1970s as divided into aggressive 'cock-rock' and romantic 'teeny-bop' cite the 'heavy metal macho style of Led Zeppelin' and the 'technically facile "prog rock" ' exemplified by bands like Yes (p. 383). Yet they concede that '[e]ven the most macho rockers have in their repertoires some suitably soppy songs with which to celebrate true (lustless) love' (p. 382). Although some claim the use of a distorted guitar on the Carpenter's 'Goodbye to Love' (1972) as the origin of the power ballad or the rock-pop crossover achieved by Boston on 'More Than A Feeling' (1976), others point to Led Zeppelin's 'Stairway to Heaven' (1971). Not only is 'Stairway' one of Zeppelin's most popular songs and a staple of AOR radio to this day, it is a very elaborate, multi-sectional ballad. Its status as a proto-power ballad is based on the emotive affect of this dynamic architecture, building as it does from acoustic beginnings and melodic vocals to a middle section that incorporates drums and 'clean' electric guitars; a suitably epic guitar solo launched from the bridge, progressing to a heavy-rock third section, before returning to the opening melodic vocal hook. Another notable example is the epic anti-war song 'Child in Time' (1970) by Deep Purple, which builds dynamically from melodic 'clean' vocals and soft but percussive keyboards to a rising hard rock crescendo over the course of three repeated verses and three repeated notes; while the chorus is 'Ooh, ooh, ooh' and 'Ah-aha, ah-aha, ah-aha' (x 2) rising up an octave each time. However this ballad structure is somewhat disguised by the use of a bridge device occurring after the first and second verse to allow an extended solo improvisation, first by guitar virtuoso, Ritchie Blackmore and then by organ-virtuoso, Jon Lord, which complements the vocal acrobatics of lead singer, Ian Gillan. While Purple's other ballads, 'Strange Kind of Woman,' 'When a Blind Man Cries' and the spoof Country and Western song, 'Anyone's Daughter' (1971), occupy the love (lust) and loss territory ('I won't get no more eggs and water, Now I've laid the farmer's daughter'), the mid-tempo rock anthem, 'Smoke on the Water' (1972) is actually structurally similar to the strophic or 'storytelling' ballad.

In the case of Judas Priest, there are a surprising number to choose from: 'Run of the Mill' (1974) is an observational song about a life lived to old age in conformity; 'Dreamer Deceiver' (1976) about a pleasurable supernatural or mystical experience (the prototype of this is Black Sabbath's 'Planet Caravan' (1970)); 'Last Rose of Summer' is a gentle ballad with clean electric guitar tones, about late autumn turning to winter; whereas 'Beyond the Realms of Death' (1978) from the *Stained Class* album (a track cited in the infamous suicide-pact, backward-messaging trial of the band), is about a person withdrawing into themselves, leaving the world behind because for 'all its sin, it's not fit for livin' in.' This song, co-written with drummer Les Binks, is interesting for the prominent use of double-kick pedals employed to add emphasis to the verses; a technique later refined in the metal-ballad by Lars Ulrich. Other, more conventional love and loss type songs, such as 'Before the Dawn' (1978) and 'Here Comes the Tears' (1977), which follows the mid-paced, riff-driven track 'Raw Deal' (a song about the notorious gay-bar hangout on New York's Fire Island, now viewed as lead-singer Rob Halford's 'coming-out' song), invite reinterpretation, especially the first-person narrated, 'Here Comes the Tears' which opens with the lines, 'Once I dreamed that love would come and sweep me up away. Now it seems life's passed me by, I'm still alone today,' while the pre-chorus refrain is, 'Oh, I want to be loved, I need to be loved, Won't somebody love me' (A-Z Lyrics/ Judas Priest).

This song is also interesting in terms of its placement within the track order of the album, *Sin After Sin* (1977). We have already noted it follows the 'Raw Deal' track, which may or may not be significant. But the fact that it segues into the proto-thrash or speed-metal epic, 'Dissident Aggressor' (later covered by Slayer), does seem to be musically significant, in the dramatic shift to a rapid tempi, the dual-attack of the guitars and heavy rhythm-section underpinning this shift and the dramatic lyrical-alliteration of Halford's screamed vocals; all seem to resolve the yearning and vulnerability revealed in the preceding ballad, through an all-out power-play of aggressive bombast, virtuosity and control.

There are many other examples of such track sequencing in Priest's oeuvre and on other classic hard rock and metal albums. What these examples illustrate is that the ballad was not only a ubiquitous component of hard rock and heavy metal bands' repertoires prior to the rise of the power ballad, but that it was musically and lyrically far from formulaic. Indeed the deployment potential of the ballad as a musical form by such musicians suggests it was largely 'progressive' in Frith and McRobbie's (1990) terms, while the range of lyrical subjects was far from macho or indeed, overly 'soppy.'

Can you feel the power? Exploring the musical dynamics of the power ballad

For Metzer (2012), the 1980s power ballad combines 'excessive sentimentality' communicated through both lyrics and vocal performance, and 'excessive uplift' achieved through the powerful bombast of the music. In this respect, heavy metal groups 'turned up the musical formula of the power ballad' (p. 450); a musical formula based on the idea of 'continual escalation' (ibid.). Almost all hard rock and metal power ballads begin with a clean, relatively subdued or 'sincere' solo-vocal, accompanied by an acoustic guitar (sometimes a piano), which plays delicate arpeggios or 'open' country music-style chords (such as G, A and Em) and 'fingerpicking.' This stripped-down and sparse voice and guitar arrangement marks out the dynamic of the first two verses, delaying the entry of the chorus; although there may be a pre-chorus refrain. It is only when we get to the chorus that heavily distorted power-chords enter along with high harmony vocals, which underpin and emphasize the song's main lyrical phrase or hook. However, usually in the second verse, drums and bass enter to add rhythmic dynamism and 'bottom end,' which provide the lead vocal with a stronger sense of power and emphasis. After the second chorus, which will often layer in a second guitar or emphasized power-chord overtones, the song moves to a bridge, which may add a second sub-theme, either musical and/or lyrical, which is almost always followed by a highly virtuosic guitar solo that extemporizes around the main melodic hook or refrain, drastically increasing the volume and emotional intensity, before subsiding to allow the third verse to enter. Sometimes, especially in heavy metal ballads, the guitar solo will launch itself from the sub-theme of the bridge and then 'explode' in a highly dynamic and virtuosic fashion, often lasting for the length of a whole verse or it will lead to the 'wrenching up-modulation' (a key change) that will play the song out. Other times it will fade-down to allow a return to the opening acoustic-motif and simple, unadorned vocal, usually repeating the first lines or the chorus hook. A variation on this, which could be considered a less popular sub-type, is where the third section introduces a new set of musical ideas and does not return to the opening hook or melody.

The art of the power ballad is therefore in repetition and substitution; or rather adding and subtracting dynamic elements, which are usually signified by guitar and vocal timbre, both of which vary from clean through varieties of distortion. The range and variation of guitar timbres or levels of 'dynamic distortion' is much greater in the ballad than in the usual hard rock and metal song, as is the featuring of clean or more melodic pop vocals, which may occur in the delivery of the verse or the chorus sections (but not both). For example, 'Still Loving You' (1984) by the Scorpions begins with a four-note arpeggio in the key of A played on an electric guitar with bright tones which is then duplicated by a second electric guitar with a deeper tone before the first verse begins, when both guitars then play the repeated note pattern together. The close of the first verse leads to a short melodic refrain in two parts, first on the lower-string and then the second parts repeats this phrase but on the higher strings, with brightness and 'hot-distortion.' The second verse then brings in the drums and bass, with the snare and kick-drums strongly emphasized, leading to the chorus where power chords with heavy sustain and overtones emphasize the song's main lyrical hook, 'If we'd go again, all the way from the start.' Bass and drums fill in the spaces between the heavily distorted four-chord pattern; there are also some 'hot' lead guitar 'fills' toward the end of the chorus. These guitar fills become more prominent in each repeat of the chorus, rising to a crescendo at the end of the final chorus and the repeated refrain of the song's title. Only the first line of the three verses is different, all other lines are repeated, with the omission of the last line. The recurring vocal hook, 'Still loving you' is then added onto the final chorus which leads to a short bridge of four heavy bass notes, which signal a transition to a repeat of the chorus refrain and the 'play-out' solo, which is highly 'emotive' and 'bluesy.'[7] Another interesting variation is the addition of high-layered harmonies accompanying the guitar refrain before it is 'answered' by the second guitar, which occurs after the third verse. After the play-out extended solo has wrung itself to a close there is a very brief return to the opening arpeggio, which ends, leaving the voice to repeat the song hook, unaccompanied.

If we look at the career of the Scorpions, their early releases date back to 1972 but they do not start to break through in the US and UK charts until the late 1970s, having their most sustained success in the 1979–1991 period. Over this period they shift from a hard rock band with 1960s blues and psychedelic influences to a metal band. From the late 1970s they start to craft not only attention-grabbing rockers (and controversial album covers)[8] but also ballads, beginning with 'Lady Starlight' (which does not chart), followed by 'No One Like You,' 'Still Loving You,' culminating in the world wide hit, 'Wind of Change,' which is actually about the fall of the Berlin Wall (and is perhaps the only metal ballad that has whistling in it!). They are therefore exemplary of the argument that I develop next.

The mainstreaming of metal: Theorizing crossover and change in musical fields

Although the metal power ballad can be highly formulaic much of which is due to its pop production aesthetics – foregrounding the voice, balancing distortion and power-chords with clean tones, simplifying the rhythmic dynamics and so on – the rest of these band's repertoires is recognizably hard rock and metal. Despite recent attempts to separate them (Cope, 2012), hard rock and metal styles form a musical continuum that differentiates itself stylistically from other rock and pop genres, despite the variation at either end of the polarity (Moore, 2001). This stylistic repertoire was established in the early-to-mid 1970s, due to the unprecedented commercial success of key hard rock and heavy metal bands, who along with progressive rock and the singer-songwriter genre, defined that decade (Brown, 2015a). While these genres were album-oriented, in line with the prevailing rock-aesthetic, hard rock and heavy metal bands did achieve notable single's success in the Top 40 charts (Led Zeppelin, Deep Purple and Black Sabbath, for example).[9] But this was not based on a strategy of releasing radio-friendly ballads or of collaborating with producers and external songwriters. However, the practice of producing a single to be released prior to the album was emerging in this period.

By the late 1970s the commercial orientation of a number of hard rock and heavy metal bands, such as Uriah Heep, Rainbow, Whitesnake, Magnum, Scorpions and early Def Leppard, had significantly changed. For Earl (2009), this shift is exemplified by the decision of Rainbow bandleader, Ritchie Blackmore, to sack vocalist Ronnie James Dio and replace him with Graham Bonnett, the consequences of which 'was a departure from epic, flashy, neo-mythological songs such as "Gates of Babylon" (1978) to [...] more chart friendly fare' (p. 40). This shift toward hard rock with a commercial edge, indicated by the album-title, *Down to Earth* (1979), was exemplified by the singles 'Since You've Been Gone' (August 1979), 'All Night Long' (February 1980), and 'I Surrender' (June 1981), with Joe Lynn Turner on vocals, which went to No. 3 in the UK charts (Strong, 2002, p. 445). Significantly, two of these hits were penned by an external songwriter, Russ Ballard.

But it was the hard rock or 'melodic heavy metal' band, Def Leppard, who took this logic further, in particular, by becoming creatively involved with producer Robert John 'Mutt' Lange (Earl, 2009, p. 43), who also collaborated on song-writing, co-authoring all of their major album and hit singles, including the UK/US top five, *Pyromania* (1983), *Hysteria* (1987) and *Adrenalize* (1992). As Strong has argued, Def Leppard's *Pyromania* 'was legendary for its use of special effects and state-of-the-art technology [the] record revolutionized heavy metal and became the benchmark by which subsequent 80s albums were measured' (2002, p. 153). The follow up album, *Hysteria* (1987) a melodic heavy rock *tour de force*, contained not only a string of top-ten singles but catapulted the band to international stardom. Lange's compositional involvement, not just co-writing but arranging material, foregrounded the centrality of the recording studio in hard rock and metal in ways that it had never been before and the producer as not just a 'surrogate listener' but as an artistic collaborator. This strategy was also replicated by Aerosmith, Whitesnake, Ratt, Mötley Crüe, Bon Jovi and, in particular, Dieter Dierks's work with the Scorpions, from 1973 to 1988, as producer and arranger, enabling them to develop a successful balance between hard rockers and ballads, leading to a number of hit singles and albums. This new role of the producer as the 'Fifth Beatle' or the 'Sixth Scorp' also applies to Bob Rock's work with Metallica, particularly the breakthrough success of the 'Black Album' (*Metallica*, 1991) but in particular the melodic ballads, 'The Unforgiven' (1991) and 'Nothing Else Matters' (1991), both of which were hit singles. However, Metallica's first attempt at a ballad, 'Fade to Black,' was released in 1984 on the thrash album, *Ride the Lightning* (Pillsbury, 2006).

The fact that we can include Metallica within this discussion of a move from heavy metal to hard rock and, over the 1984–1991 period, in the perfecting of a crossover strategy centered on the emotive ballad, should lead us to the judgment that a simple opposition between authenticity and 'sell-out' to the mainstream is not adequate as an explanation. But what are the alternatives? One is Bourdieu's (1993) account of the cultural field of restricted and large-scale production, or cultural production that has 'prestige' as art and that which is (merely) 'popular' entertainment. However, as Hesmondhalgh (2006) points out, this model does not lend itself successfully to explaining how 'prestige' is gained *within* large-scale 'commercial' fields of cultural production, such as popular music. Earl's (2009) description of the pop trajectory of the bands, in particular Rainbow, Magnum and Def Leppard, as a *position-taking strategy* within the heavy metal genre-field, designed to gain recognition by adopting more commercial strategies, is a novel application of this idea. But it is not entirely convincing since it rests on the view that their success led to the acceptance of 'mainstream metal as authentic metal' (p. 40). However, the argument that such strategies taken toward the mainstream resulted in changes to that mainstream is *indisputable*. Not least of which was the ubiquity of metal and hard rock songs in the Top 40 charts and radio playlists, whether hard rock and metal fans liked it or not.

This situation can be contrasted with the wider field of rock music, where the most 'consecrated' artists were also the most popular. As Gendron (2002) has observed, this period of confluence between critical acclaim and mass popularity, had by the late 1970s become extremely polarized, leading to a shift toward economic accreditation, taken by notable publications, like *Rolling Stone*; a trend that was to increase in the 1980s. Indeed, it could be argued that the 1980s was a decade that not only saw the resurgence of a pop aesthetic but also a shift toward large-scale ('mega') economic success as its own justification. The relevance of this to heavy metal is that the commercial success of bands that defined the hard rock and metal musical continuum in the 1970s was made possible by the artistic autonomy afforded 'album' recording artists during that decade. But it was a success that was accompanied, for the most part, by a lack of critical acclaim (Brown, 2015a, 2015b). So while Earl (2009) is right to point to a shift in the strategies of notable bands away from the typical lyrical and musical aesthetics to be found in progressive rock and heavy metal, these moves were symptomatic of the break-up of the cultural/economic coherence of the rock field itself, in the mid to late 1970s. The shift to more commercial strategies, such as the release of ballads and other pop-oriented, shorter songs, reflected broader changes in the economics of the market, which also impacted on 'prog rock' bands as well.[10] What follows from this is that the cultural/commercial field that defines the term 'heavy metal' (Konow, 2002) was only fully established in the 1980s, as the strategies of hard rock and glam metal bands culminated in the formation of a new rock 'mainstream' within popular music, one centered on the Billboard Hot 100, Top 40 radio play and MTV video rotation.

Difficult to cure: The hard rock and metal musical continuum

One of the strategies often employed by critics and fans to separate commercial hard rock from that which is 'authentically' metal is to focus on their musical and lyrical differences. For example, Cope (2012) argues that although seminal hard rock and heavy metal bands, such as Led Zeppelin and Black Sabbath, both have their origins in a re-working of blues styles, each band offers a blueprint for song composition and musical performance that, traced over time, leads to a clear differentiation of bands, song-styles and sub-genre proliferation. In particular, heavy metal can be distinguished by the rejection of blues and rock 'n' roll stylings, the de-emphasis of conventional chord progressions and standard or open tunings in favor of the development of techniques, such as modal or chromatic song structures, down-tuning and palm-muting and aggressive performance styles, such as anti-melodic shouting or growling and drum techniques, such as the frequent use of double-kicks and blast-beats.

While it is possible to identify clusters of bands that could be said to base their style on one side or the other of this aesthetic dichotomy, there are others, including ones within Cope's analysis, namely Deep Purple, Judas Priest and Motörhead, who cannot be exclusively categorized, since they combine features from both; as do bands like Uriah Heep, Saxon and Iron Maiden. More contemporary examples, such as Pantera, moved from hard rock/glam to modern metal, while still retaining the ballad in their repertoire, for example 'Cemetery Gates' (1990) and 'This Love' (1992). In none of these cases can such bands be said to retain blues structures in their songs, as would be found in 'white' blues rock, although the attention-grabbing techniques of hard rock and metal guitarists, such as string-bends, extreme vibrato, pinch-harmonics ('squealies') and tremolo-arm 'dive-bombs,' do retain some connection to urban, electric-blues, and rock 'n' roll styles (Brown, 2015a). For these reasons, as Moore (2001) argues, it is more productive to view hard rock and heavy metal 'as points on a style continuum' since, although not all bands can be clearly categorized, they share features 'that clearly differentiate bands along this continuum from those outside it' (p. 148). Although, 'sentimental love-songs (what have become known as "ballads")' are much rarer 'at the heavy metal end' (ibid.).

These common features could be said to be speed, from 80, 120 to 160 beats per minute, where 80 (laid back) is more likely to occur in the hard-rock ballad and 160 (frenetic) in thrash and speed-metal styles. Slower tempos, especially in the ballad-form, tend to feature 'delicate' arpeggios and harmonies, with mid-tempos featuring power-chords (as in the chorus section of ballads) and in faster tempi, a dynamic alternation of power chords and plucked bass-strings (Moore, 2001, p. 148). Although both hard rock and metal share a density of texture achieved through guitar distortion in the high and low frequencies, hard rock offers more variety of timbre in the use of keyboard-derived tones in the high-register. This is also true of the use of the 'high male voice' in hard rock, 'highly resonant and with ubiquitous vibrato on long notes' (ibid., p. 149), as well as parallel harmony backing vocals in the chorus. All of which speaks of a more conventional song structure, often a clear repeated four-chord sequence which acts as a hook, leading to the chorus; whereas in heavy metal, song structures are more open-ended, often based on a modal or chromatic sequence featuring a rhythmic cycle of riffs that may have no obvious melodic relationship. While the guitar solo is a ubiquitous (highly virtuosic) feature of both styles, solos in hard rock tend to be more melody and harmony based, derived from the song itself, whereas heavy metal solos are more likely to arrive 'as if from nowhere' (ibid.).

Cope (2012) also wants to argue that the musical distinction between hard rock and heavy metal styles also extends to its core lyrical themes. In particular, a defining focus in hard rock on female sexual-attraction, male-sexual conquest, and conflicted sexual-relations, including betrayal, rejection and the need for male autonomy and female acquiescence. For Cope, songs that reflect gender anxieties and foreground sexism and misogyny are typical of the urban electric and rural blues derivation of hard rock styles, where such themes are archetypal. In seeking to distinguish such themes from heavy metal's primary focus on, 'Satan, the occult, the supernatural [...] suffering and death, the horrors of war, good versus evil, nightmares and fantastic monsters/creature' (pp. 82–83), Cope seeks to deny that such 'exscriptionist' themes (that is, 'total denial of gender anxieties through the articulation of fantastic worlds without women' (Walser, 1993, pp. 110–111), involve issues of masculinity and gender-identity work.

A good example of this is his discussion of the video that accompanies Metallica's powerful anti-war ballad 'One' (1988), which combines footage of the band performing the song together in an empty hanger with excerpts from the film, *Johnny Got His Gun*, about a double-amputee paraplegic soldier, kept alive by medical science while his 'inner self [is] screaming to die' (p. 78). For Cope, this video does not deliberately set out to exclude women, since its subject matter 'front-line, world war soldiers – is already male dominated'; indeed the message of the video and song is anti-war and anti- 'the power of patriarchy to order the lives of the working class' (ibid.). While I do not disagree with Cope's interpretation of the song's theme, I note his lack of recognition that this theme is communicated through a powerful depiction of male interiority, characterized by vulnerability and despair, qualities that are entirely out of place in the context of the aggressive performative aesthetics of the thrash metal genre. Or as Pillsbury puts it, 'The codes are all wrong, from timbre to tempo' (2006, p. 45).

This leads me to suggest, in the manner of Moore's musicological categorization, that the themes of sexism, misogyny, exscription, androgyny and romance, form a continuum within the repertoires of hard rock and metal bands. Not only this but each variant is an expression of 'gender anxiety' so that their performance and reception serve to map out the contours and the limits, to paraphrase Metzer (2012), of 'the types of emotional expression appropriate to ["white" masculinity and metal identities]' (p. 446). Thus, Walser's (1993) exploration of the modes of masculine performance to be found in the popular metal acts of the power-ballad era identifies the misogyny of the 'male victim' ensnared by the dangerous sexuality of the femme fatale in such songs as, 'In the Still of the Night' by Whitesnake, 'Looks that Kill' by Mötley Crüe and 'Kiss of Death' by Dokken; the 'Nothing But a Good Time' androgyny and to-be-looked-at-sexual-display of glam-metal bands like Poison, Cinderella and Faster Pussycat, and the 'romantic sincerity' projected by hard rock and metal bands, like Bon Jovi, who not only modified their image, by ditching the leather/chains/eyeliner of their early look but also the 'macho' themes of their earlier songs ('running, shooting and falling down') in favor of songs about romance and relationships, 'where the only mystical element was bourgeois love' (p. 120).

Of course, the point that Walser is making is that these variations on the theme of masculinity – as ensnared sexual victim, androgynous rebel out for a good time and romantic partner/betrayed-lover – extend and, in some ways subvert, the hitherto dominant narrative subjects of heavy metal songs, which generally exclude the female and the feminine. We may want to question why romance, rather than androgyny or the empowering sexual-fantasy of the femme-fatale, draws 'legions of female fans to metal' (p. 111); or why it is that the pop-mainstream is invariably defined in gender-terms. However, what seems to be central to the debate about the power balled and heavy metal, is that it 'offers a very different form of masculinity to that found in other metal songs, albeit one that exists almost exclusively within the power ballad aesthetic' (Pillsbury, 2006, p. 54).

Wherever I May Roam: Exploring Metallica's ballad strategy

In this section, I want to consider the move toward the ballad-form taken by former thrash-titans, Metallica, as both an artistic and commercial strategy and to what extent it represents an attempt to produce an 'authentic' metal ballad. Commencing with the song 'Fade to Black' off the *Ride the Lightning* (1984) album and continuing through the course of the next four albums, spanning the period up to 1996's *Load*, Metallica penned a number of powerful ballads, including 'Welcome Home (Sanitarium)' (1986), 'One' (1988), 'The Unforgiven' (1991), 'Nothing Else Matters' (1991) and 'Mama Said' (1996). What is interesting here is that this sequence of ballad-production, usually one per album, parallels the period of success of the ballad by hard rock and glam metal bands; groups viewed as diametrically opposed to Metallica and their musical identity and aesthetics. The fact that Metallica knew they were entering a controversial area of songwriting is indicated by Hetfield's candid remarks,

> The song was a pretty big step for us [...] It was pretty much our first ballad so it was pretty challenging and we knew it would freak people out. Bands like Slayer and Exodus don't do ballads, but they've stuck themselves in that position. We never wanted to; limiting yourself to please your audience is bullshit.
>
> (Dome and Ewing, 2007, p. 59)[11]

However, Metallica waited until 'One' to release a ballad as a single and to employ the song as their entrée into the MTV video market in 1988.

The strategy worked, launching the album ... *And Justice for All* (1989), the single gaining a Top-40 place in the Billboard charts (and Top-20 in the UK), earning the band a Grammy for Best Metal Performance the following year.

However, the release of the self-titled *Metallica* ('the Black Album') in 1991 marked a significant change in the strategy of releasing singles for the band, bolstering the album that debuted at number one on both sides of the Atlantic. This began with the riff-driven rocker, 'Enter Sandman' (released a month prior to the album), followed by the ballad, 'The Unforgiven' (November 1991), the mid-tempo 'Wherever I May Roam' (backed with a live version of 'Fade to Black') (October 1992) and 'Sad But True' (February 1993). These singles, all Top-40 hits, remain Metallica's most popular songs to date and were instrumental in gaining the band a crossover audience that propelled them to global popularity, rivaling that of U2 and R.E.M. It was not a coincidence that the strikingly dynamic hard rock production to be found on the album, as well as the new melodic range and timbre of Hetfield's vocal performances on the mid-tempo and slower songs, was due to the recruitment of Bob Rock (who had previously worked with Aerosmith and Mötley Crüe). Indeed, according to Rock, Metallica chose him because they were impressed with the sound he had achieved, especially on Mötley Crüe's *Dr. Feelgood* (1989) album (Busso, 2014).

Pillsbury (2006) names this song-cycle Metallica's 'Fade to Black Paradigm' and interestingly compares it to the 1980s power ballad. However, he argues that the 'lyrical topic of most power ballads – the ups and downs of romantic love – finds no place in Metallica's Fade to Black paradigm, even as the presence of a less-aggressive male interiority nonetheless goes some way toward linking the two' (p. 54). Indeed, the 'presentation of interiority' is viewed as 'the primary aesthetic characteristic' of this song cycle (p. 55). The opening song, 'Fade to Black' is clearly introspective in tone, given that it is a 'suicide note,' the lyrics conveying a 'distinct sense of despair and inner turmoil' (p. 53). As Pillsbury describes it, the song offers 'an inward-looking psychological journey in which the narrator describes his decision to commit suicide' (p. 41). Although there are, in fact, other songs in the thrash genre that deal with this topic, most notably Megadeth's 'In My Darkest Hour' (1988) and especially 'A Tout Le Monde' (1994), the song is not only musically unlike other thrash songs, it is also distinctive because it foregrounds personal feelings. What I would want to add to this is that as the cycle of ballads in the Metallica canon develops over the 1984–1991 period, the 'I' or first person narrator of the ballad becomes more prominent and more obvious; but also the musical dynamics of the songs become more recognizably power-ballad-like. 'Nothing Else Matters' is probably the most ballad-like of all, indeed it employs 'open' or conventional 'box-chords' that are strummed, like a country music song; whereas, of course, 'Mama Said' (1996) is a country-ballad, both in its lyrical themes, musical structure and vocal performance.

However, the ways in which Metallica approach the ballad, at least initially, is quite distinctive and seems to be a deliberate musical strategy. How much of this was a conscious effort to distinguish their power-ballad style or to what extent they looked to earlier hard rock and metal variants, is open to speculation. For example, 'Fade to Black' although it is based around conventional chords (Am, C, G, Em) has an elaborate musical opening, with a hint of strings or keyboard tones, leading into the main acoustic picked arpeggio, which is then layered with guitar harmonies, after which a lead clean electric guitar with 'warm' distortion extemporizes this as a highly virtuosic refrain leading to a repeat of the melodic hook of the song that combines both guitar tones. Hetfield's voice is not clean however but is subject to a phasing-effect as it enters. The song is built around two sets of verses and an end verse, which is contrasting. Like most power ballads, the chorus enters after the second verse, employing power-chords. But these are heavily palm-muted and aggressively heavy in the thrash-style. There are no words in the repeated chorus, which is distinctive. What is also distinctive, although this is a sub-variant of the power ballad, is that the bridge leads to a distinctly different end section, which is introduced and performed in the thrash style, with descending chromatics and driving percussive guitar. However, there is a 'soaring, transcendent guitar solo' (Pillsbury, 2006, p. 44), which 'plays out' the piece.

'Welcome Home (Sanitarium)' (1986) and 'One' (1988), could be said to offer variations on this initial template. While both songs move to a dramatic thrash-metal third section, in both this leads to a dramatic 'punch out.' Also, Hetfield's vocal is cleaner and more enunciated in 'One.' This song is also enhanced by a distinctive use, by Ulrich, of kick-pedals during the verse; a technique that he will carry over to 'The Unforgiven' (1991) and 'Nothing Else Matters' (1991). Also the first person narrator is present in both, articulating an 'inner voice' of regret, anger or despair. As Pillsbury (2006) notes, what is distinctive about these '*Black Album*' songs, particularly 'Nothing Else Matters' is that the

I of the song is seen to directly connect to the singer, offering a more emotive or interior kind of subjectivity (p. 55). But these songs also have a different gender address, the latter coming closest to the conventions of the romantic or emotive power ballad, with lines like 'Never opened myself this way' and 'Couldn't be much more from the heart.' It also has prominent strings, as well as warm clean guitars and the emphasized bass-drum kicks. The play-out solo, performed by Hetfield rather than Hammett, is also noticeably emotive and 'bluesy.' Perhaps the most obvious feature though is the return to the opening lyrical and melodic hook to the fade.

Conclusion

There is no doubt that the 1984–1991 period was hard rock and metal's most successful period of mainstream success and a measure of that success was the extent to which mainstream music was re-defined as a result. Clearly the power ballad was a central aspect of this crossover strategy in recruiting a wider audience for hard rock and metal bands. While not all metal power ballads were about notions of love and loss, the most successful ones were. While such songs appealed to a wider female audience, the cost of this was the reproduction of conventional notions of gender relations and musical clichés, perhaps in turn a consequence of collaborating with external writers and producers. Although this strategy can be said to be in part a consequence of the break-up of the musical field from which hard rock and metal styles emerged, the ballad form as it existed prior to this was noticeably more musically complex and able to address a range of lyrical themes besides love and loss. While the performative limits of masculinity, both musical and lyrical, remain central to notions of authenticity in metal music, the deployment of the ballad form seemed to offer an emotional register beyond these limitations. Metallica's deployment of this musical style suggested that it was compatible with thrash musical aesthetics, as long as the lyrical subject matter was about suicide and death. When the band attempted to venture beyond this to more emotive expressions of masculinity, it also led them to embrace more conventional musical means of doing so. The decline in the ballad (in thrash, death, black and grindcore) is probably more to do with the changing musical syntax, whereby melody and harmony are de-emphasized along with slow and mid-tempos. Where these elements are emphasized, in power, doom and symphonic metal (including some varieties of black metal), a version of the metal ballad returns.

Notes

1. This is not to suggest that all metal encyclopedias exclude hard rock and glam metal bands. Strong's (2002) The Great Metal Discography, includes them, while the Rough Guide to Heavy Metal (Berlain, 2005) offers an entry called 'Metal Ballads' (p. 220).
2. Although Motörhead have some songs that are ballad-like, such as 'Sweet Revenge,' it isn't until the concept-album *1916* (1991) that we get a bona fide power ballad, 'Love Me Forever' and the string-drenched epic war-ballad title track. Budgie, on the other hand, have some of the most unusual ballads in heavy metal, including the ten-minute opus 'Parents' (1973) and other multi-sectional, mini-prog epics, as well as more conventional fare, like 'You Know I Will Always Love You' and 'Everything in My Heart.' Black Sabbath, in some ways can be seen as the originators of the heavy metal ballad, with tracks such as Planet Caravan (1970), Solitude (1971) and Changes (1972).
3. Despite the fact that most critics define glam metal primarily in terms of its theatricality and image, tracing this to Alice Cooper, KISS, or 1970s glam rock, studies of this music genre do not pursue such connection musically. Auslander (2006), for example, refers to 'so-called glam metal' once (p. 232). My argument would be that glam metal is part of the hard rock and metal continuum, since musically it is hard rock. The fact that this connection is rarely made is because glam metal bands are said to lack the requisite 'ironic distance' displayed by androgynous performers like David Bowie (Walser, 1993, p. 124). Bowie himself argues this in regards to KISS, 'butch, manly glam with lots of [...] fireworks, muscle and metal' (Quoted in Auslander op cit, p. 49). But not only did Bowie release an album, *Man Who Sold the World* (1971) that is hard rock/metal, many of the bands who comprised the glam rock wave, such as Sweet, Slade and Mott the Hoople, were hard rock bands who had found crossover success in the pop/singles market. Another interesting parallel here is how this was achieved via the role of external songwriters/managers/producers, such as Nicky Chin and Mike Chapman, who helped to soften the band's hard rock sound with a polished pop production.
4. American professional songwriter Child has also co-written songs with Alice Cooper, KISS, Aerosmith, Meatloaf and Ratt.
5. Kitaen appeared in four Whitesnake videos, including 'Is this Love' and 'Here I Go Again' (1987) as well as Ratt's 'Back For More' (1984) and on the covers of their debut EP and album *Out of the Cellar*. In the Whitesnake videos, in particular, Kitaen plays a seductive and highly stylized femme-fatale character.
6. SoundScan is an electronic tracking system that was introduced in March 1991 to more accurately record the volume of sales of albums and singles. It works via the scanning of the bar code found on physical music products such as CDs and album sleeves. Prior to this, record shops were surveyed weekly about their sales.
7. The solo is played by Rudolph Schenker, who is a more of a hard rock guitarist. Whereas the 'fills' are played by the more 'flashy' metal guitarist, Matthias Jabs.

8. Including Virgin Killers (1977), Lovedrive (1979), Animal Magnetism (1980) and Love at First Sting (1984). This appears to be a deliberate 'misogyny' strategy employed by the band to appeal to their male fans as well as court controversy, which they then displace with humor. This strategy is also applicable to Skid Row, Mötley Crüe, W.A.S.P., Great White, Whitesnake and Guns n' Roses in the 1984–1991 period.

9. Notable examples would include Black Sabbath's 'Paranoid' (UK 4), Deep Purple's 'Black Night' (UK 4), 'Strange Kind of a Woman' (UK 6), 'Fireball' (UK15) and 'Smoke on the Water' (US 4); and Zeppelin's 'Whole Lotta Love' (US 4), 'Immigrant Song' (US 16) and 'Black Dog' (US 15).

10. A good example of this is the career of Genesis from the 1976–1977 period onwards.

11. Of course, as many commentators have pointed out, Hetfield would live to regret this view when confronted with a sustained backlash from core fans. However, this backlash does not occur until the Black album, which suggests that Metallica's ballad strategy was successful up until this point.

Bibliography

Auslander, P. (2006) *Performing Glam Rock, Gender & Theatricality in Popular Music* (Ann Arbor, MI: University of Michigan Press).

AZ Lyrics.Com (2000) Retrieved 17 August 2014 from: http,//www.azlyrics.com./

Berlain, E. (2005) *The Rough Guide to Heavy Metal* (London: Penguin Books).

Bourdieu, P. (1993) *The Field of Cultural Production* (New York, NY: Columbia University Press).

Brown, A. R. (2015a) 'Everything Louder than Everyone Else: The Origins and Persistence of Heavy Metal and Its Global Cultural Impact,' *The Sage Handbook of Popular Music*, eds. A. Bennett & S. Wacksman (London: Sage), pp. 216–278.

Brown, A. R. (2015b) 'Explaining the Naming of Heavy Metal from Rock's "Back Pages": A Dialogue with Deena Weinstein,' *Metal Music Studies*, 1(2), pp. 233–261.

Busso, J. (2014) 'Metallica's Black Album Track by Track: Bob Rock Reflects on 20th Anniversary.' Retrieved 1 September 2015 from: http://www.musicradar.com/news/guitars/metallicas-black-album-track-by-track-485030.

Cope, A. L. (2012) *Black Sabbath and the Rise of Heavy Metal Music* (Farnham, VA: Ashgate Press).

Dickson, D. (1995) *Biographize: The Def Leppard Story* (London: Sidgwick & Jackson).

Dome, M. & Ewing, J. (2007) *Encyclopedia Metallica* (Surrey: Chrome Dreams).

Earl, B. (2009) 'Metal Goes "Pop", The Explosion of Heavy Metal into the Mainstream,' *Heavy Metal Music in Britain*, ed. G. Bayer (Farnham, VA: Ashgate Press), pp. 33–52.

Frith, S. & McRobbie, A. (1990) 'Rock and Sexuality,' *On Record, Rock, Pop and the Written Word*, eds. S. Frith & A. Goodwin (London: Routledge), pp. 371–389.

Gendron, B. (2002) *Between Montmartre and the Mudd Club: Popular Music and the Avant-Garde* (Chicago, IL: University of Chicago Press).

Harris, K. (2000) ' "Roots?" The Relationship Between the Global and the Local Within the Global Extreme Metal Scene,' *Popular Music*, 19(1), pp. 13–30.

Harrison, T. (2007) ' "Empire" Chart Performance of Hard Rock and Heavy Metal Groups, 1990–1992,' *Popular Music and Society*, 20(2), pp. 197–225.

Hesmondhalgh, D. (2006) 'Bourdieu, the Media, and Cultural Production', *Media Culture Society*, 28, pp. 211–231.

Kahn-Harris, K. (2007) *Extreme Metal: Music and Culture on the Edge* (Oxford: Berg).

Konow, D. (2002) *Bang Your Head: The Rise and Fall of Heavy Metal* (New York, NY: Three Rivers Press).

Laurin, H. (2013) 'Triumph of the Maggots? Valorization of Metal in the Rock Press,' *Heavy Metal, Controversies and Countercultures*, eds. S. Frith & A. Goodwin (Sheffield: Equinox), pp. 50–65.

Lena, J. C. & Peterson, R. A. (2008) 'Classification as Culture, Types and Trajectories of Music Genres,' *American Sociological Review*, 73(5), pp. 697–718.

Metzer, D. (2012) 'The Power Ballad,' *Popular Music*, 31, pp. 437–459.

Moore, A. (2001) *Rock, the Primary Text: Developing a Musicology of Rock*, 2nd Edition (Aldershot: Ashgate).

Pillsbury, G. T. (2006) *Damage Incorporated: Metallica and the Production of Musical Identity* (London: Routledge).

Ressner, J. (1989) 'Metal Romances Radio,' *Rolling Stone*, 9 February, p. 22.

Sernoe, J. (2005) ' "Now We're on the Top, Top of the Pops": The Performance of "Non-Mainstream" Music on Billboard's Albums Charts, 1981–2001,' *Popular Music and Society*, 8(5), pp. 639–662.

Sharpe-Young. G. (2007) *Metal: The Definitive Guide* (London: Jawbone Press).

Strong, M. C. (2002) *The Great Metal Discography: From Hard Rock to Hard Core* (Edinburgh: Canongate Books).

Walser, R. (1993) *Running with the Devil: Power, Gender and Madness in Heavy Metal Music* (Middleton, CT: Wesleyan University Press).

Weinstein, D. (2000) *Heavy Metal: The Music and Its Culture* (New York, NY: De Capo Press).

4

Same as It Never Was: Machinations of Metal Memory

Brad Klypchak
Texas A&M University-Commerce

In his keynote presentation at the *Heavy Metal and Popular Culture Conference in Bowling Green, Ohio* (US) (and its later publication as a web series), Keith Kahn-Harris (2013) identified a number of areas which metal studies would be well served to explore. One of these, a theme of memory, proposes that metal studies as a field should be mindful of not only metal's own history, but as to the ways in which the recurring stories of metal coalesce and come to influence the evolving discursive understandings and changing subjectivities of emphases and omissions, of what is valorized or forgotten, and the mechanisms by which these processes take place.

In my own session at the conference, a question of historical self-reflexivity was raised: in what manner do memories and the personalization of such memories come to be reflected in these tales of history? For example, when I was asked in my session 'wasn't Twisted Sister always camp?' I was forced to wonder, does a historically distanced hindsight contextually silence the perceived 'authenticity' of what I encountered as a fan of the band approximately 30 years ago? An added dimension to such inquiry stems from the prominence of retromanic re-representations of metal's past (be it reissued recordings, memoirs from artists, boxset retrospective, nostalgia tours or other celebrations of 'anniversary' events, etc.). The confluence of the present with a remembered and nostalgic past results in a Krokerian panic memory (1989), a hybrid exhibiting elements of Simon Reynolds' notions of retromania (2011), Svetlana Boym's notions of reflective nostalgia (2001), and, often, Baudrillardian simulacra (1994), further blurring metal's historical memories all the more. Through establishing these connections in detail, I offer the result as panicmetalmemories, the postmodern blurring of metal's past and present into an unsettled and re-reflexive cycle of self-reference.

For this chapter, I propose a series of examinations wherein panicmetalmemories have emerged and how their respective circumstances come to reversion histories of bands and/or the larger metal culture itself. I have actively chosen to focus on artists from the 1980s (which, in and of itself, illustrates one of metal's own self-definitional memory shifts, in that many of the acts I cover here might be deemed 'hard rock' by today's standards) given the benefits of retrospective distance availed by 30 years of hindsight and the litany of examples these metal veterans provide over this timespan. My examinations will work across two thematic arcs, one in which some specific band events come to illustrate memory machinations and one derived from the confluence of experiential and nostalgic blends of memory thereby blurring versions of 'the known' into constructed hybrids of truth, non-truth, and selective inclusion and/or omission.

For instances where changes of band memberships have transpired across lengthy career arcs, much of the energy contributed to memory machination attempts to control the significations of a b(r)and. Be it financially or artistically motivated, those involved seek dominance over the representations of the musical career and its legacy. Manipulations range from anachronistically altering publicity materials in order to ex-script those dismissed in favor of those participating in current line-ups (for example, website manipulations to reduce Bill Ward's presence in recent Black Sabbath publicity) to bands fracturing into multiple rivalling versions, each claiming 'authentic' status of some established legacy (including the ongoing saga of Queensryche, but also acts such as Saxon, Ratt and LA Guns, amongst others).

In terms of metal's constructed histories, the recent rash of memoirs from those with metal pasts rescript narratives in such a way as to convolute the folkloric tales of yore into discursive battles for authority of authorship of 'what really happened' (the collective memoirs surrounding Mötley Crüe and Pantera as apt exemplars). Applying Ben Yagoda's (2009) considerations on the memoir, I offer that beyond metal artists, those invested within the metal subculture are also just as prone to selective inclusion and exclusion of metal's past. Wherein the canon by which the present and future generations learn 'history' becomes markedly idiosyncratic, which further illustrates the postmodern complexities of metal's manipulations of its own memories as an ongoing process.

Largely informed from the work undertaken in *The Postmodern Scene* and its many theoretical influences (foremost of which is Jean Baudrillard), Arthur Kroker and colleagues (1989) illustrate the fleeting dissolve of meanings within snapshot instances of postmodernity in *The Panic Encyclopedia*. The key construct, panic, represents the 'key psychological mood of postmodern culture' (p. 13) and is evidenced through panic culture, 'a floating reality, with the actual as dream world, where we live on the edge of ecstasy and dread' (p. 14). Submersed in a consumptive culture where 'products are sold to finance the ad' (p. 55), the world of the simulacra fosters panic states. Be it economic (with virtual money/stock crashes), pragmatic (virtual pilots), or political (nuclear armament for peace), the projection of likelihood becomes more influential than reality. The real is devalued in favor of the hyper-real, the virtual, or the technologically enhanced.

In the case of my explorations within metal, I ascribe panicmetalmemories as one such illustration where history as a dedicated and genuine representation of truth goes seemingly awry. In *The Dustbin of History*, Greil Marcus (1995) problematizes the contradictory notion of the phrase, 'its history' and its implied finality: 'It means there is no such thing as history, a past of burden or legacy. Once something is "history", it's *over* and it is understood that it never existed at all. We swat it away like a fly – along with the possibility that, in history, nothing is ever truly over' (p. 22). Yet history is not over in such finality, akin to what Kahn-Harris (2013c) notes as metal's 'process of obsolescence' being overcome by the current era's 'age of abundance' and the ever-presence of what might have been swept into the dustbin previously: 'The past is not gone for ever (*sic*) or discredited; it is part of the now. The half-life of cultural productions extends indefinitely, as nothing goes truly out of style and artists linger well past their sell-by date' (para.14).

For Marcus (1995), when an event works outside the 'strictures of power, it is swallowed by the imperatives of history which are partly the imperatives of truth. History is a story: we want a story that makes sense, is poetically whole, that fits what we already think we know' (pp. 42–43). Within the age of abundance, these stories come to be consumed through a flattened sense of layered memories, panicmemories informed by the past yet regenerated and re-inscribed simultaneously through its ever-accessible presence. Along these lines is where nostalgia further muddies the prospects of static memories and histories. In *Retromania*, Simon Reynolds (2011) examines the popular cultural trend toward conflating the past onto present popular cultural practices.

For example he identifies YouTube, with its seemingly infinite reach, as 'a paradoxical combination of speed and standstill' (p. 63) and cites its existence (along with other technological cataloguing access points like iTunes and Google) as a key means by which retro-consumption transpires. 'Thoroughly entwined with the consumer-entertainment complex, we feel pangs for the products of yesteryear, the novelties and distractions that filled up our youth' (pp. xxix–xxx). I offer that this sort of nostalgic desire becomes a prevailing lens through which panicmetalmemories color the perceptions of contemporary practices of 1980s metal acts.

What's in a name?: Nostalgia, authenticity and the rock b(r)and

Routinely over the past decade, a number of hard rock and heavy metal artists who achieved popularity during the 1980s have attempted to rekindle careers by reforming acts that had previously disbanded and performing their respective classic material once again. Often framed through a lens of nostalgia, concert festivals like Pryor, Oklahoma's Rocklahoma, Merriweather, Virginia's M3 Festival, and a number of international concert festivals provide an active outlet for artists who seemingly had lost popular performative relevancy. In many instances however, these groups experienced a variety of membership changes over their history leaving some question as to who exactly the audience has come to see, the 'original' members, the line-up from the most popular recordings, or simply a key member or two with an assortment of replacement players. Additionally, contemporary performances often differ considerably from those of the remembered past and raise questions as to which version of performance is deemed 'authentic' by consumers – the contemporary, the historical, or some form of simulacra born of the two. By exploring notions of perceived authenticity as applied to the collective memory of hard rock and heavy metal and the ways in which negotiations of past and present come to be manipulated by performing artists, questions of where authenticity may come to lie can be advanced.

Authenticity in hard rock and heavy metal

While seemingly contrary to postmodern tenets, rock music discourse frequently centers on claims and judgments of authenticity within its musical and performative forms (see for example Grossberg, 1992; Hill, 1996; Klypchak, 2007; Moore, 2002; Walser, 1993). As Allan Moore's

(2002) survey and deconstruction of authenticity in rock music attests, there are numerous potential qualities which come to represent 'authentic' ranging from being able to perform with virtuosity, to being driven by artistic intentions rather than extrinsic, commercial ones (selling out), to the degree to which the performance on and offstage reflected and adhered to subcultural expectations. In each of these constructions of authenticity, discourse defines and redefines the standards by which authenticity is determined through comparison to the historically accumulated references gathered from rock's previous practices as well as those contemporarily emerging. For the hard rock and heavy metal subcultures, considerable emphasis is placed upon establishing a distinctive identity in contrast to a comparative other. Accordingly, the traditions and history of metal hold great importance for establishing metal's distinctive identity in contrast to the mainstream whole. To demonstrate performative markers of authentic rock/metal practice becomes mandated upon those seeking status within the hard rock/metal community.

As applied to the resurgence of late 1980s acts, the historical divide of decades offers varying challenges to authenticity performances. Appearances and fashions change over such a span, yet the nostalgic remembrance of these acts fosters a comparative consideration of the performative qualities of the past. While teased hair and bright-colored spandex pants may not be as subculturally mandatory in contemporary performances, the hyper masculine, rebellious hedonism conveyed by the scene 'back when' still holds considerable value. More significantly, the lasting legacy of the sound recordings and the values of being able to 'pull it off live' mark the necessity for bands to replicate their earlier achievements to some degree or else risk diminished standing.

The nostalgic framing of many of these performances raises additional concerns. For those bands who have remained active yet had fallen out of mainstream popularity, they find themselves forced to negotiate the demands for the 'classic' past at the potential expense of an ongoing creative history (both Klypchak, 2007 and Reynolds, 2011 offer further development of this particular phenomenon). In instances where band members have changed, the nostalgic framing of the band frequently becomes centered on the vocalist as, more often than not, vocals represent the melodic hook and point of access for many a fan; in terms of living up to past expectations, changing a drummer or a bass player will likely be less evident to the casual fan as would a vocalist switch. For example, Iron Maiden's shift from vocalist Bruce Dickenson to Blaze Bailey is far more immediately audible than the drummer transition from Clive Burr to Nicko McBrain, or the Dennis Stratton to Adrian Smith to Jannick Gers to Smith/Gers procession of guitarists playing alongside Dave Murray. As to authenticity perceptions, a band with a differing vocalist may well be interpreted as 'fake' despite the presence of original instrumentalists or the degree to which songs are played with their original or most well-known musical forms.

Versions of reversioning

Elsewhere, I have written that popular cultural entities not only become understood from their initial appearance within a cultural milieu, but also become consciously re-scripted as historical appropriations of the past, thereby becoming infused with current agendas and current ideologies (Klypchak, 2007, 2013). The changed meaning from original experience through each subsequent version of experience adds additional layers of meanings thereby creating new versions of what the entity itself comes to signify, a process I term a 'reversion.' For rock bands with historical legacies, each subsequent presentation of the band as a nostalgic yet contemporary entity reversions the ways in which the whole of the band's past comes to be understood, often through the very selective manipulation of the artists or the record companies themselves. Inevitably, the later versions of the ways in which a band comes to present itself often offer contrasting details, emphases, or remembrances than what was expressed during those original moments. What had initially been claimed as factual in publicity materials concurrent with an album's release become challenged through 20 years of retellings of stories and subsequent reversioning.

With regard to the construction of perceived authenticity, reversions complicate the process of determining where exactly the 'true' nature of a band or a recording comes to be understood. As an example, the common practice of remastering or reissuing albums with bonus tracks or supplemental materials might serve to spark back catalogue sales but, in doing so, the common understanding of that record's 'authentic' form becomes altered. As the subsequent publicity push for the reissued records occurs, additional commentary on the material reversions the record's meanings. For example, when band members complain of having never been happy with the original product 20 years removed despite lauding its initial publication as being the best album of their respective careers (for example, Twisted Sister's 1984 *Stay Hungry* and subsequent rerecording of the same songs, *Still Hungry*, 20 years later), an anomalous construction of where 'real' or 'genuine' may ensue.

Similarly, when bands change members the whole of a band's ethos gets altered and reversions about the band's identity and history often follow suit.

Rock bands are both driven by motivations of art and commerce. The desire for popularity allows for not only more exposure of one's creative art, but also greater potential for profits. When it comes to the impact of line-up changes on arguments of authenticity, commerce-based arguments often take precedence as control of the band name can prove to be a key point of contention. As a marketing device, control over the band name is crucial for promotion and recognition. The established b(r)and name will not only resonate with the potential paying audience, but also will facilitate venue booking, booking fees and coverage in local publicity outlets. This becomes all the more important for the nostalgic band attempting to effectively reconnect with the contemporary public.

At its most extreme, bands like Queensryche, Saxon, L. A. Guns and Ratt have at times presented multiple iterations of the original group on tour, each performing shows claiming 'authentic' standing. In each of these instances, debate over the band's name revolved over arguments of precedent: being a member when the band had originated, having a long or longest tenure as a group member, being in the iteration of the band when greatest past popularity was achieved, or the relative contribution to the group's image and identity in establishing the brand name. Commonly, arguments were voiced positing that confused fans expecting certain performers or performances and receiving 'inauthentic' versions would cheapen the brand name. In one such example, the trademark lawsuit between Greg Ginn and his former Black Flag bandmates specifically cites 'copying and unauthorized use of the marks FLAG, BLACK FLAG, or the BLACK FLAG or variations thereof, causes irreparable injury to the plaintiff, including injury to his business reputation and dilution of the distinctive quality of the marks' as groundwork for the complaint being served (*SST v Rollins* [2013] CV13-5579 at 5–6). Similarly, Geoff Tate's complaint against his former Queensryche bandmates claims that 'to tour without Geoff Tate will lead to the destruction of the Queensryche name and brand, just as it has for countless other bands that dump their lead singer' (*Tate v Jackson* [2012] 1829–3 SEA at 2).

Here, attempts to reversion the band stem from whatever argument best caters to the respective party's personal, often financial, interests. The draw of being the 'classic line-up' understandably holds marketing power. However, the respective claims on the basis of brand name seem to go against the mythos of rock music as being artistically and not commercially driven. The celebratory camaraderie of a band performing onstage (or memories of the band at its commercial peak) becomes undermined by these squabbles, and an adversarial climate becomes written onto what otherwise might have been publically remembered in more idyllic fashion.

While bands like Saxon or Ratt certainly have dedicated fan-bases, the degree to which the bands represent cultural institutions pales in comparison to other bands representing reversions through their assorted line-up changes and public performances. In a form similar to the instances of Ratt or Saxon, the release of Guns N' Roses' *Chinese Democracy* album in 2008 provoked considerable fan debate as to whether it was a 'real' Guns N' Roses record since only vocalist Axl Rose remained associated to the band's name. Don Kaye's (2009) review of *Chinese Democracy* on Blabbermouth.net, a leading Internet source for hard rock and heavy metal happenings, epitomizes the common arguments:

> First of all, let's call it what it is: this is not a **GUNS N' ROSES** album. You can alter the line-ups of some bands more than others, replace singers or guitarists or even large chunks of personnel, but you can rarely replace an entire band, especially one made up during its peak years of such distinctive personalities, and still expect people to pretend it's the same. **GUNS N' ROSES** as we knew it has been gone for more than 10 years, with the departures of **Slash** and **Duff McKagan** providing the final nail in that particular coffin. The ever-shifting line-up of musicians we've seen over the intervening years has nothing to do with the image, attitude and dangerous magic of the original **GN'R**, and everything to do with who was patient and well-paid enough to cool their heels while **Axl** painstakingly worked out his demons and ground out this album.

Within a week of the review's publication, many of the 228 comments offered by readers of Kaye's review condemned the 'Axl Rose Band' for tarnishing their collective memory of GN'R, perhaps best summarized by Blabbermouth user Pigchop (2009):

> And this is why today's band running under the Guns N' Roses name is a travesty, or at least a nostalgic drop in the proverbial bucket of 'there was a time…when I was a king.' Guns N' Roses are one of those few bands who live on in the hearts of people…as they were at a specific point in time….Axl may own the name, but it's the

people who took up with the music – who happily lived with it – they own the memories of Guns N' Roses.

Romanticized notions of who and what constitutes 'authentic' encroach upon contemporary consumption. Similarly, in light of the nostalgic remembrances versus contemporary happenings, an icon like Axl Rose becomes subject to comparison to his own past; the rail-thin, slithery frontman of 'then' becomes lampooned for succumbing to the aging process (or resorting to plastic surgery as a simulated means of resisting the appearance of aging). A retromanic audience holds little patience for whatever does not conform to their nostalgic expectations of playing the hits as if nothing had transpired over the decades passed (Klosterman, 2001; Reynolds, 2011).

Like Guns N' Roses, KISS represents a band wherein line-up changes and performance practices raise authenticity challenges. From their emergence in the mid-1970s, the band has enjoyed a dedicated and substantial fan-base, the KISS Army, and considerable notoriety for their creation of distinctively costumed characters. Over the years, band leaders Gene Simmons and Paul Stanley remained consistent participants with a variety of differing drummers and guitar players taking the place of original members Peter 'The Cat' Criss and 'Space' Ace Frehley. In 1996, a reunion tour in which the original band members revisited their 1970s glory in full costume proved a box office success, grossing $43.6 million of revenue and ticket sales eclipsing $1.2 million (Sanders, 1996). While the subsequent *Psycho Circus* releases (including a record, a comic book, and an action figure series) thematically linked the materials to the mythology of the characters' origin stories, original members Frehley and Criss were once again dismissed from the band. They were respectively replaced by Tommy Thayer and Eric Singer. One key distinction in the changeover process emerged. In the past when line-up changes occurred during the make-up era, new band members took on new personas and new character styles. In this instance however, Thayer and Singer adopted the Celestial and Cat/King of Beasts personas previously held by Frehley and Criss respectively as direct replacements. As explained by Stanley:

We've built those characters over 35 years and the idea that anybody owns those is ridiculous. We were there when they were created and we've worked our butts off for 35 years, so the idea that we should have 'snail man' in the band is ridiculous. We did that at one point and realized that it really was a disservice to the fans because the fans know those four iconic figures. That's **KISS** to everybody, and whether someday somebody wears my makeup, I'd consider it an honour, quite honestly. It would mean that the band is continuing with the same philosophy and thriving without me.

(Rodman, 2009)

For a band with the historical investment in marketing the specific characters and the rhetorical foregrounding of 'KISStory' throughout their lengthy career, the choice to reversion the meanings of the original members as being simply 'characters' in the greater narrative of KISS challenges the past understandings of how exactly to interpret the communal band element versus being simply mechanically exchangeable parts. Predictably, the reactions of the metal community have been contentious. Across nine stories taken from Blabbermouth specifically dealing with the issue of the characters, commenters frequently complained about the 'cab' and the impropriety of recasting the iconic roles. One typical example comes from a Blabbermouth commenter using the moniker themonster00 (2009):

Each member created their own persona. It was unique to that person. Each were a star. All of them sang their own songs. Having Thayer and Singer use Ace & Peter's personas is asinine. Gene and Paul want it to look like the original band when it really isn't. Do you think Thayer and Singer will be singing their own songs on the next album? I think not. KISS is a tribute band now. There are no longer 4 stars in the band, unfortunately.

KISS's 2014 induction into the Rock and Roll Hall of Fame rekindled these same discursive themes once again as only the original four (Simmons, Stanley, Criss and Frehley) were honored and the likes of Thayer, Singer, Bruce Kulick, Mark St. John and Vinnie Vincent were selectively omitted. A very public exchange of ego-fueled condemnations between Stanley and the ousted original members ensued, wherein the legacy of the 'classic' era was simultaneously praised and problematized. New interpretations and new tales 40 years removed from the actual performances intermix in four memoirs of conflicting contents, with four voices claiming their particular version as being more authentic than the others (Epstein, 2014). Add to these voices Simmons' multiple books, the *KISS: The Early Years* photography collection with Simmons and Stanley as offering primary commentary, and the authorized biography penned by David Leaf and Ken Sharp, and the waters are muddied even further. Without any sense of irony or self-reflexivity, Stanley's condemnations of his bandmates' memoirs as 'nothing more than self-serving fantasies or delusions or love letters to themselves' (Grow, 2014) might be easily turned upon itself, wherein Stanley selectively aims to rework the past (recalling the earlier mention of Greil Marcus), into the story he thinks he knew.

Like Guns N' Roses, the idea that the integrity of the authentic band is compromised and becomes something inauthentic ('a tribute band now') speaks to the problems within Stanley's professed reversion. The historical authenticity represented by the original members becomes tarnished into a form of simulation undermining the past versions of KISStory that had been well established and learned. Reversioned KISS becomes PanicKISS, which equates to, in Baudrillard's (1994) terms, 'a simulacrum, never again exchanging for what is real, but exchanging in itself, in an uninterrupted circuit without reference or circumference' (p. 170). The role of individual or personal identity becomes interspersed with character and mythos and the fiction of the comic book blurs with the dialogues of disputed memoirs. KISS morphs into its own hype and propaganda wherein there is little telling where any speck of the authentic might derive.

Paralleling the KISS scenario, actions carried forth by the most recent incarnation of the band Van Halen offer yet another means where line-up changes have sparked reversioning tactics resulting in authenticity anomalies. Following original vocalist David Lee Roth's departure in 1986, Van Halen continued forth with a replacement vocalist, Sammy Hagar, and extended their run of commercial success. Nevertheless, many in the fan-base routinely called for the reformation of the initial line-up of Roth, bassist Michael Anthony, and the Van Halen brothers, guitarist Eddie and drummer Alex. Hagar's departure and a period of relative inactivity for the Van Halen camp found Anthony playing music with Hagar. In 2006, the first rumors of a Roth reunion surfaced and by October, presumptions were that a full-fledged reunion would take place. However, in November of 2006, Van Halen management announced that a tour would take place with Roth, but with Eddie's 15-year-old son, Wolfgang, serving as the band's bass player and not Anthony. For the tour, Anthony's backing vocals would be sampled and triggered so that the 'classic Van Halen' sound could be achieved despite Anthony's non-participation.

Further complicating the idea of 'classic Van Halen,' in August of 2007 the official Van Halen website presented altered album art for two of the Roth/Anthony era records. For 1980's *Women and Children First*, the cover photo of all four members was replaced by simply the band's logo and the album's title. More tellingly, the debut record retained the photos of Roth and the Van Halen brothers, but replaced Anthony with a picture of Wolfgang in his stead. Immediate controversy ensued as the reversioned album art was problematized. Anthony's name was later found as being removed from the ASCAP song writing credits for the whole of the *1984* record. Most recently, a Van Halen version of the video game *Guitar Hero* omitted all mention of Michael Anthony and all recordings from 1986 on. Curiously, the game's trailer has depictions of the *1984* era personas as well as contemporary versions of the band. For the past constructions of Wolfgang (roughly eight years prior to his actual birth), he is shown wearing one of Eddie's well-known outfits from the time.

The technological manipulation of the band's past coupled with the targeted marketing toward a contemporary *Guitar Hero* fan-base offers the possibility of erasing Michael Anthony out of younger generation's reference points for Van Halen. The relative notion of 'authentic' becomes convoluted in that the retelling of the band's history, as presented by Van Halen's management, reversions the relative importance of the roles played by Hagar, Anthony, or even one album participant Gary Cherone. In large part, one might come to understand these choices as a desire to retain profits for those in the band instead of paying royalties to Anthony for the use of his image or as a version of petty feuding stemming from an acrimonious breakup. A similar pragmatic rationale might be ascribed to the 30th anniversary reissue of Judas Priest's *British Steel* which diminishes the presence of drummer Dave Holland, most likely motivated by eschewing the stigma of Holland's 2004 sexual assault conviction. Regardless, the choices made and the actions taken raise questions as to where the 'real' Van Halen comes to be understood in terms of its construction within the larger historical narrative of the band.

The circumstances surrounding the reissues of two Ozzy Osbourne albums offer yet another technological consideration for where we might find reversioning and issues of perceived authenticity in line-up changes. Following the 2002 reissues of *Blizzard of Ozz* and *Diary of a Madman*, a number of publicized arguments surrounded song writing credits and royalty payments ensued. The key players to this dispute were Sharon Osbourne, manager and wife of band figurehead Ozzy Osbourne, and the band members who recorded the bass and drums on the records, Bob Daisley and Lee Kerslake. Unlike the remainder of the reissues in which remastering occurred or bonus tracks were added to the tracklist, the reissued *Blizzard* and *Diary* records were substantially altered. As a means to avoid further royalty payments to Daisley and Kerslake, the bass and drum parts were rerecorded by the contracted members of Ozzy's current band, Robert Trujillo and Mike Bordin. The re-recordings offered minimal changes to the parts themselves and no definitive declarations were made on the album art indicating that the reissues did not contain the original recordings from 1980 or 1981. As such, those buying and hearing the re-versioned tracks 'Crazy Train' or 'Flying High Again' in a historical framework of the initial forms are left with an altered perception of where the authentic comes to be understood.

L. A. Guns, Queensryche, Guns N' Roses, KISS, Van Halen, Ozzy Osbourne – in each instance, the collective memory of these acts becomes altered by the ongoing adaptations and additions made to their respective narratives. The reversions of where a band's 'true' nature lies becomes a blending of those past stories coupled with whatever additional selective manipulations get layered onto the preceding knowledge base. For a subculturally focused music form like hard rock or heavy metal, perceived authenticity is a key component to establishing and maintaining status within the whole. As seen in the preceding instances however, conflict between subcultural ethos and contemporary practices raise questions as to where one places one's evaluative assessments – in the past, the present, or somewhere in between. PanicRockBand (be it PanicKISS, PanicVanHalen or whatever other reversioning outfit) ensues.

Metal memories and memoir: Personalizing the then to now

Prominent in Kahn-Harris's 2013 keynote is the considerable impact of technology on the metal community. In the age of metal abundance, the sheer amount and the degree of access to metal-related materials (be it music recordings, video clips, reference/archive materials, publicity outlets, vendors, artist and label webpages, community networks, etc.) affords the metal fan a remarkable array of prospects for experiencing metal in ways that were before now geographically, economically, and/or consumptively possible. Despite unprecedented abundance and diversity, Kahn-Harris (2013a) laments the loss of the 'aura' which metal scarcity and rarity held. The joy of discovery of some obscure new band, the successful completion of the hunt in obtaining a sought after demo, or the thrill at finding that new piece of metal scholarship diminishes as the Internet alleviates the 'work' of such endeavors. In his words:

Yet metal's contemporary abundance has made me realize how important *scarcity* used to be in the pleasures that metal scenes offered. It may be only a memory now. However, it still preserves that necessary halo that makes metal still feel fresh and new. I expect others feel that way too.

(Kahn-Harris, 2013a)

Where I have offered versions of PanicRockBand, the same sorts of inquiries might be explored across all participants of the metal community. Given the generational spans of metal cohorts (of which I would label myself, as a teen in the 1980s, as being of a MTV-era/mainstream cohort), retrospection to our historical points of contact with metal seems imperative. Like Keith, my own experiences as a collector and a learner shapes/informs the ways in which I engage and conceive metal happenings. Like Keith, I understand those seemingly bittersweet moments when learning of the new book, the next set of metal journal articles, or that upcoming publication series that adds to the stack of resources I seem to be falling further behind in hunting down and adding to an ever-growing archive (let alone finding the time for reading). I see this sort of reaction as deeply seated in nostalgia and one which inevitably imparts the personalized memoir of metal memories.

Svetlana Boym (2001) depicts nostalgia as 'a sentiment of loss and displacement, but it is also a romance of one's own fantasy' (p. xiii) that occurs in two core forms, restorative and reflexive. Where restorative nostalgia emphasizes the sense of place and the desire to return/rebuild/relive the past as a 'perfect snapshot . . . freshly painted in its "original image" (to) remain eternally young' (p. 49), reflective nostalgia attends to history and the individual. 'Reflective nostalgia does not pretend to rebuild the mythical place called home; it is "enamored of distance, not of the referent itself" . . . a nostalgic rendezvous with oneself is not always a private affair. Voluntary and involuntary recollections of an individual intertwine with collective memories' (p. 50).

The 'imperfect process of remembrance' (p. 41) which Boym's restorative nostalgia entails coincides with the ways in which Ben Yagoda considers memoir. In his historical account of memoir as a literary form, Yagoda (2009) routinely highlights the role of story and authorial choice within memoir and the pragmatic reasons for its being. Exact recall of any event, let alone those long ago (or in the case of rock star memoirs recounting tales of severe substance incapacitations) is implausible. 'In fact, there is an inherent and irresolvable conflict between the capabilities of memory and the demands of narrative. The latter demands specifics; the former is really bad at them' (p. 109). I offer reflective nostalgia as an intermediary bringing forth some of those elements of imperfection along the way. The desire to infuse the romanticism of nostalgia into the memoir memories being conveyed creates the backdrop for where panicmetalmemories emerge.

This contextualizing brings me back to the question introduced earlier: 'wasn't Twisted Sister always camp?' When faced with the question, my own version of panicmetalmemory ensued as I was unable to displace myself from the duality of my reaction: the seemingly obvious interpretation of the 40-something adult scholar conflated with the wholly invested teenage celebrant I hold as part of my own metal memoir. Even now, months removed from the event, I find myself conflicted. This illustrates the sort of challenge metal studies faces regarding metal and memory – how to stay attuned to our personalized memories despite hindsight's glaring critical/theoretical/philosophical clarity. In the keynote, Kahn-Harris (2013d) extends a call for reflexivity with 'unflinching looks at the past and the present,' (para. 13) yet a situation like confronting my past naiveté has me flinching considerably in trying to accommodate the layered experiences of my metal past. Consider one of the strategies Kahn-Harris (2013e) offers as a 'future' metal prospect: the exploration of mediocrity, mining what otherwise might have fallen into the dustbin of history to see where those records of the past might inform and inspire us. I see such a prospect in connection to panicmetalmemories wherein the divide between my year-of-release consumption of something like Tattoo's *Blood Red* record (1988) is vastly differentiated from what I might think of such a record today. My personalized 'truth' to that record may well have shifted given my awareness of gender politics, of metal aesthetics beyond the anthemic power chords, or of sensitivity to the performativity of rebelliousness, but the innumerable and repeated cycling through the cassette while driving throughout the suburban Central Illinois remain. Once engrossed by cultural studies scholarship and a litany of theoretical and philosophical referents, the 'aura' of reflective nostalgia falls susceptible to silencing. Perhaps this is where fan memoirs like Chuck Klosterman's *Fargo Rock City* (2001) or Seb Hunter's *Hell Bent for Leather* (2004) might serve as reminders of how fan narratives and the recollections of the past connect to how metal remembers itself. Each successive iteration/generation/cohort of metal fandom imparts their own contribution to the memory mix, and there is value to staying connected to initial impressions, recognizing self-reflexively how those impressions infuse the panicmetalmemories to come.

Bibliography

Baudrillard, J. (1994) 'Simulacra and Simulation,' *Jean Baudrillard: Selective Writings*, ed. M. Poster (Stanford: Stanford University Press), pp. 66–185.

Boym, S. (2001) *The Future of Nostalgia* (New York: Basic Books).

Epstein, D. (26 March 2014) 'Kiss and Tell: Comparing the Original Band Members' Memoirs,' *Rolling Stone*. Retrieved from: http://www.rollingstone.com/music/news/KISS-and-tell-comparing-the-original-band-members-memoirs-20140326.

Grossberg, L. (1992) *We Gotta Get Out of this Place: Popular Conservatism and Postmodern Culture* (London: Routledge).

Grow, K. (11 March 2014) 'Paul Stanley Likens Other Rockers' Memoirs to Toilet Paper,' *Rolling Stone*. Retrieved from: http://www.rollingstone.com/music/news/KISS-paul-stanley-likens-other-rockers-memoirs-to-toilet-paper-20140311.

Hill, P. (1996) ' "Authenticity" in Contemporary Music,' *Tempo, New Series*, 159 (December), pp. 2–8.

Hunter, S. (2004) *Hell Bent for Leather: Confessions of a Heavy Metal Addict* (New York: Harper Collins).

Kahn-Harris, K. (29 November 2013a) 'Too Much Metal,' *Souciant*. Retrieved from: http://souciant.com/2013/11/too-much-metal/.

Kahn-Harris, K. (6 December 2013b) 'Invisible Metal,' *Souciant*. Retrieved from: http://souciant.com/2013/12/invisible-metal/.

Kahn-Harris, K. (12 December 2013c) 'Metal at a Standstill,' *Souciant*. Retrieved from: http://souciant.com/2013/12/music-at-a-standstill/.

Kahn-Harris, K. (20 December 2013d) 'The Metal Future,' *Souciant*. Retrieved: http://souciant.com/2013/12/the-metal-future/.

Kahn-Harris, K. (27 December 2013e) 'Slow Metal,' *Souciant*. Retrieved from: http://souciant.com/2013/12/slow-metal/.

Kahn-Harris, K. (10 January 2014a) 'Breaking Metal Boundaries,' *Souciant*. Retrieved from: http://souciant.com/2014/01/breaking-metals-boundaries/.

Kahn-Harris, K. (17 January 2014b) 'Metal Beyond Metal,' *Souciant*. Retrieved from: http://souciant.com/2014/01/metal-beyond-metal/.

Kaye, D. (2009) Review of *Chinese Democracy*: Blabbermouth. Retrieved from: http://www.blabbermouth.net/cdreviews/chinese-democracy/.

Klosterman, C. (2001) *Fargo Rock City: A Heavy Metal Odyssey in Rural North Dakota* (New York, NY: Scribner).

Klypchak, B. (2007) *Performed Identity: Heavy Metal Musicians between 1984 and 1991* (Saarbrucken: VDM Verlag).

Klypchak, B. (2013) ' "How You Gonna See Me Now": Recontextualizing Metal Artists and Moral Panics,' *Heavy Metal: Controversies and Countercultures*, eds. T. Hjelm, K. Kahn-Harris, & M. Levine (London: Equinox), pp. 36–49.

Kroker, A., Kroker, M., & Cook, D. (1989) *Panic Encyclopedia: The Definitive Guide to the Postmodern Scene* (New York, NY: St. Martin's Press).

Marcus, G. (1995) *The Dustbin of History* (Cambridge, MA: Harvard University Press).

Moore, A. (2002) 'Authenticity as Authentication,' *Popular Music*, 21(2), pp. 209–223.

Reynolds, S. (2011) *Retromania: Pop Culture's Addiction to Its Own Past* (New York, NY: Macmillan).

Rodman, S. (29 September 2009). 'Still Made for Lovin' You,' *Boston Globe*. Retrieved from: http://www.boston.com/ae/music/articles/2009/09/29/paul_stanley_and_KISS_still_made_for_lovin_you/.

Sanders, A. (26 December 1996) 'Year's Top-grossing Tour Sealed with KISS,' *Variety*. Retrieved from: http://variety.com/1996/scene/vpage/year-s-top-grossing-tour-sealed-with-kiss-1117436237/.

themonster00. (28 November 2009). 'KISS' Paul Stanley: Creating New Characters for Eric Carr and Vinnie Vincent Was "A Misstep" [Online Forum Comment]. *Blabbermouth*. Retrieved from: http://www.blabbermouth.net/news/KISS-paul-stanley-creating-new-characters-for-eric-carr-and-vinnie-vincent-was-a-misstep/.

Walser, R. (1993) *Running with the Devil: Power, Gender, and Madness in Heavy Metal Music* (Middletown, CT: Wesleyan University Press).

Yagoda, B. (2009) *Memoir: A History* (New York, NY: Riverhead Books).

5

Metal at the Fringe: A Historical Perspective on Puerto Rico's Underground Metal Scene

Nelson Varas-Díaz
University of Puerto Rico

Sigrid Mendoza
University of Puerto Rico

Eliut Rivera
Ponce School of Medicine

and

Osvaldo González-Sepúlveda
Ponce School of Medicine

'Heavy Metal in the Caribbean?' This is probably the most common reaction we have had as a research team when discussing our work with other scholars. Even academics living in Puerto Rico seem completely unaware that the island has had a strong local metal scene for the past 30 years. This is not surprising, as most people perceive Puerto Rico as an island paradise where tropical rhythms like Salsa, Bomba and Plena are mostly prevalent in the sonic landscape. In this sense, heavy metal fans and the community they have developed must be addressed as a marginalized group that has been almost completely forgotten by the general population. Their multiple contributions to music in Puerto Rican music will mostly go unnoticed by local historians and scholars. To most individuals, members of the local metal scene are predominantly anonymous individuals who have contributed little to local culture. Their stories are not part of the island's official history.

Because of this overlooked history, constructing the story of Puerto Rico's local metal scene is almost an act of cultural defiance. It entails informing the island's official history with the voices of the cultural outcasts. Of course, challenging official historical accounts is not necessarily a new endeavor. For example, feminist studies have documented how historical accounts usually foster a patriarchal view of the world by negating women's roles in social development (Torres, 1998). Anticolonial researchers have highlighted how imperial regimes silence native voices when the empire recalls their history (Fanon, 1965, 1967; Memmi, 1965). Indigenous peoples of the Americas have seen first-hand how their life stories are told through the Eurocentric gaze of the colonial researcher (Tuhiwai Smith, 2012). In this same logic, the story of heavy metal in Puerto Rico has been systematically overlooked in light of archaic conceptualizations of what is culturally appropriate music. Fortunately, scholarly research on metal music is beginning to change this situation.

Scholarly work on the field of metal music studies has aimed to describe the development of this genre (Christe, 2004; Walser, 1993). These efforts are important and necessary in order to have general accounts of how this music genre came into existence and flourished. The globalization of heavy metal is in full effect and it can now be found and heard in many places around the world. Research on places like Nepal (Green, 2012), Israel (Kahn-Harris, 2012), Japan (Kawano & Hosokawa, 2012), Malta (Bell, 2012), Turkey (Hecker, 2012), South Africa (Hoad, 2014) and Egypt (LeVine, 2008) evidence how metal has crossed the borders (Wallach et al., 2012). Therefore, a current historical perspective on metal music would now be incomplete without the inclusion of the multiple social and cultural geographies that produce and consume metal. Keith Kahn-Harris has contributed to awareness of this issue by recognizing that metal scenes can vary according to their location in relation to the core places where metal is produced and consumed (Kahn-Harris, 2007). Scenes that exist at the periphery, and which sometimes are removed from epicenters of wealth and resources, face different challenges and have dissimilar outcomes than those at the cores. Just like any other community in the world, material and geographical variables influence metal scenes. Kahn-Harris's recognition of the scenes at the periphery has played an important role in placing attention to metal scenes throughout the world.

Jeremy Wallach's work on metal and globalization has also allowed researchers to have a more pluralist approach to metal music (Wallach et al., 2012). He has called for an approach to metal scenes that highlights the role of diversity and fluidity, and avoids focusing exclusively on the commonalities of its manifestations throughout the globe. This is accompanied by a call to expand research on metal scenes outside of Anglo–American contexts, in order to understand how socio-cultural factors in these settings shape metal music.

Academic research on heavy metal music that aims to document how scene members recall their history can benefit from a social constructionist framework (Holstein & Gubrium, 2007). From this approach, history can be theorized as a social artifact developed though the narration of common experiences and events. This approach has been inherently present in the construction of communal identities, specifically nations as documented by Benedict Anderson (Anderson, 1983). Sharing a common historical narrative, be it objectively verifiable or not by outsiders, can serve to strengthen emotional bonds within communities. Metal scenes are no exception, albeit in a smaller scale, as they can construct historical narratives as part of their community-building processes. Research that addresses the historical aspect of metal scenes can: (1) provide in-depth descriptions of these communities, (2) yield important information on how their context influence their development and (3) foster a better understanding of the efforts that scenes at the periphery undergo to survive. Therefore, historical research on scene formation can be part of the community building process, without neglecting its academic objectives.

Unfortunately, although small scenes at the periphery have begun to receive attention (i.e. Riches & Lashua, 2014; Snell, 2014), those in the Caribbean setting are still understudied and there is little work on their histories. For the purpose of this chapter, we focus on Puerto Rico's metal scene.

Puerto Rico: A case of academic neglect in heavy metal music research

Puerto Rico lived under Spanish rule from 1493 to 1898 and therefore has a predominant Hispanic tradition and uses Spanish as its everyday language. At the end of the Spanish-American War in 1898, the island was conceded to the United States, and became a non-incorporated territory. Puerto Ricans were given US citizenship in 1917 (Fernández, 1996). Although some argue that this was a gesture of good will toward local people, others stress that this enabled the US to draft Puerto Ricans into war while also fostering an anticolonial appearance in the face of international pressures. US Congress possesses control over areas such as the applicability of federal law and jurisdiction of federal courts, citizenship, commerce, currency, migration, patent laws, communications, mail, customs, air and sea transportation, military service, international relations and treaty development (Varas-Diaz & Serrano-Garcia, 2003). The colonial relationship of the US with Puerto Rico has been widely researched and documented in social sciences literature. The research reflects Puerto Rico as a country with distinctive Hispanic influences, confronted with its vague integration into the US. Puerto Rico is deeply embedded in what academics have labeled the 'colonial dilemma,' which means that it is a Caribbean community existing as a non-incorporated territory of a larger and culturally different nation (Meléndez & Meléndez, 1999).

In this context, research in music as a cultural phenomenon has historically neglected heavy metal as a valid issue to study. Scholars have pointed to this problem before in other settings. For example, Michelle Phillipov has documented how heavy metal music and death metal in particular have been overlooked by academic researchers who have focused on punk and hip-hop (2012). These specific forms of musical expressions have been deemed worthy of analysis as they are interpreted as expressions of political resistance for socially oppressed groups. In this scenario, heavy metal is perceived as a musical genre too concerned with individualism to be political and therefore less worthy of analysis. A similar critique has been pointed out by Andy Brown, who has written on how subculture and post-subculture studies have neglected and almost systematically ignored heavy metal music (Brown, 2011).

The neglect of heavy metal music as a valid and important subject of research and study has also been manifested in Puerto Rico for political and cultural reasons. For example, academic researchers have focused on salsa as a more native manifestation of music (Quintero Rivera, 1998). Due to the important role that Puerto Ricans in the island and New York have had in the development of this style of music, local researchers have focused on this as a legitimate area of study to understand Puerto Rican musical preferences and celebration of local national identities. In this sense, researching a musical style that is deeply associated with 'being Puerto Rican' is interpreted as a challenge to the ever-growing integration of local people to the United States' 'melting pot.' Highlighting the history of local autochthonous music has been considered as a mechanism to critically examine the effects of colonization.

Similar attention has been placed recently on reggaeton music, which mixes traditional reggae with other genres like salsa, bomba and electronica. This native and more modern musical genre has received local attention from research for different reasons. Specifically, Puerto Rico is in the midst of a moral panic scenario over concerns for the music's glorification of violence and its highly sexual content. It has been the focus of critique over concerns on its perceived detrimental effects on youth (Román, 1998). Unlike salsa music, which is studied as a source of national pride, reggaeton has been addressed by most as a social problem.

Heavy metal music has been neglected as an area of interest in local research, as it is considered neither a source of national pride nor an issue of concern due to its potential problematic consequences. As of today, heavy metal in Puerto Rico remains an unexplored phenomenon in metal studies. In this scenario, documenting the history of heavy metal music and the underground community that produces it becomes an important contribution to the history of metal in general.

A communal approach to historical documentation

This chapter is situated within a larger section of this edited book focusing on the subject of memory. Through a focus on memory, we aim to examine the past in the process of understanding the development of heavy metal music in different contexts. This is not an easy endeavor, as a historical approach toward the development of heavy metal music in different contexts throughout the world will always be mediated by recollection. That recollection or remembrance will be based on existing physical documents such as fanzines or demos, and throughout the memory of events that participants have from a specific scene. Therefore, establishing the history of a particular heavy metal scene will inevitably need to be approached as a co-constructed phenomenon whose final rendition will be a combination of facts and experiences from past scene members, current participants, and the researchers.

Our team implemented a mixed method research design using ethnographic observation, in-depth qualitative interviews and a quantitative survey[1] (Atkinson, 2001; Tashakkori & Teddlie, 2003). Interviewees also provided documents that were related to the emergence of the local scene such as fanzines, event flyers, pictures and videos. The implementation of these research techniques was accompanied by epistemological principles from Community Based Participatory Research (CBPR) (Jason, 2004; Whyte, 1991). This approach stresses the important role of community members in the development of their own historical recollection and participation in research-technique development and implementation (McIntyre, 2008). Participants in the study become engaged actors in the development of the design and its research techniques, fostering collaborative relations of equality with the research team.

Some examples of the application of this CBPR approach in our study included: 1) meeting with scene leaders as part of the ethnographic component of the study, 2) developing data-gathering forms in collaboration with scene members, 3) engaging in data analysis in collaboration with scene members, and 4) coauthoring results from the study with key participants. Also, we held several meetings with multiple generations of the local metal scene in order to have them recollect their story about the development of a local metal scene. These events allowed us to transmit to the scene our participatory approach in which they would collaborate in the co-construction of their historical narrative. This would not be a story told 'about them' by distant researchers, but rather, jointly narrated by the research team and the local metal community.

Although members of the metal scene describe their origins (i.e. initiation of a collective identity) in 1985, it should be recognized that rock music in Puerto Rico dates back to the 1960s. The Beatles, Elvis Presley and the Beach Boys were part of the sounds consumed by local teenagers. Local musicians, like those that were part of the 'Nueva Ola' (New Wave), would replicate those sounds as part of their music. Heavier sounds would be enjoyed at the 'Festival Mar y Sol' (Sea and Sun Festival) held in the town of Manatí in 1972. The event was inspired by the Woodstock festival and it allowed locals to see bands like Emerson, Lake & Palmer, Mahavishnu Orchestra and Alice Cooper, among others. Black Sabbath was included in the list, but never made it to the island in light of the festival's lack of organization. Also, local rock bands were present in the island at the time. Bands like Black Century (1977), Pelican in Flight (1978) and Quantum (1978) would highlight the rock-oriented sounds of local music. It is with this historical backdrop that metal music would reach the island's shores in the 1980s.

Period 1: Emergence (1985–1992)

This period is characterized by a truly grassroots process that aided in the development of the local scene. Participants frequently described this moment as the 'kids with dreams' period when young adolescents emulated what they saw and heard in formal albums (mostly rock oriented). Most metal fans reported becoming exposed to rock and metal music via older brothers and parents who consumed rock music (i.e. Led Zeppelin, KISS, Van Halen):

I would say that metal, and rock music in general, influenced my way of being a lot, definitely. I started listening to this music since I was in third grade because I had an older brother who was five years older than me. Since very early on I had my rock T-shirts and things, and that is something that permeates you, you know? I bought my first album when I was eight, ha ha.

(Ionex Cruz, Guitarist for the Christian Thrash Metal Band, Xacrosaint)

These younger kids then felt the need for more aggressive sounds, allowing for heavy metal music to immerse their lives. This transition from rock to heavy metal was fostered by social interaction with friends who competed for heavier sounds amongst themselves. Also, more graphic album covers, identified in the few stores that sold rock and heavy metal music, were associated with heavier sounds and were therefore purchased and consumed. Some of these albums were purchased without having heard the music, and solely based on the perceived 'heavy' nature of the artwork. As reported in other countries, tape trading played a vital role in the fast dissemination of metal music in Puerto Rico.

The initial exposures to heavy metal music, and the call to emulate these new sounds, led young people in Puerto Rico to start local bands. These initial bands were very much determined by geography and accessibility. Friends from the same neighborhoods would inevitably start playing together, not because of their shared musical abilities, but due to the impossibility of finding other like-minded people beyond their immediate surroundings. Most bands emanated in lower-middle class metropolitan areas, and practiced in their parents' garages. These garages were not enclosed as those usually found in the United States – basements are uncommon in Puerto Rico's metropolitan areas – and therefore their music was immediately experienced by a large sector of their local communities. These 'marquesina' (garage) practice sessions would usually turn into small shows where neighbors would come in and listen, regardless of the bands quality:

... we also played in 'marquesinas.' We called those 'marquesina' parties, but it was mostly hanging out with friends. I don't see that as something transcendent. It was something like 'let's play in this guy's house because he's a drummer.' He would set up his drum kit and then other musicians would follow, and we would play there. But it was nothing formal. We didn't say 'let's have a party and charge for the entrance.' It was like a get together in a musician's house and everybody took a turn at the instruments.

(Marisol Marrero, Drummer for the Christian Thrash Metal Band,
Xacrosaint)

Some bands from this period describe their practice sessions as truly communal events, even dressing up in metal-related attire to put on a show for those who came. It was in 'marquesinas' and in front of neighbors that emerging metal bands polished their craft.

Once these bands became more proficient, they began to play shows outside of their houses. Very few businesses would provide them legitimate spaces to play, so the emergence of bars that would allow heavy metal music to be played was an important stepping-stone in the formation of a metal scene. Some of these included 'Steps' (later known as 'Fuego Fuego'), 'La Casona,' and 'Anything Goes.' When these spaces were not available, metal bands would stage shows wherever they could. For example, some now legendary shows in the local metal scene took place in a 'lechonera,' a local rural shop that specializes in raising, preparing and selling roasted pork. Metal bands from this period used these spaces to their advantage, gained experience and were ready to disseminate their sound to a larger audience.

At this stage in the scene's development, bands were acutely aware of the impact of tape trading with the United States and Europe. Bands decided to begin developing demos of their own in order to disseminate their music to a larger audience. The process of recording demos was accompanied by a lack of available technology and economic resources. Demos were recorded live in practice sessions directly to boom boxes, and only those who were luckier found resources to record using reel-to-reel technology. The artwork for the demos was frequently hand drawn by band members or friends. Bands like Cardinal Sin (1989), Powerlord (1991), Crypta (1993) and Undamaged (1991) put out the most influential demos of this period.

This period was also characterized by a strong sense of community and camaraderie among scene members and bands. Bands from different genres within metal music would come together during shows. It was common to see events in which glam, thrash and hardcore bands would share the stage, a phenomenon that would rarely be seen in later periods in the scene:

We were playing in a really heavy metal band and met another band that was playing glam rock, but we went to them and said 'look do you want to play together? You have your crowd and we have ours if we get together we will have a great party.' Although the music was very different the environment was there, you know? Then, those people that saw us started forming their own bands and as soon as there were many other events our job was way easier. (...) That union also produced a lot of fans from different camps...and we respected them when they came to present their craft.

(John Dones, Guitarist for Thrash Metal Band *Cardinal Sin*)

This sense of unity emanated from the need to stick together in a cultural setting that perceived heavy metal as completely alien. For example, in 1987 Governor Rafael Hernández Colón was interviewed while participating at the 'International Day of Salsa' concert. When asked about the music that best represented Puerto Ricans he stated

Salsa comes from the heart of the people of Puerto Rico...from the soul of Puerto Rico...and it's our own expression, ours...universal... that has led us to all parts of the world. Rock is a phenomenon that comes from outside. Many Puerto Ricans enjoy it, which is great, too, but it's not intrinsic to the heart of our people.

Politicians were concerned with the potential implications of the Americanization of Puerto Rican youth. MTV had reached the island in 1981 and now direct access to rock music (and metal in 1987 via the Headbanger's Ball show) was available for youth. This concern was best exemplified by the war between salsa music consumers and those who listened to rock music. The 'Cocolos (salsa listeners and followers) vs. Rockeros (rock or heavy metal consumers)' debate could be best described as a form of cultural war for the musical heart of Puerto Ricans between those who consumed local music (salsa) versus foreign imports (rock and metal music). The debate neglected to see the ways in which Puerto Rican youth had assumed metal music as their own and had their emerging local heroes.

Local thrash metal band Cardinal Sin, has been recognized as the most important group of this period. Formed in 1984, the band released two demos entitled *Infanticide* (1989) and *Querer es Poder* (Where there's a will there's a way) (1991). In 2004, they released their demos on a CD entitled *Resurrection* (Cardinal Sin, 2004). The band migrated in 1989 to Boston, Massachusetts, as part of their effort to infiltrate the US thrash metal scene.

Cardinal Sin played with a lot of bands in Boston. A lot of them were local but we also played with bands like Death Angel, Forbidden, White Zombie, Biohazard, Meliah Rage, Wargasm...we were included in the camp as national acts and afterwards there were about ten local bands. As soon as we started playing we started generating a buzz and were getting better shows with the bands, with better local bands.

(José Rodríguez Grau, drummer for thrash metal band
Cardinal Sin)

Cardinal Sin was the first Puerto Rican metal band to be reviewed in well-known magazines, specifically *Metal Maniacs*. They would return to Puerto Rico in 1992 as part of the tour 'La Isla en Cantos' (The Island in Pieces). Although unsigned, Cardinal Sin would go to inspire the local metal scene in terms of the quality of their recordings and the possibility of migrating to find exposure in the metal world. Still today, their peers regard them as the most influential metal band in Puerto Rico emanating from this period.

In the later years of this period, the emergence of what could be considered a metal community was in full bloom. The scene was now more organized with well-known establishments to play music and a healthy dose of tape trading of local band demos. The metal community gravitated toward shopping malls as hangout spaces, in particular Plaza las Américas, which was the largest mall at the time. The mall housed a local record shop called Discomanía which would serve as the meeting place for metal-related interactions.

In the metropolitan area there was a ritual, which I also participated in, of meeting in 'Plaza las Américas' [shopping mall] every Friday. It was somewhat funny because the first time I went there I thought 'okay, everyone here is dressing like a member of a band that is about to play.' You know, with a bullet belt...ha ha. All that clothing just to hang out and buy albums! Then people would handout flyers for upcoming shows. Bands like Cardinal Sin, Rebel Rose, Rockshot and Soul Hunter were there. Those were bands that were way up there with their skill levels and their instruments...organizing shows and handing out flyers. It was there that you found out about the activities.

(Ramón Ortiz, Guitarist for local metal band Puya)

Fanzines sprung up and allowed for communication between local scene members and other international scenes. Out of all these fanzines, *Enthroned*, which was edited by Rafael Bracero, stood out as the most comprehensive.

...there was always a need for information and obviously the local scene lacked a lot of it. There were several fanzines then, but mine was in English because I had a vision which was more international. I wanted to project myself in an international level, not only in Spanish. Spanish was my native tongue, but it would limit me...I would do a lot of trading with editors of other fanzines, and they would always ask what was going on here. When they would see bands like Organic in the fanzine, they would ask about it. I would tell them 'here's the demo, here is their address.'

(Rafael Bracero, Fanzine Editor)

In 1991, Puerto Rico's first heavy metal music store opened in the town of Las Piedras. The shop was founded under the leadership of Ray López and it was named Thrash Corner Records (TCR). The store was situated inside Ray's family-owned print shop, and it started as a small display cabinet with only a few international records. TCR would provide local metal fans with extreme music that was unavailable to them in traditional music outlets. Visiting TCR would entail a trip outside the metropolitan area, which was difficult for young consumers. Still, it would be considered an important rite of passage for local metal fans. TCR would play a vital role in the development of the local scene by establishing collaborations with other labels and distributors outside of the island and hosting the first visit of an underground metal band from the US (i.e. Nuclear Death and Impétigo). The show was opened by local band Organic Infest, the first extreme band in Puerto Rico to be signed to a US label (JL America). TCR continues to play a vital part of the development of the local scene even today.

In this period, metal fans got their first radio show under the leadership of John Rodríguez (better known as 'Papo' the Metal Kid) at the Mega Station 106 FM radio station, which was active from 1990 to 1994. The show allowed local metal bands to hit the airwaves and showcase their talent. He would also create Brutal Noise Records, the first local label to sign Puerto Rican bands.

Rock was recognized as an established art form in the island when the University of Puerto Rico hosted the First Meeting of National Rock in 1991 (*Primer Encuentro de Rock Nacional*). Although metal bands were absent from the event, local experimental band Whisker Biscuit would play. The band is usually considered as the initial manifestation of what would later become the local band Puya, the most widely recognized metal band outside of Puerto Rico. A year later, in 1992, Iron Maiden would visit Puerto Rico. This was the first time an international heavy metal band of this size would visit the island and play for an organized

Table 5.1 Salient local metal bands from each period of Puerto Rico's metal scene[*]

Period 1: 1985–1992

Apocalips	Golpe Justo	Rebel Rose
Cardinal Sin	Habacuc	Red Steel
Cat Zaphire	Kileria	Rock Shott
Corrupt Society	Lápida	Sekel
Crackhouse	Legacy	Soul Hunter
Crisalis	Mattador	Spitfire
Crypta	Mindscrape	Tour de Force
Deathless	Morbid Death	Undamaged
Decadence	Mutant	Velyal
Dukes	Nonpoint Factor	Xacrosaint
Firecross	Organic Infest	
Godless	Power Lord	

Period 2: 1993–2000

After Omega	Infectoria	Sicamol
Cadaver	Morbid Death	Tavú
Cannibal Massacre	Occultism	Tierra de Nadie
Darkened Skies	Osamenta	Tinieblas
Deathkross	Perpetual	Tortura
Ematoma	Puya	Wings of Death
Encrypted	Sacrificio	
Homicide	Serpenterium	

Period 3: 2001–2013

Abismo Nuclear	DOD (Dealers of Death)	Opaque Mirror
After Omega	Doomlord	Opera Mistica
Alas Negras	Dracmas	Organic
All that I Bleed	Duel of Fate	Pacto de Sangre
Alma Blanca	Errant Society	Pit Fight Demolition
Another Fallen Soldier	Fasttaker	Rabia
Athaxia	Filacteria	Rodney el Infernal
Aura Azul	Gualaka	Sacred Guardian
Back in the day	Humanist	Sacrilegio
Bastard Chain	Infamia	Sacrosent
Blood Rapture	Iternia	Sepulchral
Catarot	Kabal	Severe Mutilation
Dantesco	Mantarraya	Solvo Animus
Death Arrangement	Massive Destruktion	The Mirage Theory
Death Legion	Matriarch	Transgresion
Dismal Divinity	Narval	Unzane
		Voracious
		Zafakon

[*] This table was developed with the contributions of Eric Morales and Rafael Bracero.

and cohesive local metal scene. To the delight of many Puerto Ricans, local band Mattador would be the opening band of the Iron Maiden concert.

Heavy metal music had grasped the hearts of a section of Puerto Rican youth who had established a scene with specific spaces, local bands, original music and outlets for its dissemination via radio and fanzines. Few people could predict the challenges that the coming years would entail for the local scene. Some of these challenges would reflect changes in musical preferences in the United States, while others would be intrinsic to the Latin American region. Puerto Rico's metal scene, embedded in the middle of these two worlds, would have to face both.

Period 2: Survival (1993–2000)

The second period in the development of Puerto Rico's metal scene would be less active than its first. Many factors could be identified as causal agents of this decrease in activity. Heavy metal at the international level would be impacted by the emergence of grunge music, which captured the airwaves and was perceived as a somber response to the excesses of glam metal. In the case of Puerto Rico, the challenge emerged from other sources, specifically Latin America and Europe.

Rock en Español (Rock in Spanish) would arrive to Puerto Rican shores during this period. The promotional slogan of *Rock en tu idioma* (Rock in your language) seemed to validate local national identities and ties to the Latin American region, which were usually overlooked in Puerto Rican life. Traditional rock and metal in English was positioned once more as a foreign artifact, while rock in Spanish would represent a way to appropriate the music styling of rock and provide it with a local flare.

Although the effects of the Rock in Spanish movement would seem to some as a simple matter of shifts in musical tastes, we argue that it is much more than that. First, it reflects the cultural and political debates that were ongoing in Puerto Rico at the time. Puerto Rico, a Spanish-speaking country embedded in a colonial relation with the United States, was not immune to the debates over language. In 1991, the Puerto Rican government declared Spanish as the official language of the country. The debate seemed to cut through the heart of a larger discussion over what it meant to be Puerto Rican, and speaking Spanish was a vital criteria. But this would be problematic for local politicians. For example, more Puerto Ricans now lived in the United States than on the island. Some subsequent generations of those that migrated in the 1950s to the USA did not speak Spanish. One year later, in 1992, the incoming political party, a proponent of the island's integration with the USA as the 51st state, declared that both Spanish and English would be official languages.

The debate over national identities would not be limited to language. In this period, Puerto Ricans voted twice in referendums to determine their political relation to the United States (1993 and 1998). In 1999, Puerto Ricans massively mobilized to force the US government to close its military bases on the municipal island of Vieques, which was used as a military practice site. These events helped contextualize the importance placed on debates regarding Puerto Rican national identities during this short seven-year period. Local rock music would reflect these debates by incorporating Spanish as the language of preference and looking toward Latin America and Spain for inspiration. Heavy metal music was not immune to this context.

The most important band from this period was Puya. Emerging from the remnants of experimental rock band Whisker Biscuit, Puya managed to merge the local sounds of salsa into metal music. After releasing their self-titled demo debut (1994) the band was signed by MCA records. They are the only local metal band to have signed with a major record label. Local metal writer Jeyka Laborde explains the importance of this band:

> ...it is a band with a musical fusion that was able to incorporate Puerto Rico in every sense of the word. Not only in the musical fusion, but also in the lyrics, their projection, and themes. It's not a band singing about dragons and swords...It was a band that was talking about Puerto Rico in their lyrics, rhythms, and music. To me it is the most important band in the Island.

After releasing their debut album entitled *Fundamental* (1999), the band was selected to open the second stage of Ozzfest in the same year sharing the stage with bands like Slipknot. Their impact at Ozzfest would garner them international acclaim and opening spots for bands like Sepultura, Red Hot Chili Peppers, KISS and Pantera. Puya would be recognized in 2000 by the Billboard Latin Awards for 'Rock/Fusion Album of the Year' for their album *Fundamental*. Their second album *Union* would come out in 2001. They would release another EP in 2010 entitled *Areyto*, not before playing in the famous *Rock al Parque* festival in Colombia (2010) and releasing a live DVD (Puya, 2010).

During this period, many of the metal bands formed during the metal scene's initial years would disband. Some of them saw their musical style as less relevant in the new times and others would simply become tired of the constant grind without local or international recognition. Some members of the local thrash metal bands would move on to sing in Rock in Spanish style groups.

A lot of people kept playing metal music but changed it to Spanish... It was like 'It's fashionable to sing in Spanish? Well then let's jump on that.' But they still kept playing the same metal music. People that started listening to rock in Spanish knew that what had changed was putting a singer in a different language. Instrumentation remained the same. I understand that some people are born metal and die metal, and see that those playing another genre of music is demeaning, or that you are lowering yourself to another category, but I don't see it that way.

(Marisol Marrero, drummer for the Christian thrash metal band
Xacrosaint)

Henceforth, a new generation of younger metal fans would come into the scene and establish new bands, which continued to forge the metal movement on the island, which was now even more underground.

Local metal fanzines (*Perversor, Enthroned, New Blood, Eniznikufesin*, among others) continued to provide the underground scene with more extreme versions of the metal music they loved and produced. TCR, having played an integral part in the development of the metal scene, would continue to foster the spread of metal. Ray López would provide extreme metal music to stores in major shopping malls. Local store 'Music Zone,' under the leadership of Rafael Bracero, developed complete sections on metal music focusing on international and local acts. Music Zone would become a point of reference for metal music fans during this period much like Discomanía was in the 1980s. Local promoter Pepe Dueño would bring international acts like Pantera (1993), Sepultura (1994) and Slayer (1994) to the Island, helping to keep the metal scene alive. Local bands Powerlord, Crypta and Puya would open these shows respectively. Local record label Brutal Noise Records would release a compilation of rock and metal bands entitled 'Puerto Rock' in 1997. Only one question was left... how would the metal scene emerge from this period?

Period 3: Systematic survival (2001–2013)

The third period in the development of Puerto Rico's metal scene is characterized by the emergence of new technologies and organization. With the advent of websites like MySpace and Facebook, local bands could disseminate their work beyond the confines of the Island. They would take full advantage of this technological support not only in the dissemination of their work, but also in the creation of their music. With the death of local radio shows, internet radio then played a vital role in community formation. Juan Manuel Solá (better known as 'Lechón Atómico') would start a web based radio show titled Heavy Metal Mansion highlighting local metal bands. The show has been airing uninterruptedly for more than a decade.

Local band members would get ahold of illegally downloaded computer software to record their music at makeshift studios, mostly made at their homes. These new technologies made it possible to record new albums at a faster pace and share them with people from established scenes. For example, local band Sacrilegio had their album *The Ultimate Abomination* (Sacrilegio, 2009) mixed by Andy LaRocque, the world renowned guitarist for King Diamond from Sweden. These new avenues of collaboration would have been impossible without the immediate access to global connections.

One Puerto Rican band that should be highlighted from this period is Dantesco. Dantesco is a Doom Metal band from the rural town of Cayey. They have released five albums including the self-titled *Dantesco* (2004), *De la Mano de la Muerte* (2005), *Pagano* (2008), *The Ten Commandments of Metal* (2010), *Seven Years of Battle* (2011) and *We Don't Fear Your God* (2013). Dantesco has been signed to international labels such as Cruz del Sur (Italy) and Inframundo Records (Mexico). They have played shows in Panamá (2004), Costa Rica (2004), Colombia (2005), Germany (2006) and the USA (2008, 2009, 2011, 2013). They also shared the stage with Judas Priest in their visit to Puerto Rico in 2005.

> I remember when Dantesco opened for Judas Priest. It was a great event in terms of production, although attendance left much to be desired. The response to Dantesco was...in the next couple of days I had to send out for more CDs because we ran out. They did what they had to do, and that's the point.
>
> (Rafael Bracero, President of the Puerto Rico Metal Alliance)

Dantesco stood apart from other local bands due to their consecutive release of albums, having more than any other band in the history of the local scene. Their lyrics address philosophical issues related to death, violence and religion. Vocalist Eric Morales, a trained tenor singer, made the ensemble stand apart from others through his skills in lyrical compositions, which are heavily influenced by his master's degree in philosophy. Dantesco has garnered underground followers across Latin America and Europe.

The local scene was well aware of the challenges they had faced in the previous years and how the local context had been less than receptive to their music. In 2005, Eric Morales decided to create the first 'Festival de Metal Boricua' (First Boricua Metal Festival), which was held in the town of Cayey at a location called 'La Finquita' (The Small Farm).

> With the festivals at 'La Finquita' I saw the possibility of doing something like the European festivals, or the festivals in South America or the United States, but with local bands from Puerto Rico. I started recruiting bands through a local website called Pulso Rock. The first two festivals were fantastic, open-air, in a farm in the town of Cayey. (...) There were almost 700 people there. I felt great because the whole scene was there.
>
> (Eric Morales, Singer for Doom Metal band Dantesco)

The festival was extremely significant for several reasons. First, it brought together more than 15 local bands that would spend the decade strengthening the local metal scene. Participants would call them the 'Class of 2005.' Second, the festival's name would be significant in strengthening local identities. 'Boricua' is a local term that emanates from the word 'Boriken,' a word used by native habitants to name the Island, before the Spanish colonization. Therefore, the term 'Boricuas' is used to denote authenticity within the debates for Puerto Rican identity. The use of this term as part of a metal festival evidenced that local musicians had appropriated metal music as theirs, and that concerns over Americanization or metal as a foreign cultural practice had been challenged and surpassed. Two more festivals, now with larger international acts like Omen, Twisted Tower Dire, Deadly Blessing, Strike Master, would be organized in the same place during 2006 and 2007. The local metal scene, now aware of themselves as a small community that could very well disappear, would use these events to cement their collective identity in this new decade.

The energy created in the local scene by these festivals would foster the need among its members to become even more organized. Eric Morales would write an open letter to the metal community stressing the need for unity and further organization. After several meetings, the 'Puerto Rico Metal Alliance' (PRMA) would be created under the presidency of Rafael Bracero in 2009. The PRMA would provide local bands with formal training on band management and dissemination of their work. Furthermore, it would put together a CD compilation in 2010 highlighting the talent of local metal bands. PRMA continues to this day as an organizational beacon in the local metal scene.

Other individuals who had been present from the onset of the metal scene would continue to contribute in this later period. For example, Ray López from TCR developed the 'Pulguero Metal' (Metal Flea Market) in 2005.

> ...I wanted to get local bands together and give them exposure so that they could sell their merchandise. People liked the concept. The first one we did we had more than 300 people there. It also gave vendors the opportunity to sell or exchange merchandise. It would be a great get-together...bands and vendors, and let's have a nice day. You know, everybody together and at the same time we would help the scene grow.
>
> (Ray López, Organizer of the 'Pulguero Metal')

The idea behind the event was to bring together metal fans, musicians and collectors to an event in which they could share a day's worth of live local music, food and merchandise exchange. The successful event is repeated on a yearly basis. It has become a community-oriented event where scene members from previous periods bring their children and interact with old and new friends.

These examples of internal organization, accompanied with extensive Internet access, have garnered the attention of international entities. Local bands have benefited from this attention with support from small distribution labels, collaborations with international musicians and tours. For example, local thrash metal band Zafakon would tour the east coast of the United States in 2013. They also had guitarist Joel Grind from the band Toxic Holocaust (USA) as a guest musician in their album *War as a Drug* (2013). Aura Azul would sign a distribution deal in 2013 with Total Steel Records from Japan. Other local bands like Tavú, Severe Mutilation and Dantesco would get rave reviews by international outlets from countries in Latin America and Europe. Godless, a local black metal band with an underground audience in Europe, would continue to win fans in the region and be included in a vinyl released compilation in France.

In this current and later developmental period of the local metal scene, many achievements and advances have been systematically documented. Still, it must be stressed that although communal productivity and activity have increased, the general population of the island is still unaware of the existence on the metal scene. This has worked, in part, as an advantage to the local metal scene that seems to work outside the constraints of the moral panic that characterized previous stages of their development.

Building memory through metal-related research

This study is, to the best of our knowledge and, as informed by the local community, the first to document the history of Puerto Rico's underground metal scene. As one might expect, it is a great challenge to include almost 30 years of history in the limited amount of space provided by a chapter in an edited volume. Many stories and important individuals still remain to be identified and discussed as part of an effort to provide an encompassing historical perspective on this local scene.

We understand that the documentation of heavy metal scenes in the Caribbean region, like the one done here with the case of Puerto Rico, will serve to widen the scope of Metal Music studies as an emerging field. Although authors interested in these smaller scenes have begun to populate the existing literature with new information from the periphery of traditional metal, more work needs to be carried out in order to provide new perspectives that emerge from areas like the Caribbean and Latin America. Countries in these areas have very extensive histories in which metal has served to give voices to indigenous populations (e.g. Mexico, Colombia) and even fight dictatorships (e.g. Argentina, Brazil). We hope our work is an initial step in the right direction to foster other efforts in the region.

Furthermore, examining how these metal scenes have emerged and survived researchers interested in local culture will be able to better understand how it has influenced the development of the music. In the case of metal in Puerto Rico, issues related to religion, language and nationality have been cornerstones for discussion among metal fans. These cultural issues have heavily influenced how metal is made and consumed since its origins and continue to do so today.

Finally, and more closely linked to the issue of memory, which is a central theme of this edited book, understanding small metal scenes at the periphery can also help the general population in these countries understand that metal fans are an important part of the history. Although largely ignored, metal musicians in Puerto Rico have gone to achieve important goals in other styles of music that are greatly recognized by the local population. Little do they know that metal music paved the way for many of those musicians. Through the recollection of their history we have been able to incorporate metal as a discussion point within local culture, challenging those who have overlooked its existence.

We have aimed to provide this historical perspective with the intention of diversifying the ways that we tell the story of heavy metal music in general. A truly encompassing historical account of metal music, now part of a globalized world, needs to include the experiences and stories of those living outside the epicenters of metal production and consumption. This will be an important part of respecting local histories and experiences.

Note

1. This study was approved by the University of Puerto Rico's Institutional Review Board for the Protection of Human Subjects in Research. All subjects were informed of the purpose of the study before providing oral consent to participate. All subjects were of legal age at the time of participation.

Bibliography

Anderson, B. R. O. (1983) *Imagined Communities: Reflections on the Origin and Spread of Nationalism* (London: Verso).

Atkinson, P. (2001) *Handbook of Ethnography* (Thousand Oaks, CA: SAGE).

Bell, A. (2012) 'Metal in a Micro Island State: An Insider's Perspective,' *Metal Rules the Globe*, eds. J. Wallach & H. Berger (Durham, NC: Duke University Press), pp. 271–293.

Brown, A. R. (2011) 'Heavy Genealogy: Mapping the Currents, Contraflows and Conflicts of the Emergent Field of Metal Studies, 1978–2010,' *Journal for Cultural Research*, 15(3), pp. 213–242.

Cardinal Sin. (1989) *Infanticide [Demo]* (San Juan, Puerto Rico: Independent).

Cardinal Sin. (1991) *Querer es Poder [Demo]* (San Juan, Puerto Rico: Independent).

Cardinal Sin. (2004) *Resurrection* (San Juan, Puerto Rico: Khaosmaster Productions).

Christe, I. (2004) *Sound of the Beast: The Complete Headbanging History of Heavy Metal* (London: Allison & Busby).

Crypta. (1993) *Join the Madness [Demo]* (San Juan, Puerto Rico: Brutal Noise Records).

Dantesco. (2004) *Dantesco [Demo]* (San Juan, Puerto Rico: Independent).

Dantesco. (2005) De la Mano de la Muerte. (TDNE).

Dantesco. (2008) *Pagano* (Italy: Cruz del Sur Records).

Dantesco. (2010) *The Ten Commandments of Metal* (San Juan, Puerto Rico: Jurakan).

Dantesco. (2011) *Seven Years of Battle* (California, USA: Stormspell Records).

Dantesco. (2013) *We Don't Fear Your God* (México: Inframundo Records).

Fanon, F. (1965) *The Wretched of the Earth* (New York, NY: Grove Press).

Fanon, F. (1967) *Black Skin, White Masks* (New York, NY: Grove Press).

Fernández, R. (1996) *The Disenchanted Island: Puerto Rico and the United States in the Twentieth Century* (Florida, USA: Praeger).

Green, P. (2012) 'Electronic and Affective Overdrive: Tropes of Transgression in Nepal's Heavy Metal Scene,' *Metal Rules the Globe*, eds. J. Wallach, H. M. Berger, & P. D. Greene (Durham, NC: Duke University Press), pp. 109–134.

Hecker, P. (2012) *Turkish Metal: Music, Meaning, and Morality in a Muslim Society* (Burlington: Ashgate Press)

Hoad, C. (2014) 'Ons is saam' – Afrikaans Metal and Rebuilding Whiteness in the Rainbow Nation,' *International Journal of Community Music*, 7(2), pp. 189–204.

Holstein, J. A. & Gubrium, J. F. (2007) *Handbook of Constructionist Research* (New York, NY: The Guilford Press).

Jason, L. (2004) *Participatory Community Research: Theories and Methods in Action. APA Decade of Behavior Volumes* (Washington, DC: American Psychological Association).

Kahn-Harris, K. (2007) *Extreme Metal: Music and Culture on the Edge* (Oxford: Berg).

Kahn-Harris, K. (2012) 'You Are from Israel and That Is Enough to Hate You Forever': Racism, Globalization, and Play within the Global Extreme Metal Scene,' *Metal Rules the Globe*, eds. J. Wallach, H. M. Berger, & P. D. Greene (Durham, NC: Duke University Press), pp. 200–226.

Kawano, K. & Hosokawa, S. (2012) 'Thunder in the Far East: The Heavy Metal Industry in 1990s Japan,' *Metal Rules the Globe*, eds. J. Wallach, H. M. Berger, & P. D. Greene (Durham, NC: Duke University Press), pp. 247–270.

LeVine, M. (2008) *Heavy Metal Islam: Rock, Resistance, and the Struggle for the Soul of Islam* (New York, NY: Three Rivers Press).

McIntyre, A. (2008) *Participatory Action Research: Qualitative Research Methods Series* (Los Angeles, CA: Sage Publications).

Meléndez, E. & Meléndez, E. (1999) *Colonial Dilemma: Critical Perspectives on Contemporary Puerto Rico* (Brooklyn, NY: South End Press).

Memmi, A. (1965) *The Colonizer and the Colonized* (New York, NY: Orion Press).

Phillipov, M. (2012) *Death Metal and Music Criticism: Analysis at the Limits* (New York, NY: Lexington Books).

Powerlord. (1991) *Power Lord [Demo]* (San Juan, Puerto Rico: Independent).

Puya. (2010) *Pa' Tí en Vivo: Live in Puerto Rico* (San Juan, Puerto Rico: Ahorake Corp).

Quintero Rivera, A. (1998) *Salsa, Sabor y Control: Sociología de la Música Tropical* (Mexico: Siglo XXI).

Riches, G. & Lashua, B. (2014) 'Mapping the Underground: An Ethnographic Cartography of the Leeds Extreme Metal Scene,' *International Journal of Community Music*, 7(2), pp. 223–241.

Román, M. (1998) *Lo criminal y otros relatos de ingobernabilidad* (San Juan, Puerto Rico: Publicaciones Puertorriqueñas).

Sacrilegio. (2009) *The Ultimate Abomination* (San Juan, Puerto Rico: Khaosmaster Productions).

Snell, D. (2014) 'The Black Sheep of the Family: Bogans, Borders and New Zealand Society,' *International Journal of Community Music*, 7(2), pp. 273–289.

Tashakkori, A. & Teddlie, C. (2003) *Handbook of Mixed Methods in Social & Behavioral Research* (Thousand Oaks, CA: SAGE Publications).

Torres, J. B. (1998) 'Masculinity and Gender Roles among Puerto Rican Men: Machismo on the U.S. Mainland,' *The American Journal of Orthopsychiatry*, 68(1), pp. 16–26.

Tuhiwai Smith, L. (2012) *Decolonizing Methodologies – Research and Indigenous Peoples* (London: Zed Books).

Undamaged. (1991) *Die Before Seeing the Light [Demo]* (San Juan, Puerto Rico: Independent).

Varas-Diaz, N. & Serrano-Garcia, I. (2003) 'The Challenge of a Positive Self-image in a Colonial Context: A Psychology of Liberation for the Puerto Rican Experience,' *American Journal of Community Psychology*, 31(1–2), pp. 103–115.

Wallach, J., Berger, H. M., & Greene, P. D. (eds.). (2012) *Metal Rules the Globe: Heavy Metal Music Around the World* (Durham, NC: Duke University Press).

Walser, R. (1993) *Running with the Devil: Power, Gender, and Madness in Heavy Metal Music. Music/Culture* (Hannover, NH: University Press of New England).

Whyte, W. F. (1991) *Participatory Action Research, Sage Focus Editions* (London: Sage Publications).

Part III
Critique

6
Blasting Britney on the Way to Goatwhore: Identity and Authenticity among Female-identified Fans in Semi-rural North Carolina

Jamie E. Patterson
University of North Carolina Chapel Hill

In his now classic ethnography of a death metal scene in Akron, Ohio in the 1990s, folklorist Harris Berger utilizes a critical phenomenological approach that acknowledges the ethnographer as a 'subject among subjects' (1999, p. 258) who voices opinions and criticisms with all other 'subjects' involved.[1] Through face-to-face communication, the ethnographer engages in a dialectic in which she and the research participant share their own partial knowledge in order to reach a clearer understanding of the situation or perspective in question. But, like identity scholars Holland and Lachicotte, Jr. (2007) argue, that understanding is informed through social interaction and personal histories and will continue to shift based on the multiple subjects' internalization and reflexive responses to social historical discourses, emerging identities and power dynamics. While I have been a long-time fan of death metal music, I have never felt entrenched in a death metal community for various reasons. For one, my metal friends and I grew up in Wilson, a rural part of North Carolina, where we had to carpool to the nearest death metal shows and record stores one hour west in the state capital of Raleigh. Given the distance and the lack of social media at the time (early 1990s), we often depended on tape trading among each other. Though they treated me as a valued member and fan, I, like the few other women in our small group of friends, was also in a romantic relationship with one of the male members. When that relationship split, I kept in touch with a couple friends, but mostly I was left to pursue death metal music on my own. Incidentally, in the late 1990s, big name death metal acts toured less through North Carolina and the scene waned. So, while I still listened to the music, over time, I became surrounded by more people who treated my musical tastes as a novelty or a source of jest. I became accustomed to defending my tastes and defining myself as an oddity. However, years later, in graduate school, as I embarked on an ethnography of self-identifying female fans of death metal near the same region where I grew up, moments emerged that revealed just how significant death metal had been to my continually shifting identity and gender construction. I realized that I shared common cultural notions of what it means to be a woman in the scene, but when those notions were challenged by research participants, I felt a visceral response. At those times, I was reminded of Berger's phenomenological approach to ethnography. Paraphrasing Alan Watts, he says, 'The solution to any truly vexing paradox is found by moving through the difficulty, not away from it' (1999, p. 259). The following is an example of one such moment that became a gateway into re-examining women and gender construction in death metal.

26 August 2010. Wilmington, North Carolina

It is late summer in the relentless heat of Wilmington, North Carolina. I am riding with research participants Kelicia, and Amanda, both in their early 20s, both avid death metal fans.[2] The three of us are heading to see blackened death metal band Goatwhore at the Soapbox Lounge, a sort of dive bar that is located above a laundromat on North Front Street, the coastal town's main strip.

Kelicia is nervous. She always gets nervous before shows.[3] Not to mention, this is our first time hanging out with Amanda beyond Facebook and Kelicia's first time in Wilmington (she is from the Piedmont region of North Carolina and spends little time at the coast). By this point, Kelicia and I had been acquainted for six months.[4] On the way there, Kelicia and Amanda bond in their love for Disney's *Beauty and the Beast*, death metal bands like Suffocation and Dying Fetus, and pop music.

Amanda is driving. As a rule, she never plays death metal in the car – it's too intense. So instead, she is playing music from the pop radio station. A few songs in, as we're all still talking, getting to know each other,

Kelicia gets excited and starts singing along with the song. It is Britney Spears' 'Gimme More.'

'Ooh! I love her!' she says.
Amanda turns up the radio as Kelicia continues singing. She turns
    to me.
'You don't love this?'

[I immediately pressed my body against the side of the car, my face anguished. I wanted to jump out, flee from the moment. Though we had talked about her contrary love of pop music, hearing Kelicia interact with it was too much.]

Amanda laughs. 'Oh yeah, that's happening. Right here, on the way to Goatwhore!'

In that moment, as Kelicia bellowed out, I felt a repulsion so immediate, it seemed involuntary. The fan in me was screaming, 'How could someone who loves death metal also identify with such soulless music?' It just felt horribly wrong. To me, pop music is grounded in a dominant culture that excludes much of what I value. It feels empty, transparent and promotes hegemonic standards of beauty, gender and sexuality; it celebrates pettiness, competition and a ravenous capitalism. The lyrics, which stress these standards in practice, are sung in a style that engages in the embodied human voice, keeping me aware of the person (or socially produced image) behind the words.

Death metal, though equally ephemeral and socially constructed, feels weighted, ancient, primordial, timeless and inhuman. Listening to the intensity of the music, with its machine-gun double bass kick-drums, low-tuned guitar riffs that churn forward in jarring succession, and guttural, disembodied utterances like the growls of a being stripped of cultural language, I feel face-to-face with what Bakhtin called the 'cosmic terror,' or 'the fear of that which is materially huge and cannot be overcome by force' (1984, p. 335). The overwhelmingly low force of the bass frequency evokes for me a feeling of rising from unfathomable depths. Like the fans of Dethklok in Adult Swim's *Metalocalypse*, the music rips me apart and I lose all sense of self, dissolving into the moment. As I continue to listen, I feel a cathartic release of pleasure. Listening to pop, on the other hand, I feel grossly embodied, gendered, trapped.

How I came to view death metal as 'music with soul,' or more particularly, how I came to view pop music as 'lacking soul' involved a series of choices and value judgments based on my personal history.

But as I came to know more women in the death metal community and sought others' perspectives, I realized how these deeply personal, emotionally-charged responses were also 'culturally interwoven' (Finnegan, 2003, p. 183) with social constructions of what it means to be both a death metal fan and a 'female' death metal fan. Through oppositional discourse, fans I spoke with established a dialectic between pop music and extreme metal and between mainstream constructions of gender and their own reflections of their gender construction. This dialectic perspective informed their judgment of other women in the scene, creating a hierarchy of power in which women who presented themselves as more feminine, or aligned with mainstream feminine gender construction, became foils or specters of the larger culture and, therefore, were perceived as less 'authentically death metal' or 'less authentic members' of the death metal community. Within the scene, research participants interpreted more feminine displays in terms of mainstream heteronormative romance, which they argued took a back-seat to the pleasurable experience of and dedication to the music. Using exclusionary language, they discounted these feminine women as simply 'girlfriends,' those there to 'hook up' with other fans and musicians, whereas they defined themselves as 'true fans' or 'there for the music.' One fan dehumanized the feminine women entirely, calling them 'fluffies' or 'arm candy.'

Previous research (Klypchak, 2007; Krenske & McKay, 2000; Purcell, 2003; Vasan, 2009, 2011) interviewing female-identified metal fans has drawn attention to these emic classification patterns in which participants determine others' involvement in the scene based on gendered categories of self-presentation. Whereas some participants dismissed the social practice itself as 'being catty,' an interpretation based on mainstream gender power structures that trivialize such disagreement as 'feminine,' it regularly came up in discussion as a source of anger and frustration. When asked what is important when studying women in death metal and what, specifically, should an ethnographer focus on, all interview participants cited these divisions, recounting situations in which they were judged or had judged others according to heteronormative, culturally gendered cues. Over the course of this paper, I seek to problematize this process of categorization and previous research such as Krenske and McKay (2000) which treats these categories as though they are stable or fixed, rather than products of shifting social processes informed by identities and personal histories that fans engage in outside of the scene. I argue that these fans participate in these exclusionary classification practices as methods of self-authoring.

Holland and Lachicotte, Jr. (2007), who elaborate on Mead's social identity construction and Bakhtin's concept of heteroglossia, define self-authoring as 'a social, dialogical process.' They note:

> Identity is an achievement of the person's activity – but only within the contexts and events of social interaction. One's identities are social products drawn from social history, actively internalized, and redrawn as one's expressions of these identities enter into new circumstances and new activities. They are complicated by the ongoing dialogue of many actors in many activities, and the continual interplay of personal and interpersonal negotiations of their meaning and effects. At times, identity development becomes intermeshed in the strategic involvement of self-authoring, as a means to organize activity and gain a better footing with specific audiences.
>
> (Holland & Lachicotte, 2007, p. 118)

The fans I repeatedly interviewed use categorization to build mundane and transgressive subcultural capital with others in the scene (Kahn-Harris, 2007; Thornton, 2006) and also to delineate spaces (which they may set apart from mainstream society) to explore gender, not simply based on male-dominated definitions of gender roles in the scene (as previous research has emphasized), but on participants' own dialogic relationships with mainstream constructions of gender that are channeled through their own personal histories and social choices. These often emotionally-charged narratives of the 'authentic fan' are informed by a participant's 'identity work' (Berger, 1999; DeNora, 2000) that often pits the fan in direct opposition to common female gender presentations as perpetuated in popular American culture, as in pop music. At the same time, the increasing popularity of death metal in mainstream modes of leisure has brought new listeners from various backgrounds, thus changing the dynamics of audiences and ultimately impacting discourses of authenticity. While their self-presentation ranged from hyper-feminine, moderately feminine, to more masculine and genderqueer, all research participants self-identified as true fans regardless of their gender construction.

This paper is divided into two main sections. The first section examines fans' engagement with historicized constructions of authenticity that act to distinguish death metal from mainstream society. Exploring authenticity discourse as a series of dialogical relationships between participants and mainstream society, participants and the local death metal community, and participants and selves, I examine common 'becoming-a-fan' narratives among research participants and the role gender construction plays in discussions of authenticity. Phillipov's (2012) research on listening practices and pleasure shows how a listener becomes a fan of death metal through an active 'reorientation of listening' or deciphering of non-traditional musical cues that distances a death metal fan from casual listeners. Also, Larsson's (2013) research on authenticity in metal, among others (Berger, 1999), discusses how fans build relationships based on oppositional identity construction. In the second section, using sociologist DeNora's (2000) work on music, emotion and identity along with Berger's (1999) phenomenological ethnographic methods as my interpretive lens, I return to Kelicia and Amanda, examining how they use popular music in their identity work and their narratives of authenticity in relation to death metal. In her narratives, Kelicia cites her African-American heritage as a source of conflict that led her to death metal. Dawes's (2012) foundational research with women of color in North American metal scenes helps to position Kelicia's authenticity narrative in a larger socio-historical context. In conclusion, while this article seeks to understand female-identified fans' dialogic processes involved in identity construction and authenticity, and ultimately discourses of power, I contend that the oppositional categories they collectively construct and engage with – dichotomies between pop and metal, mainstream and underground scenes, authenticity and superficiality, conformity and nonconformity, masculinity and femininity – are fluid, in-flux, and, like other factors in identity construction, are often experienced simultaneously or in contradiction. The continuing practice of categorization excludes fans who are attracted to the music aesthetically or instrumentally and who may greatly benefit and actively contribute to the scene.

This argument is based on ethnographic research conducted from 2010 to 2013 among female-identified fans in semi-rural North Carolina along with my own personal experiences of ambivalence in the death metal scene from 1992 to 1998 and since returning to it in 2010.

Authenticity: Building and maintaining the 'secret'

Through repeated in-depth interviews, the concept of authenticity kept emerging as a source of empowerment and frustration among research participants. While participants felt empowered defining themselves as death metal fans and discussed the effects their involvement with the music has had in relation to other aspects of their lives,[5] they also felt they had to 'prove themselves' as 'authentic fans,' defined by them as 'authentically interested in the music,' in order to be treated equally, or merely to be 'left alone' by other scene members. Most pointed to more feminine-displaying women – women who they say 'wear high heels' to shows and who only go to 'pick up men' – and constructed judgments based on their appearance and their location in relation to the stage – 'true fans stand at the front to watch the band.' These fans argued more feminine-presenting women make it 'harder to prove oneself as a fan' because it influences males in the scene to interpret them strictly in gendered terms. Others simply said such women just looked uncomfortable, like they weren't 'having a good time.' Here, participants are comparing themselves to women they see as inauthentic and are judging their own self-constructions through an internalized and social process informed by both the death metal community and their personal histories. They are reflecting on their own biographical constructions and are reaffirming themselves as 'authentic' in relation to self, the death metal community (for which they may not always feel inclusion), and mainstream society. To understand this process of authenticity building in relation to such judgments, I explored how research participants became fans initially. These 'becoming-a-fan' narratives involved a series of activities in which participants took power in transgressing popular domains both musically and culturally. First they had to transgress boundaries of sonic experience, translating sounds from noise to pleasure.

Phillipov defines extreme metal, and by extension death metal, as 'a diverse collection of musical styles, each of which seeks to disrupt the expected conventions of pop, rock, and heavy metal in an attempt to remain as inaccessible and unpalatable as possible to 'mainstream' audiences' (2012, p. xv). Bogue describes the rhythm as a series of 'catatonic fits' that can produce a musical affect upon the listener where the 'self becomes nothing more than a character whose actions and emotions are desubjectified, even to the point of dying' (2004, p. 99). Overell calls this sensation 'brutal affect' in which listeners experience an 'evacuation of self' or 'a blowing away of self' (2011, p. 202). The low-tuned pitch of the guitars and the often syncopated bass sounds of the vocals and drums played at loud decibels vibrate within the listener, further transgressing the boundaries of bodily experience and pop sounds. Phillipov notes that while the voice deepens, it no longer becomes engendered, and 'ceases to sound human, resembling instead some 'unspecifiable animal or machine' (2012, p. 64).

Bogue contends that the music is antipop, especially in the lyrics, both in structure and content:

Formally, death metal lyrics largely avoid rhyme and seldom follow rock's traditional alternation of verse and chorus. For most parts, songs are structured as autonomous verses of varying meters and numbers of lines. In terms of content, the lyrics transgress most pop terms. Just as the music rejects anything that might sound pretty, tender, or cheerful, so the lyrics shun all expressions of hope, optimism, or romantic love...Seldom do death groups celebrate alcohol, drugs, or sex (save in connection with death)...While ignoring heavy metal's Dionysian themes, death bands specialize instead in metal's traditional dark side, themes of chaos, death, violence, and destruction.

(2004, p. 102)

Phillipov discusses how death metal's musical structure requires 'especially attentive and focused listening to find meaning and pleasure in the music' (2012, p. 85). The listener actively reorients herself to decipher non-traditional musical cues as sources of pleasure rather than noise. This leads to repeated listening and over time the listener adopts a position or 'taste' that differentiates her from casual listeners.

The experience of 'brutal affect' sonically 'allows for an intense sense of belonging with others to a particular space and music' (Overell, 2011, p. 202). Within the community of death metal listeners, those who can discern the nuances between songs gain prestige among others in the scene, defined as an example of gaining 'subcultural capital, a term developed by Sarah Thornton in her research on club culture (2006, p. 84). Becoming 'in-the-know' about the sounds and pleasures of death metal allows a listener to gain what Kahn-Harris (2007) calls mundane subcultural capital, because it builds inclusion and strengthens everyday cultural bonds among fans in the death metal community.

Phillipov argues 'the pleasures of death metal's inaccessibility can be linked to its contribution to the exclusivity of the death metal scene, and in particular, to a romance of the scene as being maintained and populated only by those truly dedicated to the music' (2012, p. 84). In other words, there is a kind of privileged knowing or 'secret' about death metal that has evolved within the scene, distancing itself from mainstream society.

Indeed, research participants defended death metal as a 'secret' which separated them from casual listeners. To engage in a 'secret' implies a privileged knowledge and air of authenticity. It creates a division between what 'appears' and what is 'secretly true.' Even when the secret is a lie, such as when a band uses Satanic imagery but does not actually participate in Satanism, fans hold privileged knowledge over its truth (Brown, 2007). They experience power in knowing the secret, which they harness in relation to those in authority. This power reflexively becomes a role in their identity construction.

In their personal narratives, research participants often step out from positions of exclusion that become empowered through their knowing the 'secrets' of death metal. They describe themselves as outside or contrary to cultural norms, in their interests, philosophies and self-presentations, often defining themselves in relation to that in which they are opposed. Many share personal histories in which they have had to face ordeals of adversity, whether in everyday life or in singular trauma situations. In such cases, participants had found that listening to death metal helped them develop resilience. One participant Louise, notes:

> I think people have some shit that they've been dealing with as a kid. But so I think it's like a natural kind of movement to get into darker heavier music if you've been through darker, heavier shit in your life. Then, it has this kind of reverse effect where it's actually therapeutic, because like maybe for once in your life, you're part of a community. Maybe for once in your life, you're finding music that you can really identify with. And you don't feel alone, and you've got a way to kind of express how you feel just by listening to it. You think you're in on a secret that's yours. The whole rest of this screwed up world doesn't get to do what I get to do; this is awesome. So it actually kind of builds you back up a little bit. It's like almost even therapeutic and for people that stick with it. If you stick with it, it's because it's serving you in a really positive way, for the most part.
>
> (2 July 2010)

Previous researchers report similar findings among participants. In Berger's ethnography, Dan Saladin argued listening to death metal had become a 'vent for life anger' (1999, p. 270), or daily frustrations. Hickam and Wallach reported fans using the music to gather strength to fight back against adversity in their lives (2011, p. 268). Research participants also reported being attracted to death metal first in their formative years, at or near the onset of puberty (Laura was an exception – death metal had not yet existed. But she had become interested in the progenitors of death metal around this time). In her ethnography of female punk fans, Leblanc (1999) considers this a critical time period when girls are expected to leave the freedom of childhood and adopt the restraints of femininity, what she labels the 'femininity game,' which she argues, places women in a no-win situation. In adopting normalized constructions of femininity, they are cheating themselves into being passive, compliant, and involved in beauty and relationships. When they win, they lose (Leblanc, 1999, p. 137).

Like Leblanc's respondents, who resisted popular constructions of femininity using punk music, all my research participants had developed gender constructions that incorporated their relationship with death metal so that death metal and their gender constructions were, to them, seen as naturalized. For example, when asked what attracted them to death metal, many research participants noted that they had always been 'tomboys' or interested in 'less girly things.' Using oppositional discourse, they contrasted femininity construction's focus on romance with their own pre-occupation with 'darker elements,' existential and social themes related to death, the grotesque, and the macabre, all of which they ranked as more important. For the most part, such constructions were self-defined as more 'masculine,' but not all considered themselves as 'masculine.' Instead, they defined themselves as simply resistant to gender norms. They used these constructions, along with their personal histories, to develop what Susanna Larsson labeled 'constitutive authenticity,' in which their relationship with death metal was considered a natural progression of their life narratives (2013, p. 102). Such fans considered death metal so intertwined with their sense of self, that they called it the sound of their 'soul.'

Stepping forth from positions of exclusion, research participants' positions as women in the death metal scene were far from naturalized. The death metal community in the Piedmont region of North Carolina, similarly to other extreme metal communities in the south, primarily consists of white males (though more males of Hispanic descent are participating) ranging from college students to older men in working-class positions. Scholars have successfully discussed elsewhere how authenticity in death metal communities becomes a gendered process in which pressure extends to women to conform to heteronormative standards of femininity and masculinity (Hutcherson & Haenfler, 2010; Klypchak, 2007; Krenske and McKay, 2000; Vasan, 2009, 2011). Women who either emphasize their femininity or exscribe it altogether are accepted members according to hegemonic standards of masculinity. However, this ignores participants' own definitions of masculinity and femininity. Clifford's (2009) research argues that queer-identified fans often use the scene as a queerscape in which multiple combinations of gender can be challenged and performed. Fans may interpret masculinity as 'camp performance' (2009). Likewise, Chloe, a transgendered female fan who I interviewed, used engagement with hyperfeminity in the scene to 'come out' for the first time in public at a black metal show in Chapel Hill, decked out in pink platform boots and pig-tails. I found regularly that research participants used their involvement with death metal at shows, with other members, or in everyday listening, to play with gendered identity construction rather than simply conforming to normative male prescriptions. Participants had constructed identities that directly opposed popular constructions of femininity, whether in choosing to be more assertive over what they called 'complacent agreeableness,' or 'always being nice,' or in redefining the terms of beauty. They expressed power in being 'women' and constructed gendered identities with varying degrees of femininity and masculinity. Even more masculine-presenting participants who recounted stories in which they had 'passed as men' garnished power in being able to outsmart or 'trick the audience.'

In her research with women's participation in mosh pits, Riches discusses how women's involvement at shows affords them a sense of freedom and immediate 'genderlessness' (2011, p. 328). Research participants reported similar experiences in which they escaped the gendered body simply by listening to the music. This goes back to the brutal affect discussed earlier in which listeners can interpret the voice as genderless. By listening to and internalizing that voice, they experience freedom, which they use to affect other aspects of their lives.

After having discussed a bit of the process behind authenticity building, I return to Kelicia and Amanda, stepping back to that night in the car described earlier. At that moment, when Kelicia was bellowing out Britney (and as I was feeling repulsed), she was feeling a release of her nervousness and a sense of empowerment, similar to when she listens to death metal. By local standards of authenticity in death metal, Kelicia was being sincere or 'authentic' in the moment, expressing a 'radical individualism' that Kahn-Harris shows is often rewarded in transgressive subcultural capital (2007, p. 127). In her own authenticity building in the scene, Kelicia regularly employs the use of transgressive cultural capital over mundane capital practices, because, as one of the only African-Americans in the local scene, she rarely feels a connection with other local fans. Because of this, she actively refuses to learn about the history of death metal, preferring instead to focus on the bands she simply likes. Like the other participants interviewed, Amanda and Kelicia do regard pop and death metal as distinct genres. Kelicia does not call Britney the sound of her soul, but she does identify with the image of Britney as a character who has been criticized by popular society and who was defended by a community of fans. Meanwhile, Amanda, in a tradition of camp and spectacle, juxtaposes pop and metal identities for transgressive affect. Though she often employs a more transgressive or 'radically independent' position, stressing her passion for pop music, she has also made it her business to learn about the history of metal and connect with members of the larger metal community, locally, nationally, and internationally. For her senior project in high school, she examined the history of metal, employing the help of writer and publisher Ian Christe to act as her official mentor for the project. In the following section, I plan to briefly explore a little of where those death metal and pop identities intersect in each of their experiences. They both use authenticity discourses to legitimize their choices and integrate them with their love of death metal.

Kelicia: 'You don't love this?' Experiencing friction and empowerment

That night in Wilmington, Kelicia may have just met Amanda, but the social environment of being in a car with girlfriends singing along to pop was quite familiar to her, even on the way to a death metal show. Kelicia had become attracted to death metal's intensity at age 11. 'Having a long time to grow with it,' she says, 'it has definitely shaped what things I like, how I choose to live, and who I choose to let be a part of my life' (17 February 2010). She treats the music as a main point of departure, describing it as 'a core part of what makes up the "self." ' But she's never had more than a few friends who've listened to it. Her main show buddy growing up was an old friend from elementary school who she had exposed to death metal. Still, on the way to shows, the two would often listen to what she called 'guilty pleasures,' bands from their childhood like NSYNC and Backstreet Boys. But Britney was not a guilty pleasure, she tells me. 'No, I own that!' (17 March 2010).

Claiming ownership, Kelicia is involved not only in the construction of Britney but in projecting a self-in-Britney. DeNora notes, 'Music is a material that actors use to elaborate, to fill out and fill in, themselves and to others, modes of aesthetic agency and, with it, subjective stances and identities' (2000, p. 74). Kelicia first says she likes Britney because of Chris Crocker, the fan made famous for posting videos of himself engaging in emotional outbursts in defense of Britney, at a time when the general public had turned against her. When defending her musical taste, Kelicia uses her biography, specifically events which led to her death metal affiliation, to connect to the myth of the comeback pop star.

Kelicia identifies herself as a fantasy writer, which is what she says compels her to focus on lyrics. According to her, Britney has 'some damn good writers.' In the song 'Gimme More,' the narrators display power and command. Britney announces herself, 'It's Britney, bitch,' and through the lyrics and the video exudes sexual freedom by choosing who she wants to dance with and what she will do. In the chaotic situation of the audience and the energy of the moment, she loses control. But even then, she's at the center. It ends with the lines 'you gonna have to remove me 'cause I ain't goin' nowhere.' Discussing the song, Kelicia parallels this empowering narrative with how she feels after listening to death metal. Through what DeNora calls a 'reflexive process of remembering/constructing who one is' (2000, p. 63), Kelicia traces her first empowerment narrative to listening to death metal lyrics, for example, Mortician's 'Drilling for Brains,' a song featuring a sadistic dentist.[6]

> Yeah, because I mean I didn't want to go out and murder someone (laughs). But you know, when I heard the songs – you can't understand the lyrics, but when I'd read the lyrics – they're all about killing other people. I was like, 'Yeah, that could be you couldn't it?' You know? 'That could be me doing that to you, drilling for braaaiiins!' You know? And I was like 'Yeah, okay, I'm angry.' And I would always have this built up energy, and when I would listen to it, I would just sit in my room headbanging and stuff, and it was just great. And then I would be like, 'Whew. Everything's good again.' It took my anger from me.
>
> (17 February 2010)

Kelicia gravitated to death metal during a period of intense anger and social pressure. She had attended a Christian private school up until third grade. There, teachers would punish her for not speaking 'proper English,' though she was simply speaking the vernacular with which she was familiar, what she referred to as 'African-American dialect.' In fourth grade, Kelicia transferred to a public school where the demographics included more children of African-American and Hispanic descent. When she transferred to public school, she said the black kids mocked her voice and accused her of trying to be white. Over the next two years, when they saw her, they would chew things up and spit them at her. As she grew up, Kelicia internalized similar stigma from peers, parents and teachers who reinforced ideas that she didn't fit into any social framework. She dealt with this frustration through giving her anger over to death metal, a process she called energetic and empowering. And it has helped her deal with adversity head on. Though she still experiences empowerment listening to death metal, as a self-identified black woman who is not 'super girly' or 'one of the guys,' she has never found much of a community in the local death metal scene.[7]

In her groundbreaking work *What Are You Doing Here? A Black Woman's Life and Liberation in Heavy Metal*, Dawes (2012) shares similar narratives from women in metal scenes who were treated by others as though they were betraying their black heritage by not following a set of cultural expectations. One fan, Pisso, notes, 'Some people who have met me for the first time automatically assume that I'm dissing my hood or I'm not being 'real.' They have no idea of where I grew up, my values, or my cultural background. They are expecting an authenticity from me that I can't even give them' (Dawes, 2012, p. 52).

Dawes writes, 'A black metalhead can be perceived not only as an affront to the past and present struggles black people have endured, but as a personal insult to those closest to them' (2012, p. 79). Discussing black culture, she notes:

> Every black person in North America is somewhat aware of prevailing societal assumptions, and must struggle to rise above them. Sharing certain commonalities – like dialect, dress, dating, and music preferences – signifies to other blacks that you show pride in who you are as a black person. For anyone who chooses not to adopt those cultural signifiers for whatever reason, the choice is seen as a rejection, even an insult. The status quo has questions ready for this: Do you think you are better than me? Why don't you want to be like us?
>
> (ibid.)

Kelicia's experiences resemble those of Dawes's informant Camille Atkinson who says, 'You have people on both sides of your life, your family life and your peers, telling you that you are not black enough because you listen to this music. So you do question yourself. What ends up happening is that you create for yourself an identity of what a black person should be' (Dawes, 2012, p. 54).

In her fiction writing, Kelicia's characters often struggle with expectations from members of black communities and local metal communities. Her protagonists meet harrowing ends, and in their dying moments, they experience a sense of freedom usually through listening to death metal. Likewise, Kelicia, not only felt freedom in death metal, but as culturally marked in the scene, she developed confidence in adopting a sort of token status. Dawes calls this the 'only one' (2012, p. 101) syndrome, in which black members can use their uniqueness in the scene to feel special. She notes how she often felt territorial when she saw other black women at shows. Growing up straddling cultural categories and feeling no sustained connection with any of them, Kelicia also developed an identity of power in her sense of uniqueness and fierce individualism.

At the University of North Carolina in Chapel Hill where Kelicia is an undergraduate student (as of publication, she has now graduated), she has chosen friends who are fun and supportive, even though she doesn't really identify with them.

> 'We don't have the same sense of humor,' she says. 'Reading about guys' heads blown off is funny like in death metal, but they'll say 'that's just mean.' So what? Sometimes you need to be mean. If someone's annoying you, you'd like to be able to tell him to stop, right? It's okay.
>
> (17 March 2010)

Here, Kelicia was not calling for violent behavior, but instead she was using the hyperbolic language of death metal as a springboard for discussing the possibilities of asserting or defending herself in ways inconsistent with her friends' social upbringing of being passive or non-confrontational. Kelicia, like other research participants, struggles with social, regional, and gendered standards of 'being nice' that she feels restrict her available responses and limit her freedom to act in ways that are interpreted as 'dissident.' She reports that her involvement with death metal has given her more confidence to transgress these restrictions when necessary. Not only that, she has integrated this process with her identity construction by claiming, 'I'm weird, mean, and exceptionably nice' (26 August 2010). Though she prides herself on being a nice person, she is 'mean' when she has to be. She and her friends regularly engage in these kinds of discussions and debates. Through this dialogical process of identity construction, Kelicia reinforces an identity of power to herself, and her friends may in kind internalize an alternative voice. Framing Kelicia's Britney fandom through her death metal identity of power, it becomes easy to see why she identifies with a narrative of a celebrity woman who is criticized, consumed and spat out, then gets back up and reasserts herself on display.

Amanda: 'This is happening.' Playing with boundaries

Death metal for Kelicia is a central point of departure, and much of how she interprets the world has been shaped by her relation to the power she feels in the music. Amanda describes death metal as her 'thing,' but she never goes so far to say it comprises any core of 'self' or has changed how she relates (even though it *has* opened doors regarding *who* she relates with.) Instead, she sees the 'me' which dominates her interactions as 'super girly' and uses play and shock as her interpretive lens. Extreme metal's intensity and dark subversive imagery gets absorbed in her presentation of self which sometimes borders feminine camp, for example when she wears what she calls 'ridiculous' heels to the grocery store. This presentation changes little if at all, no matter what the environment. She will cut up a larger graphic Goatwhore (or other extreme metal) t-shirt into a more feminine fit and throw on a pair of jeans and heels, then head to the beachside or a family restaurant. But she is not merely appropriating death metal tropes. She engages with death metal community members, building authenticity through learning the history or progression of death metal sounds, and considers the scene a large component of her social life. And she equally headbangs to Lady Gaga around a group of death metal fans or her pop friends.

For Amanda, death metal's tradition of transgression and horror ties in seamlessly with Lady Gaga, whose style of pop incorporates images of the avant-garde and the macabre. Amanda likes that Gaga's 'fucking crazy,' that her music is 'very accessible, but at the same time it's very deep.' By deep, she points to Gaga's involvement in the song-writing process and believes that much of her identity is entrenched in the music. This includes dropping in ideas that are alternative to mainstream culture. For example, like many extreme metal bands, Gaga is critical of organized religion (Amanda, 27 August 2010). To illustrate this, Amanda brings up the Alejandro video where Gaga wears inverted crosses and swallows a crucifix. She notes,

> It's interesting what she's doing with it. She's a huge pop star but she's sneaking in these things. She's dressed as a pope. Gay dudes attack her. But people don't notice it. They think it's just pop music. 'It's just her crazy outfits.' Some groups boycott her, but in general, people don't get it. She's metal.
>
> (27 August 2010)

Here, Amanda defines Gaga in terms of authenticity discourse, invoking a privileged knowledge in discovering the secret hidden in plain view, even when the general public refuses to acknowledge it.

Amanda and Kelicia both admire Gaga's use of objects that imbue symbols of femininity with masculine power. For example, in a visit to Amanda's house, Kelicia noticed a portrait of Gaga on the cover of Rolling Stone wearing a bra with guns protruding forth, symbolizing nipples. 'I've *got* to get one of those!' she says. Halberstam (2012) argues Gaga is part of an emergent feminism called 'shadow feminism' that lurches and jerks into action and plays with madness and agitation. Gaga engages in 'creative mayhem' (Halberstam, 2012) as documented and analyzed in the online journal *Gaga Stigmata* (Durbin & Vicks, 2010). These descriptions are reminiscent of death metal's sonic lurches and jerks, its transgressive themes, and layering of intensity. Dibben's research in pop highlights that 'music which apparently affirms stereotyped gender roles can also afford resistant or subversive uses' (2002, p. 129). Kahn-Harris states, 'Equally radical is the (extreme metal) scene's exploration of the boundaries of "the serious" and its demonstration of how "play" can be brought into unexpected areas' (2007, p. 162).

It is not uncommon for death metal bands to do camp versions of pop songs (even everyday impromptu performances), like recently when Dying Fetus members sang along with a Madonna song that was on their mp3 player (Kelicia, 10 November 2010). Kelicia and Amanda do similar 'death metal' renditions of pop songs when hanging out with their friends at home. When Amanda and Kelicia break out into a death metal performance of the Britney Spears song 'One More Time' in the 'feminine-coded' domain of the bedroom, they are not only engaging in a crossover or 'play' performance, but are imbuing feminine identities with death metal power.

Conclusions

Over the course of this ethnography, through engaging with fans such as Kelicia, Amanda and other research participants, I have learned that the rigid categories between authenticity and superficiality, resistance and conformity, mainstream pop and extreme metal, that I had internalized as sources of power, are more fluid, nuanced and complex, involving a reflexive relationship among participants emerging through social interaction. Kelicia's participation may follow the normative prescriptions of 'true fans' at shows. She stands near the front, listens intently to the band, and participates with her body. However, both she and Amanda have been read by some of the other research participants as 'girlfriends' or not 'true fans.' Class definitions, race, age and personal backgrounds play additional roles in this exclusionary process. For example, Kelicia and Amanda are both the youngest participants interviewed and are both of middle-class backgrounds, although class ranged greatly from lower-working class to upper-middle class among participants. Gender construction in Raleigh, North Carolina also played a role in how they were defined. Comparing scenes in the smaller but more homogenously liberal scene of Asheville, North Carolina to that of the larger metropolis of the Raleigh area, Louise, who identifies as genderqueer, remarked that in Asheville, she was considered 'fem' while in Raleigh she's 'practically read as butch' (2 July 2010). She notes that the Raleigh area has more strict definitions of gender compared to the city of Asheville. Encountering such ambivalent acceptance, contradictory 'readings,' or at times rejection by some scene members fuels Kelicia and Amanda's fierce individualism and inspires them to carve their own spaces in the scene to continue to feel the freedom and power they acquire from the music. But not all participants would persevere through such odds. Without feeling welcomed in the scene, many participants would forego the live show and choose instead to listen to the music in private, thereby missing out on what could be a dynamic expansion upon the experience of bodily intensity that the music fosters.

Amanda and Kelicia's narratives represent shifting notions of authenticity. Though Bogue defines death metal as antipop (2004), it is a form of popular music that is growing in popularity with increasing exposure through broader mediums such as social media, music sharing sites, video games and references in popular adaptations. As death metal reaches wider audiences through wider mediums, fans emerge from multiple backgrounds and influences offering challenges to exclusionary categories through their complex identity processes. Amanda and Kelicia both challenge rigid categorical oppositions as they bring death metal into bedroom culture, into pop culture, and everyday interactions. Kelicia's embrace of power and her refusal to be passive and nice in all situations can stimulate her friends to envision alternatives, thereby changing the definitions of femininity among her friends. As Amanda puts on a studded bathing suit and drapes fake blood over herself, her presentation ruptures some of the common stereotypes of beauty, while admittedly reinforcing others. Their interpretations are hardly unproblematic. For example, while Kelicia freely asserts herself, at the time of ethnography (2010–2013) her ideal romantic relationships asserted stereotypical gender roles. And while Amanda values Gaga's subversive imagery, she is critical of her androgynous presentation, which some research participants may find refreshing and transgressive. Both downplay the business elements and multiple authors behind the production of Britney and Gaga as pop images. Regardless, they offer examples of death metal's influences reaching out to unexpected areas, creating dialogues, infiltrating, sneaking in transgressive themes that increase agency and shed light on alternatives in gendered presentation.

While Kelicia and Amanda's personal narratives illustrate the complex relationship between popular music and extreme metal, their use of authenticity discourses to frame their tastes and self-presentations reflect the continuing relevance and application of categorization in power discourses among metal fans. To understand the persistence of such exclusionary practices, metal music scholars would benefit from examining fans' practices of self-narrativization to find what historical social processes inform their construction of self in relation to 'other.' Exclusionary processes of authenticity building, in other words, engaging in the 'secret' sonically and socially, have been sources of obtaining power that research participants have proven can be used to make significant improvements in their lives. However, what attracts some fans to the music and how they define it in opposition to what they consider as mainstream constructions of gender or superficiality can simultaneously become instrumental in excluding others who they interpret as 'mainstream,' other women who could also benefit from involvement with the death metal community. Instead of excluding female participants based on their self-presentations, which are ever shifting and complex, fans could engage in their own dialogic processes with others in the scene and outside the scene to redefine gender and sexuality. Through engaging with fans from multiple backgrounds and with varied gendered self-presentations, female fans can help transform those mainstream gendered presentations that they initially sought to challenge by being involved in death metal. Scholars, too, by engaging with fans' multiple subjectivities, can gain a clearer understanding of death metal identities as not fixed or separate from other identity processes, but as part of continuing social activity of self-authoring in the person.

Notes

1. The term's double-meaning is intentional. On one hand, blasting can mean to 'criticize fiercely,' but it can also refer to playing music at full volume. Given the context of the work, both meanings are applicable here.
2. It should be noted that all research participants in this article have provided informed consent to have the material collected through ethnography and interviews be presented here within this specific article's context under the purpose of researching life narratives and personal experiences of self-identifying female fans of death metal. None wished to be kept anonymous, but to protect their identities, I chose not to use their full given names.
3. She connotes this feeling to a combination of excitement in hearing her favorite bands live and a claustrophobic social anxiety of being enmeshed in a throng of bodies, strangers pressed against her, contesting her usual range of personal space.
4. She had contacted me after seeing a flyer I had posted in the undergraduate literature building on UNC's campus seeking research participants who considered themselves fans of death metal for a graduate master's thesis in Folklore. After conducting several interviews with her at length, she had become a major contributor to my research. Though she runs a blog on underground death metal with a male friend, Kelicia is less socially involved in the North Carolina metal scene than Amanda, who contacts bands in other regions to book shows, and, despite living two hours away in Wilmington, often travels to Raleigh to visit friends or watch local bands.
5. I discuss this at length in an upcoming publication.
6. Kelicia's interpretation of the lyrics may be of interest to scholars analyzing women's identification with violent lyrics. The song features a sadistic dentist who tortures a female or feminized victim and forces the victim to perform fellatio. Kelicia ignores the sexual transgression in the lyrics and does not identify with the victim or with the fact that the victim is depicted as a woman. Kahn-Harris defines this process of consciously choosing to ignore sections that may otherwise be offensive 'reflexive anti-reflexivity' (2007). Phillipov points out the difficulty in analyzing the lyrics alone without listening to what's going on musically alongside their presentation (2012).
7. While this paper focuses on the experience of authenticity building in relation to gendered classification in the scene, elsewhere, I have attempted to deconstruct the common stereotypes, originating from both within death metal scenes and from scholars writing about them, of female-identified fans as either being masculine as 'one of the guys' or hyperfeminine, classified as 'the girlfriends,' 'super girly' or 'band whores.' My argument is that women's experiences in the scene are more nuanced and cannot be reduced to such categories. Even those who would seem to 'fit' a stereotype are reflexively interacting with complexity to such tropes.

Bibliography

Bakhtin, M. (1984) *Rabelais and His World* (Indiana, IN: Indiana University Press).
Berger, H. (1999) *Metal, Rock, and Jazz: Perception and the Phenomenology of Musical Experience* (Hanover, NH: University Press of New England).

Bogue, R. (2004) *Delueze's Wake: Tributes and Tributaries* (Albany, NY: State University of New York).

Brown, A. (2007) 'Rethinking the Subcultural Commodity: The Case of Heavy Metal T-shirt Culture(s),' *Youth Cultures: Scenes, Subcultures and Tribes*, eds. P. Hodkinson & W. Deicke (New York: Routledge), pp. 63–78.

Clifford, A. (2009) 'The Leather Sisterhood: Heavy Metal, Masculinity, and Lesbian Fandom,' *First International Conference on Gender and Heavy Metal, University for Music* (Cologne, Thursday 8th to Saturday 10th October 2009).

Dawes, L. (2012) *What Are You Doing Here? A Black Woman's Life and Liberation in Heavy Metal* (New York: Bazillion Points).

DeNora, T. (2000) *Music in Everyday Life* (New York: Cambridge University Press).

Dibben, N. (2002) 'Gender Identity and Music,' *Musical Identities*, eds. D. Macdonald, D. J. Hargreaves, & D. Miell (Oxford, UK: Oxford University Press), pp. 117–134.

Durbin, K. & Vicks, M. (2010) *Gaga Stigmata: Critical Writings and Art About Lady Gaga*. Retrieved 7 January 2013 from: http://gagajournal.blogspot.com/.

Finnegan, R. (2003) 'Music, Experience, and the Anthropology of Emotion,' *The Cultural Study of Music: A Critical Introduction*, eds. M. Clayton, T. Herbert, & R. Middleton (New York, NY: Routledge), pp. 181–192.

Halberstam, J. (2012) 'Going Gaga: Scream, Shout, Lose Control,' *JPMS Online: POP/IASPM-US* [Online] (*Sounds of the City Theme Issue*). Retrieved 26 November 2012 from: http://iaspm-us.net/jpms-online-popiaspm-us-sounds-of-the-city-issue-jack-halberstam/.

Hickam, B. & Wallach, J. (2011) 'Female Authority and Dominion: Discourse and Distinctions of Heavy Metal Scholarship,' *Journal for Cultural Research*, 15(3), pp. 255–278.

Holland, D. & Lachicotte, W. (2007) 'Vygotsky, Mean, and New Sociocultural Studies of Identity,' *The Cambridge Companion to Vygotsky*, eds. H Daniels, M. Cole, & J. Wertsch (Cambridge, MA: Cambridge University Press), pp. 101–135.

Hutcherson, B. & Haenfler, R. (2010) 'Musical Genre as a Gendered Process: Authenticity in Extreme Metal,' *Studies in Symbolic Interaction*, 35, pp. 101–121.

Kahn-Harris, K. (2007) *Extreme Metal: Music and Culture on the Edge* (Oxford, UK: Berg).

Klypchak, B. (2007) *Performed Identities: Heavy Metal Musicians between 1984–1991*. A Thesis Submitted in Partial Fulfilment of the Requirements of Bowling Green State University for a Degree of Masters of Popular Culture (Bowling Green, OH: Bowling Green State University).

Krenske, L. & McKay, J. (2000) 'Hard and Heavy: Gender and Power in a Heavy Metal Music Subculture,' *Gender, Place and Culture*, 7(3), pp. 287–304.

Larsson, S. (2013) 'I Bang My Head, Therefore I Am: Constructing Individual and Social Authenticity in the Heavy Metal Subculture,' *Young*, 21(1), pp. 95–110.

Leblanc, L. (1999) *Pretty in Punk: Girls' Gender Resistance in a Boys' Subculture* (New Jersey, NJ: Rutgers University Press).

Overell, R. (2011) '[I] Hate Girls and Emo[tion]s: Negotiating Masculinity in Grindcore Music,' *Popular Music History*, 6(1–2), pp. 198–223.

Phillipov, M. (2012) *Death Metal and Music Criticism: Analysis at the Limits* (New York, NY: Lexington Books).

Purcell, N. (2003) *Death Metal Music: The Passion and Politics of a Subculture* (Jefferson, NC: McFarland).

Riches, G. (2011) 'Embracing the Chaos: Mosh Pits, Extreme Metal Music and Liminality,' *Journal for Cultural Research*, 15(3), pp. 315–332.

Thornton, S. (2006) 'Understanding Hipness: "Subcultural Capital" as Feminist Tool,' *The Popular Music Studies Reader*, eds. A. Bennett, B. Shank, & J. Toynbee (London: Routledge), pp. 99–105.

Vasan, S. (2009) 'Den Mothers and Band Whores: Gender, Sex, and Power in the Death Metal Scene,' *Second Global Conference on Heavy Fundamentalisms: Music, Metal and Politics* (November 2009. Austria).

Vasan, S. (2011) 'The Price of Rebellion: Gender Boundaries in the Death Metal Scene,' *Journal for Cultural Research*, 15(3), pp. 333–350.

7
Powerslaves? Navigating Femininity in Heavy Metal

Jenna Kummer
University of Lethbridge

Introduction

Since the musical genre of heavy metal first appeared in the late 1960s, it has been associated with symbols and images of masculinity by both insiders and outsiders of the heavy metal subculture (Hickam & Wallach, 2011, p. 255). This is apparent on heavy metal album covers as women are often shown inferior to men by being placed in the background, signifying weakness and dependency. The lyrics of heavy metal songs also generally present women as inferior to men and '[r]eferences to sex are typically of a lustful nature, for the pleasure of men, and without commitment' (Krenske & McKay, 2000, p. 290). Aside from album covers and lyrics, there is another obvious reason for heavy metal's primary association with masculinity. Walser (1993) states:

> The purpose of the [heavy metal] genre is to organize the reproduc-
> tion of a particular ideology, and the generic cohesion of heavy metal
> until the mid-1980s depended upon the desire of young white male
> performers and fans to hear and believe in certain stories about the
> nature of masculinity. (p. 154)

Through the marginalization and pressure to conform for women in this subculture, it is clear that heavy metal is, inescapably, a discourse shaped by patriarchy (Walser, 1993, p. 154). The patriarchy that Walser (1993) is referring to is the general consensus of heavy metal fans who agree the genre is male-dominated. This male-domination denotes the primary roots of the music.

This research questions how women navigate within the broader sub-culture of heavy metal, and uses Michel Foucault's notions of discourse, resistance, normalization, and the subject/subjectification in order to provide new insight into understanding how women within the heavy metal subculture might resist and/or subject to power in different ways. Aligning with the theme of critique, I will focus on two of four findings of my research: how female heavy metal fans construct an 'other' femi-nine type that they compared themselves to, and, how they were found to reappropriate their femininity.

I argue that women feel empowered to be a part of the heavy metal subculture. They feel that heavy metal ultimately allows them to resist mainstream society which allows them to emphasize their uniqueness as a female heavy metal fan. I also argue that the women inter-viewed were all found to reappropriate their femininity which was how they felt they resisted the male-dominance within heavy metal. This reappropriation of femininity therefore becomes a new understanding as to how female heavy metal fans navigate their femininity within this popular subculture.

Heavy metal music and its gendered fans

Originating in the heavily distorted guitar style with bands such as Black Sabbath, Led Zeppelin and Deep Purple, heavy metal has been around in various forms since the late 1960s (Epstein, 1998, p. 103). The con-struction of the music's instrumental structure generally includes power, distortion, freedom and volume '...built up through vocal extremes, guitar power cords, distortion and sheer volume of bass and drums' (Walser, 1993, p. 153). Heavy metal musicians have been described as '...swaggering males, leaping and strutting about the stage, clad in span-dex, scarves, leather and other visually noisy clothing, punctuating their performances with phallic thrusts of guitars and microphone stands' (1993, p. 153). The audiences for heavy metal music are also predom-inantly male (Vasan, 2011, p. 342). Metal enthusiasts, known as 'metal heads,' typically wear articles of clothing such as T-shirts with illustra-tions of band album covers or logos, jeans, leather or denim jackets, as well as heavy boots. Female enthusiasts usually wear similar articles of clothing as the men. However, they are also seen wearing revealing dresses, cut up T-shirts exposing their shoulders or back, corset tops and short skirts (Vasan, 2011, p. 342). Men dominate the mosh pit, although women who wear jeans and a T-shirt also have been seen participating (ibid.). If men dominate in this subculture, why do women choose to be a part of it?

Krenske and McKay's (2000) research leads to further suspicions about why women would want to be a part of the heavy metal subculture as they argue that it is an oppressive subculture that is dominated by males. They also state that women 'do gender' on men's terms by discussing how female fans of heavy metal are rebellious in order to be on the same level as men within the group (p. 287). Weinstein (2000) further discusses how women are dominated within heavy metal by arguing that they associate themselves with a feminine persona, which allows them to be dominated:

Women, on stage or in the audience, are either sex objects to be used or abused, or must renounce their gender and pretend to be one of the boys. The few female metal performers must conform to the masculinist code, and have generally opted to appear as sex objects. (p. 221)

Observing that female fans that dress and behave like men are more likely to be respected by male fans is also suggested in the literature (see Vasan, 2011, p. 347). Further, Walser (1993) argues that for heavy metal, '[s]pectacles are problematic in the context of a patriarchal order that is invested in the stability of signs and which seeks to maintain women in the position of the object of the male gaze' (p. 153). This suggests there are only two roles for women to fill in heavy metal: pretend to be 'like the boys' to fit in, or to be a sex object. Krenske and McKay (2000) expand on this by stating that there were a few telling indications of women's subordinate status to men. First, although some women hold some power, it was limited. Second, when women did have power over men, it was always exercised through a male friend or boyfriend due to a defensive or reactive situation. Third, women never exercised any collective power over men (p. 302). Ultimately, it is argued that women are unable to hold any form of status within the heavy metal subculture.

Scholars maintain that heavy metal celebrates and reinforces male power while restricting female power (Krenske & McKay, 2000, p. 300; Weinstein, 2000, p. 221). As a result, women's femininity has ultimately been a factor as to why they have not been able to bond with men on the same level that men bond with men in the heavy metal subculture (Weinstein, 2000, p. 135). It is also argued that doing gender for a woman in the heavy metal subculture generally defines them as a sex object (Weinstein, 2000, p. 221; Zillman & Bhatia, 1989, p. 284). Vasan challenges this idea by arguing that heavy metal frees women from many of the restrictions of mainstream society (2011, p. 334). Hickam and Wallach elaborate on mainstream society and the subculture by noting that '...some hostile outsiders find the music offensive – and that, admittedly, is part of the fun – the music's primary aim is defensive, to shield from assault, to provide the strength to endure and prevail' (2011, p. 266). Therefore, although the music is seen as offensive, heavy metal fans still enjoy the music because it gives them an outlet. Heavy metal empowers both men and women. Although women are marginalized and restricted within the heavy metal subculture, they still continue to listen to and support the music (Vasan, 2011, p. 334).

Methodology

As an emerging sociologist and fan of heavy metal, I began to be critical of the literature surrounding this popular genre of music. With the key ideas from the literature in mind, I was led to the conclusion that femininity in general within the heavy metal subculture is not widely discussed or understood. Hill (2014) also argues this, stating that dominant frameworks in heavy metal studies are inadequate for understanding female fans and their experiences (p. 174). When I first began listening to heavy metal, I did not feel that I was doing so in order to be resistant or defiant, but I really, truly enjoyed the music. I enjoyed the power, distortion and freedom that Walser refers to. I also enjoyed that I had found a place to belong within such a welcoming subculture. As a result, I became more and more confused as to why outsiders were so critical of the music and its fans, like Hickam and Wallach note. I began to think of resistance as a stepping stone toward a better understanding of these critiques, a first step in determining if women within heavy metal do resist and, if so, what this resistance might look like.

The idea that women resist within the heavy metal subculture was first discovered for this research not only in review of literature, which does not seem to discuss resistance for women, but also due to speculations made by Vasan (2011) which I could personally identify with. Arguably, women are searching for liberation and personal fulfilment through the music and the heavy metal subculture. This search for liberation could stem from a lack of empowerment in mainstream society, as well as a lack of empowerment in alternative groups or subcultures (Vasan, 2011, p. 347).

My analysis of how women navigate their femininity in heavy metal was generated using three aspects of qualitative methodology. First, in order to provide context and knowledge for my interview questions as well as determine important elements of discourse present in a heavy metal scene, I began by immersing myself in the setting of the subculture in Calgary, Alberta, Canada with the position of a researcher. While observing, I focused on the most likely heavy metal settings such as concerts or shows and I did not limit myself to attending shows within any particular genre of heavy metal. Second, interviews were conducted with five self-proclaimed female heavy metal fans, or scene members, in their early to mid-20s. All participants signed informed consent forms outlining the purpose of the research as well as how their identities would be protected by the use of pseudonyms and the removal of personal and/or identifying information. Participants were selected through purposive and snowball sampling methodologies, and all interviews were face-to-face. In the interviews, participants had the opportunity to explain exactly how they felt they navigated their femininity in heavy metal as well as explain why they had to navigate their femininity in ways that accorded with the discourses that exist within the subculture. The term navigation was used because it encompassed many aspects, including performance and negotiation, but it was not leading in any sense to the participants. For example, I did not want the women to feel that I thought they were 'performing' their femininity because in stating this, they may suspected me to be implying that they were not truly heavy metal fans. Finally, in order to set the stage for understanding Foucauldian theories of discourse and power for this research, heavy metal images and lyrics were shown to participants during the interviews and then discussed in order to allow the participants to engage in somewhat of a discourse analysis themselves. In what follows, I will elaborate on the concepts that inform this study. These include: discourse, resistance, normalization and the subject/subjectification.

Hall (2013) argues that for Foucault, discourse is a system of representation that constructs topics not in language but in social practices (p. 29). He states that 'it attempts to overcome the traditional distinction between what one says (language) and what one does (practice)' (p. 29). Further:

> Discourse … defines and produces the objects of our knowledge. It governs the way that a topic can be meaningfully talked about and reasoned about. It also influences how ideas are put in to practice and used to regulate the conduct of others. (p. 29)

Ultimately created through language and interactions, discourses create certain rules that define the purpose of each object (Hall, 2013, p. 29).

These rules are the power of discourse. The discourse that will therefore be referred to throughout this paper will be the male-dominated,
masculine subculture that heavy metal encompasses.

Discourse also produces knowledge which in turn produces power.
Insofar as individuals have knowledge about power, the opportunity
presents itself for them to resist power. Clarke (2006) asserts this by noting that, for Foucault, '[w]here there is power there is resistance, the
individual is a product of power and a transmitter of power' (p. 104).
Therefore, within the masculine heavy metal subculture, the possibility for women to resist presents itself. Operations of power ultimately
produce the discourse which also outlines what proper behaviors would
be for an individual, as well as what an improper behavior would be.
Known as normalization, what is considered the ideal type of behavior is based on binary normal versus abnormal behaviors (Heyes, 2007,
p. 32). These manifestations of power include our gender, sex, race, class,
intelligence, musical genres; every aspect that constructs an individual's identity (ibid.). As a result, what is considered acceptable within a
society is a process in which normal and abnormal binaries are created.

Foucault's notion of the subject provides a key insight in determining
how much an individual internalizes the masculine discourses within
heavy metal and how much they might resist this. In *The Subject and
Power*, Foucault (1982) asserts that '[t]here are two meanings of the
word "subject": subject to someone else by control and dependence; and
tied to his own identity by a conscience or self-knowledge. Both meanings suggest a form of power which subjugates and makes subject to'
(p. 781). As there are two meanings of the word subject, how women
heavy metal fans are subjects in these ways is important to address.
First, women in heavy metal can be considered as fans '... who personify the particular forms of knowledge which the discourse produces'
(Hall, 2013, p. 40). Second, the women are 'defined by the discourse'
(ibid.) as female heavy metal fans and this is tied to their identity.
If female heavy metal fans resist and/or subject themselves to the culture, symbols and images that heavy metal presents, it is an inquiry
in how they navigate their femininity within the subculture because
the ideas and attitudes that ultimately shape a female heavy metal fan's
subjectification and/or resistance to the music is produced through discourse. Butler (1997) follows up on this by arguing that the creation of
this individual subject is not possible without simultaneous submission.
She states that for Foucault, power is not what presses on the subject
from the outside, but instead it also forms the subject '... providing the
very condition of its existence and the trajectory of its desire' (p. 2).

Due to this, '... power is not simply what we oppose but also, in a strong sense, what we depend on for our existence and what we harbor and preserve in the beings that we are' (p. 2). Thus, in any given situation, an individual can both resist and subject themselves to the discourse simultaneously, hence my use of the phrase 'subject and/or resist.'

Findings

This study's broader findings indicated that female heavy metal fans were originally drawn to the music because they were looking for something heavier, more powerful instrumentally, and faster paced. All participants also admitted to heavy metal as a whole being male-dominated alongside the arguments that are generally (re)presented in heavy metal studies literature. Heavy metal was also described to empower the participants, allowing them to be rebellious as well as giving them an outlet for their anger and frustration, and it was commonly described as 'bad ass.' How the participants described their reasons for enjoying the music were useful in determining why they continue to support heavy metal bands as well as in understanding what motivates them to continue to participate in the subculture.

In order to further access how women navigate their femininity within this confirmed male-dominated subculture and link the results with the theme of critique, I maintain two arguments: construction of the 'other' and reappropriation of femininity. These arguments will each highlight how the participants subjected and/or resisted heavy metal discourses.

Construction of the 'other'

Each of the interviewees in this study described their femininity to be different than a woman who exists outside of the heavy metal community. The participants also mentioned that they were different than women within the subculture who were not as committed to heavy metal. This demonstrates how women navigate their femininity in heavy metal because the participants were very defensive when they described how they were different than other women inside and outside of the heavy metal community. I argue that the participants understood these women in such a way that they 'othered' them, resulting in the defense of their femininity and status in the heavy metal subculture.

The notion of 'othering' is described as '... the social, linguistic and psychological mechanism that distinguishes "us" from "them," the normal from the deviant. Othering marks and names the other, providing a definition of their otherness, which in turn creates social distance and marginalizes, dis-empowers and excludes' (Barter-Godfrey & Taket, 2009, p. 166). Foucault (1982) also provides a definition of the 'other,' stating that it is 'the one over whom power is exercised' (p. 789). This distinguishing of two types of women, the 'us' – participants – from 'them' – women outside of the heavy metal community and women who were not as committed to heavy metal – was seen in a few ways. First, it was seen in knowledge. The participants argued that they had gained the knowledge that it takes to hold status in the heavy metal community in comparison to the 'other' women. As described by Maria, women feel that they have to work their way up in the subculture to be at the same level as males, and this was described to be a very difficult process:

> I think that girls definitely have to try harder to work up to it... You have to be able to sit down and have a conversation about albums and members and, if you can talk about instrumental parts too cause I feel that's a big... separation kinda too, like listening to metal and then being able to break down like the music and stuff.

> (Maria)

These individuals who had not gained this status were commonly referred to in the interviews as 'not a true metal head' versus a 'legitimate woman in metal.' The participants categorized feminine qualities that heavy metal devalues as qualities that women who do not listen to heavy metal encompass. These feminine qualities that heavy metal generally devalues include weakness, dependency and nurturance. Due to this, the participants continued to describe themselves as different than these two types of 'other' women. In the process of defending their femininity, the women navigate their femininity as unique, allowing them to separate themselves from conventional notions of what it means to be feminine. This separation illustrates resistance because it allows the participants to continue in the subculture as still feminine, but in the sense that they are not targets of the discourse.

Second, 'othering' was seen in how the participants perceived themselves. Outside of the heavy metal scene, participants expressed their concern with how they felt out of place. This was outlined by how the participants wanted to separate themselves from the conventional constructions of what it means to be feminine. They described themselves as more aggressive and as tomboys, and mentioned that even though they looked and felt out of place in society, it did not bother them. This consideration of how women are perceived from outside of the heavy metal community links with how they navigate their femininity within heavy metal because the participants argued that the music led them to be strong and independent women. One participant mentioned that before listening to the music, she felt less confident and heavy metal changed that for her:

> Just as a person and my self confidence in myself and who I am and being stronger and being able to survive situations and whatever life throws at you…And feeling empowered to take anything that can swing at you down.

(Sheena)

Thus, as it is discussed in the literature, participants identified with the argument that heavy metal '…provide[s] the strength to endure and prevail' (Hickam & Wallach, 2011, p. 266).

Third, 'othering' was seen in how the participants stereotyped. When the participants were shown images of strong men and dependent women, which are often illustrated on album covers, they immediately explained that the women in those pictures are not women who would listen to heavy metal. They explained this to be due to their physical position in the images and were described by the participants as sex objects, sluts or slaves. In this case, Foucault's notion of normalization is presented as a consideration of a binary of abnormal versus normal behaviors within the heavy metal community that women who are fans of the music also face. The binary is how women within the heavy metal community are constructed as the 'other' concurrently with women who are not fans of the music.

To bring knowledge, perception and stereotyping together, the participants argued the women on the album covers are not true metal heads. They felt that the portrayal of women on heavy metal album covers in such a way that they are sexually objectified allows people from outside of the community to consider all women to be dominated by the men within the subculture. They mentioned that the difference is they have the knowledge about bands, instrumentals, albums and artists in order to not be treated, as Brittany put it, 'like a girl,' and to ultimately be at the same level as the males within the community. If a woman did not have this knowledge, they were immediately considered as an 'other,' and participants described them, once again, as not true fans of the music.

Furthermore, larger discourses of heavy metal are also embodied and played out in localized scenes. Aside from 'othering' women in the album covers, participants also admitted to looking at 'other' women within the subculture differently. At one point in my conversation with Maria, she mentioned that it is common to notice lots of women who seem 'out of place' at heavy metal shows. When asked what she thinks of these women, she stated:

> First impression, it might be kinda bias of me to think this, but first impression...I just kind of assume that they're here with their boyfriend or they're here to impress somebody. I don't think that they're here for the band. And if you kinda watch, as creepy as it sounds, if you kinda watch some of them throughout the show, they're not really...They won't really pay attention when the band's on. They'll be like by the bar or by a wall or something.
>
> (Maria)

The participants explained that looking at 'other' women different within the subculture was mainly due to the community being so close knit that if a new woman were to be seen at a heavy metal concert or event that were not following how the 'other' women within the subculture dressed or acted, she would stick out.

How the women continued to defend the fact that although they were females, they were true heavy metal fans, would be considered subjec-tification alongside resistance because of how they defend and position themselves as legitimate fans of the music. Even though the women are resistant to the discourses by defending their feminine fan status, they are becoming subjects of the discourse by attaining the knowledge that they need in attempt to align their status with the males in the group. They also defended this when it came to considering how oth-ers outside of the subculture view women in heavy metal. By 'othering' women who do not listen to heavy metal and categorizing them as sim-ilar to women who are in the heavy metal community but are not 'true' fans, they are reinforcing the discourses of heavy metal.

Similarly to the 'othering' that they felt coming from outside of the heavy metal community, the participants felt that they should not be treated differently than the males within the community. Due to this, I found that the women had a strong desire to be considered separate from the discourse of patriarchy and misogyny within the commu-nity. This consideration illustrates resistance once again because of how they defended their femininity and defined it as more independent and empowered. Women navigate their femininity in the very action that they work hard to have the knowledge about heavy metal in order to have the same status as men. Not only did they not want to be looked at as different or 'othered' outside of the group, but their primary concern was being looked at as different or 'othered' within the group:

> So, the most important thing is just treating them like everyone else. Like, not giving them any benefits or any hindrances to being in the subculture if I can call it that.
>
> (Brittany)

This example also presents a binary because the desire to be treated similarly to women who do not listen to heavy metal presents a manifestation of power that constructs the women's identity. This is because the participants felt that they should not be placed in the abnormal category just because of the type of music that they listen to. Interestingly, this presents a huge contradiction, therefore illustrating subjectification alongside resistance. Although the women did not want to be 'othered' themselves, as discussed, they still 'othered' 'other' women. In other words, the participants were so concerned about not being 'othered' by the men within the subculture, yet they had a tendency to 'other' women within the subculture which they considered not to be a 'true' metal head. For example, as discussed, the participants all, in some way or another, 'othered' women in the album covers by stating that they were not women who would listen to heavy metal. This was because the women in the images were seen as dependent on the men that were illustrated in the images because the men are the dominant gender in heavy metal: they were illustrated as stronger and more powerful than the women. To elaborate on the earlier discussion of the images shown to the participants, I showed the participants the Manowar album cover, *Gods of War* where strong, burly men stand on top of a mountain triumphantly with women lying at their feet. I also showed participants the *Revenge in Blood* album cover by WarCry, and the *Balls Out* album cover by Steel Panther. Some participants described the women in the pictures to be different than women within the heavy metal subculture by suggesting that it is just an advertising ploy to get more young males to purchase the albums. One participant suggested that only a certain kind of girl would kneel at men's feet like the picture portrays:

> This kind of girl, they would rather have down there, but I dunno. If you had like another girl up here, they would have to

be way more like men to be beside them, or at least exhibiting the same status. So you'd have to be more manly to be up here rather than super ridiculously feminine with thongs on.

(Nicole)

Another participant states that a good sense of humor is required to interpret these images as well as a woman's position in the subculture:

Some women would be really disgusted by that, but for the most part, legitimate women in metal they, most of them that you meet, they've got a pretty good sense of humor. And most of them have to have a pretty good sense of humor, 'cause you know what? You get used to getting knocked down and challenged for who you are and what you're into all the time that you have to have a sense of humor or else you'd just be so angry that even the music you listen to itself isn't gonna balance out how mad you are about having to justify that all the time.

(Sheena)

Overall, the participants felt that the album covers and images within heavy metal did not impact them because the images were always the same within the subculture, and they did not consider themselves to be 'those girls.' They argued that they were veterans in the community and felt that they were appreciated by the males due to having a knowledge base about the albums, artists and instrumentals that the music encompasses. Resistance therefore allowed the women to feel that they were not like the women on the album covers. However, as the participants maintained that they should not be treated differently from the males, they miss that they are subjecting themselves to the patriarchy and misogyny that the music is constructed through by 'othering.'

More examples of 'othering' were demonstrated by the participants when they referred to a local venue that was holding feminine heavy metal nights, as well as when I mistakenly referred to bands with female vocalists in them as 'female fronted.' At one point, Nicole mentioned to me that is was unnecessary to say 'female fronted' because it separated the female fans from the male fans. When women are 'othered' within the group, it challenges their notion of being empowered, strong and independent. To illustrate this example, a conversation I had with Brittany about feminine heavy metal nights that were organized by a local bar in Calgary comes to light. She mentioned:

It really bothers me because like, why?! Do [they] really need to do that? Can't [they] just pretend that we're all the same like we are? Not pretend, but actually behave like we're all the same? I don't get it.

(Brittany)

Nicole also reflected on similar circumstances, and stated:

It's just old news now...It's like, 'Oh, women are in metal!' And everyone's just like, 'Yeah, we know...Okay. So what?'. At one point maybe it was important to call attention to it and to say, 'Hey, girls you can actually like metal too, you don't have to think it's weird.' But now everyone knows that women listen to metal. Everyone gets it. You don't have to point it out.

(Nicole)

Therefore, the participants argued that by pointing out the fact that women are into heavy metal is not beneficial because it does not make them feel any more empowered. Also, it just reinforces women's marginalization and novelty status within the metal scene.

This discussion can further be developed by considering how women perform their gender. As discussed, Krenske and McKay (2000) argue that women in the heavy metal community 'do gender' on men's terms (p. 287). Their research found that women might be rebellious in the heavy metal subculture because they are trying to attain an equal status to the males within the group. Although Krenske and McKay's research presents a new vantage point for understanding women's status in heavy metal, I sought to further understand what doing gender on men's terms means. In so doing, I found women admitting that they worked hard at learning about what heavy metal music had to offer in order to be taken seriously by the males in the community. Maria notes:

I think that girls definitely have to try harder to work up to it...Like, you have to be able to sit down and have a conversation about albums and members and...instrumental parts too...

(Maria)

Aside from knowledge about the music, Sheena also argued that men appreciated women who know something about heavy metal. She mentioned this by saying:

...guys are more attracted to a girl that can actually talk about metal than look the type. So, from having a lot of male metal friends that have that opinion, they're way more attracted to that than the actual physical looks...

(Sheena)

This appreciation is one reason why women have to work so hard to gain the knowledge they needed to be a part of the subculture. It is also an example as to how women might do gender on men's terms, even if they are in fact true fans of the music.

Foucault would argue that female heavy metal fans are only conforming to the male-dominated subculture insofar as they have knowledge and internalize the discourses to be the truth. As participants in this study felt that, for the most part, they were the same as men within the heavy metal community because they had knowledge about the music, they did not internalize the male-domination within the subculture to be the truth. Yet, they each challenged it by arguing that they had the knowledge to determine what was patriarchal within the symbols and images in the music. They also challenged it by 'othering' women who did not fit the descriptions of what it means to be a fan of the music.

Overall, female heavy metal fans are 'othered' outside of the heavy metal subculture as well as inside which causes them to navigate their femininity in a very defensive way. This defensiveness is illustrated through a woman's attempt to escape from being 'othered' within the heavy metal community. The contradictions that were presented by the participants in relation to this argument illustrates that they are still subject to the discourses that are present outside and inside heavy metal, even though they were resisting by defending their femininity. Thus, their quest to hold the same status as males within the group is abnormal due to how femininity has been constructed over time to be less significant within society and also less significant within heavy metal. How the participants constructed an 'other' is also beneficial for understanding how women heavy metal fans also reappropriated their femininity.

Reappropriation of femininity

As the female participants described themselves to have a different understanding of their femininity as compared to 'others,' I argue that they reappropriated their femininity. In this circumstance, reappropriating femininity is a process in which a woman considers herself to have a different outlook on femininity and what it means to be feminine. Participants in this study expressed that much of their femininity is not necessarily similar to masculinity, but is somewhat of a hybrid version of both feminine as well as masculine traits. Within heavy metal, women are objectified in the lyrics, symbols and images which reinforce a paternalistic and masculine discourse. In order to avoid being objectified, female heavy metal fans must find a way to associate their femininity differently, so they reappropriate it by considering it as different, thus allowing their subjectification to the discourse to be justified. However, in the very practice of reappropriation, the participants did show some signs of resistance. To illustrate how women reappropriated their femininity and thus defined their identity within the discourses of heavy metal, I will expand on conversations that I had with the participants in terms of their clothing choices, their actions and attitudes inside the scene, and their relationships inside the scene.

First, how these women chose to dress is one inquiry as to how they appropriate their femininity because the clothes that female heavy metal fans described themselves to wear represented another interesting contradiction. Some of the articles of clothing that the participants admitted to wearing seem to be more along the lines of what the participants described women who are not heavy metal fans would wear, aligning with the conversation of 'othering.' Sheena talked about corsets:

> Yeah, corsets are something that I've gotten used to seeing at metal shows and you would think, 'Ah, she's just milkin' the attention,' but some of the ones, they...heck, even I have two corsets. Although, I think I've only worn one to a show once.
>
> (Sheena)

Maria talked about cutting up her T-shirts:

> I cut my shirts so they...show a little cleavage...at metal shows, you'll also see a lot of backless shredded shirts...
>
> (Maria)

Nicole discussed her makeup:

> I wear a lot more make-up when I go to a show and like, try to make it extreme...If I go out to a show I wanna go pretty crazy if I'm feeling

up to it. I do find myself trying to pick through what to wear to go to a concert, like it really matters for some reason.

(Nicole)

Brittany talked about 'feminine pieces' of clothing:

The only difference with women is that I think there's feminine pieces that they'll throw in like fishnets once in a while, or skirts, or corsets.

(Brittany)

Ultimately, this style is not very different when comparing what the participants described another woman to wear if she is being sexually objectified on an album cover because they are obviously provocative. This consideration of how the participants described the 'other' women is where another contradiction presents itself because each participant agreed that they were not that type of woman, even though they admitted to wearing similar clothing. Thus, they have a different consideration of what it means to be feminine as a true female heavy metal fan.

Four of the five participants mentioned that they were totally aware that they were feminine in terms of how they dressed. Some believed that this was due to their style of clothing, while others mentioned that they simply prefer to wear short skirts or tight black pants. Two participants even mentioned that their clothing choices were feminine not because they always wore a plain male-sized T-shirt and jeans, but because of their long blonde hair. For the other participants, they felt that if they wore boots, which they considered to be masculine, it was still feminine because they dressed them up with a skirt and fishnets or pantyhose.

The participants' descriptions of how they felt that they dressed specific to themselves was not described as masculine or feminine necessarily, but at times it was also described as something else. One participant described her choice of clothing to be practical:

The way I dress is because I like to wear things that are very utilitarian. Like, I need to be able to headbang, I need to be able to run, I need to be able to fall off the stage drunk. You know, like these things are important to me.

(Katie)

Whereas Maria described a reason as to why women might cut up their T-shirts:

> I never really wear shirts that have collars like that and all guys shirts do. I feel more comfortable in like the cut up shirts than a regular one.
>
> (Maria)

Both of these examples provide insight as to how female clothing choices in heavy metal were not necessarily considered masculine or feminine by the participants. In redefining their attire, women are subjecting themselves to the discourse of heavy metal by purchasing the T-shirts and cutting them up to be more comfortable because, arguably, they are also doing it to be more feminine and sexy because they want to stand out in the subculture. They are also describing their attire not as feminine or masculine, but something else. At the same time though, women are resistant insofar as they are attempting to embody the discourse differently, thus they are challenging it. Their choice of clothing and style allows them to feel empowered and visible within the subculture. This modification of clothing creates a new style and purpose for the women and therefore is an example as to how women reappropriate their femininity in the heavy metal subculture.

Second, I explored how women navigate their femininity in heavy metal by their actions. The participants ultimately argued that they could still be considered feminine by how they acted at shows or events. However, they did not elaborate on what exactly these feminine actions were and simply described them as not masculine. For example, Maria stated:

> I don't go into a show and be like, 'Grrr, get out of my way! I'm gonna drink all these beers and go in the pit and I have to punch people in the face' or else people aren't going to accept me. It's not like that. You can get in the pit and still like go off and have a conversation and be feminine. You don't have to butch up to go to a show.
>
> (Maria)

Whereas Katie stated:

> It's really hard to call someone who has like shoulder length blonde hair masculine. I'm pretty and I know that, and people say it to me

all the time. Not just metal heads, a lot of people say that to me on a regular basis. They're like, 'You're really beautiful,' and I'm like, 'Well, I'm still gonna wear like my fuckin' shitty T-shirt and my shitty patches.'

(Katie)

Katie's positioning of her metal attire as masculine in terms of being 'shitty' ultimately troubles her feminine look. These women described their actions and choice of clothing as neither masculine nor feminine, but a hybrid of both genders; in light of these contradictions, they still accept the discourse that heavy metal is patriarchal and therefore they are subjects of the discourse. This is because the discourse of heavy metal presents femininity to be less legitimate than masculinity and the women seemed to internalize this by being unsure of how to explain their clothing and their actions. This subjectification is seen through their explanation of gendered actions as being not completely masculine rather than explaining how they thought they were feminine in comparison. Women are drawing upon these discourses in order to distinguish themselves as legitimate and/or authentic fans and members of the subculture, but in doing so they are also challenging these discourses through embodied practices such as their style, moshing, drinking and headbanging. Because of this immediate association to masculinity, female heavy metal fans do not necessarily dismiss masculine traits. Instead, female fans are resisting masculinist discourses by embodying both masculinity and femininity, thus illustrating a reappropriation.

Third, the construction of relationships is also central in understanding how female heavy metal fans reappropriate their femininity. Every participant admitted to having more male friends than female friends since they had become more involved in the heavy metal community. Maria discussed this by stating:

I think that I would be more likely to be friends with them if they listened to metal, so I assume that, 'Oh, this person is somewhat like me and probably likes a lot of the stuff I do.'

(Maria)

Brittany also discussed this by mentioning she is 'wary' of women:

I'm always kind of more wary of women because I don't know how they are gonna react or behave because I generally have mostly male friends and my friends that are not male, most of them are not metal.

(Brittany)

The participants also stated that it was very difficult for them to navigate their romantic relationships because they had so many male friends. Katie reflected on this by stating:

… with relationships it does impact it because I do notice a lot of the time that I'll go to a show and if I happened to be there with a guy I like, or with a boyfriend, or a guy who is a friend, a lot of the time other men won't talk to me. So I'll just go out of my way to be like, 'Hey, what's going on? I like your shirt, let's talk about music.' …

(Katie)

This idea is also an inquiry as to how women navigate their femininity because their relationships – both romantic and friendly – shape their attitudes and interests that encompass the discourse within heavy metal. Although they try to be 'one of the guys,' there is still a need for them to act feminine in some sense. In relation to the women's attitudes in the heavy metal subculture, participants admitted to wanting to feel sexy when they are in a situation that presents them with romantic opportunities and links with the first discussion in this section which is dress. The intent of the participant's clothing choices in some instances was to be revealing and provocative which would make it feminine. However, the participants do not consider it to be this way and it was common for them to deviate from admitting that their clothing choices were in fact feminine. Katie further elaborates on this by stating:

I mean, sometimes, like when I first started hanging out with them, like I wanted to be like sexy 'cause I wanted to be like, 'Yeah,' like, 'I'm a sexy girl hanging out with all these dudes!' Right?! But, then at some point you're just like, 'I don't even care,' like, 'I'm going the way I am.' But, some part of you still wants to be sexy.

(Katie)

Another contradiction is present here because the women specifically felt that they were different from the women who put themselves out there sexually to get attention from a male romantically. They felt that no matter how they dressed, they were not the dependent women which they described as the 'other.' This was because they had worked so hard to try to get to the same status as men. Also, because they had more male friends than female friends, it was less likely for them to attain a romantic relationship within the heavy metal community.

Although there was a need for the participants to still be feminine yet also be 'one of the guys,' the participants were being defined by the discourse therefore illustrating subjectification once again. This subjectification is presented through how the participants described their friendships and relationships because no matter how much the women try to be at the same status as the men, they felt that they could never attain a similar status. To recall, Katie discussed having to actively pursue conversations with men, and it is because heavy metal is so male-dominated. The participants felt that men prefer to talk to other men because women are more likely to be considered as non-legitimate fans. These attitudes encompass and continue to define the discourses in heavy metal, allowing the masculine actions to continue being considered as something that is acceptable within the subculture.

All in all, the participants did not dismiss the fact that they are feminine, but they also did not totally describe themselves as masculine. This provides an example of reappropriation as resistance because the participants considered themselves to be feminine in different ways, each feeling that their feminine clothing choices did not make them overtly masculine. Therefore, the participants reappropriated their femininity insofar as they redefined what it means to be a female metal fan. At the same time, although the participants feel that they are resisting patriarchy by cutting up their T-shirts, they are still following along with the discourse of patriarchy by presenting themselves as sexier or as more of an object to be exploited by men, thus illustrating once again their subjectification and how they are defined by the discourse.

Conclusions

Navigating femininity within the heavy metal subculture for women is very complex. For them, it is seen as an adaptation and acceptance to the male-dominated subculture in which a patriarchal and misogynist discourse is present. Through this adaptation, acceptance and reappropriation of this male-dominated industry, women are resisting from the present discourse of patriarchy and male-domination. At the same time, this reappropriation also illustrated subjectification to the discourse that the heavy metal subculture is comprised of as the women allow themselves to be defined by the discourse of heavy metal by doing things such as 'othering.' Thus, in many instances, the women were seen as simultaneously subjecting and resisting. This is in line with Foucault's two meanings of the subject as the women were seen to both personify particular forms of knowledge that the discourse of heavy metal produces as well as define themselves by the discourse. As all of the participants not only agreed that the subculture was male-dominated, they also agreed that this does not bother them much. They were prepared to continue to challenge this discourse and resist where they could. This shows that heavy metal is male-dominated, as seen straight from the female participants in this study themselves, thus linking with the theme of critique. Despite this, it is clear that the women participants in this study illustrated tremendous hopefulness and independence with regards to resistance by way of how they were found to reappropriate their femininity and redefine what it means to be feminine in the heavy metal subculture.

A recommendation that has been made clear to me throughout this study is my limited sample size and, therefore, my limited findings. With this being said, more research is necessary in order to further explore how women navigate their femininity in heavy metal. As discussed earlier, there are many gaps in the current literature for addressing women and their experiences in heavy metal. Therefore, the intention of this chapter was simply to begin to explore why women listen to heavy metal in spite of its male-dominated subculture and whether this could link to theories of resistance.

Bibliography

Barter-Godfrey, S. & Taket, A. (2009) 'Othering, Marginalisation and Pathways to Exclusion in Health,' *Theorising Social Exclusion*, eds. A. Taket, B. R. Crisp, A. Nevill, G. Lamaro, M. Graham, & S. Barter-Godfrey (Abingdon, OX: Routledge), pp. 166–172.

Butler, J. (1997) *The Psychic Life of Power* (Stanford, CA: Stanford University Press).

Clarke, S. (2006) *From Enlightenment to Risk: Social Theory and Contemporary Society* (New York, NY: Palgrave Macmillan).

Epstein, J. S. (1998) *Youth Culture: Identity in a Postmodern World* (Malden, MA: Blackwell Publishing).

Foucault, M. (1982) 'The Subject and Power,' *Critical Inquiry*, 8(4), pp. 777–795.

Hall, S. (2013) *Representation* (2nd Ed.). (Thousand Oaks, CA: SAGE Publications).

Heyes, C. J. (2007) *Self-transformations: Foucault, Ethics, and Normalized Bodies* (Oxford, NY: Oxford University Press).

Hickam, B. & Wallach, J. (2011) 'Female Authority and Dominion: Discourse and Distinctions of Heavy Metal Scholarship,' *Journal for Cultural Research*, 15(3), pp. 255–277.

Hill, R. (2014) 'Reconceptualizing Hard Rock and Metal Fans as a Group: Imaginary Community,' *International Journal of Community Music*, 7(2), pp. 173–187.

Krenske, L. & McKay, J. (2000) ' "Hard and Heavy": Gender and Power in a Heavy Metal Music Subculture,' *Gender, Place & Culture*, 7(3), pp. 287–304.

Vasan, S. (2011) 'The Price of Rebellion: Gender Boundaries in the Death Metal Subculture,' *Journal for Cultural Research*, 15(3), pp. 333–349.

Walser, R. (1993) *Running with the Devil: Power, Gender, and Madness in Heavy Metal Music* (Middletown, CT: Wesleyan University Press).

Weinstein, D. (2000) *Heavy Metal: The Music and Its Culture* (New York, NY: De Capo Press).

Zillman, D. & Bhatia, A. (1989) 'Effects of Associating with Musical Genres on Heterosexual Attraction,' *Communication Research*, 16, pp. 263–288.

Part IV
Metal Beyond Metal

8

'Among the Rocks and Roots': A Genre Analysis of Cascadian Black Metal

Anthony J. Thibodeau
Bowling Green State University

In the early to mid-2000s, an innovative expression of extreme heavy metal sprouted from the coastal range of the Cascade Mountains of the Pacific Northwest, seemingly influenced as much by the peaks, forests and rivers of the region as its Scandinavian musical forbearers. A strong connection with the local Cascadian wilderness is evident in the lyrical content of songs such as 'I Will Lay Down My Bones Among the Rocks and Roots' by the band Wolves in the Throne Room (2007) from Olympia, Washington, referenced above in the title to this essay.[1] In 2009, I came across a review of a record by Wolves in the Throne Room and I was drawn to the band's website. The first sentence of the band's bio read:

> During the Summer of 2002 at an Earth First [*sic*] rendezvous in the Cascade mountains of Washington State, guitarist Nathan Weaver was inspired to create a band that merged a Cascadian eco-spiritual awareness with the misanthropic Norwegian eruptions of the 90's.
> (Wolves in the Throne Room website, 2012)

The influence of a radical social movement, the Earth First! environmental group, and the raw energy in the band's recordings reminded me of the early days of American hardcore. I soon discovered that this energy and DIY ethos of hardcore punk had been a specific influence on Wolves in the Throne Room (Stosuy, 2007), and that there were others creating similar music, many arising from the Pacific Northwest, or 'Cascadia,' a term adopted in the 1970s to describe this bioregion, later inspiring a regional independence movement.

Often referred to in the blogosphere, and by some fans, as Cascadian black metal, this music has converted many fans and inspired other like-minded musicians, while the term itself has garnered mixed reactions from bands, fans and the music press. I am conscious of the fact that the term has not been universally accepted or even recognized within the metal community or the general popular music press. Yet its usage has been used to such an extent that it provides a compelling example in an analysis of genre. In this essay I will establish a theoretical framework from which to approach Cascadian black metal, illustrate that the concepts of genre and scene are applicable for this type of collective expression in popular music, explore how the radical environmental movement may have influenced the development of Cascadian black metal, and show how this genre uses a place-based aesthetic construction that sets it apart from other forms of heavy metal music.

The Cascadian black metal genre

The adaptation of the concept of genre in popular culture from the tradition of literary criticism has proven to be a simple yet effective means of categorizing cultural forms for the purpose of analysis. Though John G. Cawelti's influential ideas on genre and formula were developed in the late 1960s with narrative forms such as literature and film in mind (Cawelti, 2004), they are still very useful in approaching genre in popular music. Cawelti's description of conventions and inventions inform this analysis, as well as his construction of genre as a 'supertext,' or, 'a consolidation of many texts created at different times' as 'one way of conceptualizing artistic traditions' (Cawelti, 2004). In this way Cascadian black metal as a genre can be read as an individual text to examine its qualities as a unique collective musical expression.

In positioning Cascadian black metal as a genre, I further draw from criteria developed by Fabian Holt (2007) to create a framework to understand and analyze genre in popular music. His concept of *networks* functions as the communicative channels through which individual artists crystallize into *collectivities* (Holt, 2007, pp. 20–21). Holt also includes conventions as part of this framework, though he is careful not to advocate creating 'catalogs of conventions' as he warns this would lead to reductive and dull analysis (2007, p. 22). However, recognizing genre signifiers through textual analysis, in conjunction with an analysis of the shared *values* of a social group may help to understand the complexity of a musical collectivity (Holt, 2007, pp. 22–23). Finally, Holt uses the concept of *practice* to shift analysis away from textual analysis of the music itself to include agency and the process of creation and performance (p. 24).

Black metal as a sub-genre of heavy metal, at least the black metal that became notorious from the early 1990s in Norway, has long had relatively strict genre conventions enforced by fans. Those that deviate from these conventions risk being derided as not 'trve' (true) or 'kvlt' (cult), common expressions by fans to indicate authentic black metal, which likely has had the effect of limiting innovation in the genre. Ross Hagen (2011) has documented the production, instrumentation, and overall sound of black metal in detail, describing the 'blast beat' drumming, the raspy, mid-high pitched screamed vocals, fast tempo tremolo or 'buzz picking' guitars with full-chord voicings rather than power chords, played through heavy distortion, and a frequent emphasis on very 'lo-fi' production values (pp. 183–187). Cascadian black metal has generally adhered to these conventions, with some notable differences in production, such as the inclusion of long intervals of ambient sound and field recordings, often from natural sources. Songs are often much longer in length than those in Norwegian black metal, sometimes exceeding 20 minutes, or in the case of the album *The Hunt* by the band Fauna (2007), the entire album is one 60-minute uninterrupted piece.

The importation of black metal to the United States seems to have created a space in which artists can experiment with the genre without the fear of fan rejection. This is not to say that some black metal 'purists' have not been critical of American musicians' interpretations, but it is possible that since the music has been taken out of its European context, fans have been willing to accept more deviation from established conventions. In Cascadian black metal, this has come primarily in the form of lyrics and artistic image, which address environmental degradation and connection to an ancient wild spirit. Norwegian artists have typically concentrated on Satanic themes, which may be found in the many anti-Christian messages in their songs. Hagen (2011, pp. 188–190) has noted other visual signifiers such as the common practice of band members wearing 'corpse paint' makeup, upside-down crosses in band logos and album covers, and spiked armor and bullet-belts in band photos, evoking a menacing and violent image. In contrast, most Cascadian black metal artists eschew these visual cues, and though the Satanic themes persist in other American interpretations of black metal, it remains virtually absent from Cascadian expression, itself conveying very little in the way of theatrical image. Some visual conventions persist however, and are immediately apparent in many band logos, which emulate the indecipherable quality of other extreme metal bands. Cascadian bands incorporate elements evoking the natural world, such as tree roots and branches. Most album cover art features strong signifiers of nature, such as forested landscapes, and many names of albums and songs refer to nature in some way, often specifically to the Cascadia region (Shakespeare, 2012, p. 2).

Ritualistic objects and images are common throughout Cascadian black metal, as they have been in black metal in general. Many of the symbols used in Norwegian black metal alluded to Satanism and death (upside-down crosses, corpse paint), but in contrast these are absent in Cascadian black metal imagery and live shows, with these bands instead favoring animal skulls, altars with candles or other fire features, runes, herbs and incense, or soil and plant material from Cascadian forests, to complement the ritual being performed. The band Alda describes an altar that they construct at their shows:

> The idea is to bring a piece of the forest, a representational piece of wildness into these performance spaces that are typically located in a very urban environment, such as Seattle. The altar is a circle of old-growth Douglas Fir bark which encloses young evergreen branches that we usually gather the day of the show, which in this photo are Hemlock. The skull in the center is a Coyote who was killed locally by a hunter in a way we found reprehensible, and so we decided to honor the animal in our own way and ritualistically use its remains as part of our shows. The bone above it is from a Blacktail Deer that we found in a hollow tree.
>
> (D'Alessandro, 2012)

It is understandable that many Cascadian bands express a preference for playing live outdoors in remote areas, where many of these objects and symbols exist naturally. While most of the images found on album covers and artist websites portray misty forested landscapes and scenes evocative of the Cascadian wilderness, some bands also portray iconography associated with Paganism. Blood of the Black Owl feature animal skulls, runes and symbols of the four cardinal directions on its albums, and most of the albums by Wolves in the Throne Room depict ethereal, spirit-like creatures in forested settings.

British scholar Steven Shakespeare writes of his search for Cascadian black metal artifacts, and a wooden box he acquired which was used to package an LP by an obscure band:

> It was a vinyl LP, and it came packed in a large red cedar box tied with rope fashioned from the bark of the same tree. Once opened, the box turned out to contain soil, leaves, thin strips of bark, a bundle of fragrant herbs charred at the tip: the real matter of Cascadia, encased and shipped abroad.
>
> (Shakespeare, 2012, p. 3)

Inside the box Shakespeare also found a handwritten treatise by an unnamed author, covering mostly theoretical and spiritual issues related to Cascadian black metal in a somewhat esoteric and arcane schema. The author addresses the issue of whether Cascadian black metal has a local or global worldview, and comments, 'the music lyrics and art are explicitly formed by an ingestion of the Cascadian earth, in which there is a union between the presumed narrative voice and the nature which makes it possible' (Anonymous in Shakespeare, 2012, p. 3) and proceeds to quote lyrics from 'Rain' by the band Fauna as an example of this intense local connection:

> Before the stars fled our sky
> When we spoke the old tongue
> When our mouths were filled with dirt
> Our tongues danced as trees
> As owl flies to cedar bough...
> Fauna, 'Rain' (Shakespeare, 2012, p. 4)

The forests and mountains of Cascadia are not a simple trope used to create an image for the music, but the true essence of Cascadian black metal itself.

To revisit Holt's concept of practice (2007) in genre, there has been a clear preference for Wolves in the Throne Room and other bands to play live, under specific conditions, rather than an emphasis on recorded output. Some shows have been held outdoors, with minimal amenities, and are not widely publicized (Davis, 2007). When Wolves in the Throne Room toured in 2012, it made a point to travel with its own PA system, so it could play nontraditional venues, and avoid the club/bar scene, which it had experienced in their previous tour (Smith, 2011).

The intended result was a more intimate atmosphere, allowing for a closer connection with the audience. This DIY ethos, borrowed from the hardcore punk movement, informs many elements of Cascadian black metal. According to Holt, 'ritual and performance aesthetics' are a part of genre, and they 'inform interpretations of aural and visual materials and negotiations of boundaries' (2007, p. 24). These aesthetics are critical to Cascadian black metal and recognizing them allows us to go beyond simple identification of conventions and gain insight into a wider range of meaning.

The preference for live performance over recording signals another crucial difference between Norwegian black metal bands of the 1990s and most North American black metal bands. As Wolves in the Throne Room drummer Aaron Weaver explains:

> Our band, unlike most black metal, was created in order to play live. It is through live performance that we are able to conjure the cathartic, transformative energy that we seek. It is more about introspection and melancholy feelings. I always hate it when people behave in a violent, aggressive manner at our performances. I would rather that they lay on the floor and cry.
>
> (Gehlke, 2007)

Weaver not only points out the different approach that many North American black metal bands have toward live shows, but he touches on the emotional impact that his band is trying to create for its audience.

> Playing live is the reason why the band exists, that's why we do it. We look at it like an opportunity to journey somewhere else, to receive some sort of knowledge, to receive some sort of transfusion of energy.
>
> (Raduta, 2007)

The atmospheric quality of the overall sound common to much black metal is especially prevalent in Cascadian black metal, often interspersed with passages of ambient sound or field recordings, usually from nature, inducing a transformative or meditative state in the listener. This same sound is reflected in recordings as well, and as Hagen has noted about production of black metal in general, this blurring of individual elements, partially obscuring the rhythmic features, results in an 'atmospheric wash of sound' (2011, p. 187). This is likely one reason Cascadian musicians initially adopted black metal, since it has the capacity to capture both the tranquil and the chaotic aspects of nature in a musical expression.

Themes of nature and earth-based spirituality have often been present in global black metal, and the ideal of a pre-Christian pastoral utopia has been embedded in far-right nationalistic ideology and identity (Hagen, 2011, pp. 194–195). The ideology of Norwegian black metal has been covered well by the popular music press, as well as most recently by scholars such as Hagen (pp. 190–196), and though these tropes of nature and a pre-industrial, pre-modern existence have resonated with musicians in the United States, they do not take on the same nationalistic tone as they have in Europe. In fact, though bands such as Wolves in the Throne Room have rejected any inference of a political ideology (Stosuy, 2009), it seems clear that the local traditions they are emerging from have historically occupied the far left of the political spectrum. Cascadian and Norwegian bands may share common ecological beliefs, and they are expressing it through the same style of extreme heavy metal, but there is an apparent difference in ideology that is rooted in how environmental issues have been framed socially in Europe and the United States. In short, Cascadian black metal typically embraces an anti-modern 'anarcho-primitivism' (Shakespeare, 2012, p. 2), while dispensing with the extreme nihilism and 'blood and soil' racism found in other corners of black metal.

In the late 1980s the radical environmental movement, particularly Earth First!, experienced a major shift in ideology and direction, with an influx of younger activists promoting more emphasis on civil disobedience, and an awareness of social issues and left-wing politics. These ideas were perceived as standing in direct opposition to the 'Old Guard' of Earth First!, most of whom were older, male and uninterested in social or political issues. This became known within the movement as 'the anarchy debate' (Scarce, 2006, pp. 87–88), since newcomers to the movement had a different idea of what anarchy should mean, and it did not mesh well with some of the ideals held by older activists influenced by the environmental movement of the 1970s. Martha F. Lee describes them as 'younger individuals, most of whom had joined the movement in the mid-1980s, and whose geographic roots, education, and political backgrounds differed substantially from those of the original Earth First!ers' (1995, p. 113). In terms of this geographic difference, it is important to note that while the founders of Earth First! primarily originated in the Southwest, new activists who joined the movement came from the West Coast, specifically the Pacific Northwest. The ideals of the radical environmental movement in this region have persisted and likely influenced many aspects of underground culture, in particular the local music scene, as suggested by the Wolves in the Throne Room website concerning the band's origins, and further elaborations made by Aaron Weaver in interviews (Raduta, 2007).

This has led to some frustrating incidents when Wolves in the Throne Room have toured in Europe, since an assumption is made that since it is advocating a rejection of modern society and a renewed relationship with nature, and is playing black metal, the band members must hold the same racist far-right ideologies as many European bands. Though it makes an effort to distant itself ideologically, the association persists and the band frequently must address it with the European music press (Stosuy, 2009). Interestingly, this issue rarely comes up with the American music press, and that may suggest an American recognition and acceptance of the practice of picking and choosing from previous art forms, adapting certain elements and rejecting others.

The radical critique of modern industrialized society known as 'anarcho-primitivism' is cited often in the Cascadian black metal scene as influential to members' music and lives in general. This ideology runs as a common thread through the scene, generally advocating for the collapse of modern civilization and a return to a pre-industrial, pre-agricultural tribal existence. Promoted through author Fredy Perlman's 1983 book *Against His-Story, Against Leviathan!*, which retells history through the metaphor of the Leviathan as modern civilized society, its influence in the Cascadian scene can be seen in album titles such as Leech's 2007 demo *Against Leviathan!*, as well as in interviews with bands, such as the band Skagos, who cites Perlman's book as the major influence on all the band's lyrics:

> It was only natural for a work of this kind to influence Skagos so heavily, as the exploration that we seek to undertake within the project follows so closely with the intent of *Against Leviathan*. I truly find it difficult to speak of the topics that I do through lyricism and song titling without using the terminology found within that book, as it has encapsulated my world-view to such an extent that I feel hindered trying to avoid them. It has permeated every depth of our lyricism.
>
> (Kookie, 2012)

Anarcho-primitivism has common elements with Transcendentalism, and the idea of transcendence is something that is often associated with Cascadian black metal, and North American black metal in general, most visibly through the Hunt-Hendrix manifesto 'Transcendental Black Metal' (2010). Though this treatise has become the object of some scorn by other bands and fans, due to its perception as a pretentious affectation on the part of the author, the goal of transcendence itself through the black metal experience persists, and continues to resonate, as suggested by the band Fauna concerning its 2012 album *Avifauna*:

> Avifauna is a description of the flying animals, the birds. Avifauna is an exploration of the themes of flight and transcendent journeys to the Otherworld as a winged creature or as taken on the back of the Harpy or other flying figures. Our research into Shamanic lore and as well as the variegated spiritual traditions of this world led us to consider flight as the preeminent symbol of transcendence, and the bird as the ultimate harbinger of the otherworldly journey.
>
> (Atomei, 2012)

While the idea of transcendence may be mutable and prone to a wide range of interpretations, I suggest that in the case of Cascadian black metal, these artists express a distinctively American vision of transcendence in the traditions of Thoreau and Emerson, entwining a Western concept of wilderness with art. This practice pushes the notion of transcendence in nature, realized through music, far beyond the original intentions of Norwegian black metal artists in the 1990s, many of which became bogged down in the trappings of Satanism and 'kvlt' authenticity. Cascadian black metal artists, drawing from a local tradition of radical environmental activism, have been free to circumvent conventions tied to Norwegian black metal, and reproduce a musical expression that reflects not a spirit grounded in the traditions and landscape of Northern Europe, but embraces a bioregionalism that captures the unique essence of Cascadia and the potential for mythic and primeval inspiration in the pristine mountains and forests of the Pacific Northwest.

The Cascadian black metal scene

Within discussions of genre theory, particularly in popular music studies, there has been increased attention to the concept of scene. Holt (2007) notes that the term goes back to at least the 1950s as a common term among jazz musicians, but it emerged as a useful concept in popular music studies in the 1980s, as a possible alternative to the concept of subculture (Holt, 2007, p. 116; Kahn-Harris, 2007, p. 19), as developed in the 1970s by Hebdige (1979) and others. Straw's attempt in 1991 to define scenes 'as geographically specific spaces for the articulation of multiple musical practices' (Straw, 2001, p. 249), captures the bare essence of the term, but fails to allow for its application to non-local musical collectives. In Kahn-Harris' 2000 analysis of Sepultura's career, he makes a distinction between the academic and the common use of scene, the latter of which denotes a local tradition of music production and consumption, implying a collective belief system (p. 14). However, Kahn-Harris (2000) also explores how the global and local can coexist in the concept of scene, and how a worldwide idea like the 'extreme metal scene' has relevance and connections to music experienced at the local level. The apparent flexibility of the concept of scene makes it an appealing approach to understanding what may have once been understood as subculture, since the rigidity with which subculture has been used may not make it applicable to describing music collectivities in an increasingly globalized environment. This is not to say that subculture has somehow outlived its usefulness in cultural studies, but it may not serve as a replacement analytical tool for genre or even scene.

Some scholars such as Straw (2001) have observed the concept of scene as problematic, mostly due to its wide range of use in academics and the vernacular, as well as its unconstrained applicability, describing both 'highly local clusters of activity and to give unity to practices dispersed throughout the world' (p. 248). Hesmondhalgh (2005) suggests that 'the same holism is possible via other, less confusing terms, such as genre' (p. 29), and though he admits that the concept may provide deeper insight into musical collectivities, suggests its loose nature may limit its usefulness. However, I agree with Holt's assessment that since the concept of scene is used in everyday conversation among musicians, this makes it an important tool for popular music studies, and it should stand separate from, though an effective complement to, the concept of genre (pp. 116–117). As Holt notes, the concept of scene 'creates a close and fairly straightforward connection between the abstract notion of genre and its concrete relation with practices occurring in a particular place' (p. 117). Though it will become apparent in the discussion below how scene and place have a complex relationship, it is worth establishing that the concept of scene is relevant in popular music studies, not despite its vernacular use in popular music and apparent flexibility, but because it has universal appeal.

Keith Kahn-Harris has observed that all music exists within a scene or likely even intersecting scenes (2007, p. 21), so the question of whether a specific music collectivity can be viewed as a scene is immaterial. What is interesting is what we can learn by examining the complex fabric of a scene, and how scenes interact with each other. In his discussion of place-based and genre-based scales of scene (2007, p. 99), Kahn-Harris notes that both types of scenes can intersect on many levels, and any given scene may represent itself on both scales. Though there may be many ways to uncover the intricacies of a scene, Wallach and Levine (2011) have suggested a set of four functions and six generalizations that apply to metal scene formation, based on their own ethnographic research in Indonesia and Toledo, Ohio. While the four functions described in their framework are especially dependent on ethnographic data, Wallach and Levine's sixth generalization is useful to consider in this analysis. This generalization characterizes the relationship scenes have with each other on a global-to-local or a local-to-local level (Wallach & Levine, 2011, p. 128), and the Cascadian scene certainly intersects with the greater extreme metal scene, as well as other North American black metal scenes. In this discussion I refer to the concept of 'dubbing culture' created by Tom Boellstorff (2005) in his ethnographic study of gay and lesbian groups in Indonesia, in an attempt to understand the globalization process and 'interpretation and reconfiguration' of cultural expression. Though Boellstorff uses this concept specifically in relation to contemporary ethnography, I think it can be helpful in this discussion to describe the process of reproducing a cultural form from one location (in this case, Norway) to another context (the United States), and the resulting interpretation of the cultural expression (black metal). For Cascadian black metal bands, this likely begins with the consumption of the recorded output of Norwegian black metal, such as Burzum and Darkthrone (Bubblegum, 2009). However, as Boellstorff specifies, agency and discourse are crucial to dubbing culture, and 'to 'dub' a discourse is neither to parrot it verbatim nor to compose an entirely new script' (2005, p. 58). Boellstorff (2005, p. 86) draws on Althusser's (2012) idea of interpellation or 'hailing' (p. 85) to describe how culture spreads, and this is a useful way to understand the appeal that Norwegian black metal, a seemingly foreign expression removed from American experience, may have to a North American audience. While I have discussed the differences in image, conventions, and ideology between Norwegian and Cascadian black metal earlier in this analysis, I believe the crucial common thread can only be understood in terms of emotion, and the anguish felt when faced with the realities of contemporary life. As expressed by Ray Hawes, of the band Skagos from British Columbia, when black metal was imported to North America, 'it was often characterized by and presented as formless despair, the completely misanthropic disdain for human life, or the formulated rejection of anything but nondescript sorrow...' (Kookie, 2012).

It is important to understand that Cascadian black metal should not be equated with American black metal, since there are other scenes across the United States and Canada that have their own interpretations of black metal. However, there is some reluctance to lumping all these scenes under one moniker like 'USBM,' and the following quote from Michael Korchonnoff from the band Alda from Tacoma, Washington illustrates this sentiment:

There isn't really a single unified Black metal scene, merely pockets of subcultures manipulating the oppositional stance of Black metal to suit their own ends. The all-encompassing oppositional stance of this art is really the only unifying factor, and a big part of what makes it attractive to so many people outside of specific affinities to the genre's sound. The bummed-out nihilist and the atavistic Pagan are both proclaiming through their music that this reality we're living in isn't what it's cracked up to be.

(Fitz, 2011)

Though some artists have a fairly cynical outlook on the practice of creating labels for scenes, or even recognizing communities, others make attempts at understanding how black metal meshes with the American experience, such as He Who Crushes Teeth, drummer for the band Bone Awl from Novato, California:

If you listen to the music, I think you can hear discernable qualities of American life. The stance is humble and masculine. It's a strong walk rather than elegant flight. Americans always take pride in being focused, potent, and straightforward. The simplification of terms is our strongest American quality.

(Stosuy, 2010, p. 145)

As well as Wrnlrd, from Arlington, Virginia:

I see ghosts of American music everywhere. I hear Dock Boggs in black metal, the droning banjo, voice like an earthquake. I hear Blind Lemon pounding his feet on the floor, and I know he is my cousin. I find black metal in traffic noise. Whether the streets are German or

Japanese. I think the essence of black metal is something that goes beyond geography and stylistic tradition, even beyond music.

(Stosuy, 2010, p. 156)

The above artists' willingness to examine the essence of black metal and the appeal to American beliefs sheds some light on the nature of the process of interpellation that has led to an interpretation of an otherwise 'other' cultural expression. Considering the reluctance to recognize a general North American black metal scene, it may be better addressed as a network of overlapping scenes, or as Holt describes it, a 'translocal level of interaction between local scenes' (2007, p. 117). For example, bands which share the aesthetics of the Cascadian black metal scene have cropped up in places like Maine (Falls of Rauros), Kentucky (Panopticon, Merkaba) and Colorado (Velnias), and this suggests another level of interpellation, analogous to the Norway/United States example, but originating from the Pacific Northwest and inspiring musicians in other regions of the United States.

In the Introduction I alluded to the reception that the term 'Cascadian black metal' has received from fans and bands, and this reluctance to be associated with any category that is created or applied from outside the core of participants is directly related to distinct ideologies. There is a general tendency in current popular music for musicians to try to avoid categorization that they may perceive as locking them into a specific style. Since the association with a greater collective can sometimes imply a lack of autonomy, or artistic integrity, it has become almost a cliché in interviews with bands, when asked about what genre their music fits into, to respond with ambivalence, or in the case of some bands, outright hostility. In this excerpt from an interview with guitarist/vocalist 'K' from the band Ash Borer, based in Arcata, California, he is asked about the term 'Cascadian black metal':

It does not really exist, nor is it something we seek to be associated with. It is a term invented by bored individuals (who are probably not from the so-called region in the first place) who seek to pigeonhole every project they hear.

(Stosuy, 2012)

Though the notion that bands are solely responsible for the cultural environment that their music is associated with is another topic worth examining, what is important for this analysis is an apparent policing of scene borders, while simultaneously denying the existence of the scene itself. Kahn-Harris (2007) notes a difference between scenes that are recognized by participants within them and those that are not, referring to the latter as an 'external discursive construction,' and cites the 'Tampa death metal scene' as an example of a construction that is widely recognized, yet only vaguely acknowledged within itself (2007, p. 100), and this seems to describe the Cascadian black metal scene as well. The inference that K makes, suggesting that the term 'Cascadian black metal' has been invented by others 'who are probably not from the so-called region,' speaks to the issue of the boundaries of this scene. This relates to Wallach and Levine's fourth generalization, that metal scenes patrol their boundaries, but with a different intent from other scenes, generally with less attention to ideology than punk scenes (2011, p. 124). The Cascadian scene might have more in common with punk in this regard since ideology, and especially ties to the Cascadia region, seems to be most prominent for scene exclusivity. Kahn-Harris also emphasizes the importance of maintaining boundaries since scene is at least partially a spatial concept (2007, p. 21), and I suggest this is the root of the issue that artists have with any classificatory process. The idea that an outside force, especially if it is seen as representing a form of authority, exerting influence on the scene runs counter to the ideologies of many artists, as this is perceived as a means of control, and ultimately, commodification. The typically elitist nature of black metal in general helps to foster such ideology, and can be traced to the primacy of bands staying 'trve' and 'kvlt,' which serves as a sort of gauge of subcultural capital. The first determining factor for the creation of subcultural capital in the Cascadian black metal scene, at least as indicated by K's quote above, is the importance of being from the Cascadia region, and not an outside observer or carpetbagger looking to cash in on a trend.

Conclusion

While there may be some ambivalence within the Cascadian black metal scene about the use of this term, the similarities and relationships between bands make it a compelling example of a contemporary musical collectivity. While I understand the sentiment that abhors the aggregation of individual artistic entities, at the risk of producing a diluted, totalized message, the flexible nature of the concept of scene makes it very useful in the study of popular music without homogenizing and equating all scenes with each other. The advantage of using scene over other concepts like subculture is its relative acceptance among musicians and artists, though researchers need to recognize that some musicians are acutely resistant to any process of labeling, and are especially suspicious when they perceive it as originating from outside their scene. By applying the concepts of genre and scene to Cascadian black metal, we gain understanding of a fascinating musical collectivity, not simply through identifying its conventions and what it may or may not share with its Norwegian predecessors, but by understanding shared values, which may hail other musicians in an Althusserian sense, spreading the influence of a local aesthetics to a much broader audience. The natural environment is so critical to Cascadian black metal that this kind of expression would not likely evolve in an urban setting, but it should not be surprising that similar scenes are taking root in other places in North America where unfettered access to wilderness is not only available, but generally valued by the larger community beyond the metal or even greater music scene.

Clearly, Cascadian black metal, or even global black metal, does not have a monopoly on allusions to nature in its music, and one only has to look at a handful of Scandinavian folk metal bands to understand the appeal of this type of aesthetic. However, it is apparent through comments made by Cascadian black metal artists, and the example of the wooden box of Cascadian artifacts described above by Steven Shakespeare, that this cultural expression, whether we consider it a genre or a scene, or some other type of musical collective, is intensely local. Band members consistently emphasize a strong connection to Cascadia, that their greatest influence is spending time out in nature, sometimes for weeks at a time, and truly connecting with their native environment. Though it captures the attention of fans and other musicians throughout the United States and beyond, Cascadian black metal is intrinsically tied to the Cascadia bioregion, and this differs importantly from other place-based categories of American metal. For example, fans and the music press have often referred to 'Tampa death metal,' which may be better described as a scene or style than a genre, but the geography of Tampa, Florida has not been an integral element to the aesthetics to this music. For Cascadian black metal, a very specific region, not simply 'nature' in general, is referenced consistently through a great many bands' work. This has not been the case with other regions in the United States where the same aesthetic has taken hold. In places like Colorado, Maine and Kentucky, cultural reproduction is represented by a relatively small number of bands, too small to qualify as a separate collective entity that may represent an emerging place-based genre. While some artists outside of Cascadia may reference their own bioregion in their work (most notably Panopticon, especially its brilliant 2012 release *Kentucky*, which beautifully captures the essence of Appalachia), no region has emerged like Cascadia where so many bands have been influenced by such geographic specificity.

So we are left with a predicament: when the Cascadian black metal aesthetic is imported to another region, the qualifier 'Cascadian' no longer makes sense. Other terms such as 'eco-metal' have not caught on, and some are simply too ambiguous, such as 'atmospheric black metal.' I believe this helps support the idea of Cascadian black metal as a distinctive genre, though we have come to associate place-based music collectivities with the concept of scene. Clearly, as I have shown above, there is value in discussing the 'Cascadian black metal scene,' but the place-based aesthetic construction which I have identified in Cascadian black metal sets these bands apart from other American black metal bands in a way in which we can discuss such a musical expression in terms of both scene and genre.

In the summer of 2014, Wolves in the Throne Room released its fifth full-length, *Celestite*, on its own label, Artemisia Records, after a brief hiatus. A follow-up to 2011's *Celestial Lineage*, *Celestite*'s shift in style did not come as a shock to the band's fans, since the band had been hinting that it was prepared to explore new sonic territory with future projects. According to the band, *Celestite* was conceived as a companion piece to *Celestial Lineage*, calling it 'a completely newly envisioned, parallel-universe version' of their 2011 record, even utilizing some of the same melodies, though describing them as 'barely tethered to the original compositions' (Wolves in the Throne Room website, 2014). Utilizing a vast array of vintage synthesizers, and employing a guest wind ensemble, *Celestite* serves as something of a ghostly refrain to *Celestial Lineage*, and the two records together lift the band's sound from the roots and rocks of the Cascadian soil into the divine cosmos, leaving all earthly constraints behind. Both Weaver brothers are credited on synthesizers, and guitars as well, which make occasional appearances on several tracks with familiar punctuations of distortion, so the band did not entirely abandon the icon of rock instrumentation. The overall sound of *Celestite* can best be described as shimmering, with occasional subtle throbbing rhythms, somber tones giving way to washes of fuzz, and droplets of glimmering synth patterns emerging and fading away. *Celestite* is otherworldly, with only the subtlest visual hints on the cover art to the Cascadian wilderness, and it seems intent on transcending the physical world entirely.

The ambient experimentalism of *Celestite* is not unprecedented in Wolves in the Throne Room's work, since the band used soundscapes, including passages of electronic instrumentation and field recordings, on its second full-length release *Two Hunters* (2007), and subsequent releases. In fact, 2011's *Celestial Lineage* was intended as a final install-ment of a trilogy that began with *Two Hunters* and continued through 2009's *Black Cascade* (Stosuy, 2011), and this thread now extends to *Celestite*, since it is so closely related to the band's 2011 release. Though Wolves in the Throne Room is not alone among artists exploring the Cascadian spirit with ethereal electronics, artists like Sacrificial Totem and Blood of the Black Owl (and Chet W. Scott's more ambient projects Ruhr Hunter and Cycle of the Raven Talons), have mostly kept to the fringes of the scene, and arguably on the outside of Cascadian black metal as a genre. However, a high profile band like Wolves in the Throne Room made a bold statement with *Celestite*, and this practice strengthens a genre, since evolving conventions are often preceded by innovation among artists that have great influence. Their use of ambi-ent experimentation shows growth of Cascadian black metal as a genre. I consider this process an example of what Kahn-Harris has identified as 'trangressive subcultural capital' (2007, p. 127) in a scene, though I think it applies in a discussion of genre as well, since it pioneers a new direction while staying true to the genre in spirit, on a scale that had previously been unrealized. Some purists may argue that without the standard sonic markers of black metal, *Celestite* must be considered outside of the genre, and though it may be Cascadian *something*, it is just not 'metal enough.' I contend that *Celestite* challenges the accepted borders of a genre, while constructing enough of the aesthetics that it can still be considered Cascadian black metal. Experimenting with ambi-ent electronics is not unique in global black metal, and Varg Vikernes' albums under the moniker Burzum while serving prison time and since his release in 2009 may be the best known example, though this may be a dubious distinction due to Vikernes notorious reputation. How-ever, I believe Burzum's later output should be viewed as an outlier to any consolidated scene or genre, since Norwegian black metal has frag-mented significantly since its heyday in the 1990s. In contrast, I view *Celestite* as an excellent example of what Kahn-Harris (2014) calls 'metal-beyond-metal,' in which metal is not defined as identifiable aesthetics, or even by affiliation in an existing metal genre or scene, but through specific kinds of social values, as hard as these may be to pin down. This echoes Holt's framework for genre that I discussed at the beginning of this essay, in which shared values are a critical element for establishing genre. Wolves in the Throne Room still capture the values of Cascadian black metal with the spirit of *Celestite*, incorporating this composition into a unified genre despite the lack of metal signifiers in the music. That spirit of primal energy and transcendence is what ultimately defines Cascadian black metal as a genre.

Note

1. Special thanks to Aaron Weaver of Wolves in the Throne Room for his kind permission to use a portion of the lyrics to the band's song 'I Will Lay Down My Bones Among the Rocks and Roots' from the 2007 release *Two Hunters* in the title to this essay.

Bibliography

Althusser, L. (2012) 'Ideology and Ideological State Apparatuses (Notes Towards an Investigation),' *Media and Cultural Studies: Keywords*, eds. M. G. Durham & D. M. Kellner (Oxford, UK: Wiley Blackwell), pp. 80–86.

Atomei, D. (18 September 2012) Interview with Fauna. *Kogaionon*. Retrieved 7 August 2014 from: http://www.kogaionon.com/en/kogaionon-interviews/fauna.

Boellstorff, T. (2005) *The Gay Archipelago: Sexuality and Nation in Indonesia* (Princeton, NJ: Princeton University Press).

Bubblegum, B. (22 May 2009) An Interview w/Wolves in the Throne Room's Aaron Weaver. *Brooklyn Vegan*. Retrieved 7 August 2014 from: http://www.brooklynvegan.com/archives/2009/05/an_interview_w_13.html.

Cawelti, J. G. (2004) *Mystery, Violence, and Popular Culture: Essays* (Madison, WI: University of Wisconsin Press).

D'Alessandro, C. (14 September 2012) Interview: Alda. *Severed Heads Open Minds*. Retrieved 7 August 2014 from: http://severedheadsopenminds.blogspot.com/2012/09/interview-alda_14.html

Davis, E. (13 November 2007) 'Deep Eco-metal,' *Slate*. Retrieved 7 August 2014 from: http://www.slate.com/articles/arts/music_box/2007/11/deep_ecometal.html.

Fauna. (2006) *Rain*. CD. Self-released.

Fauna. (2007) *The Hunt*. CD. Self-released.

Fauna. (2012) *Avifauna*. CD (Auburn, CA: Pesanta Urfolk).

Fitz, S. (14 June 2011) CVLT NATION Interviews Alda. *CVLT NATION*. Retrieved 7 August 2014 from: http://www.cvltnation.com/cvlt-nation-interviews-alda/.

Gehlke, D. E. (2007) [Interview with] Wolves in the Throne Room. *Blistering.com*. Retrieved 7 August 2014 from: http://www.blistering.com/fastpage/fpengine.php/link/1/templateid/13346/tempidx/5/menuid/3.

Hagen, R. (2011) 'Musical Style, Ideology, and Mythology in Norwegian Black Metal,' *Metal Rules the Globe*, eds. J. Wallach, H. M. Berger, & P. D. Green (Durham, NC: Duke University Press), pp. 180–200.

Harris, K. (2000) ' "Roots"?: The Relationship Between the Global and the Local Within the Extreme Metal Scene,' *Popular Music*, 19(1), pp. 13–30.

Hebdige, D. (1979) *Subculture: The Meaning of Style* (London, UK: Routledge).

Hesmondhalgh, D. (2005) 'Subcultures, Scenes or Tribes? None of the Above,' *Journal of Youth Studies*, 8(1), pp. 21–40.

Holt, F. (2007) *Genre in Popular Music* (Chicago, IL: University of Chicago Press).

Hunt-Hendrix, Hunter. (2010) 'Transcendental Black Metal,' *Hideous Gnosis: Black Metal Symposium 1*, ed. N. Masciandaro (Create Space Independent Publishing Platform), pp. 53–65.

Kahn-Harris, K. (2007) *Extreme Metal Music: Music and Culture on the Edge* (Oxford: Berg).

Kahn-Harris, K. (17 January 2014) Metal Beyond Metal. *Souciant.* Retrieved 1 February 2015 from: http://www.kahn-harris.org/metal-beyond-metal/.

Kookie, K. (27 August 2012) Interview with Ray Hawes of Skagos. *Hammer Smashed Sound.* Retrieved 7 August 2014 from: http://www.hammersmashedsound.com/2012/08/interview-with-ray-hawes-of-skagos.html.

Lee, M. F. (1995) *Earth First!: Environmental Apocalypse* (Syracuse, NY: Syracuse University Press).

Leech. (2007) *Against Leviathan!* Cassette (Denver, CO: Woodsmoke).

Panopticon. (2012) *Kentucky.* CD (Traverse City, MI: Bindrune Recordings).

Perlman, F. (1983) *Against His-story, Against Leviathan!* (Detroit, MI: Black & Red).

Raduta, Stefan. (1 December 2007) Wolves in the Throne Room: The New Black Metal. *Kogaionon.* Retrieved 31 January 2015 from: http://www.kogaionon.com/en/kogaionon-interviews/wolves-in-the-throne-room-the-new-black-metal-by-stefan-raduta.

Scarce, R. (2006) *Eco-warriors: Understanding the Radical Environmental Movement* (Walnut Creek, CA: Left Coast Press).

Shakespeare, S. (2012) 'Of Plications: A Short Summa on the Nature of Cascadian Black Metal,' *Glossator*, 6(1), pp. 1–45.

Smith, J. (11 October 2011) Wolves in the Throne Room: The Hellbound Interview. *Hellbound.ca.* Retrieved 7 August 2014 from: http://www.hellbound.ca/2011/10/wolves-in-the-throne-room-the-hellbound-interview/.

Stosuy, B. (26 September 2007) Interview with Wolves in the Throne Room. *Pitchfork*: *Show No Mercy.* Retrieved 6 August 2014 from: http://pitchfork.com/features/show-no-mercy/6697-show-no-mercy/

Stosuy, B. (12 June 2009) Interview with Aaron Weaver from Wolves in the Throne Room. *Pitchfork: Show No Mercy.* Retrieved 6 August 2014 from: http://pitchfork.com/features/show-no-mercy/7668-show-no-mercy/

Stosuy, B. (2010) 'Meaningful Leaning Mess,' *Hideous Gnosis: Black Metal Symposium 1*, ed. N. Masciandaro (CreateSpace Independent Publishing Platform), pp. 143–156.

Stosuy, B. (23 September 2011) Wolves in the Throne Room: Celestial Lineage (Review) *Pitchfork.* Retrieved 1 February 2015 from: http://pitchfork.com/reviews/albums/15835-celestial-lineage/

Stosuy, B. (13 August 2012) Sophomore Class: Interviews with Ash Borer and Samothrace about their Respective Second LPs. *Pitchfork: Show No Mercy.* Retrieved 7 August 2014 from: http://pitchfork.com/features/show-no-mercy/8914-sophomores/

Straw, W. (2001) 'Scenes and Sensibilities,' *Public*, 22, pp. 245–257.

Wallach, J. & Levine, A. (2011) ' "I Want You to Support Local Metal": A Theory of Metal Scene Formation,' *Popular Music History*, 6(1–2), pp. 116–134.

Wolves in the Throne Room Website 'Bio.' Retrieved 4 November 2012 from: http://www.wittr.com/bio.

Wolves in the Throne Room Website 'News' (30 January 2014). Retrieved 31 January 2015 from: http://www.wittr.com/2014/01/30/wolves-in-the-throne-room-reveal-details-on-new-recordings/.

Wolves in the Throne Room. (2007) *Two Hunters*. CD (Los Angeles, CA: Southern Lord Recordings).

Wolves in the Throne Room. (2009) *Black Cascade*. CD (Los Angeles, CA: Southern Lord Recordings).

Wolves in the Throne Room. (2012) *Celestial Lineage*. CD (Los Angeles, CA: Southern Lord Recordings).

Wolves in the Throne Room. (2014) *Celestite*. CD (Olympia, WA: Artemisia Records).

9
Metal and Comics: Strange Bedfellows?

Colin A. McKinnon
Vevey, Switzerland

In terms of popular culture, few phenomena have reached the heights of popularity and influence achieved by comic books. Whether they read comics or not, everyone knows the stories of the boy who saw his parents gunned down in front of him and who vowed to rid his city of crime as Batman, or the baby sent in a rocket from the dying planet Krypton who made a new home on Earth as Superman, or the teenager bitten by a radioactive spider who subsequently learned that 'with great power comes great responsibility' as Spider-Man. On the face of it, heavy metal and comic books might seem to have little in common, but they do share some similarities in terms of demographics, themes, communities and certain public perceptions, although some of these connections may be more obvious than others. For many years, however, there seemed to be outwardly very limited crossover and influence between the two, but there are signs that this has begun to change, or at least that connections have become more visible, in recent years.

It has been said that the DC and Marvel continuity universes are the largest narrative constructs in the history of human culture (Kaveney, 2008). It is perhaps not entirely surprising then that mythologies as vast and complex as those that exist in the realm of comic books should be influenced by another form of cultural mythology that, while perhaps not as vast, is certainly just as complex, if not more so. It is also apparent that both forms of mythology require a sound understanding of the history and landscape for those who wish to explore the mythology further, and that a display of the depth of this understanding is one of the key criteria by which potential explorers will be judged by those who have gone before. Deena Weinstein has mentioned previously that one of the reasons that metal has endured much longer than some other rock genres is because of the subculture and community that surrounds it (Weinstein, 2000). So it is with comic books as an entertainment form. Likewise, the concept of 'authenticity' remains of crucial importance in both camps, despite the elusiveness of how exactly this should be defined.

As an aside, it might seem strange to talk about metal as mythology; metal certainly embraces and celebrates mythologies of various kinds, but it is also possible to think of metal itself as a kind of mythology. It has its origins, its apocryphal and oft-repeated stories, and its characters, themselves frequently spoken of in terms of 'epic' vocabulary as 'legends,' 'heroes,' 'gods,' and 'warriors.' Indeed, metal musicians may sometimes be portrayed as such, especially 'warriors,' in photographs, through postures, dress, tattoos, gestures or expressions (Hill, 2013), in addition to persistent warrior-like themes throughout the music and album artwork. In the political science fiction series *Saucer Country*, written by Paul Cornell, the character Joshua Kidd, a professor of modern folklore, says that mythology 'bridges the gap between truth and lies. It creates a disturbing liminal zone, – a grey area. And in that space all of a civilization's weak spots and shortcomings and hypocrisies are made visible' (Cornell & Kelly, 2012). In terms of metal, the mythology that is inadvertently created around metal bridges the gap between the sometimes tedious boring, run-of-the-mill truth about the hard work and business logistics of the industry, and the romanticized 'lies' about the wild, hedonistic lifestyle of the bands. On a deeper level, though, it could be said that both metal and comics, perhaps even more than other artistic media, reflect and highlight the hypocrisies and shortcomings of the prevailing societies and cultures of the times.

So, who reads and listens to this stuff?

Considering similarities between comics and metal, let's first take a look at the demographic aspects. Most people think they know what the typical demographics are for metal fans: mostly white, mostly male, mostly working class ('blue collar') or middle class, mostly adolescent to late teens. Indeed, this has been perpetuated and reinforced by some of the early academic studies of metal. For example, Deena Weinstein states that the 'stereotypical metal fan is male, white and in his midteens,' and that 'most are also blue collar' (Weinstein, 2000, p. 99). Similarly, Natalie Purcell tells us that 'fans of Heavy Metal tend to be white, male, middle class and adolescent' (Purcell, 2003, p. 100). Most people also think they know the typical demographics for comic book fans: mostly white, mostly male, mostly working class, mostly adolescent. Metal and comics are both often viewed as something that the fan in question will 'grow out of,' that when the person grows up and presumably discovers more worthy and cerebral pursuits, that they will be discarded. Although the similarities certainly do not imply a connection, an impartial observer looking at these data might be forgiven for making certain extrapolations based on them. However, we also know one more thing about these demographics: we know that they are not entirely correct.

In terms of age, for instance, while it is and probably always will be difficult to obtain objective and accurate data, we do know that the breadth of age of metal fans has shifted over the years; the younger age group is still there, certainly, but as metal itself has grown older as a genre, so many of its dedicated fans have aged with it. Although this may be more sub-genre specific (with certain sub-genres such as deathcore or melodic metalcore attracting younger fans), personal experience from seeing concert audiences, particularly in the last ten or so years, is that the audience age range runs from around 15 or 16 to mid-40s and over (sometimes significantly over in the case of bands such as Black Sabbath or Judas Priest). This also does not take into account the many older fans who still passionately listen to and follow the music, but whose concert attendance may be much less frequent for various reasons. Evidence from other research has also confirmed that metal's followers are not predominantly adolescent males. Recent findings challenge this view; for example, Mika Elovaara states that 'an average age of 23.4 means that for every 15-year-old fan that Weinstein, among others, claims to primarily populate the metal audience, there is a 31-year-old counterpart' (Elovaara, 2014). Even fans of the Japanese metal idol phenomenon Babymetal, arguably marketed exclusively at teenagers, do not conform to the stereotypical metal age demographic; in an online question about the age of Babymetal fans, responses show an age range from 14 to 62 (Reddit, 2014). In other findings, Elovaara's statistics 'also suggest that metal is no longer – if it ever truly was – a scene for blue collar men only' (Elovaara, 2014). Similar suggestions that the typical metal audience is firmly post-adolescent and 'often consists of a group of people with a variety of occupations' (ibid.), extending well into upper-middle class and beyond, have also been made (Halnon, 2006; Hein, 2003; Kahn-Harris, 2007). Rosemary Hill has also challenged the perception of the male exclusivity in metal and emphasized the importance of the female metal fan experience (Hill, 2013).

We also see a similar trend in comic book fans, particularly when considering the hardcore collectors, although we know now that the perception of the comic book fan as predominantly adolescent males has, to an extent, been wrong from the beginning. Studies by the industry in 1947 did show that 95 per cent of American boys were habitual comic readers, but they also showed the same of 91 per cent of girls. For teenagers, the figures were 87 per cent of males and 81 per cent of females, respectively. Additionally 41 per cent of males aged 18–30 regularly read comic books; the figure for females in the latter age group was lower at 28 per cent, still a respectable figure considering this was before the real advent of romance comics aimed at these readers (Van Lente & Dunlavey, 2012). This was aided by the fact that, following Superman's first appearance in 1938, comic books began to attract both creators and fans of science fiction/fantasy literature, who tended to be older (Duncan & Smith, 2009). In a continually updated analysis of comic book fans on Facebook (Graphic Policy, 2014), for example, it was apparent that just over 80 per cent were in the 18–45 age group; indeed, comics readers in the 30–45 age group outnumbered the 17 and under group by over three to one (27.24 per cent compared to 8.76 per cent). Of particular note, over 40 per cent of comics readers in the 30–45 age group were women, and the proportion of overall fans who stated they were in a relationship was greater than those who identified as single (Graphic Policy, 2014). Although the analysis is US-centric, there seems a good probability that similar results may be reflected in other Western countries; in some areas, general readership may be even higher, such as in Belgium, France and parts of Switzerland where *bande dessinées* have widespread recognition as a visual art form, or in Japan with the prevalence of manga titles, including many specifically aimed at a female audience.

Another earlier survey by the ComicMix website indicated that 32 per cent of their readers were aged between 35 and 44, and 29 per cent were over 45 (ComicMix, 2011). Indeed, one thing to consider with both metal and comic books is that, for those most passionate and dedicated to it, it can require a reasonable amount of disposable income for going to concerts or conventions, and buying the books, music and assorted paraphernalia associated with both; the kind of income necessary also tends not to be associated with the youngest age group. This is borne out by recent research from Ohio University into comic book collectors, indicating that the most active are between 25 and 34, with an average household income of $150,000+ (Ohio University, 2013). With comic books as well as metal, the percentage of female fanship has also increased; in the Facebook analysis mentioned earlier, over 40 per cent of comic book fans were female (Graphic Policy, 2014; The Beat, 2014). Although we know that any analysis performed via social media has its own inherent flaws and biases, these figures still make interesting reading. Indeed, one hopes that such data may help to forever dispel the image of the teenage fanboy living in his parents' basement. We can see, therefore, that both the actual and, more importantly perhaps, perceived demographics between metal and comic book fans are very similar. This may be, however, purely circumstantial, but hopefully closer examination can show us some more substantial connections and mutual influences.

History repeating

Similarities also exist in how comics and metal are perceived by others; both struggle, even now, to be taken seriously, and both have been accused of being a bad influence on children and adolescents. Metal has been accused many times in the past, and indeed still is, periodically, of being a corrupter of youth, a defiler of morality and generally an evil influence. Certain metal albums played a big part in the American recording industry bowing to pressure from the Parents Music Resource Center (PMRC) in the mid-1980s to warn innocent buyers about the potential harmful content of the music in the form of the famous 'Parental Advisory' sticker. Metal has been accused numerous times of being positively correlated with delinquent behavior, drug-taking, suicidal ideation, depression, anxiety and even schizophrenia (Baker & Bor, 2008; King, 1988; Martin et al., 1993; Scheel & Westefeld, 1999; Stack, 1998; Stack et al., 1994; Weidinger & Demi, 1991). The flaws in many of these studies have since been outlined, and these claims have largely been refuted, although they still rear their heads periodically in slightly mutated forms every time we think that the arguments have been successfully put to death once and for all.

However, we should spare a thought for what the comic book industry went through. The industry suffered the same kind of persecution, sparked by the same kind of panic, but many years before metal came under similar scrutiny. As comics grew exponentially in popularity, so they began to attract the attention of those who feared that the nation's youth was being corrupted. David Hajdu talks of the 'aesthetic lawlessness' of this period, 'through the lack of clear, established standards and the limited accountability within the trade' (Hajdu, 2008). The creators and publishers 'were competing by improvising, trying practically anything, rejecting almost nothing, in a freewheeling spirit of innovation entwined with opportunism, born, for many, of desperation' (Hajdu, 2008). Comic books accounted for one-third of all periodicals sold in 1947 (Van Lente & Dunlavey, 2012); despite their popularity, however, comic books became increasingly stigmatized, affecting both their creators and readers (Lopes, 2006). Psychologist Dr. Fredric Wertham's book *Seduction of the Innocent* in 1954 accused comic books of being a major cause of juvenile delinquency, encouraging crime, violence, drug-taking and having detrimental effects on the juvenile psyche.

This was not the first accusation leveled against comic books. Articles citing the detrimental effects of comic books, including claims that they are deleterious to mental health of children by increasing aggressive tendencies (Blumberg, 1948; Elkisch, 1948) and inspiring rebelliousness and delinquency (Legman, 1948), had already appeared. Furthermore, banning and even burning of comic books because of their detrimental effects occurred even in the late 1940s. Wertham's book, however, acted as the catalyst that led to a US Senate investigation into the effect of comic books and juvenile delinquency. The outcome of this went further than a 'Parental Advisory' sticker in the form of the creation of the Comics Code Authority, instigated by the comic book industry itself in an attempt to appease the persecutors; all comic books that met the CCA guidelines carried an 'Approved by the Comics Code Authority' stamp. The comics that met the guidelines were sanitized; excessive violence and horror were forbidden, as was anything that could be construed as disrespect for authority figures and pretty much anything to do with sex. Comic books that did not conform to the guidelines found themselves going out of business fairly quickly, since most distributors would no longer handle them. The list of artists, writers and other individuals in the comic book industry who lost their jobs or left the industry during this period, and who would never work in it again, is disturbingly extensive (Hajdu, 2008).

There are parallels between the type of cultural stigma attached to metal during the height of its persecution and that experienced by comic books, in the sense that the stigma was equally attached to both the artists/creators and the fans. What is apparent, however, is that the comic book community subsequently grew through the creation of comic book conventions, specialist comic book stores and fanzines, allowing the formation of a subculture of 'individuals, groups and "sympathetic others"' that arose in response to the stigma surrounding them (Lopes, 2006). It could be argued that metal underwent the same process, with a similar subculture constructed through a similar process, with metal festivals taking the place of conventions, specialist clubs taking the place of specialist stores, and a similar, if not greater, level of fanzine activity. More recently, the online space has become a crucial environment for both sets of fans.

Adherence to the CCA guidelines decreased over time and is now thankfully abandoned; however, the negative attitudes still have not completely dissipated. Recent examples have suggested that violent comic books can have an adverse influence on a male reader's perception of ambiguous provocation situations, that is, males were more likely to perceive harmful intent in such situations (Kirsch & Olczak, 2000). Interestingly, however, the number of regular comic book readers among the study participants, which consisted of psychology students, was very low (only 9 per cent had read a comic book in the previous six months), perhaps unnaturally so given what we know about comic book demographics. The study may also be notable for its description of *Archie & Friends* as 'a mildly violent comic book.' Similar results on the effect of extremely violent comic books on social information processing were reported in a later study by the same authors, where the level of comic book readership was even lower at 6 per cent (Kirsch & Olczak, 2002). The authors did, however, recognize this low proportion as one of the limitations, indicating that no inference can be gleaned about the effect of frequency of exposure.

The most visible influences and crossover between metal and comic books broadly (but not exclusively) fall into one of two types. First, there are the examples where metal music and its fans, or metal bands (both real and fictional) have been depicted in comics or graphic novels. Secondly are the examples of metal/rock artists who have created or contributed to comics, or where specific comic books or graphic novels are linked to or inspired by bands or albums, for example as an extension of the album's concept. There is also perhaps a lesser-known but no less interesting third group, consisting of comic creators who have been influenced by metal in some way, which may sometimes be reflected in their work in subtle rather than obvious ways.

Although traditionally it could be argued that comics have always been more influential on other media than influenced by them, the opposite tends to be more true regarding connections between metal and comics, although we can't forget that some iconic metal songs having been inspired by comics, some notable examples including Megadeth's 'Killing is my Business,' based on Marvel's The Punisher, and of course 'I Am The Law' by Anthrax, inspired by Judge Dredd.

Entombed's *Wolverine Blues* has also been cited, albeit incorrectly, as an example; even though the band effectively disowned the association with the X-Men character, a version of the album was produced with Wolverine on the cover, and which also included a mini-comic, as a result of a deal struck between Earache Records and Marvel Comics.

Unlike many other musical genres that often use photographic images, often involving the artist(s) themselves, metal album covers often lend themselves more toward artwork that would not seem out of place in the pages of a horror or sci-fi comic. There are numerous metal album covers that have overtly used various types of comic book-style imagery and artwork. Aside from the *Wolverine Blues* example, other recent examples have included the iconic Silver Surfer image on Joe Satriani's *Surfing with the Alien,* drawn by comic book artist John Byrne (although used without his permission), Iced Earth's *The Dark Saga* (which featured Todd McFarlane's character Spawn, on whom the album was based, on the cover) and *Days of Purgatory,* which featured Artist Jim Balent's rendition of the vampire goddess character Purgatori. Comic book artists have contributed to several rock and metal album covers, some of the more notable being artist Adriana Melo's super-heroine image for the cover of Bonrud's *Save Tomorrow* album, Alex Ross' contributions to Anthrax in the form of covers for *We've Come for You All, Music of Mass Destruction* and *Worship Music,* as well as several promotional items, and the cover of Korn's *Follow the Leader,* designed by Greg Capullo and Todd McFarlane, who also designed the cover for *Ten Thousand Fists* by Disturbed.

It's all KISS's fault...

It is impossible to talk about the examples of bands in comics, or indeed to have any discussion at all about metal and comics, without mentioning KISS. There may have been depictions of rock stars in comics before, but KISS was the band that really brought it to prominence. One could, of course, argue the point about whether KISS classify as metal or not, but for the purpose of this discussion the question is essentially irrelevant – what cannot be denied is the tremendous influence the band has had on metal in general.

Through their makeup and lavish stage shows involving fire-breathing and pyrotechnics in the mid-1970s, KISS had already portrayed themselves as larger-than-life fantasy figures, so in a sense it was a logical step for this to go one stage further and have themselves immortalized in comics. Gene Simmons was (and still is) a massive comic book fan, and had even partially based his on-stage costume on Black Bolt, created by Jack Kirby (Howe, 2012). The band had indicated an interest in the creation of a KISS comic as early as March 1976, and manager Bill Aucoin later approached Marvel Comics with the idea of producing such a comic. The company agreed, and the project went ahead, although the band's management expressed their extreme displeasure in an early meeting when it was discovered that the band were being portrayed in the story as the musicians they were. 'If you're gonna be doing a story,' Aucoin's VP declared, 'they're not musicians, they're superheroes!' (Howe, 2012). Portraying the band as superheroes (the Demon, the Starchild, the Cat and the Spaceman) was, in fact, a natural extension of their stage personae and made perfect sense for comics. Although KISS actually made their first comics appearance in an issue of *Howard the Duck* a few months before, the band was featured in their own comic, the *Marvel Comics Super Special,* in 1977.

The KISS comic, which was printed in a larger magazine-style format than the standard comics format, was heavily bolstered by the publicity surrounding it. Each band member famously donated some of their blood (drawn by a registered nurse and officially witnessed by a notary of the public), which was subsequently mixed with the red ink that was to be used for the comic, so that it could be, as the cover proudly proclaimed, 'Printed in real KISS blood.' An unconfirmed rumor later alleged that there was a mix-up or delay with the batches, however, and that the KISS ink actually ended up in a copy of Sports Illustrated (Howe, 2012). Regardless of where their blood ended up, KISS comic books became an integral cog in the KISS merchandising machine ever since. The first issue went on to sell half a million copies and became Marvel's best-selling comic (until Todd McFarlane's Spider-Man #1 15 years later) (Howe, 2012; KISSopolis, 2013), and was swiftly followed by a second Super Special the following year.

Since then, a number of KISS comics have followed over the years, most notably the *KISS: Psycho Circus* series from Image Comics in the late 1990s/early 2000s. Although nominally based on the *Psycho Circus* album, the series (which ran for about three years) had a number of features in common with the *Music from 'The Elder'* album, depicting the band members as supernatural beings the Demon, the Starbearer, King of Beasts and the Celestial, collectively known as The Elder, or the Four-Who-Are-One. Other series were published by Dark Horse in 2002 and the now defunct Kiss Comics Group in 2007; this series, *KISS 4K*, was notable for the 'Destroyer' edition of the first issue, which at 20 inches by 30 inches was the largest (in terms of format size) single comic book issue in the world thus far published – subtlety is clearly not a part of the KISS portfolio. Most recently we have seen a new ongoing KISS series by IDW Comics, which harks back to many of the supernatural elements of the Four-Who-Are-One from the *Psycho Circus* series (the band's characters are not physical beings but avatars that can manifest in ordinary humans), and combines it with some of the most iconic KISS songs and concepts, and in the wonderfully kitsch *Archie Meets KISS*.

Or maybe it's all Alice Cooper's fault...

Over the years since the KISS comics debut, we have seen many other metal acts portrayed in comics, including GWAR and Megadeth (or at least their mascot, Vic Rattlehead) in the 1990s, Lordi, Alice Cooper, both in his own comic in the late 1970s and in his later collaboration with author Neil Gaiman on *The Last Temptation*, based on the album of the same name. *The Last Temptation* perhaps deserves some special attention and credit for helping to kick-start the rock and metal foray into comics in a more serious manner. Gaiman was first approached by Bob Pfeifer from Epic, Alice Cooper's record company at the time, and asked if he would work with Alice on developing the concept for a new album (Campbell, 2014; Gaiman & Zulli, 2005). The concept featured 'Steven,' a character who has surfaced on a number of Alice Cooper albums, a mysterious 'showman' and a strange theatre, and a deal offered if he is willing to 'sign on the bloody line' (Campbell, 2014).

The idea to develop a comic based on the album came as soon as the album was finished, and Gaiman saw the opportunity to not only examine the concept of Alice Cooper as a horror icon, but also write a good rock-and-roll comic. Talking about the project and the lack of good rock comics, Gaiman said, 'Whenever one thinks of them, one thinks of those silly things that Malibu did, or the strange things that Marvel do. You know, rock-and-roll bands turn into superheroes. So what I wanted to do was take a look at Alice as an icon' (Campbell, 2014). The accompanying comic became 'a whimsically demented story of faith and temptation, a horror-tinged version of *A Christmas Carol* in which Steven is shown what his life would be like through a series of dark and twisted morality plays' (Campbell, 2014).

Although not the first to do this, *The Last Temptation* brought to the fore a theme that has become fairly common among comics that deal with actual bands, which is a strong element of the supernatural, best exemplified in the recent *Eternal Descent* series by guitarist and author Llexi Leon and artist Jason Metcalf. Here the god Loki, an ever-popular character in mythological metal, is attempting to use singer Lyra Constance and her band Constellation 9 to influence their fans and create an army of followers. The warrior Sirian, cast out of heaven, takes the role as her protector and an epic journey and series of battles ensues, encountering other metal musicians in the guise of heroes or villains with supernatural powers, most notably Gus G, Atreyu's Dan Jacobs and Travis Miguel, Wayne Static, God Forbid, and Arch Enemy's Angela Gossow and Michael Amott (Leon & Metcalf, 2011). Here, we have examples of the 'real' characters transcending their normal selves, becoming a myth within a myth in a sense, taking transgressive elements in the music to different levels. Through this medium, the musicians can be depicted as either avatars of evil or as saviors and heroes, moving from one form of mythology to another.

Interestingly, elements of fantasy, horror and the supernatural can also be found as common themes in comics written by metal musicians or that have a close association with the music. Considering the huge thematic prevalence of supernatural and mystical elements in metal, it's not surprising that this should be the case. A good example is avid comic book fan Glenn Danzig's *Verotika* and *Satanika* series, published by his own Verotik comics label, a name derived from 'violent' and 'erotic' – as the name might suggest, extremely violent and/or overt sexual content prevail, and the comics are certainly not aimed at younger readers. We also see elements of supernatural violence and horror in comics by Rob Zombie, including *The Haunted World of El Superbeasto* and *Spookshow International*, Scott Ian's run on *Lobo* for DC comics and in Corey Taylor's *House of Gold and Bones*. In the story of 'the Human' in the latter series, we also see another common theme that occurs in mythological literature and mythological metal, that of an epic journey at the end of which may be salvation/redemption, or eternal damnation. *The Unforgiving*, based on the Within Temptation album of the same name, also contains strong supernatural elements based around themes of guilt, forgiveness and repentance, and also raises some interesting philosophical questions on the limits of vengeance, punishment of the guilty, and the true nature of redemption. Likewise, *The Amory Wars* by Claudio Sanchez, although more science fiction, still exhibits recognizable fantasy and supernatural elements. The same kinds of fantastical, supernatural, and mythological elements have been a staple element of metal since its inception and continue to crop up regularly. In fact, there are almost too many to name, but some recent examples crop up on parts or all of Alice

Cooper's *Welcome 2 My Nightmare*, Iced Earth's concept albums *Framing Armageddon* and *The Crucible of Man* (as well as on the more recent *Dystopia* and *Plagues of Babylon*) and Rush's *Clockwork Angels*, which was also subsequently brought to life as a comic book, co-authored by drummer Neil Peart.

Interestingly, these same elements crop up in comics unrelated to metal but whose authors have been influenced by it in some way. A notable example is the *Metal* story arc from the Viking series *Northlanders* by writer Brian Wood. The *Northlanders* series consists of several self-contained storylines at different time points in Viking history, both at home and in other lands in which they settled. This particular story concerns Erik, a blacksmith in medieval Norway who rescues a girl from the oppressive clutches of corrupt Christian missionaries, and subsequently vows to 'exterminate each and every one of them from the Northlands before I die' (Wood, 2011). Erik laments that the ways of the Christian invaders are not the ways of his people: 'Do we forget our own gods so quickly? For a handful of silver, a bit of hollow praise and the promise of a salvation we barely understand?' (ibid. 2011).

Similar themes have been strongly portrayed in metal, for example in Bathory's *Blood Fire Death* and *Hammerheart* albums, and more recently (and perhaps more overtly) in *By the Light of the Northern Star* and *Valkyrja* by Týr. Although Brian Wood admits that he is not a fan of Viking or black metal, but declared that 'Heavy metal and Vikings go hand in hand,' having been introduced to the imagery in high school, where he had to walk across a particular bridge filled with 'rednecks, headbangers, weed smoke and heavy metal t-shirts. From Led Zeppelin to Bathory, the imagery was dominant' (Vertigo, 2010). For this particular story arc, Wood indicated that he took certain elements from heavy metal to take the comic's concept further. As he says 'I'm taking what I'm able to take from the musical genre and apply it to comics'; specifically, he indicated that the story 'taps into the same dark mythology and nihilistic worldview that inspires the genre' (ibid. 2010). In addition, his artist partner for the *Metal* story arc, Riccardo Burchielli (also a bass player in a heavy metal band), asked Wood to write him 'something with a lot of swords and blood' (ibid. 2010). In his story outline, he described the concept as 'Norse Mythological Fundamentalism.' In particular, one of the things that makes this particular storyline different from others in the series is overt use of mystical and supernatural elements from the mythology, previously treated in the series as 'nothing more than casual superstition' (ibid. 2010).

Rebellion, resistance, revolution

It has been said that one of the defining and much-discussed subjects about metal is the element of transgression; indeed, it could be argued that metal is all about transgression in various forms. This transgressive element in metal often takes the form of resistance or rebellion, particularly against injustice, authority, oppression, whether in real, historical or fantasy contexts. Indeed, this resistance often manifests in lyrics expounding a willingness, even an overzealous desire, to go down fighting, to die a warrior's death. This kind of willing martyrdom can be found in way too many examples in metal to count, but some of the more obvious examples come from songs by Manowar, including 'Gates of Valhalla,' 'Swords in the Wind,' 'The Kingdom of Steel,' and 'Heart of Steel,' and songs by Týr, such as 'Fields of the Fallen,' 'Another Fallen Brother,' and 'Hold the Heathen Hammer High.'

If we think of transgression as transcending limits or crossing boundaries, or even just violating laws or commands, then we see that, perhaps unsurprisingly, these same elements around the theme of justified rebellion appear with a connection to both metal and comics, either through the creators or the subject. Take, for example, the comic *Orchid* written by guitarist Tom Morello. The story is a sometimes-not-very exaggerated examination of class inequality, set in a dystopian future in which the rich and powerful exert complete and absolute control over the poor, for whom life is a constant struggle to survive, and who have to eke out whatever existence they can in squalid conditions. The eponymous Orchid is a young prostitute who becomes embroiled in a resistance movement against the overlords, reluctantly at first, but later fully embracing her defiant role. The character Opal, who takes Orchid under her wing, tells her that 'To stir the oppressed to the point of getting off their knees and taking what is rightfully theirs is a sacred act.' In a later rousing speech to the bridge people, those who are condemned to slavery and poverty, Orchid tells them 'We are without hope and so we are free. Free to shed this existence in a blazing fire of revenge ... We do not seek liberty, we seek only destruction, and through destruction we will be liberated' (Morello & Hepburn, 2012).

The zealous willingness to die a warrior's death is exemplified again here when Orchid calls for eight martyrs, asking 'Who among you has nothing to lose?' and is inundated with volunteers (ibid.). As Morello himself says in his afterword to the second collected volume, 'Your role is simple, clearly defined, and comfortable: ratify decisions and consume. Or opt out and fall through the cracks. Or ... Resist. Because resistance is feasible even for those who are not heroes by nature' (ibid.). One can hear the echo of the simple but powerful refrain of 'Fuck you, I won't do what you tell me' from Rage Against the Machine's 'Killing in the Name Of.' In a sense, many of the themes prevalent in metal can give the listener the power to envisage that resistance, while many of the related themes in comic books can give the reader a concrete glimpse of how that resistance can be achieved, and the consequences of not doing so. Metal and comics also correlate heavily in their response to and spotlight of, injustice in its various forms, often reflected in allegorical fashion. As Tom Morello indicates, 'The tilted playing field of our world is not so different from Orchid's' (Morello & Hepburn, 2013).

Black Metal: So grim, so trve, so real

In closing, special mention should be given to Rick Spears and Chuck BB's *Black Metal* trilogy, which possibly merits particular attention in any discussion of metal and comics. The reason for this is because it takes a number of clichés surrounding metal and manages to use them in a genuinely funny and affectionate homage without ever making them ridiculously laughable. Plus, you have to give any comic credit for beginning with 'First there was blackness. Then...there was metal' (Spears & BB, 2007). It concerns twin brothers Sam and Shawn Stronghand, the archetypal weird kids constantly transferred from school to school whose 'only solace has been in the sweet, grim sounds of black metal' (ibid.). Through an album by the legendary Frost Axe, a 'frostbitten onslaught of brutality,' they learn the story of the Sword of Atoll, commissioned by the hell baron, The Roth (ibid.). By playing the record backwards (of course), the brothers are physically transported to the sword, thus attracting the fury of The Roth's enemy Von Char. Thus begins an epic quest, involving the band Frost Axe themselves (the 'caretakers of metal'), hell demons, and a blending of Norse and Christian mythology, including Satan, in which they ultimately learn of their true destiny and fight to take back what it rightfully theirs (Spears & BB, 2011).

The third and final volume in the trilogy takes the epic journey even further, with pseudo-Nietzschean philosophy and an examination of the truly duplicitous nature of both good and evil. Again, one of the main themes is transgression, most obviously in the brothers' journey through and beyond the abyss, 'a place beyond perspective, beyond right and wrong, beyond hope or fear,' and the becoming of 'something new' (Spears & BB, 2014). The common themes mentioned earlier, especially vengeance, rebellion, supernatural fantasy, are also here in abundance, alongside familiar motifs such as jealousy and betrayal. As artist Chuck BB indicates, 'the meat of our story and the music genres is so supernatural and hellbent' (Comic Book Resources, 2011). What is apparent, and what makes *Black Metal* different from other representations of metal in comics, is the genuine love and reverence that the creators have for the genre, to the extent of slipping in several sly references to black metal bands, both in the text and the artwork. The authors have said that 'the music reaches for a dark area that's ancient, scary and dangerous. It's brutal and theatrical, and that's fertile soil for storytelling.' The creators also wanted the comic to reflect the 'brutality, the epic darkness that is so present in black metal' (Comic Book Resources, 2011). The characters are not only rooted in traditional teenage angst and rebellion, but also, in the words of author Rick Spears 'embody that pure, raw black metal ethos' (Comic Book Resources, 2011).

Conclusion: Comics beyond metal

In his series of articles on *Metal Beyond Metal*, Keith Kahn-Harris describes a mostly unseen crisis that appears to be affecting metal today, specifically the crisis of abundance. He explains why it is a crisis, how it has come about, and some examples of ways to negotiate through it. Again, there are correlations here with the comic book industry, and perhaps the metal scene can take some lessons from this, arising from the existing and growing connections and inter-relationships between the two.

Perhaps the metal scene can also take some comfort in the fact that the comics industry has also experienced this 'crisis of abundance' in recent years and is beginning to emerge through the other side. Although the industry is certainly not the same as it was before, it has not only survived but is arguably stronger and more relevant than before. In a similar way that Kahn-Harris (2013a) describes the easy access to a wide range of different types of metal and the importance of the concept of 'scarcity' in metal (Kahn-Harris, 2013a, 2013b), so it is for comic books also. Comic books, particularly in the form of graphic novels or collected editions, are easier to get hold of than ever before, especially since the development of digital editions that can be read online or on tablets. This has led to broadly two different types of comic book reader – firstly, the more casual reader for whom the

most important thing is reading the stories or following particular creators, and secondly the traditional dedicated fans. Crucially, the latter
group has also embraced the new technologies that allow access to more
comics than previously thought possible, but it could be argued that
importance of scarcity remains. On a personal note, for example, while
I appreciate the fact that I can read Alan Moore and Brian Bolland's
pivotal *Batman: The Killing Joke* digitally, it doesn't approach the feeling of physically holding a mint condition first edition copy in my
hands. Likewise, the abundance of digital editions does not replace the
thrill of finding the exact comic one needs to complete a particular
story arc, author run or collection after trawling through the back issue
boxes in a comic store. Perhaps, then, metalheads could also embrace (or
maybe re-embrace) the thrill of the hunt in trying to track down physical copies of albums, for example special limited editions or original
vinyl.

Kahn-Harris also mentions the importance of traditional practices in
metal (2013b). The comic book industry, particularly in the US, also
adheres to some traditional practices that have been a part of the culture
for a long time, for example a Wednesday release date for the majority
of comics (even digital copies) and advance solicitations (usually several
months ahead) of upcoming releases. These advance solicitations also
contribute greatly to the sense of anticipation that Kahn-Harris identifies as important in metal as well (2013a). In addition, digital-only
releases, which have been growing in number, are still subsequently
collected and printed in the traditional manner. Although it may be
controversial and counter-intuitive to suggest for a music genre in which
development is primarily driven by artists and fans, perhaps there may
be a greater role for the industry, in the form of the metal record labels,
to play in safeguarding the future of metal and in influencing the shape
and movement of the metal scenes.

Although the complete way forward for metal may not be to simply
transfer metal aesthetics into another medium, it may be that broader
ventures for the 'social value' of metal, which Kahn-Harris refers to
as something 'defiant, inexhaustible and unashamed' into other areas
could help act as a bridge to other ways for metal to realize its commitment to 'resilience and endurance' (2014). He also mentions that
responding to the current crisis in metal requires 'an enhancement of
metal's capacity for reflexivity' (Kahn-Harris, 2013c). The strengthening
connections between the two art forms may be one way in which comics
could help metal negotiate through its crisis of abundance, specifically
for creators and fans of metal to use this different medium to cast fresh

light on their reflexivity around metal, allowing perceptions to be challenged in a different way. It may be that that they can then take some of the outcomes of the experience back to metal, better equipped to face the 'questions, issues and challenges' that Kahn-Harris states are often prohibited or beyond prescribed boundaries in metal as a result of its 'reflexive anti-reflexivity' (2013c).

Indeed, it could be argued that comics are one of the most reflexive art forms, regularly displaying a number of reflective strategies (Jones, 2005). One of them is demystification, which is seen in the inclusion of original scripts, character development sketches or an explanation of the progression from idea to finished form in many graphic novels and collections. Other reflexive strategies include the presence of the author within the work itself, as in Art Spiegelman's *Maus*, and an awareness of the reader (or 'breaking the fourth wall'), which is seen regularly in comics such as *Ambush Bug* and the currently running *Harley Quinn* series from DC. Intertextuality, commonly seen via references in one title to other in-continuity events in other titles, and intermedia reflexivity, where one medium is represented through another, are also signifiers of reflexivity (ibid.). Simplistically, the latter may be seen as the most relevant to metal in comics; however, an enhancement of metal's reflexivity may occur more through learning and adapting the relevant ways in which comics have wholeheartedly embraced reflexivity in various forms. It could be argued that this reflexivity is one of the reasons that comics have endured and gained their unique status in popular culture.

Even a cursory glance suggests that metal and comics often inhabit the same spheres of reference in terms of imagery, thematic explorations, stigmatization and fan experience, and in willingness to push the boundaries of what could be achieved – the 'aesthetic lawlessness' that Hajdu described could, perhaps, also be a fitting phrase for metal. It is worth briefly mentioning, however, that another obvious similarity between metal and comic books does exist, specifically the problem of the either overt sexualization or embarrassing marginalization of women. While apparent, often blatantly so, it is not discussed here because it is a vast and complicated topic that deserves a chapter (if not an entire book) to itself.

Although the connections may not always be obvious, it is apparent that metal and comics have been influencing each other for a number of years and have resulted in several instances of iconic representations in both camps. In particular, the transgressive elements can be very similar in both forms, and that these contribute greatly to their power and success. Combined with these connections are the strong bonding experiences within each group, rising in no small part from the alienation, stigmatization and persecution suffered by both. In addition, it may be that future connections could allow metal to learn and adapt some of the strategies that have led to comics becoming the resilient, successful and enduring art form it is, and allow metal to do the same. Perhaps, then, metal and comics are not such strange bedfellows after all.

Bibliography

Baker, F. & Bor, W. (2008) 'Can Music Preference Indicate Mental Health Status in Young People?' *Australasian Psychiatry*, 16(4), pp. 284–288.

Blumberg, M. (1948) 'The Practical Aspects of the Bad Influence of Comic Books,' *American Journal of Psychotherapy*, 2(3), pp. 487–488.

Campbell, H. (2014) *The Art of Neil Gaiman* (Lewes: ILEX).

Comic Book Resources (2011) 'Spears & BB Play 'Black Metal.' Retrieved 22 June 2011 from: http://www.comicbookresources.com/?page=article&id=32918.

ComicMix. (2011) 'Yet Another Reason for Comics to Go Digital: 40 Is the New 15.' Retrieved 8 June 2011 from: http://www.comicmix.com/2011/06/08/yet-another-reason-for-comics-to-go-digital-40-is-the-new-15/.

Cornell, P. & Kelly, R. (2012) *Saucer Country Volume 1: Run* (New York, NY: DC Comics).

Duncan, R. & Smith, M. J. (2009) *The Power of Comics: History, Form and Culture* (London: Continuum International Publishing).

Elkisch, P. (1948) 'The Child's Conflict about Comic Books,' *American Journal of Psychotherapy*, 2(3), pp. 483–487.

Elovaara, M. (2014) 'Am I Evil? The Meaning of Metal Lyrics to Its Fans,' *Hardcore Punk and Other Junk: Aggressive Sounds in Contemporary Music*, eds. E. J. Abbey & C. Helb (Plymouth: Lexington Books), pp. 35–50.

Gaiman, N. & Zulli, M. (2005) *The Last Temptation* (Milwaukie, OR: Dark Horse).

Graphic Policy. (2014) 'Facebook Fandom Spotlight: Who Are the US Comics Fans?' Retrieved 1 July 2014 from: http://graphicpolicy.com/2014/07/01/facebook-fandom-spotlight-who-are-the-us-comic-fans-10/.

Hajdu, D. (2008) *The Ten-Cent Plague: The Great Comic-Book Scare and How it Changed America* (New York, NY: Picador).

Halnon, K. (2006) 'Heavy Metal Carnival and Dis-Alienation: The Politics of Grotesque Realism,' *Symbolic Interaction*, 29(1), pp. 33–48.

Hein, F. (2003) *Hard Rock, Heavy Metal, Metal: Histoire, Culture et Pratiquants* (Paris: IRMA).

Hill, R. L. (2013) *Representations and Experiences of Women Hard Rock and Metal Fans in the Imaginary Community*, Ph.D. thesis, University of York. Retrieved 5 January 2015 from: http://etheses.whiterose.ac.uk/4744/1/Hill_RL_Women_Hard_Rock_Metal_Fans_Imaginary_Community.pdf.

Howe, S. (2012) *Marvel Comics: The Untold Story* (New York, NY: HarperCollins).

Jones, M. (2005) 'Reflexivity in Comic Art,' *International Journal of Comic Art*, 7(1), pp. 270–286.

Kahn-Harris, K. (2007) *Extreme Metal: Music and Culture on the Edge* (Oxford, OH: Berg).

Kahn-Harris, K. (2013a) 'Too Much Metal.' *Souciant.* Retrieved 29 November 2013 from: http://souciant.com/2013/11/too-much-metal.

Kahn-Harris, K. (2013b) 'Invisible Metal,' *Souicant.* Retrieved 06 December 2013 from: http://souciant.com/2013/12/invisible-metal.

Kahn-Harris, K. (2013c) 'The Metal Future,' *Souciant.* Retrieved 20 December 2013 from: http://souciant.com/2013/12/the-metal-future.

Kahn-Harris, K. (2014) 'Metal Beyond Metal,' *Souciant.* Retrieved 17 January 2014 from: http://souciant.com/2014/01/metal-beyond-metal.

Kaveney, R. (2008) *Superheroes: Capes and Crusaders in Comics and Films* (London: I.B. Tauris & Co.).

King, P. (1988) 'Heavy Metal Music and Drug Abuse in Adolescents,' *Postgraduate Medicine,* 83(5), pp. 295–301.

Kirsch, S. J. & Olczak, P. V. (2000) 'Violent Comic Books and Perceptions of Ambiguous Provocation Situations,' *Mediapsychology,* 2(1), pp. 47–62.

Kirsch, S. J. & Olczak, P. V. (2002) 'The Effects of Extremely Violent Comic Books on Social Information Processing,' *Journal of Interpersonal Violence,* 17(11), pp. 1160–1178.

KISSopolis (2013), 'Today in KISStory – 1977: 1st KISS Marvel Comic Released.' Retrieved 30 June 2013 from: http://www.kissopolis.com/2013/06/today-in-kisstory-1977_30.html.

Legman, G. (1948) 'The Comic Books and the Public,' *American Journal of Psychotherapy,* 2(3), pp. 473–477.

Leon, L. & Metcalf, J. (2011) *Eternal Descent Volume 1* (San Diego, CA: IDW Publishing).

Lopes, P. (2006) 'Culture and Stigma: Popular Culture and the Case of Comic Books,' *Sociological Forum,* 21(3), pp. 387–414.

Martin, G., Clarke, M., & Pearce, C. (1993) 'Adolescent Suicide: Music Preference as an Indicator of Vulnerability,' *Journal of the American Academy of Child and Adolescent Psychiatry,* 32(3), pp. 530–535.

Morello, T. & Hepburn, S. (2012) *Orchid Volume 2* (Milwaukie, OR: Dark Horse).

Morello, T. & Hepburn, S. (2013) *Orchid Volume 3* (Milwaukie, OR: Dark Horse).

Ohio University. (2013) 'The Daring Adventures of Current Collectors.' Retrieved 18 January 2015 from: http://www.ohio.edu/people/av205009/portfolio/portfolio/magazine/comicproject_draft2.pdf.

Purcell, N. J. (2003) *Death Metal Music: The Passion and Politics of a Subculture* (Jefferson, NC: McFarland & Co.).

Reddit. (2014) 'Age of Babymetal Fans?' Retrieved 05 May 2014 from: http://www.reddit.com/r/BABYMETAL/ comments/24to0v/age_of_babymetal_fans.

Scheel, K. R. & Westefeld, J. S. (1999) 'Heavy Metal Music and Adolescent Suicidality: An Empirical Investigation,' *Adolescence,* 34(134), pp. 253–273.

Spears, R. & BB, C. (2007) *Black Metal* (Portland, OR: ONI Press Inc.).

Spears, R. & BB, C. (2011) *Black Metal 2: The False Brother* (Portland, OR: ONI Press Inc.).

Spears, R. & BB, C. (2014) *Black Metal 3: Darkness Enthroned* (Portland, OR: ONI Press Inc.).

Stack, S. (1998) 'Heavy Metal, Religiosity and Suicide Acceptability,' *Suicide and Life-Threatening Behavior,* 28(4), pp. 388–394.

Stack, S., Gundlach, J., & Reeves, J. L. (1994) 'The Heavy Metal Subculture and Suicide,' *Suicide and Life-Threatening Behavior*, 24(1), pp. 15–23.

The Beat (2014) 'Market Research Says 46.67% of Comic Fans are Female.' Retrieved 5 February 2014 from: http://comicsbeat.com/market-research-says-46-female-comic-fans.

Van Lente, F. & Dunlavey, R. (2012) *The Comic Book History of Comics* (San Diego, CA: IDW Publishing).

Vertigo (2010) 'Northlanders as Metal (or Norse Mythological Fundamentalism & the Notion of a Container Series).' Retrieved 10 June 2010 from: http://www.vertigocomics.com/blog/2010/06/10/brian-wood-talks-northlanders-metal.

Weidinger, C. K. & Demi, A. S. (1991) 'Music Listening Preferences and Preadmission Dysfunctional Psychosocial Behaviours of Adolescents Hospitalized in an in-patient Psychiatric Unit,' *Journal of Child and Adolescent Psychiatric & Mental Health Nursing*, 4(1), pp. 3–8.

Weinstein, D. (2000) *Heavy Metal: The Music and Its Culture* (New York, NY: Da Capo Press).

Wertham, F. (1954) *Seduction of the Innocent* (New York, NY: Rinehart & Co.).

Wood, B. (2011) *Northlanders Book Five: Metal and Other Stories* (New York, NY: DC Comics.

Index

CPSIA information can be obtained
at www.ICGtesting.com
Printed in the USA
LVHW050408191220
674543LV00006B/263

9 781137 456670